"Remarkable," The Rev said. "I used to think people were exaggerating the humanity of Fuzzies." He made a quick, noncommital gesture. "But, then, I've always thought they exaggerated the humanity of Terrans, too."

"They aren't exactly like us," Rainsford said. "Nature never makes exact duplications—even in character. However, Fuzzies are a totally sane race. And, they cannot be driven insane. They know the difference between right and wrong, good and bad—and their ethical system is highly developed, more highly developed than ours, I'm bound to think. For example, they have no concept at all of crime or doing hurt to another in any premeditated way."

"It's strange," The Rev said reflectively. "Beings that are totally good; the Vision finally realized. And we had to come this far through space and time to find it."

"Little Fuzzy" is one of the most beloved characters in science fiction. Now, at last, the story of the Fuzzies continues. . .

Be sure to read the original "Fuzzy" adventures by H. Beam Piper, available from Ace Science Fiction:

LITTLE FUZZY

FUZZY SAPIENS

FUZZY BONES

A novel by William Tuning
Based on works by H. Beam Piper

FUZZY BONES

by **WILLIAM TUNING**

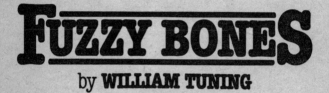

SF

ace books

A Division of Charter Communications Inc.
A GROSSET & DUNLAP COMPANY
51 Madison Avenue
New York, New York 10010

FUZZY BONES

An ACE Book

First Ace printing: December 1981
Published Simultaneously in Canada
2 4 6 8 0 9 7 5 3 1
Manufactured in the United States of America

This book is dedicated to
ANUBIS,
the guide from the first life to the second life. (Also the
Egyptian god of embalming, but there's no need to
dwell on that.)

ACKNOWLEDGEMENTS

Being, myself, something of an utter fool about science—among other things, I'm told—I should like to publicly thank those persons who have given valuable technical advice and assistance, and those who have air-checked my head from time to time as I wrote this novel. They are, *alphabetically:*

James Patrick Baen, Chev. G.S.B. Csillaghegyi, K.S.J., Dr. Robert L. Forward, Randall Garrett, Frank Gasperik, Robert A. Heinlein, Sherry L. Pogorzelski, Stan Strong,

and
Antoinette Symons

PART ONE: FUZZY REDUX

PART TWO: FUZZY BONES

FUZZY REDUX

I

" 'Tis a pity she's a whore,' " the Marine said.

"Don't bet your ass or your pension on it," the priest said.

The two of them were perched at the bar of the first–class passengers' lounge on the *City of Asgard*, outbound for Zarathustra. They sipped their drinks and chatted while the rest of the first–class passengers "ooohed" and "ahhhed" at the ever-changing panoramas of space that were presented in the observation screens around the edge of the lounge deck.

The Marine nodded toward the object of the conversation, a strawberry blonde named—correction—calling herself Christiana Stone. "That might be your first convert on Zarathustra," he said.

The Marine was Master Gunnery Sergeant of Fleet Marines Philip Helton. The priest preferred to be called The Rev.

They had hit it off immediately. The Rev was dressed like a priest—collar and all—but thought like a Marine—one who had been able to take the time to absorb and appreciate some of the galaxy's variety of culture.

You can take the boy out of the Marines, Helton had thought when he met him, *but you can't take the Marine out of the boy. Retired, perhaps. Officer, maybe. Tough, yes.*

The Rev snorted derisively. "Do the old Magdalene caper? Not a chance."

"Why not?" Helton said. "Souls are where you find 'em."

"Several reasons," The Rev replied, as he chewed noisily

on an ice cube from his drink. "First, it's not my style. Round the souls up every spring, put The Brand on them, and drive them to market? That's a mug's game. Second; unnecessary. If that young thing is a prostie, then I'm the Archbishop of Nifflheim."

"You sound pretty sure of yourself," Helton said.

The Rev snorted again. "My lad, I daresay you've observed just about as many whores in your profession as I have in mine. What the lady *says* she is and what she *is* don't have to come to the same thing." He wagged his finger as Helton started to interrupt. "She may, however, *intend* to become one when we get to Zarathustra."

"But you don't think she's a—ummmmmm—journeyman," Helton said.

The Rev slapped his hand lightly on the bar and leaned forward slightly. "Of course not!" he said quietly. "Otherwise she would have been working the ship. Lots of lonely business types in the first–class. A young lady with her looks and just the slightest amount of enterprise could rack up quite a bundle during a six–month hypertrip."

"That's where you've missed," Helton said with a chuckle. "You don't have all the data to draw a conclusion."

The Rev's face took on an expression of mock menace. "Well, son, you get to be pretty damned observant in my trade."

"And in *my* trade," Helton said, "I travel quite a bit of the time by commercial carrier."

"So?" The Rev was not impressed.

"So I happen to know the ship captain on this trip. His name is Hermann Kaltenbrunner and he makes the Orthodox–Monophysites look like a bunch of reckless hedonists. I was on the *City of Malverton* once—when the old boy was stalking his quarterdeck—and I saw him put a professional gambler out the airlock for starting up a card game on Sunday."

"Great Ghu!" The Rev gasped. "He does sound to be just a trifle on the puritanical side. Uh—what happened to the rest of the players?"

"Nothing," Helton said flatly. *"They* were not professional card–players. Oh, they got a sermon about evil–doing that would set fire to your underwear, but that was about it."

"So someone tipped her off mighty quick," The Rev said, "perhaps in hopes of receiving some—ahhhh—non–professional thanks."

Helton smiled. "Oh, I don't know. There are people who just have that old soft spot in them."

"Hunh!" The Rev grumped. "I'd hate to have to hold my breath between meeting the first one and the next one."

"Now that you've muffed your first great deduction," Helton said, "what do you think her game is?"

The Rev shrugged and swigged from his drink. "She might be a spoiled rich kid who's out to get even with Mommy and Daddy—come home from Zarathustra with a bundle of money and rub their noses in how it was earned. Or, she might have a decrepit old Mum back home on Terra, and this is the only way she can earn enough sols fast enough to let the old lady live out her last years in style and respectability."

"Sadie Thompson, and all that," Helton mused.

"Star–travel makes strange bedfellows," The Rev said. He rapped his knuckles on the bar for two more drinks. "Who was that you were quoting a minute ago?"

"You mean, 'Tis a pity . . .'?" Helton asked.

The Rev nodded.

"John Ford," Helton said.

The Rev stroked his chin a moment. "John Ford the First Century screenplay director?"

Helton smiled. "John Ford the obscure Elizabethan dramatist; Fourth Century Pre-Atomic."

The Rev's eyebrows shot up. "Pretty exotic reading for a Gunnie."

Helton looked at him levelly. "I get a lot of time for reading," he said.

"So do I," The Rev said, "so do I."

II

Helton smiled as he recalled the conversation, which took place only a few days out from Terra.

He stood, now, with his feet apart, his hands clasped behind his back, and rocked up and down on the balls of his feet. It was a habit of his which tended to cause nervousness in units and commands he was auditing; one of the principal assets in his trade was the ability to keep people just a little bit off balance.

At one point in his life he had owned a pair of boots which squeaked softly as he rocked on the balls of his feet. They had been among his most favored possessions, because with them he could, at will, cause others to be visibly disturbed in his presence.

There was no one to audit at the moment. There was not even another Terran human on the first-class lounge deck; only Philip Helton standing in front of the armor-glass observation screen, auditing the star-pinioned darkness of space beyond the vessel—and rocking slightly on the balls of his feet.

One of the moons of Zarathustra was slowly traversing the screen, but at this distance Helton couldn't tell which one. It might be Xerxes, the site of his next assignment at the huge Navy base that occupied all of it; or it might be Darius, where Terra-Baldur-Marduk Spacelines maintained Zarathustra's commercial port.

The *City of Asgard* would dock on Darius in about two hours—just in time to disrupt everyone's lunch schedule.

Helton turned toward the small noise behind him.

"Good morning, Sergeant," Christiana Stone said, as she walked across the carpeted deck toward him.

"I would think," he said, "that after six months of travel

4

in hyperspace, you might not find it improper to call me by my first name.''

The dim starlight from the observation screen reflected on her reddish-blond hair as she smiled good–naturedly. ''I suppose so—Phil,'' she replied. ''I find it difficult to be informal with people, though. It's a business habit.''

During the trip, Helton began to suspect The Rev was right; Christiana didn't likely know much more about the oldest profession than one might learn in a steamy romance novel. But there was a big boom happening on Zarathustra, with fortunes to be made by all sorts of means; if Christiana said she was going there to clean up on the influx of population generated by the Pendarvis Decisions, Helton was willing to go along with it.

It made little difference to him, anyway. He was just as glad to be by himself as around others. He was used to operating alone. There were very few Master Gunnery Sergeants of Fleet Marines, so it was not the usual thing for him to settle in with his peer group at cocktail hour and talk shop. Maybe once every year or two he would run into another Master Gunnie. Mostly he just did his job, auditing weapons systems, gunnery performance, and readiness levels. Most often he traveled by civilian transportation to avoid excessively widespread knowledge of his destination and wasn't much obliged to answer to anyone below the rank of Fleet Admiral or Force-General.

''Is our fellow passenger about, this morning?'' Christiana asked.

''I didn't see him at breakfast,'' Helton replied, ''but then I never see him at breakfast.'' He looked at the readout on the wall. ''Nearly ten hundred, galactic standard, though. The bar will open in a few minutes and that should fetch him out.''

I rarely see you at breakfast, either, he thought, *but I suppose you're in the habit of sleeping late in the morning.*

III

At the first rattle of ice into the bin as the barman began to open up, the third passenger appeared in the companionway as though answering a mysterious call to nature. He was sporting a Zarathustran sunstone in the neckcloth below his clerical collar. At the start of the trip he had introduced himself—rather grandiloquently—as "The Right Reverend Father Thomas Aquinas Gordon," but allowed as how he would answer just as readily to "Rev," "Tom," "Father G," or "Thursday."

"Thursday?" Christiana had said, falling for it.

"I certainly am!" The Rev boomed. "Let's have a drink!"

"Good *morning*, children," The Rev said, without breaking stride as he headed for his favorite barstool. He clapped his hands together and rubbed the palms against each other vigorously. "Sustenance, Harry," he said to the barman, "sustenance."

Phil Helton was a bit youngish—early forties—to be a Master Gunnery Sergeant, but he didn't think of himself as "children" in any sense of the word. *To The Rev, though, maybe I am*, he thought. *But, then, when he talks about "gathering his flock" on Zarathustra, I don't reckon he means herding sheep, either.*

The Rev himself was some indeterminate age which could fall anywhere between thirty and sixty, even allowing for a good deal of hyperspace travel. His hair was gray at the temples, but thick and healthy. He was a little on the fat side, but had the fast, light–footed movements of a young man. There were wrinkles around his eyes but the eyes themselves were an alert and piercing dark blue.

He took a respectful swig of his first drink and shuddered

violently for several seconds. "Ahhhhhhhh," he said. "Like blood to a vampire."

While The Rev swapped pleasantries with the barman— and gambled him out of the next two drinks playing Double–O—Helton and Christiana drifted around the rim of the lounge toward the bar, drinking in the different views in the observation screens.

Helton had been on Zarathustra before, but not recently, so his replies to Christiana's barrage of questions about the planet were less than informative. Everything would be changed by the current land rush, in any case.

The two of them had drifted over to The Rev's roost at the bar.

"Only a couple more hours," Helton said, nodding toward the image of the Zarathustran moon. "Then the last leg down to Mallorysport for you and the shuttle to Xerxes for me. What's the name of the place where you'll be setting up your mission, Rev? I may get down and see you."

The Rev shrugged. "I don't know what it's called or where it is. But I know Mallorysport is the largest city on the planet—seventy–five thousand or so. Might be double or triple that by now, with all this immigration. So there's bound to be a slum section for me to work in—some place that's crying for a soup kitchen and medical mission."

"A slum?" Christiana said. "Already? Zarathustra's only been settled for a little more than twenty–five years."

"Oh, it's there, all right," The Rev said, tapping his index finger alongside his nose as though he could smell the place already. "Wherever Terrans go, vice and squalor are in hot pursuit and soon pitch camp with the rest of the pilgrims."

IV

He was right, of course. The slum of Mallorysport had the name Junktown and in it teemed the throngs of the unwashed and the unfortunate—losers, thieves, gamblers, cut-throats, prostitutes, dope-runners, racketeers, hoodlums, the impoverished, and the eternally down-on-their-luck.

Though there were only the three in the first-class lounge, the economy–class decks of the *City of Asgard* were crammed with a fresh crop of immigrants to be deposited in Mallorysport. As soon as the word of the Pendarvis Decisions reached Terra, colonists had stampeded toward Zarathustra. A Class–IV, inhabited, planet. No more Company monopoly. Free land. A chance to make your fortune. A chance to get away from Terra—where no one ever had enough room.

When they discovered that it might take longer than a couple of standard galactic days to become deliriously rich, their grubstakes would start running out.

The people who scraped together every sol they could lay hands on to migrate to a colony world weren't just worthless bums, though; they all had skills, knowledge, and abilities that were needed. The Chartered Zarathustra Company had carved out the modern city of Mallorysport with such people and with the intelligent management of their talents.

Sixteen years earlier, Mallorysport had been a cluster of log and prefab huts beside an improvised landing field. The town had not grown up out of the ground like a tree. *People* had built it. And, it was built, for the most part, by people like those who were now crowded into the lower decks of the *City of Asgard*—people who were betting every last centisol they had that they could make a go of it on a new world.

Some, though, would wind up in Junktown when they

found the streets of Mallorysport were not actually paved with sunstones.

The Rev ran his finger around his throat, between the cleric's collar and his neck. The warmth of his hand, brushing across the sunstone in his neckcloth, caused the gem to flare brighter, which cast a glossy light against the ring on his right little finger.

"You figure there are a lot of souls to save in Mallorysport, then?" Helton said conversationally.

The Rev pulled his finger out from under his collar with a disdainful gesture. "I told you I don't save souls," he said. "Leave that for the Orthodox–Monophysites. I just help God look out for people who can't look out for themselves—temporarily or permanently. Theology has to pay its own freight; I don't preach."

"What about the souls of the Furries?" Christiana put in. "Don't—"

"Fuzzies," Helton interrupted irritably. "You mean Fuzzies."

"Sure," she said. "Fuzzies. What about the souls of the Fuzzies. Don't they need saving?"

"Don't know," The Rev said. "Their souls may be in better shape than ours are. On the other hand they might not be what people think they are, these Fuzzies. I make up my mind about such things when I've seen for myself."

"Sounds odd coming from a priest," Christiana said.

"So it might," The Rev agreed, "so it might. I don't worry too much about this intellectual stuff. We have priests in my order who sit around with computers and try to mathematically calculate the ages of the prophets and the angels. That's swell for them; I just go to where there are people who are hurting and try to put something in their bellies and keep them from catching the polka–dot plague."

She smiled. "Is that why they sent you to such a helluva—such a Nifflheim of a place? According to my packet, there isn't a religious congregation on Zarathustra."

The Rev took a long, noisy suck at his drink, then smacked

his lips. "Don't be particular about cussing around me, daughter," he said. "I don't give a damn one way or the other."

He paused, staring at the observation screen. "If my superior had his way—or wanted to spend that much more money—I suppose he would have sent me even further into the celestial boondocks. Someplace like the Gartner Trisystem. I hear *that's* real rough–and–ready country since crazy old Genji Gartner died at Storisende. Everyone's been wearing out holsters to see who's going to control Poictesme."

"But don't they have a chartered company there?" Christiana asked, "With a Resident General and Federation troops?"

The Rev laughed mirthlessly. "Of course, sweetheart," he said, "and all the settled planets in the trisystem are Federation members. So what?"

She wasn't so sure of what she meant, now. "Well, if they have a colonial government, how can law and order break down that way—just over the death of one man?—even if he did establish the first settlement on the planet."

"Systematically," The Rev said—genuinely amused, now. "Systematically. You know how long it takes just to get some heavy Federation troops out here?"

Helton frowned for a moment, being logical. "Out there—not less than a year's turnaround time."

"Right," The Rev said. "Six months going and six more coming back. If you squawk for troops out here, it takes at least a year to get any—*if* you get any. The Federation may decide the request is unwarranted and just send back a message that says 'Sorry.' "

"Even at that," Helton said, "it's usually all over by the time they get there. Most often, the only thing left for troops to do is put some muscle behind the reorganized government and make sure it's going to honor the old trade agreements that made the place worth commercial traffic to begin with."

Christiana looked shocked, and just a little bit frightened by what they had said. "Th—that couldn't happen on Zarathustra, could it?"

The Rev shrugged. "The Federation depends on every

planet to do its own policing. A charter company or colony world is only as tough as the fist on the end of its own arm. I don't suppose things could really fall apart on Zarathustra.'' He gestured toward the moon in the observation screen. ''The Navy's right close at hand, there, on Xerxes—or Darius—whatever—but things could get pretty wild and woolly under the right set of circumstances. You know— push come to shove and all that. . .

''Which, I suspect, is why our friend here is arriving— after just enough time has passed for word to get to Terra and for someone to be assigned to the job—to audit weapons systems and readiness levels. Am I right, Gunnie?''

Helton smiled.

V

While the passengers of the *City of Asgard* prepared for the last leg to Zarathustra—or Xerxes—it was early morning on Beta Continent and coffee–break time in Mallorysport.

Up Cold Creek Canyon from the Snake River, the KØ sun of Zarathustra slanted orangish light across the growing settlement which the latest maps called Holloway Station. A year ago the place had been a quiet one–man camp from which Jack Holloway prospected for sunstones and lived a peaceably solitary life.

There wasn't much stirring at this hour of the morning, but later on the place would be bustling with activity. Jack Holloway still lived here, but not in the privacy and seclusion he would have preferred. The place was now the administrative center for the Native Affairs Commission.

For the first several weeks, the Commission had been operated out of Holloway's own bungalow from a jumble of cardboard–boxes–turned–filing–cabinets, extra tables, and steno equipment scattered around the living room—and confusion. Now it took up a half–dozen big prefab huts and was straining at the seams of those.

The headquarters and barracks for the Zarathustran Native Protection Force was across the creek. It was home base for the police force which protected the Fuzzies and maintained surveillance of their territory against Terran intrusion. That alone accounted for over two hundred men, if you counted the Marines loaned to the ZNPF by Commodore Napier.

Besides that cluster of buildings there was the bungalow where Gerd and Ruth van Riebeek lived and the big laboratory and infirmary where they conducted studies of Fuzzy biology and psychology, a Reception Center, a Fuzzy School for learning Lingua Terra, and other such structures as might be of use or interest to a Fuzzy.

This conglomeration, the scientific corner of Holloway Station, was referred to informally as Fuzzy Institute.

Add to all this the constant comings and goings by officials of the new Colonial Government, people from the Company headquarters in Mallorysport, Constabulary officers, the Adoptions Bureau that had been set up for Fuzzies who wanted to live with human people and love them, and everyone else who had business involving Fuzzies—to say nothing of a couple hundred curious and playful Fuzzies—and Holloway Station was the kind of place that might need traffic cops before long.

Major George Lunt was puzzled.

That's why he was in his office so early this particular morning. When George Lunt was puzzled about something, he had to turn his detective's mind loose on it one bite at a time, and he couldn't do that with a dozen people pestering him about two dozen things at once.

He hoped he would have a handle on it by the time the day watch started coming in to go on duty at 0800. After that there would be the whole tedious business of inspecting the watch in ranks and sitting in on the watch briefing; not that he needed to—the watch commander was perfectly competent—but as Commandant of the ZNPF he was sort of expected to do it on occasion. It was good for morale.

George reached out with his left hand and blanked the shade on his window, then pulled out a section of printout from the stack of survey logs in front of him and bent down his head to study the rash of squiggly lines which the computer had superimposed on the strip map of a section of northern Beta Continent, the Fuzzy Reservation.

There it is, again, he thought . . . *plain as can be.*

He slewed the stacks of paper around and matched up the registry marks on two parallel strips of geography. *That's nuts,* he said to himself. *If all the various kinds of titanium compounds on Zarathustra were put together in one spot, it still wouldn't cause these readings—I think.*

George leaned back in his chair and rubbed his eyes. Two possibilities seemed to him equally likely to account for the odd data recorded in the survey printout of north Beta: malfunction of the scanner or recorder, or sloppy procedure on the part of Paine's Marines. George thought it would be better all around if he could kiss off Paine's Marines. George Lunt was uneasy about commanding men over whom he did not have direct control. He hadn't been a major long enough to have a clear handle on delegating duty and staff work to others.

The third alternative was too preposterous—that there really *was* a big concentration of titanium compounds on north Beta. Why, you could practically take all the titanium in the entire crust of Zarathustra and put it in your hip pocket. And here this damned readout was telling him there was a big slug of it up there, in several different forms.

Well, he'd ask Jack Holloway about it. Jack knew a good deal about geology—had to to be a successful sunstone prospector. Gerd van Riebeek could tell him more, too. Gerd was a zoologist—used to work for the Chartered Zarathustra Company—so he knew a lot about paleontology from working with fossils and rock layers.

George Lunt yawned and stretched. While his arms were extended, he snapped open the shade on his office window once more, then pushed back the chair and got to his feet.

VI

Major Lunt wasn't the only person, at that hour, to be slaving over puzzling entries on hard–copy printouts and trying to interpret their meaning and importance.

Three time–zones to the east, in Mallorysport, it was mid–morning. Hugo Ingermann—attorney-at-law—sat alone in his office, absently massaging his smooth, round, pink cheeks, and studied the printout pages before him on the large desk. The commercial manifests—cargo and passenger—of the *City of Asgard* had been broadcast to the port on Darius and the capital at Mallorysport as soon as the ship dropped into normal space. Cargo and passengers were known to those who planned to receive them—persons who expected goods or passengers, the customs inspectors, brokers for commercial shipments, lading and freight contractors, and other interested parties. Preparations could then be speedily made to receive that which occupied the decks and holds of the vessel before it actually docked.

Very efficient.

Hugo Ingermann was in the category of "other interested parties." As the moving and guiding force behind all activities illegal or even slightly shady in Mallorysport, Ingermann was interested in everything and everybody that might be on an incoming hypership from Terra.

This was not to say that Hugo Ingermann would turn honest business from his door. During the seven years or so that he had maintained his busy law practice in Mallorysport he had represented at least eight clients who were completely honest and respectable persons. He owned some land north of the capital city. And he was a partner in several perfectly legal businesses—to say nothing of being a major shareholder in a dozen more.

Ever alert to the opportunities which abound on a colony planet, Ingermann was also the architect and principal advisor of several loosely and informally organized conglomerates in Mallorysport.

Ivan Bowlby's entertainment enterprises—telecast productions, prize–fights, nightclubs formed the visible surface of his activities. Out of sight—prostitution, murder for hire, the black-market, and a little dope business here and there.

Spike Heenan's specialty was gambling: crap games, numbers, bookmaking, and fixing sports events. His respectable front—in which Hugo Ingermann was a partner—was a company which leased vending machines and electronic games.

Raul Laporte's talents leaned toward racketeering, extortion, plain old-fashioned country-style crime, and stolen goods. He had expertly developed a system of fences for illegal sunstone buying when the Company had been the only legal buyer for them. Rather than let that part of his operation lay fallow since the Pendarvis Decisions, Laporte had sketched out a plan to expand into straight robbery of sunstone prospectors right at the diggings—cut out the middleman—just as soon as he could find time to organize the operation personally.

The most respectably–fronted of Ingermann's protégés was Leo Thaxter, Loan Broker and Financier—also shylock, smuggler, bag-man, and protection racketeer. He used Laporte's strongarm employees for collections.

When Thaxter came to Zarathustra ten years earlier, he had fooled around with some small–time rackets, set up some crooked labor unions and a couple of marketing co–operatives to put the squeeze on planters. Nothing really big, though, until he fell under the tutelage of Ingermann some four or five years later—who had showed him how to make good money by laundering bad money and investing the profits in six–for–five loans to people who couldn't borrow anywhere else.

His sister, Rose Thaxter, had married Conrad Evins, who later became the chief gem-buyer for the CZC. At the height of the Fuzzy craze, the three of them had kidnapped some

Fuzzies and trained them to get into the Company gem vault through the ventilation system. Ambitious enterprise that; the vault contained upwards of one hundred million sols worth of sunstones.

They almost got away with it. Two minor henchmen, Phil Novaes and Moses Herckerd, had been caught inside Company House with the loot. Herckerd managed to get well-ventilated by a Company policeman with a submachine gun. Novaes lived to stand trial on charges of enslavement, with Mr. and Mrs. Evins, and the three of them received the mandatory sentence for that crime—death administered by a pistol shot in the back of the head; no discretion of the court allowed.

Ingermann angrily jerked out a fresh printout. *The fools*, he thought. *If only the idiots had consulted me, I could have showed them the weak spots in their plan*.

As it was, he had just barely managed getting Thaxter off, and had actually been arrested himself when the police started rounding up everyone connected with Thaxter.

The whole matter had been a great source of aggravation for Attorney General Gustavus Adolphus Brannhard, who "knew" they were all guilty, but didn't quite have enough on them to take it to court.

The hincty bastard tried to put me under veridication for questioning to have me disbarred. Ingermann became enraged every time he thought of the incident. *Patience will put the whole goody, goody lot of them in my hands, sooner or later; then I'll squeeze the juice out of their pious guts*.

What irritated Ingermann was not that the caper had gone wrong, not that four people had been caught, not that he himself had come close to veridicated questioning about his enterprises, a thing that would have meant ruin and jail; but that the whole scheme had gone sour before he could get hold of the sunstones. He would have considered it a profitable bargain to trade the lives of four of his own people for—say—a double handful of sunstones.

Ingermann shook his head sadly and went back to perusing the printout sheets.

Now, here was an interesting item. Three first–class pas-

sengers from Terra. The passage voucher number of one of
them had an "R" suffix. Restricted entry; data not available
except to official inquirers, and then on a "need to know"
basis only. No way to match the number up to a name at this
end of the trip. Payment vouchers were like boarding passes
or baggage tickets. Passengers presented their vouchers to
the chief steward upon entering the ship and he recorded the
number on his manifest. After that it was a matter of head–
counting and tally–keeping. Three boardings first–class for
Zarathustra; and if three got off at Zarathustra all was in
order. Anything more detailed was a violation of the Privacy
Act.

An "R" suffix indicated the possible presence of a Federation official or government employee of fairly high rank
among those three first–class passengers.

Interesting.

The chief steward who recorded the voucher numbers
might remember which passenger showed him the "R"
voucher, but that steward had long–since switched over to an
inbound ship at some intermediate port.

There was a way, of course, to dig out the information
from the other end, on Terra, but it would take a year just to
get the inquiry back to his source and receive a reply. Easier,
really, to just knock them in the head one at a time here in
Mallorysport and steal their ticket copies—if they hadn't
already been tossed in the trash converter.

It might not amount to anything, but Ingermann made a
stenomemophone note of it, anyway. If any one of these three
people began to take an interest in things within his sphere of
influence, it might warrant some further digging.

VII

When Major Lunt returned to his office, there was a slender gentleman sitting at his desk—with his feet propped up on it—and puffing on the short pipe that had yellowed the corners of his white moustache.

· At the sound of boots scraping behind him, he bounded to his feet and turned. "Hi, George," he said.

"Good morning, Jack. What's up?"

Holloway leaned on the corner of the desk. "Well, I need to get something worked up on paper for the mining reserve that we're leasing to the Zarathustra Company up there in the Fuzzy Reservation."

When they were just getting this thing together, Holloway hadn't thought of himself as the Commissioner of Native Affairs, and he hadn't thought of the ZNPF as his private police force, although it was. There was a job to be done looking out for the Fuzzies' interests and it was too important to entrust to anyone else. In the early days he and George Lunt had shared a makeshift hut and called it an office, communicating by shouting back and forth from their desks. Now they had to hike through a hundred–twenty–foot stretch of desks and office machines and roboclerks and human secretaries to get to each other's offices.

"When I put this deal together in my head," Jack said, "Ben Rainsford was very busy being the new Governor General and very busy hating Victor Grego and the CZC as the unscrupulous enemy. Now that I've finally got them doing business with each other, the royalties we'll get from the Company for mining that rich patch of sunstones Gerd and I found in Fuzzy territory just might be enough to keep everything afloat until after the constitutional elections. The government can't levy taxes till then. In the meantime, I want to get the mining operation underway."

"Might be more than we can chew, Jack," George said. "I'm stretched pretty thin, now. We'll have to monitor that operation mighty close; make sure nobody goes sneaking off on his own inside the Reservation. Have to keep track of everything going in or out, watch that they don't bother any of the Fuzzies—that sort of thing."

"I know, George," Holloway said.

"Have to patrol the borders—tight electronic surveillance—be certain no one goes in or out except at our check-points. Take more men than I've got right now just to do that."

"I know, George," Holloway repeated. "Start working something up for me in the way of what you'll need, both men and equipment, if we have crews up there cracking—say—three hundred tons of flint a month."

"Jack—we can't afford it!"

Holloway nodded. "*We* can't, but the Company can. The CZC is going to reimburse us for what we spend policing their leasehold."

Major Lunt chuckled. "I see. Do they know it yet?"

"No," Holloway said, "but Grego will see the wisdom of it once it's explained to him. In the long run, it's a toss-up as to whether it's cheaper for the Company Police do the job or for the Company to hire us to do it. Besides, I won't grant the lease unless our own people are specified to do the law enforcement.

"Grego knows a good thing when he sees it. His bottom line won't be much different at the end of the year. This deal will be good for the Company, good for the Fuzzies, and good for the Government—all the way around."

"Okay," George agreed. "I'll get something together that you can take to Grego—maybe not down to the last paper clip, but in general terms of how much it's going to cost."

"Good," Holloway said. "Grego won't say yes or no right away. He'll take the breakdown to his own Company Police Chief first—have Harry Steefer look over the figures to see whether we're gouging the Company."

He turned to leave, then added a question. "Today, George?"

Lunt nodded. "I imagine so."

"*Hokay, bizzo,*" Holloway said, lapsing into Lingua Fuzzy. "How about bringing it over to the house—right around cocktail time. That way we can talk it over without being interrupted by more than four or five screen calls."

After Mr. Commissioner Holloway had left, George sat down at his desk and sighed; not in aversion to this new task, but in the realization that he was mentally waving goodbye to any immediate chance of getting rid of Lieutenant Paine and his Marines.

I've got to get Ahmed back over here, he thought. *It's very good public relations to have Captain Ahmed Khadra, Chief of Detectives, ZNPF, acting as the Mallorysport liaison with the Company Police, and the Constabulary, and the Mallorysport P.D., and all that, but I've got to have a strong Exec over here if we're going into another expansion phase. He'll just have to set the date with Sandra, get hitched, and bring her over here permanently.*

Then, I've got to start getting the manpower strength up—send John over to Mallorysport and goose up the recruiting office—and beef up my training program with more instructors and cadre sergeants, scrounge up some more uniforms and equipment, and. . . .

VIII

Victor Grego sat in the lawn chair on his penthouse apartment's terrace and thought. He leaned back, with his eyes closed, and thought.

To look at him, one would think he was a gentle, heavy-set man who was dozing in the sun on his day off. One would not immediately think that this man was the Manager-in-Chief of the Zarathustra Company or that he was hard at work. One might suppose that running a colonial company which did about a quarter of a billion sols in gross annual business was little more than presiding over luncheon meetings with subordinate executives and reading reports.

That was what one would think if one went to work each day, worked one's shift, and then went home—conveniently leaving the job at the office.

Victor Grego's office was inside his head, and he carried it with him night and day.

The meat-packing plants on Delta Continent were working around the clock, now. With all this influx of population, there was a constant and heavy demand for prepared and packaged foodstuffs of all kinds. Not only was that a blessing for the general profit picture, but it kept the supervisors so busy they didn't have time to worry about the Company losing its charter or to pester the Manager-in-Chief with minor problems.

The agreement with Governor Rainsford's Colonial Government that allowed the Company to mine on that rich sunstone deposit inside the Fuzzy Reservation was going to work out all right, too—no matter if it did cost a hefty royalty for the privilege. The continued input of sunstones owned by the Company would keep the Company in a tough position which virtually amounted to control of sunstone prices. That had been an early horror that haunted Grego right after the

Fuzzy Trial; one hundred million sols in the sunstone vault combined with the prospect of a free market in sunstones could have badly eroded the Company's worth if a gang of prospectors had gotten together and formed a co–operative to sell directly to someone like the Couperin Cartel—who had the money to drive down the buying price and drive up the selling price by controlling inventories.

The private communication screen chimed softly from inside the apartment. Grego's eyes snapped open and he got to his feet to answer it, casting a glance toward where three Fuzzies were laying out an intricate pattern of colored tiles and plastic rods.

As he suspected, the caller was Colonial Governor Ben Rainsford. Ben had left off his own two Fuzzies, Flora and Fauna, to spend the afternoon with Grego's Diamond. Diamond was very happy with *Pappy Vic,* but he did get lonesome for the company of other Fuzzies. Have to do something about that one of these days.

"Of course, Governor," Grego was saying to the image in the screen—a rumpled little man with bristling red whiskers who still wore bush clothes, even though he was the chief executive of a planetary government. "1730 will be quite convenient. Perhaps you'd care to join me in a cocktail if you can spare the time."

"I'd be delighted," Ben Rainsford said. "In fact there's something I think we should chat about, and this will be a good opportunity to talk."

Grego bid Rainsford good–day and switched off the screen. He chuckled to himself as he returned to the terrace. *How times change*, he thought. *When Fuzzy business started, Rainsford wanted nothing so much as to nail my skin to the fence and use it for target practice.*

He stopped on the terrace, stretched and yawned, then looked down the wide valley below Mallorysport. Clouds were rolling up from the horizon. It looked like rain.

Just as the first large drops of rain *splatted* down onto the terrace, the doorway chimed and Grego admitted Ben

Rainsford. The two men exchanged greetings and some small talk. Then Grego turned toward the terrace and motioned for Rainsford to follow him. "Before the rain really gets going, I want you to take a look at what the kids have been doing," he said.

As they stepped out into the afternoon light, which was now dimmed by the overcast, a fork of lightning split the sky, followed by the roll of thunder marching up the valley.

The Fuzzies looked up at the sky, decided it was really going to rain, and trotted toward the open terrace doors.

"Come on, Pappy Vic. *Do-bizzo*," Diamond said, "*Bizzo; fazzu*. Get fur all wet."

"*Hokay*, Diamond," Grego said. "*So jash–ah; jos* Flora æ Fauna. I'll just show Unka Ben this pretty thing."

Rainsford stooped to get a better look at the design which the three Fuzzies had created, paying no attention to the big raindrops which were making dark spots on his khaki jacket.

"Well?" he said to Grego. He spread his hands, then put them back on his knees. "What's unusual about it?"

"Nothing," Grego said, "except that I've noticed the spiral design seems to be a favorite of Fuzzies, but I can't imagine where they've seen it before. You're the expert xeno–naturalist. What's the answer?"

"The first answer," Rainsford said as he shuddered under the increasing rain, "is to get in out of the wet. Let's have that drink."

Both men moved briskly across the terrace, into the living room, and Grego closed the doors just as another clap of thunder boomed.

The Fuzzies had already drifted into the Fuzzy–room, just off the kitchen, and were watching a screenplay. They knew quite well that this was the time of day when the Big Ones drank *tosh–ki–waji*—bad-tasting water—and made Big One talk.

"Thank you, Victor," Colonial Governor Rainsford said, accepting a glass, then settled back on the couch.

Grego dropped into his favorite chair. "Well, Bennett," he began, "where *do* they get that spiral design?"

"Why, from nature, I suppose," Rainsford said. "All

manner of spiral-shaped things in nature—flower stamens, snail shells, rams' horns, seed pods—that sort of thing.''

"Not on Zarathustra," Grego said.

Rainsford looked at him with a quick movement of his head. "What?''

"The Mother Nature who drew the plans for Zarathustra," Grego replied, "favored the concentric circle design over the spiral design. Featherleaf tree, pool-ball fruit, tandavine beans—all manner of plants grow in layered round shapes.''

Rainsford stared at him, as if to say, *who's the scientist here, you or me?*

Grego smiled disarmingly. "I got curious and looked it up. I just thought you might have an idea about it.''

Rainsford sipped his drink, then shook his head. "I don't know, Victor. Science for me has been something of a luxury—a luxury I can't afford—ever since Alex Napier stuck this Governor job onto me. You'll have to ask the Fuzzyologists about that one.''

Grego waved a hand. "I noticed that the first day I took Diamond to the office with me. He got into the computer room and rearranged all the lights on the input board; the pattern he made was a spiral one, kind of like a nebula.'' Grego chuckled as he recalled the panic which had followed until Joe Verganno had restored the Executive One and Two computers to their normal functioning. "It was sort of pretty, too, except there was hell to pay for a couple of hours.''

Another flash of lightning glared through the premature twilight and the thunderclap rattled the terrace doors.

The Fuzzies peeped bashfully around the door jamb, then decided all the noise wasn't Pappy Vic and Pappy Ben fighting and went back to their communication screen.

"That's something else I've been wondering about," Grego said, nodding toward the Fuzzies.

"Whazzat?'' Rainsford said absently.

"For a people of low paleolithic development, the Fuzzies don't seem to have the slightest fear of natural events. Consider the Thorans, for example. With all their intelligence and absolute fearless courage, whenever there's a thunderstorm they drop to the ground like stones and start praying to Great Ghu the Grandfather God like the end of the world is coming in five minutes.''

Rainsford rubbed his chin and nodded agreement.

''That's another thing,'' Grego said, warming to his subject. ''Fuzzies don't seem to have any primitive nature–gods or religious myths about the creation of the world and so forth. What do you make of that, Bennett?''

''Hmmmf,'' Rainsford said. ''Next thing, you'll be applying to the Institute of Xeno–Sciences for a fellowship.''

Grego reddened slightly.

''The first thing a xeno–naturalist learns about extrasolar creatures is to find the yardstick,'' Rainsford said, ''instead of trying to make existing yardsticks apply. Comparisons, yes. Circular reasoning, no.''

''Well, then,'' Grego said. ''There are nine sapient races besides Terrans. They all react the same to loud noises, don't they? With the exception of Fuzzies, that is.''

''Yes,'' Rainsford snapped, ''and they can all be driven insane. Fuzzies are totally sane and can't be driven insane. Maybe that's the difference. There is always *some* difference. Non–Terran psychology is not all whittled from the same stick.''

Grego raised his eyebrows and pursed his lips. *Can't argue with that line of reasoning,* he thought.

''Even the Yggsdrasil Khooghra,'' Rainsford went on, ''with the lowest mentation of any sapient race, can be driven nuts.''

''I see your point,'' Grego said. ''I've been pondering some of these things. I was interested in your opinion.''

''Thank you,'' Rainsford said. ''There is something else I wanted to ask you about, though, and I'm getting a bit pressed for time.''

''So, you see,'' Rainsford concluded, ''we've got a damnthing by the tail here with no way to let go unless we stay strictly on top of the situation. With our budget situation being what it is, we can't hope for law enforcement organizations to grow fast enough to meet the requirements of this damned population boom.''

Grego nodded. "I know, Bennett. Nine years ago, before you came to Zarathustra, we had an immigration boom. If it hadn't gone bust, there would have been a Nifflheim of a law enforcement problem come out of it—at least for a while."

"Well, we can't allow it," Rainsford said. "We've got to get the most we can out of available manpower with the least possible waste motion."

Grego smiled. *Spoken like a true manager,* he thought. "You have some ideas, then, I take it?" he said.

Rainsford knocked the heel out of his pipe. "Indeed," he said. "We've got a helluva lot of overlap, here." He ticked the agencies off on his fingers. "There's Ian Ferguson's Colonial Constabulary, the Mallorysport City P.D., the ZNPF, Harry Steefer's rather sizeable mob of Company Police for your own company, and almost a hundred Marines on loan for various peace–keeping chores." That used up all the fingers on one hand, and Rainsford waved it in the air. "Besides that, there's the Colonial Marshal's office, and it's not unusual for Max Fane to send one of his men all the way over to Delta Continent just to serve papers on someone."

Grego nodded.

"The way I see it," Rainsford continued, "We should establish a central records and dispatch agency right here in Mallorysport—a Colonial Investigation Bureau—and put all our law enforcement records and mission requests through it. That way, if the CZC swears out a warrant for some veldbeest herder who stole a company aircar on Beta, you won't have to send your own men on a ten-hour round trip to get them where the crook is. The Bureau can just put out a want on him to the local agency—Constabulary, ZNPF, whatever. Someone can bring the miscreant along when they come over to Alpha Continent on other business. You see?"

"And," Grego said, nodding agreement, "if someone holds up a planter or a prospector on Beta, then hightails it for Junktown, the Constabulary can have our people here pick him up and hold him. Yes, I can see where that would be more efficient—now that we have law enforcement almost everywhere on the planet."

"Exactly," Rainsford said. "But it won't work unless all

the agencies involved agree to co-operate. The big advantage, as I see it, will be to get the officers who are fooling around in offices out of administrative work and into the field. Why, that ought to give us a twenty percent increase right there in people who are actually out chasing crooks—without hiring any more people or paying any more salaries."

"I'm convinced," Grego said. "What do you want me to do about this, Bennett?"

Rainsford snatched his pipe and tobacco pouch from his jacket pocket and reared back on the couch. "Why, talk to Harry Steefer about it—see what he thinks. I've talked to Colonel Ferguson, and I'll talk to George Lunt when I'm over on Beta in a week or so. I've already talked to Captain Khadra about it. It was his idea, by the way. We'll set up a meeting with all the force commandants. Ought to have Gus Brannhard in on it, too, I suppose."

"Luncheon would be a good time," Grego said. "I'd like to attend, myself, if that's all right."

"Why, of course, Victor," Rainsford said. "I was hoping you'd say that. I may be the Colonial Governor General, but that's only been for a year. If both of us tell all of them it's a good idea, I'm sure they'll all go for it."

After Ben Rainsford had left with Flora and Fauna, Diamond yawned and stretched in the foyer, then climbed up into Grego's lap. "What you talk with Unka Ben, Pappy Vic?" he asked.

"Business, Diamond," Grego answered. "About ways to do a better job of catching bad Big Ones."

"Tosh-ki-Hagga?" Diamond asked, "like the Big Ones who brought me here from the big woods?"

"That's right," Grego said. "It's an awfully big job."

Diamond squirmed around until he was comfortable on Grego's ample lap. "Not so bad—the way it work out," he said sleepily.

Grego thought about the way Diamond had been kidnapped by Herckerd and Novaes and held prisoner until he escaped. *"So–noho–aki dovov tosh–ki,"* Grego said. You tell me how not bad.

Diamond yawned, again. "If not come here, no find Pappy Vic," he said. "No find you *hoksu–hagga—* wonderful big one."

Grego scratched the back of Diamond's head, between his ears. In a moment he set down his brandy snifter and brushed something out of the corner of his left eye.

IX

They were in Jack's living room, and it looked almost exactly as it had the first night Gerd van Riebeek had seen it, when he and Ruth and Juan Jimenez had come out to see the Fuzzies, without the least idea that the validity of the Company's charter would be involved.

All the office equipment and supplies and files that had cluttered Jack Holloway's home right after the Pendarvis Decisions were long since cleared out into the Administration Office buildings. Now there was just the sturdy, comfortable furniture which Jack had built himself, the damnthing and bush–goblin and veldbeest skins on the floor, and the gun-rack with a tangle of bedding under it where his own family of Fuzzies slept. The other Fuzzies didn't intrude here—they understood it was private to Pappy Jack's Fuzzies.

There were only four people present—soon to be joined by another: Jack and the van Riebeeks as before; and Lynne Andrews, slender and blonde and sitting on the couch where Juan Jimenez and Ben Rainsford had sat that first night. Jack sat in the armchair at his table-desk, trying to keep Baby Fuzzy, on his lap, from climbing up to sit on his head.

"We're getting closer, but there's an enormous amount of information we don't have yet," Gerd was saying. "The Fuzzy infant mortality rate is running something like ninety percent. The NFMp hormone inhibits normal development of the fetus every time—" He pointed to the example of Baby Fuzzy. "—*except* when the NFMp production cycle is out of phase with the mother's fertility cycle."

"How many viable infants are there in Fuzzy–shelter, now?" Jack asked.

"Seven," Ruth answered. "Since we set up the lab, we've had sixty–two deliveries. Fifty–five of those have been stillbirths, live births that die within hours, or preemies who aren't strong enough to stay alive, even in incubators. The mothers with healthy babies have been kept here, so we can study their kids—even if there aren't enough of them for a decent sample group.''

Jack nodded as he arranged the information in his mind. ''Good—actually, not good. What I mean is that it's good you're retaining the Fuzzies with viable offspring, instead of letting them disappear into the adoption pool. Do you have an infant experimental group getting large doses of hokfusine, as well as the adult sample?''

''Yes,'' Lynne said, ''but it's too soon yet to measure any differences in development.'' Lynne had been shanghaied from the hospital in Mallorysport, where her practicing M.D. was in pediatrics. She still hadn't completely shaken off the notion of equating Fuzzies with human children about one year of age; they were much the same size. Some of them, of course, were older than she was, but the present state-of-the-art Fuzzyology didn't include any method of age-determination. And Fuzzies had a very cavalier attitude about numbers: they counted to five on the fingers of one hand, using the other hand to count with. Then they counted past that to a ''hand of hands''—twenty-five. After that it was ''many,'' and somewhere beyond that it was simply ''many-many.'' ''Many-many summers'' of age wasn't very satisfying to a scientist trying to set up research records.

''Hell, Jack,'' Gerd said. ''We're not even real sure what the gestation period is for Fuzzies, much less what their growth rates and mental development schedules are. We have some adolescent Fuzzies. We have some pubescent Fuzzies. And we have adult Fuzzies. But we have no Fuzzies who can give us precise elapsed-time information about their own life cycles. We'll just have to skull it out for ourselves by observation of experimental groups. We've got a long job ahead of us, here.''

Jack asked, ''Do we know anything definite yet about how they use hokfusine—more than that they metabolize it into something that inhibits NFMp production?''

''We think it's like a vitamin to them,'' Lynne said. ''They prefer eating land-prawns over anything else, because of the

titanium in its middle intestine. But the molecule isn't the
same as the hokfusine molecule. They can't convert it into
anti–NFMp, even though they're very fond of the taste it
gives the land–prawn. We're making a series of endocrine
comparisons now to determine what's involved with the
titanium in hokfusine that allows its conversion into anti–
NFMp and doesn't allow the titanium in land–prawns to be
converted.'' She gave a short laugh. ''You have to understand, though, that when I say endocrine system for Fuzzies,
that's only the vaguest kind of label; we have precious little
information on the subject at this point.''

Land–prawns were very important to Fuzzies and a great
nuisance to Terrans. They got into gardens; they got into
machinery; they got into campsites; they got into bedding—
painfully pinching the owner of the bedding when *he* tried to
get into it. They got into wiring and ate the insulation; they
got into dirty laundry and ate holes in your socks.

What the Terrans called a land–prawn the Fuzzies called a
zatku; a big pseudo–crustacean, about a foot long, twelve-
legged and possessed of two pairs of clawed mandibles.
Fuzzies hunted *zatku* avidly and preferred them to any other
food—until they tasted EMERGENCY FIELD RATION, EXTRATER-
RESTRIAL SERVICE TYPE THREE. Fuzzies liked *zatku*, but they
loved Extee–Three. If it hadn't been for the land–prawns
starting to move south into the big woods to get away from a
drought, the Fuzzies would have stayed in the unexplored
country of northern Beta Continent and it would have been
years longer before any Terran made contact with them.

At first, it was a mystery why Fuzzies were crazy about
Extee–Three, until the greater mystery developed of why
they loved some Extee–Three and spit out other Extee–Three
when both had been prepared identically.

Actually, *almost* identically.

A Company Science Center chemist named Charlotte
Tresca had proceeded along completely unscientific lines and
found that Fuzzies were nuts about only Extee–Three that had
been prepared in titanium cookers. It contained a molecule,
mostly carbon–oxygen–hydrogen, with five atoms of
titanium hooked onto it. Sixty–four atoms in the long–chain

organic molecule; five of them titanium. The molecule amounted to about one part per ten million of the Extee–Three.

Fuzzies could tell the difference by taste.

Pretty keen tasting.

Ms. Tresca had named the molecule hokfusine, from the name for Extee–Three in Lingua Fuzzy—*hoksu–fusso,* wonderful food. That had annoyed the lab chief no end; Dr. Jan Christiaan Hoenveld had planned to name the substance hoenveldine, thus assuring his niche in scientific history, but the term hokfusine was already in widespread usage before he could make up his mind that Charlotte Tresca's research was valid.

Outside Jack Holloway's bungalow, the Zarathustran sunset was blazing orange and red in the western sky. The slanting, ferruginous sunlight cast a coppery glow on the stocky man with a square face who was walking across the footbridge over the creek toward Holloway's house; and silhouetted the five little figures who followed behind him, tinting the soft, golden fur which covered their bodies to a russet red in the falling twilight.

They were erect bipeds, about two feet tall, with round, humanoid faces, little snub noses, big ears, and wide eyes that were very large and appealing. They all wore green canvas pouches made of TFMC ammunition pouches— "*shodda–bags*"—on a shoulder–strap, two–inch silver I.D. discs on a chain about their necks, and nothing else. Each of them had a weapon in one hand—a six–inch, leaf–shaped blade on a foot–long steel shaft, with a steel ball welded to the butt end for balance. They were the Fuzzies adopted by George and his men at Constabulary Station Beta Fifteen. The silver discs around their necks were each engraved with the name of the bearer: Dillinger, Dr. Crippen, Ned Kelley, Lizzie Borden, and Calamity Jane.

Just like a bunch of cops, to hang names like that on innocent Fuzzies. But Fuzzies didn't care much what names the Terrans gave them. Fuzzies were glad to be with the Big Ones—the *Hagga*—and have fun with them, and be protected, and be loved, and to love the *Hagga* and make them happy. Plenty of time later to find out what all those names meant. There was still a lot for Fuzzies to learn—so many things to learn from the Big Ones.

Jack's Fuzzies heard George Lunt and his family of Fuzzies approaching the house before the Terran humans did, as always. They all jumped up and ran out through the little spring–loaded doorway Jack had built for them.

The Fuzzies went pelting across the open space in front of the house to greet the visitors. They lapsed into their own ultrasonic speaking range, which was inaudible to Terrans except as an occasional "Yeek." There were a lot of "yeeks," with different inflections, as all eleven adult Fuzzies frolicked and pushed and rolled on the ground with their friends.

After the Fuzzy-romp had spent itself, the whole spectacle was repeated, at a lesser intensity, as the Fuzzies greeted their Terran friends: *"Heyo Unka Jack. Heyo, Unka Gerd, Auntie Woof, Auntie Win,"* all garbled together in a brief, delightful jumble of controlled bedlam.

When that was all over, George Lunt said anticlimactically, "I thought the kids might like to have a visit." He took off his pistol and beret and hung them on a peg near the door, signifying that he considered himself off duty. He laid a slender sheaf of papers on Jack's desk–table.

George's Fuzzies were looking over the complex multiple design on the floor, walking respectfully around it, squatting down to view it from different angles, and asking questions of Jack's Fuzzies about the composition.

That had been one of the first things to tip off Jack Holloway and Ben Rainsford that Fuzzies might be sapient; they had color perception and artistic sense, and made useless things just because they were pretty to look at.

Jack bent down and spoke to the group. *"Aki–josso–so t'heet?* How about *esteefee?"* Yes, they would love a treat, especially Extee–Three.

"What about you, George?" Jack asked. *"Aki–josso–so whiskey?"*

"*Hokay,*" George said. "*Hoksu. Do–bizzo.*" He flopped down in a chair and exchanged greetings with the others in the room, all of whom he knew quite well by now.

Jack went into the kitchen and got two of the blue labeled tins down from a cabinet. He divided the Extee–Three into twelve equal portions, cutting up the moist, gingerbread-colored cake with a knife, then laid out the pieces on a plate. With the plate in one hand and George's drink in the other, he returned to the living room, handed the glass to George, and set the plate down on the floor among the Fuzzies.

Each Fuzzy picked up a piece and began to munch on it appreciatively—although Baby Fuzzy was making rather more crumbs than was necessary as he maneuvered his small mouth around a chunk. Mamma Fuzzy gave him a smack and reminded him of good manners.

"What I still can't figure out," George was saying, "is, if Fuzzies are so smart—maybe smarter than we are, like Gerd says—why is it they never discovered fire?"

Lynne Andrews smiled. "Still stuck on applying the priorities of *Homo s. terra* as a criterion for sapience, George?" she said, almost tauntingly.

George looked annoyed. "Well how else can you measure things except by a universal body of rules?"

"Oh, George," Gerd said, "that talk–and–build–a–fire rule isn't a real test for sapience at all. It's something they cooked up to slow down colonists on frontier planets who would exploit hell out of the natives and then claim afterward that they didn't know the natives were really sapient."

"Came out of the Loki enslavements, didn't it?" Jack asked. He squinted at the ceiling. "Fourth century. Thereabouts, anyway."

Lynne Andrews nodded. "What you have to understand," she said to George, "is that Fuzzies don't think the same way we do. What's important to us isn't necessarily important to them. Counting and numbers, for instance."

"Records, for another," Ruth said. "Even after a year or so of intense study, what we know about Fuzzies is just a tiny spot of light, surrounded by a dim twilight area of what we *think* we know—and most of *that* is probably wrong. Beyond that there is *still* a vast darkness, filled with things that will surprise us when we stumble up against them.''

"I suppose you're right," George said. "I have a cop's mind; it likes there to be square holes for all the square pegs.''

Gerd chuckled. "Well, Fuzzies certainly don't do that; they're more like a jigsaw puzzle. This is the ninth sapient race we've found in about five centuries of star travel. I've had direct experience with seven of them; and Fuzzies are like no primitive people I've ever seen." He motioned toward the group in the center of the floor, who were just now polishing up all the crumbs from their *esteefee* treat. "You'll never hear any gobbledygook from this gang about a demon eating the sun during an eclipse.

"You know, maybe, that Victor Grego has models of the planet and the moons in his office that are suspended in the air and revolve on their own individual Abbott lift–and–drive contra–gravs. Well, the sun is represented by a fixed spotlight. When there was an eclipse of the sun, Diamond watched the umbra shadow move across the planet model for a while. Then he went over and felt it. Then he looked back over his shoulder and took a few sample sightings of the alignments and started to laugh.''

"He laughed?" Lynne said.

"Sure," Gerd replied. "He knew what it was right away. 'Just like in the big woods,' he said, 'when moon mix up light and dark.'

"Any of you ever run across low paleolithic people who understand the mechanics of a solar eclipse?''

No one had.

X

"So when the goddamn dog looked like it was going to jump me," the First Marine said, "I whipped out my nine–millimeter and shot a big hole in him."

The second Marine shook his head. "You should've called in the E.O.D., Ev—laid the old 'danger to life and property' on him, and *then* shot the damned dog."

"I didn't have time to think, Jim," the first Marine said.

"So what happened?" Jim asked.

Ev made a sour face. "Well, the guy what owned the dog made a big stink about it—said he paid a fortune to bring it out from Terra—and the Old Man suspended me to quarters for thirty days."

Everett Diehl was a corporal and James Spelvin was a junior sergeant. Apparently neither one of them ever had "time to think," because they both had more hash marks than chevrons. That made sense, for otherwise they would not now be sitting in a Junktown dive called 'The Bitter End,' waiting for Raul Laporte to collect the regular vigorish on the money they owed him—money borrowed from Laporte and lost back to him at his own gaming tables.

Though technically illegal, Laporte's gambling operations were no particular secret. If one went past the end of the bar, down the wide corridor, and through the double doors, one would be admitted to almost every game of chance ever invented—from electronic probability betting to cards and dice; and on all of them a seven percent guaranteed profit for the house built in.

All the gambling equipment was leased from Spike Heenan—honorable thieves never infringed on each other's specialties. By the same token, the entertainment in the front portion was booked through one of Ivan Bowlby's entertainment agencies; musicians and female vocalists, mostly, like the group that now occupied the low stage at one end of the main lounge.

Four instrumentalists were backing a fragile–looking blonde who was singing in a reedy voice that sounded as delicate as she looked.

"Well, it could have been worse," Jim Spelvin said. "The Major, you know—he could have cut a stripe off you, too."

Diehl nodded without enthusiasm. He wanted to change the subject. "Who's the new singer down there?" he asked.

"Why, that's Gwen," Spelvin said. "You remember Gwennie."

"Yeah?" Diehl said, squinting through the cloudy air, "I thought she was at 'Pandora's Box'."

"She's been over here for two–three weeks, now," Spelvin said with some surprise.

"I've been in barracks for a month," Diehl growled.

"Oh, yeah. I forgot," Spelvin said. "Y'know, now that she's working over here, do you suppose she's Laporte's private stock?"

Diehl started to answer, but Spelvin tugged at his sleeve and nodded toward the man moving in their direction through the smoky, crowded beer hall.

Raul Laporte was a tall, swarthy man, with a black handlebar mustache. His black hair was worn long on one side in a single braid that lay close to his scalp and ran down behind his left ear, then fell loose onto his shoulder and was tied off with a dirty ribbon. The braid was rumored to cover a large, ugly scar, but no one ever asked Laporte if this was true. He had the look of a man who would cut your throat just for the fun of it.

Laporte spun a chair around backwards and sat down facing the two Marines. He took a small notebook from his shirt pocket and looked at them. He said nothing.

Diehl and Spelvin each produced some folded currency and pushed the bills across the table, smiling nervously. "Good afternoon, Mr. Laporte," Spelvin said. "Business sure looks good today. Nice crowd."

Laporte's mouth smiled at them. His eyes did not. He leafed through the notebook, then fingered the two sheaves of bills. "You're ten sols short," he said to Spelvin, then turned to Diehl. "You're five short."

The Marines both squirmed slightly in their seats. "I sure am sorry about that, Mr. Laporte," Diehl said. "But, y'see I was on restriction to barracks and I didn't get to rotate to Xerxes this month. Y'see there's a guy on Xerxes what owes me some money, and just as soon as I get up there to get it, I'll get it to you."

"Not my problem," Laporte said. "Suppose you was to win some money from me playing Double–O, or Gombjuli, or something, and I said, 'Gosh, Corporal, I just can't pay off right now. How about next week?' You wouldn't like that much, would you?"

Diehl looked uncomfortable, then took a sudden and great interest in a raveling on his jacket cuff.

"Well?" Laporte said in a slightly louder voice. "*Would you?*"

"No, sir," Diehl mumbled.

"What?" Laporte said. "I can't hear you."

Diehl gave him a pained look. "I don't guess I'd like it. No, sir." Then, he quickly added, "But I'm sure I can get it to you by next week."

Laporte said nothing. He stared at Diehl for a moment with expressionless, cold eyes, then turned toward Spelvin, swiveling the chair slightly as he reached into his hip pocket. He brought out a large clasp knife, opened it up, and began cleaning his nails. "What about you?" he said to Spelvin without looking up.

"I can get it to you by then, too," Spelvin said. "I'm sure of it. See, they been workin' us pretty hard and nobody's had much chance to get around and—"

"I don't like bein' short–changed," Laporte said in a quiet voice.

"I ain't trying to short–change you, Mr. Laporte. I just don't have all the money," Spelvin said.

Diehl tugged at his buddy's elbow. "Jim," he said, "maybe Mr. Laporte would like to hear what we saw in the valley up there."

Laporte looked up, mildly interested. "What valley?"

"Up on north Beta," Spelvin said. "See, we been flying patrol up there and doin' survey mapping at the same time."

"Our platoon is attached to the Native Protection outfit," Diehl chimed in, "an' they got this reservation on north Beta for the Fuzzies—"

"I'm well aware of that." Laporte cut him off in mid-sentence. "What did you *see?* I can't know whether I care a damn about the information until you tell me what you saw."

"Why, in this big valley up there," Diehl said. "There's some hutments up there—little lean–tos, like—and what looks like fields—not really regular, but like they'd been—uh—cultivated. There ain't nothing growin' in them right now, but you can see where there used to be."

Laporte laughed—genuinely this time. "Why you dumb jarheads," he said. "You tryin' to tell me there's tilled ground on north Beta?"

"Well, that's what we saw," Spelvin protested.

"Nobody but Fuzzies live on north Beta," Laporte said. "And everybody knows Fuzzies ain't farmers."

Spelvin looked scared, but he answered. "Well, we *seen* it," he said, "plain as anything."

Diehl shook his head. "We wouldn' lie to you, Mr. Laporte. We know what we saw."

Laporte relaxed. "All right," he said, "I can't call you liars because I haven't been there myself, but this wouldn't be the first time you've lied to me. Now, get this straight, your 'information' isn't worth a pinch of snot. But I'm going to tell my bartender to give you a beer apiece—just because I wanna meet you more than halfway. And you let me hear about you *buying* a beer anywhere else in this town,"—he waved the clasp knife, presumably to include all of Mallorysport—"before you square up accounts with me, and I'll take enough skin off your backs—with this—to get my money back from the tannery. You hear me good?"

"Yessir," Diehl said.

"Yes, sir, Mr. Laporte," Spelvin chimed in.

After Laporte had given the highsign to the bartender to lavish two large beers on the Marines, he shook his head and put away the knife. *Blunderers,* he thought. *Can't do any-*

*thing for themselves—not without somebody leaning on them
all the time. Well, if I keep them on the hook, they'll sooner—
or—later come up with some information that's worth a
couple of sols.*

The Right Reverend Father Thomas Aquinas Gordon
snorted in disgust. "Mr. O'Gorman," he said, "this place is
a damned disgrace. I don't know why I'm bothering to waste
my time looking at it."

The object of his displeasure raised both hands heavenward in a placating gesture. Mr. O'Gorman was an incongru-
ous Mr. O'Gorman. His little black shoe-button eyes were
closely set above a magnificent nose which flourished over
much of his olive-skinned face. His full name was Hiram
Mustaphah O'Gorman, and he was a rental agent and real—
estate broker in Junktown.

"I am a parish priest," The Rev said, "looking for a place
to set up a neighborhood mission. Now why have you
brought me to this decaying firetrap?"

O'Gorman winced. "Economy, Father, economy. You
stated the need for economy."

The conversation was taking place in the large, high-
ceilinged main workroom of what had once been a bakery.
"Economy is one thing, Mr. O'Gorman," The Rev said.
"This—this cistern is something else." He carefully stepped
around a puddle of rainwater which had entered through the
hole in the roof.

"But, Reverend Sir," O'Gorman protested. "Rental
buildings are in very scarce supply. This is the only building
of the size you describe which is on my lists for rent." He
wrung his hands.

"Then I shall have to go to another broker, Mr. O'Gorman," The Rev said. "My superiors expect me to produce
results, not the refurbishment of some drafty old barn like
this. Why, if I send my bishop the bills to rebuild this rickety
mess, he'll have me clapped in a mental institution."

O'Gorman waved his hands with massaging motions. "I
assure you, Reverend Father, it will be no problem to put the
place in very fine shape. The owner is a kinsman of mine—an

honest, Christian person like myself. I shall speak to him personally, and all will be well. You'll see. Take my word for it; there is no other place in all Mallorysport that can be assembled for the size and the price you are able to pay.

"Perhaps when he learns the purpose of your tenancy, my cousin will even reduce the rent—to the Glory of God, you understand."

"It would be tax–deductable," The Rev said.

"Oh, an excellent point, sir," O'Gorman replied. "I shall bring it up to him at the first opportunity.

"We are settled, then. This must be the place for your mission. Let us return to my office and settle everything at once. My other cousin, Nima Bactrian, shall supervise all the repairing. You will be saving heathen within the week, Father."

"At least we can bake our own bread," The Rev said, eyeing the row of ovens along the back wall. "You'll put in new power converters and see that those ovens are operational?"

O'Gorman waved his hands once more, as they walked out through the remains of the old bakery's storefront and onto the esplanade. "All will be taken care of. We will make notes for the lease and agree upon everything right after we have some tea and sweet rolls from the bakery of my cousin Stoudhi—he sends them to my office fresh every morning, bless him."

"Tea?" The Rev said.

Hiram Mustaphah O'Gorman blinked at him in the Zarathustran sunlight. "Of course," he said. "The mullah himself tells us that the most satisfactory deal is never struck before the third cup of tea."

XI

"Dammit, Sandra!" Victor Grego pounded his cigarette into the ashtray so hard he almost burned his thumb. "You can't just up–and–flat leave me without a sitter for Diamond. I know you and Ahmed want to get married, but you've got to give me a chance to select someone who is appropriate and qualified to be your successor."

The tall redhead smiled at him from across the coffee table in the living room of the penthouse on top of the Company House building. She smiled broadly enough to make wrinkles at the corners of her green eyes. "Why, Mr. Grego," she said. "You've been saying that for over seven months, now. Ahmed is beginning to think you're after me yourself. He's getting quite jealous."

"Faugh!" Grego snorted. He waved his hand as though to dismiss the entire discussion. "It's not a bad idea," he said, "but I never stand in the way of young lust, or poach in another man's pasture—especially not when the man is a police captain and carries a pistol."

"And, as for the careful selection part of your argument," Sandra continued, "I remember *exactly* how careful and scientific you were about *that*. You said, '. . . you've just been appointed Fuzzy-Sitter-in-Chief. You start immediately; ten percent raise as of this morning.' "

Grego leaned back in his chair and tried to look stern. "That was different," he said. "I could tell right away that Diamond liked you and trusted you. Fuzzies have an instinct for that sort of thing."

"Governess would be a better term, anyway, Mr. Grego," Sandra Glenn said. "I think he's smarter than I am; either that or he learns faster than any Fuzzy I've seen. I just can't stay ahead of him any more."

"Ah–ha!" Grego cried triumphantly. "That's exactly

why I must be very choosy about who takes over your job—and there has to be an overlap period while whoever-it-is learns everything you know about Fuzzies and about Diamond. Why, we can't just switch Fuzzy–sitters on him without any notice, like that. It would break his little heart. He's very fond of you, you know.''

''But, Mr. Grego; really! Ahmed and I have been engaged so long, the ring is starting to grow to my finger.'' Sandra had stepped into another Grego–trap and she knew it. It was not any great surprise, either. The Manager–in–Chief of a Colonial Company might be expected to be a fairly good, fast–talking negotiator.

''We could compromise,'' Grego added quickly.

''How?'' she said, half–dreading the answer.

Grego warmed to the deal. ''You and Ahmed could get married right away—something simple and private—and get a little place right here in Mallorysport until we can break in a new sitter. You could cut your hours back to whatever meshes with Ahmed's schedule—at the same wages you get now, of course—and I would take up whatever slack that caused.''

''But what about the honeymoon?'' she said in a rising voice.

''Oh, faugh!'' Grego replied. ''Plenty of time for that after the two of you move out into the sticks, there, at Holloway Station.''

''But, that might be a year!'' She almost wailed.

Grego snorted. ''No such thing! You go along with me on this, and help me interview candidates for your job, and I'll tell you what I'll do. Well—I'm going to do it anyway, but—'' Grego stopped short.

Sandra sniffed. ''Do *what?*''

''Throw the wedding reception,'' he said. ''Right here on top of Company House. There's enough room here to properly entertain and feed a couple hundred people.''

Their conversation was interrupted by the soft chiming of the entrance door.

''That must be Leslie,'' Grego said. ''I forgot to tell you; no need to go and fetch Diamond home. Leslie told me he would pick him up on his way back from Government House.''

Company Chief Counsel Leslie Coombes entered the foyer, preceded by an energetic ball of bounding fur which jumped up onto the arm of Grego's chair. *"Heyo, Pappy Vic,"* Diamond shouted from the chair arm, then leaped on Grego's chest, danced around on his lap, pummeled his stomach playfully, and hugged him as hard as his little arms could manage.

Grego laughed heartily and scuffled a bit with Diamond. "There's Extee-Three on the kitchen counter, if you want,'' he said. "You know where the can opener is.''

Leslie Coombes frowned. "Shouldn't you—?'' he began.

"—work the can opener for him?'' Grego finished.

"He might hurt himself.'' Coombes said.

Grego shook his head. "Yes, Leslie,'' he said, "and you might fall in the bathtub and fracture your skull, too. But I don't see that's a good reason why your Mommy should still bathe you.''

Coombes' face reddened as Sandra Glenn chuckled over the mental image of a grown Leslie Coombes splashing the bath water with his rubber duckie while a gray–haired matron scrubbed him down with soap and a wash cloth.

Grego smiled. "The Fuzzies are people. We can't go on forever treating them like little china dolls, much as it might please us to have someone around who is going to be eternally ten years old, always stay with us, always depend on us, and never grow up.''

Coombes sighed. "I see your point, Victor. Most folks cherish Fuzzies like their own kids, and no one ever wants his own children to grow up and leave home.''

"And we're not going to have that luxury with Fuzzies, either,'' Grego said, "so we might as well get used to the idea.''

"They learn like a house on fire,'' Sandra said. "The people over at Science Center are beginning to wonder if they are smarter than we are.''

"It wouldn't surprise me,'' Coombes said gloomily. "You don't see Fuzzies wearing themselves out trying to

keep a charterless colonial company in the black. That's what
I came to see you about, Victor. Do you know we've had
seventy-six aircars stolen in the past two months, mostly by
veldbeest herders who take off to make their fortune and take
a Company vehicle along to speed the process?''

''I already told you,'' Grego said, ''swear out warrants for
their arrest.''

''Warrants are one thing,'' Coombes replied. ''Arrests are
another. We've got to expand the Company Police and we
can't afford it. The more vehicles they steal the more sols it
costs us, and the equipment loss cuts into budgets that ought
to be going for more cops. It's a vicious circle.''

Grego chuckled. ''Spiteful, perhaps.'' He wagged a finger
in the air. ''You must be resourceful, Leslie. Creative. For
example Sandra, here, is going to get married, leave me flat
without a Fuzzy sitter; but you don't hear me complaining, do
you?''

''Hah!'' Sandra said.

''Stick around a while, Leslie,'' Grego went on, ''until
Gus Brannhard gets here. Ben Rainsford came up with a plan
to increase police efficiency all over the planet. I'd like to
knock it around with both of you—see what you think of it.''

George Lunt snapped the cover back on the separator and
closed the printer's paper-feed. Nothing wrong that he could
see, and certainly nothing that would explain the soil readouts in that valley. George was a methodical man and he
didn't like loose ends. This was a loose end.

George jumped lightly to the ground from the aircar's open
hatch. *No point in taking it out of service for maintenance,* he
thought, *unless the readouts continue to be screwed up for
some* other *piece of geography. No; we'll just re-fly that
sector with a different vehicle–see what we come up with for
comparison.*

As he finished punching in the assignment change to the
roster, George straightened and turned to the watch sergeant.
''Log that change, Sarge, so it'll be highlighted at the watch
briefing. That section of the Cordilleras will just have to wait
a little longer for survey mapping.''

"Right–o," the sergeant said. He leaned out of his chair and made a notation on a clipboard, as Major Lunt walked back out in front of the duty desk.

George stopped for a moment, then turned back. "And, change the assigned vehicle to the command boat. I think I'll go along for the ride."

Ben Rainsford opened the front door of his apartments in Government House, then stepped back in astonishment. "Gus!" he said sharply. "What in hell is the matter with you? Do. you have to go to the bathroom?"

Gus Brannhard was dancing in the hallway. Dancing was not the precise word, perhaps, but Colonial Attorney General Gustavus Adolphus Brannhard was shuffling about briskly, rather like an amiable bear, swinging his arms vigorously. Periodically, his enormous frame would seem to float up off the floor slightly, and he would click his heels together.

"Stop grinning like an idiot and tell me what this is all about," Rainsford said. "You want people to think the planet is being run by a bunch of lunatics?"

Gus stopped dancing and came inside the foyer, but he couldn't stop grinning. A double row of white teeth glittered through his tousled gray–brown beard like a hedgehog that had swallowed a piano.

"We got him disbarred," he guffawed. "Totally, completely, and altogether disbarred."

"Who?" Rainsford shouted. "*Who* did you get disbarred? And why would one shyster be glad to see another shyster get disbarred?"

Brannhard became suddenly serious. "Why, Hugo Ingermann, of course. Who the hell else have I been trying to get disbarred for the past year and a half? I was just now at Grego's smoothing the way for this police streamlining of yours and Leslie Coombes told me he had seen the order in this afternoon's recordings. Hugo Ingermann is still a *bona fide* attorney, but he's *mala fide* in all the courts on Zarathustra—no longer admitted to practice before them."

He clapped his hands together. "Maybe he'll be so disgusted he'll leave the planet."

"Fat chance," Rainsford said.

"Well," Brannhard said, "then I can get to work on some way to have the bastard deported. Man's got to have a hobby, you know."

Gus sat and leaned back in his chair. The chair creaked. "Yes, sir," he said. "I'm a happy man. Ingermann has been a thorn in the side of the government, the Company, the military, and a stench in the nostrils of every honest lawyer on Zarathustra."

"I'm not real sure," Rainsford said quietly, "that there *are* any honest lawyers, but I'm glad to get the news that we've pulled a couple of his teeth." Rainsford glanced up at the time readout. "Max Fane will be just as happy as you are, Gus. Why not stick around and tell him youself, since you seem to enjoy the story so much."

Brannhard nodded. As though he had signaled it, the door chimed.

If Brannhard had been overjoyed when he arrived, Colonel Marshal Max Fane was in a black rage.

Gus looked perplexed. "What's eating you, Max?" he asked.

Fane paced a few quick steps up and down the room, then spun his rotund body on one heel. "Some sonofabitch took a shot at me!" he roared. "In town!"

Gus leaped to his feet. "What?"

"Right here!" Fane jabbed his finger toward the floor. "On the esplanade, as I was coming over from the Central Courts complex."

"Did you get him?" Rainsford asked.

Fane scowled. "Naw. He was too far away to chase— probably why he missed me. But there weren't any people around so I got a couple rounds off at him." As though it reminded him, Max Fane pulled out his automatic and palmed the magazine.

"Well? Did you hit him?" Brannhard asked impatiently.

Fane laughed as he thumbed two fresh cartridges into the magazine. "Nooooo. But close." He looked up as he smacked the magazine back in and holstered the weapon. "I bet he's deaf in his left ear, though."

Marshal Fane listened approvingly to Brannhard's joyous account of the disbarment of Hugo Ingermann. Ingermann had the irritating habit of springing thugs and Junktown rats on a writ almost faster than Fane could round them up and jail them on warrants. He was likewise pleased about Rainsford's plans to consolidate police services while preserving the autonomy of the various agencies. That would put more men in the field, and that was what he needed—what every cop on the planet needed, what with the population influx and the burden on the legal system generated by the sudden availability of free land.

"It seems a little odd," Rainsford was saying. "Anybody ever take a shot at you before, Max?"

Fane reared back in his chair. "Out in the bush, yes. On pavement, never!"

"That's the odd part," Rainsford said. "A unique occurance that occurs less than five hours after Ingermann is disbarred. What do you think, Gus?"

"Nothing odd about it," Gus said. "Ingermann is behind it, and it's what I expected. This makes him raw as hell, and he's going to be Out–To–Get–Us, in capital letters, from now on—until something busts loose. I don't know about you, Ben, but I plan to start packing a gun in town."

"Some citizens are already doing that after dark," Fane remarked. "Perfectly legal. There's no way to make 'em stop."

Rainsford sighed. He got up and walked to the window, then stood there, with his hands behind his back for a moment, looking out at Mallorysport. Then he said matter-of-factly, "That's the way it always starts to break down. Thugs, bums, and animals—they scare honest citizens into exercising their constitutional right of self–defense. Next thing you know, the town's full of bullet–holes."

He returned to his chair. "Get out your scratchpads, gents. The Governor General is about to make some specific suggestions and you may want to take notes."

Fane exchanged puzzled looks with Gus as he began fishing in his hip pocket for the notebook that every cop in the universe carried there.

Rainsford re–lit his pipe, then leaned forward in his chair. "First, this government has got to do everything it can to keep the Zarathustra Company afloat." He raised one hand, palm outward. "I know, I know. When Commodore Napier railroaded me into this job I wanted to take Grego and everyone on his payroll and hang 'em high, but a strong colonial company is all that's going to hold this place together for a while—at least till we can get a legislature seated. Otherwise, a civilized colony on Zarathustra is going to be out the airlock. The trade that's been built up over twenty-five years will go to hell, and Ghu knows what will happen to the Fuzzies—whose welfare our government has taken responsibility for."

"Oh, now," Fane said, "I don't think it's *that* bad. You really serious about this?"

"Damn tootin' I am!" Rainsford barked. "What's bad about it is that we're flying blind. Gus, as Attorney General it's up to you to set the itinerary and run this meeting about consolidating police records. As we go ahead with that, I want the information from each police agency as to what kind of intelligence operatives they have working under cover, what they're doing, where they're doing it, and what they find out."

Brannhard made a face. "They're going to be pretty touchy about that, Ben."

"I know they are," Rainsford said. "Let them know in a gentle kind of way that we're prepared to subpoena the records if we have to.

"Max, I want you to draw up a table of organization for an Intelligence Section within your office, where we will consolidate police espionage information separately from the operations records. After all, the Company, the Federation, the military, and Ghu knows who all, constantly use spies to keep them informed. Why, I'm willing to bet Ingermann does the same thing. The only way we're ever going to bust him and his consortium of hoodlums is to out–G–2 them.

"Start feeling around and see if you can't get that young Khadra fella to head it up. I knew him when he was a patrolman on Beta. Got a good head on his shoulders."

"I'll do it," Fane said, "but I still think you're painting a pretty gloomy picture."

"Maybe I am," Rainsford admitted, "but if Zarathustra does turn into a sinkhole populated by riffraff and cutthroats, it sure won't be because I didn't try to head it off before it got out of hand. For one thing, this government couldn't stand the blow to public confidence if things go to Nifflheim and we get another dose of Martial Law from the Navy."

"He's right, Max," Brannhard said. "The same thing happened on Fenris. The Chartered Fenris Company went off half cocked with colonization, then found they couldn't turn a profit. When the Company went bust, it stretched the Colonial Government too thin. There weren't enough stabilizing influences on the economy to keep it from getting lopsided. A lot of rip-offs and power grabs here and there. In no time at all the only people left on the planet were about ten percent of the original population—they were the only ones tough enough and smart enough to stay alive."

XII

Christiana Stone lay face down at an angle across the bed, sobbing, and thrumming her fists noiselessly on the sylkon coverlet. In one fist was a crumpled piece of message print-out.

"Damn him! Damn him! *Damn him!* Why did he have to go and die? Before I could keep him out of jail."

Coming to Zarathustra had been the only way out that she could see at the time. That was all right. But she knew now that she had failed to do her homework when she refused to go to work for Ivan Bowlby and insisted on striking out on her own. Bowlby controlled all the prostitution in Mallorysport and he became very cranky if anyone tried to buck into his monopoly. He had systematically terrorized her with rough trade and dried up the rest of her business, forcing her to drain away what little assets were left after buying passage from Terra, and grandiosely sworn, "So long as I'm alive, that broad will never turn another trick on Zarathustra."

Now, when she was broke, beaten, and demoralized completely, the news came that her father had died. The father she idolized—the father she couldn't bear to tell that she knew about his embezzlements—the father who had been drinking himself into an early grave with guilt—gone.

The communication screen exploded with a burst of colors, then steadied into the image of Captain Ahmed Khadra.

George Lunt made a minor adjustment of the screen at his end. "You're going to have to get yourself out here, Captain. I need you."

"But, George," Khadra protested, "my detached leave won't be up for two more weeks."

"Mmmmm," George said, "I know. I don't want to

52

discuss it on screen, but how soon can you get yourself back over here and go to work for me?"

Khadra looked pained. "Well, Sandra and I are about to set the date. What's the rush?"

"I should think you would," George Lunt grumped. "A year you've been engaged to that girl and I've barely gotten a tap of work out of you the whole time."

"I come from a very formal family," Ahmed said stiffly. "We wanted to wait till Holloway Station is a little more civilized before I drag her out to live in the bush. Besides, Grego keeps wheedling at her to stay on 'just a little while longer.'"

"No more frittering, Ahmed," George said, "and no more giving in to slick talk from Victor Grego. I'm going to need you. Now! I'll get a bungalow up for you and Sandra right away—though Ghu knows how I'll justify it in the budget. You get your affairs in Mallorysport wrapped up. I want you, bride, and baggage out here bright and early no later than a week from Tuesday."

"That's not much time," Khadra protested.

"Sure it is," George said. "You can take your honeymoon on the installment plan."

The Right Reverend Father Thomas Aquinas Gordon leaned forward in his chair and pushed the box of tissues across the desk. He thought to himself of the countless times he had done this drill before, although this was the first in his cool, quiet office in Junktown. The walls were a reassuring pastel tone and still smelled of newly applied vyathane spray coating.

"I didn't know where else to turn," Christiana said. She snatched two tissues from the box and blew her nose.

"You turned to the right place," The Rev said. "There are things in life that you can control, child, and there are things you can't. The things you can't have to be carried as best you can—till you can get the upper hand on them."

She dabbed at her eyes. "I feel better, already, just getting it all out and telling someone."

The Rev nodded.

She had poured out the whole story to him, in a jumble of words and tears. The accidental discovery that her father was embezzling money from his company and using it to keep another woman and pay the gambling debts of the woman's worthless brother, and Christiana's inability to bring herself to tell him for fear it would completely break his spirit. She was certain that her fiancé could be depended on for help. That had been young Rodney Schuyler of the shipping family—very old family, very wealthy family. He had proved his loyalty by breaking the engagement and dumping her. The only thing she could think of then had been to come out to Zarathustra, earn money as fast as she could—preferably in a way calculated to horrify Rodney—and try to get her father off Terra before the authorities caught up with him. If one could get off-planet, one's chances of being extradited back to Terra for anything as piddling as grand theft were quite small.

Now it was all gone—all come to nothing. Ivan Bowlby had her blacklisted. Daddy was dead. What did it all mean?

"I just can't see the use of going on," she said.

The Rev leaned back in his chair. "I don't imagine you can; and that's understandable right now. I'm not going to give you any fancy advice about waiting for Almighty Intervention, but I will tell you this: in every disaster that happens to people no matter how overwhelming it seems at the time there is the seed of something you will find you want much more, something that is far more wonderful than what you seem to have lost. But, you gotta look for it."

"But what am I going to *do*?" she sobbed.

"Well," The Rev said, "this might be one hell of a good time to get a regular job and go straight. At least if you don't like it, you can earn enough money to get off Zarathustra, and from what you tell me I don't see that you've much chance of turning a sol any other way. Look—I bet you know how to run a processor—a data terminal—a transcriber deck—that sort of thing. Don't you?"

She nodded.

The Rev spread his hands and smiled. "There you are. Get

uptown and apply for work at every tall building you can find. You don't belong down here, anyway."

". . . Ahmed has to go back out to Holloway Station," Sandra Glenn finished. "In just over a week!"

"You're going to get married right away and go with him, of course," Grego said.

"Of course," she replied.

"Mmmmm. You'd be crazy not to—the way that man worships you is beyond belief." He paused. "But, then, you are a treasure, Sandra. I wonder why Major Lunt was so insistent.

"Well!" Grego leaped to his feet. "I'll tell Myra to take charge of all the details you want with the ceremony itself. *I'll* plan the reception. I think we can do the whole thing here. How about Saturday afternoon, with the reception staggering on into the evening?"

"I'll have to talk to Ahmed," she said.

"Of course you will," Grego agreed. "I want the two of you back here to have cocktails with me promptly at 1700. That's the one time of day when I know where to lay my hands on anyone and everyone. We'll get it all discussed and start the ball rolling. Now, we want to make a big bash out of this—"

"I'm not sure we can—" she started to interrupt.

Grego bent toward her and smiled benignly. "—Afford it?" he said.

She nodded.

"The Company," he said evenly, "will insist on paying all the bride's expenses. That takes care of the reception, the entertainment, and practically all of it."

"But—" she said.

"You see," Grego said, "*I* am giving the bride away— heh, heh—and appropriate it is, too. Best damned Fuzzy sitter I ever had." He rubbed his hands together. "Yes, yes. We'll have all the Fuzzies in for it, too. And invite all the girls from the Company Executive Offices. Yes, yes. Some good-looking young women around this place will have an

ameliorating effect on the dispositions of old coots like Ben
Rainsford and me.''

By the end of breakfast the next morning, Victor Grego
had amassed a hefty sheaf of notes. As he poured a second
cup of coffee and lit a fresh cigarette, he riffled through them,
looking for the must–do–right–now items he had underlined.
On the communication screen across the breakfast room,
Myra Fallada finished some notes on his instructions and
pushed her pencil back to its roost in her elaborately curled
white hair. Myra had been his secretary since he first came to
Zarathustra.

"Oh, yes," Grego said. "There won't be time to have any
invitations printed up and be certain that they get to all the
guests at a decent time for them to reply. We'll go ahead and
do that, of course, as a matter of courtesy and etiquette, but I
want you to take the guest list and program a reasonably
flowery invitaton into the computer so it will inform
everyone by communication screen and log their replies. The
caterer is going to be temperamental at best, given the short
notice, so we'll have to let him know how many to expect
immediately."

Myra ran the pencil in and out of her hair a couple of times
as she braced for a reply. "Mister Grego," she said, "this is
more than any one person can manage—if I drop everything
else, like—" she pursed her lips "—Company business, for
example."

Grego drew thoughtfully on his cigarette. "Yes, Myra. I
know there's a lot to do. Sandra can help a little—while she's
not with Diamond. No, that won't do it. Listen, have we had
any applications for office jobs lately?"

Myra consulted some clipped-together papers. "Yes,"
she said. "Two yesterday."

"Good," Grego boomed. "Hire one of them this instant.
That'll give you a full–time assistant until we see the happy
couple off to Beta. Also, you can spread around some of the
detail work among the other workers in the office. After all
this Company has weathered in the past year, I think we can
cope with putting a large wedding together on short notice."

Myra nodded and looked at him with half–closed eyes. "Yes, Mister Grego," she said.

"That's the stuff, Myra. I'll be down in a half-hour. I'm going directly to the Conference Room for the department heads' briefing, so I should be at my desk in less than ninety minutes."

After the meeting, Grego was chatting in the corridor with his Construction Director.

". . . So, by developing Company–owned real estate, we can head off some of the land grabbers and speculators, and still keep ourselves in an aggressive posture—profitably—as the largest builder on the planet."

"I see what you mean, Don," Grego replied. "It's human nature. People will rent apartments and commercial space from us first if we have selection and price. Volume will give us the price by drying up supply to the smaller builders. It'll keep them from snowballing things for a fast buck—like what happened out in Mortgageville."

Leslie Coombes tugged gently at Grego's sleeve. "Okay, Don," Grego said. "Work up some presentations on specific projects and get back to me."

Then he turned to Coombes. "What is it, Leslie?" he said.

"I've been looking at your ops sheet for this wedding reception, Victor. Did you know that Jerry Panoyian is listed as the caterer?"

"Of course I know it," Grego said. "I specifically asked that he be the caterer."

Coombes looked like he had just tasted something very sour. "But, Victor, surely you know he's in very thick with all the underworld bigwigs."

Grego nodded. "Um–hmm. I know that. But as far as the police can find out, he's only involved in catering their social functions for them. That aspect of it is disturbing to me, I'll admit, but he *is* the best caterer in all Mallorysport. And I want this to be a party to remember for some time to come. I want to have only the finest of everything, so that means we'll be using Jerry Panoyian."

He looked sideways at Coombes. "However, if it'll make

you feel better, I'll have a couple plainclothes Company
Policemen watch him from the moment he sets foot in Company House until he and his people have gone.''

"And count your silverware before you let them leave,"
Coombes added.

XIII

Mr. Chief Justice Frederic Pendarvis stepped deftly to one side of his wife and presented her formally to the bride and groom—although they had met each other before the ceremony.

"I hope you will be as happy together as we have been," she said, after shaking hands with both Ahmed and Sandra. Then she turned her gentle face toward her husband, with the soft light in Victor Grego's living room catching her white hair with a halo–like glow, and smiled at him.

"Oh, Claudette," Pendarvis said, "you'll make these young people blush."

"No one is ever embarrassed by love," she chided him easily.

It was only fitting that Claudette and Frederic Pendarvis be the first to join the reception line. The newlyweds had chosen him to perform the ceremony, and Ben Rainsford was the only person in the room whose civil rank was higher.

They took their places alongside the bride and groom to greet the balance of the guests—a process which might occupy the rest of the afternoon, judging from the mob of people milling about the penthouse, the outdoor pavilion on the terrace, and the bars and buffet that had been set up outdoors in the shade of the north and east sides.

Next to join the line was Victor Grego, the host and the man who had given the bride away, looking as jolly as a character from a Dickens novel in his stand–up shirt collar and gray swallow–tail coat.

Properly, Ben Rainsford should have been in the reception line, too, as the ranking civil official, but he had begged off on the excuse that he had a sprained hand and that standing there for so long would make his "gimpy leg"—invented along with the sprained hand—start acting up.

Chief Earlie of the Mallorysport P.D. sloshed the ice around in his glass and remarked to his opposite number in the Company Police Force, "Y'know, Harry, if I was a crook this is the time I'd pick to stick up a bank." He motioned to where the temporary coat rack in the penthouse foyer was festooned with a perfect jungle of pistol belts and berets, hung there by their owners whose ethics forbade them to drink while wearing those badges of office. "Why, I bet every senior cop in town is here this afternoon."

With the skyrocketing population every peace officer in the city no longer had the luxury of putting on his tuxedo to attend a social event; they never knew when they might have to drop everything and jump into some crisis. And, most agencies had a current standing order to maintain a high visual profile to reassure the citizens that there was literally a policeman on every landing stage, esplanade, and escalator.

Harry Steefer nodded. "What I don't get is why George Lunt didn't come over for the wedding. He's only three hours away—and he and Ahmed are pretty close. I mean, they go 'way back—to when George was a lieutenant and Ahmed was a patrolman in the Constabulary."

They were joined by a roundish man in khaki gabardines, holding his champagne glass gingerly, as though it might explode at any moment. "I don't get that, either," Max Fane said. With his free hand he tapped his nose. "This educated member of mine smells something odd about that. It's not like George Lunt to throw his tail in the air that way—cancel Khadra's leave—tell him to beat it back to Beta on the double. Something's in the wind, if you ask me."

Harry Steefer shrugged. " 'Spose they might have made another big sunstone strike up in the Fuzzy Reservation? That would cause a lot of fuss and fury."

"Oh, hell, no," Fane said, waving his free hand in a gesture of dismissal. "George has an army of cops to take care of *that*—it's just patrolling and keeping people out who don't belong there. No, sir. Sumpin's funny in the wind."

Chief Earlie nodded. "I'll admit I'm curious, too, Max, but that's on Beta—three hours away from here. The rats down in Junktown are getting bolder; too many of them, now, to make a living off each other. They're starting to drift up into the new city, in little knots of three and four. I'm handling double the number of robberies I was this time last year—and getting fewer arrests. That's what *I'm* worried about. It looks like it's going to get a lot worse before it gets any better, at least by the rate the population is rising."

"You don't think the immigrants are all criminals, do you?" Steefer said.

"Oh, of course not, Harry," Chief Earlie said. "But, when you get a population boom on immigration, the rats always move in with the immigrants. We've all seen it before—if not when Mortgageville bloomed up out of the ground north of town eight or nine years ago—then someplace else. The rats come in their pockets, riding their coattails, and hiding under their hats. Lotta times, its the same rats that were living off them back home; when poor people pull up stakes and move on to try for something better, the rats pack their little rat carpet bags and go right along with them—like a cockleburr on a dog's tail." He stepped over to the east terrace's portable bar—a painted white rattan affair—and handed his glass over to the liveried bartender.

Max Fane chuckled. "And that's only the amateur rats, the professional rats can smell a compost heap of money halfway across the galaxy. Why, they're practically waiting for the marks at the spaceport when they arrive—with rigged rat card games, little rat shylocks, and little rat swindlers with mustaches."

"Don't forget little rat pimps," Harry Steefer chimed in, "with strings of cute rat whores."

Chief Earlie accepted a fresh drink from the bartender. "Oh, yes," he said, "we can count on a lot of new business from Bowlby, Heenan, and Laporte. Thaxter is too comfortably situated to risk much these days. He's almost as well off as Ingermann."

"Well, that's one thing," Fane said. "Now that the little porker can't practice law any more, I won't have to look at his superior smirk as he hustles in with a writ clutched in his fist to spring some thug employed by the gentlemen you just mentioned."

"It won't matter, Max," Chief Earlie said, "he'll just hire someone who can still practice law to do it for him."

Fane gritted his teeth. "I know, but at least I won't have to look at him."

"Oh, I don't think it will be too 'boring,' as you put it, for Sandra," Juan Jimenez was saying to the tall sociologist from Science Center. He couldn't recall having seen her before, and wondered if she was aware that she worked for him; no mention had yet been made that he was head of the Company Science Center.

"But, *Holloway Station*," the sociologist said, " 'way the hell out on Beta. What is there for a wife to *do* out there, except—" she shrugged "—cook and keep house?"

Juan laughed. "I imagine she'll help Dr. and Mrs. van Riebeek at Fuzzy Institute. Sandra's knowledge of Fuzzy language is extensive and involves many subtleties she's learned from looking after Diamond."

"Fuzzy Institute?" the lady sociologist asked. "You mean there's a college out there?"

He laughed again. "Almost," he said. "Research labs. Medical Center. School for the Fuzzies. Permanent staff of twelve, plus about ten more on loan from the Company."

I'm going to have to take this lady camping, sometime, Juan thought. *I bet she hasn't been out of high-heeled shoes since she got her diploma.*

"It's not exactly a wilderness, Miss—ah—Miss. . ."

"Bell," she said and smiled at him. "Liana Bell."

"Thank you. A lovely name. In any case, Miss Bell, Holloway Station is the headquarters of the Native Affairs Commission, so it's quite a busy place, really."

She looked off into the middle distance. "It's beginning to sound very interesting. I think I'd like to go over there and do a short survey on the interface between Terran and Fuzzy culture. Do you think they'd mind?"

"Not at all," Juan said. "I think they'd be overjoyed."

She bobbed her head once, decisively. "Yes. I'll ask Dr. Mallin about it right away. In fact, he's at this reception, isn't he? I thought I saw him earlier."

"In fact, he is," Juan said. "In the meantime, may I get you some more champagne?"

"I'd love it. Dr. Mallin is my immediate superior, you see, so I'll need his permission."

Juan chuckled. Ernst Mallin thought everyone had Fuzzies on the brain, did not approve, and thought people should get back to good old "hard" research. He had already made up his mind that the NFMp hormone had doomed Fuzzies to a genetic dead end and it was only a matter of time until the species died out in any case. He took Liana Bell's glass. "Be right back," he said.

"Oh," she said, "but you haven't told me *your* name."

"Jimenez," he said. "Juan Jimenez."

She laughed. *"Dr. Jimenez!* And you let me stand here, rattling on like an ado-ditty about 'my superior'. You run the Science Center!"

Juan smiled and shrugged. "They let me think so, anyway," he said. "You'll *still* have to get Dr. Mallin's permission, although I think you would have an interesting project."

"Thank you, Dr. Jimenez," she said.

"Thank *you*, Miss Bell."

"Liana," she said.

"Juan," he said.

"Champagne?" she reminded him, pointing at the empty glasses.

"Oh, yes," he said, and started to turn in the direction of the buffet. "Don't go away."

Gus Brannhard parted his gray-brown whiskers carefully as he prepared to answer the question from the Clerk of the Colonial Courts. "Champagne, Mr. Wilkins, is very bad for the sinuses." He inhaled deeply from the enormous brandy snifter easily cradled in his huge hand. "And that is why," he concluded, "I never touch the stuff. No, no—all those bubbles hopping around inside a man's head; must make a terrible racket. I imagine it would make my ears pop something fierce."

It was the eyes that were popping for Roy Wilkins. He had

never dreamed that a human being could drink as much as the
Colonial Attorney General and still retain his faculties. Wilkins shoved his glasses back up his nose to a firmer footing
and plunged back into the conversation.

"And what," he asked, "do you think about this business
of Hugo Ingermann being disbarred? Personally, I'm tickled
pink."

Gus eyed the young man solemnly. "Why, as an official of
the colonial government, I have no thoughts on the subject at
all. As public employees, we should have no comments—not
public ones, anyway—on the fortunes of any private citizen.
Do you get my meaning, son?"

Wilkins sipped his champagne nervously. "Oh, I understand perfectly, sir. It's just that—I mean—that is—I didn't
intend it to sound—exactly—like I *rejoiced* in Mr. Ingermann's disbarment."

Gus eyed him some more, then his face broke into a smile
and he winked broadly. " 'Course you didn't. People in our
position just have to be prudent."

Wilkins nodded. One lesson learned.

"There is something, though, that I would like your opinion on, Mr. Wilkins—professionally."

Opinion? This legendary giant who was the Attorney General wanted *his* opinion on something? Gosh!

"What," Gus Brannhard asked, "is the scuttlebutt on the
coffeepot telegraph around your offices about the constitutional convention? Interworld News and the rest show the
delegates all busily roaring like wounded damnthings every
night on the screen, but as far as actual resolutions and
articles filed, it's as dry as a temperance meeting. I just
wondered if they were actually generating documents and
someone forgot to send me review copies. What are they
doing?"

"Well, sir, I can't rightly say. I do know that we've copied
and sent over about a metric ton of colonial case law which
they've requested."

"And they haven't sent any of it back?"

"No, sir."

"And they haven't filed any draft articles or resolutions?"

"No, sir," Wilkins said. "Well, sir, that is, with one exception."

"Which is?"

"They sent me a draft request to extend the convention for a year, and wanted to know if it was properly framed."

Gus jabbed his finger at the ceiling triumphantly. "*Now* I know what they've been doing. The buggers have studied everything to death. Now they see that their year is almost up and they aren't even close to framing a constitution, so they want us to give them another year—another year during which the government can't levy taxes.

"Well, I guess it's time for Governor Rainsford and my-self to pay these dedicated foot-draggers a visit in open session—*in situ* as it were—and sort of explain the facts of life to them."

Wilkins pushed his glasses up his nose, again, hesitated, then gulped and spoke. It was not the usual thing for the Clerk of the Court to correct the Attorney General on process, even at a party. "But, sir," he said, "colonial law forbids any appointed official of colonial government being in atten-dance at the site of a constitutional convention—uh—to prevent sandbagging, I guess."

Gus took another swig of brandy while Wilkins spoke, and glowered at him through the snifter glass as he did so. He lowered the glass and fluffed his beard. "Of course it does, Mr. Wilkins, but only in an uninvited capacity. I'm sure the intrepid colonists in that body will be pleased—once the matter is explained to some of the leaders—to invite us in for some 'advice.'"

While Gus Brannhard guffawed at Roy Wilkins, a slender man who stood nearby, chatting with Ernst Mallin, frowned and pursed his lips.

"That man's a perfect example, Ernst," Dr. Jan Chris-tiaan Hoenveld said. "Refinement and breeding are out the airlock in Mallorysport so long as the Governor General still wears bush clothes and his colonial officials are a bunch of bumpkins like Brannhard. Rainsford's offices and quarters in Government House have *animal skins* all over the floors. It's just not civilized.''

Mallin sipped his champagne and smiled. ''I suppose, Chris, that you preferred Nick Emmert's administration—cocktail parties sparkling with mindless chatter, and all those damned canapés. Personally, I don't care if I never see creamed cheese again.''

''Well, at least the man had some *style*,'' Hoenveld sniffed.

''I used to like those parties of Emmert's, too,'' Mallin mused, ''until—something—I guess it was me—changed. I can tell you one thing, Chris, Rainsford's administration is one hundred percent honest, even if the men in it are a little rough around the edges.''

''Oh, don't talk to me about 'rough around the edges,' Ernst. This mob of ragged vagabonds that's immigrating to Zarathustra is ruining what little grace we had developed in Mallorysport. My tailor is feeling the pinch already; no one has any standards, any more. And why should they—when the *Governor* always looks like he's been sleeping in his clothes? One just throws on any old flak jacket one finds wadded up in the back of the closet and one is in perfect style.''

Mallin smiled. ''I'm sure refined taste will survive, Chris. It's come through worse setbacks than this.

''Excuse me, will you? One of my people is waving frantically for me to join her.''

Mallin had to get away from Hoenveld; he wasn't sure how much longer he could keep a straight face. Chris Hoenveld was the best biochemist ever to set foot on Zarathustra, but he sure had some strange ideas about what was important. Besides, Liana Bell really was signaling him to come over and join her and Juan Jimenez.

As he threaded his way through the guests, he caught a scrap from another conversation that was refreshingly balanced against Hoenveld's notions about genteelness.

Colonel Ian Ferguson, commander of the Colonial Constabulary, had joined the other law enforcement types gathered around the bar. "Well, I'll tell you one thing," he was saying, "with Ben Rainsford in the governor's chair, you never have to wonder what the hell he's talking about. The man doesn't know how to beat around the bush."

"Amen to that," Al Earlie said. "Nick Emmert always wanted people to get gussied up like a pet owl—just for cocktails, mind you—and then he'd talk your ear off and you never knew what he'd said afterwards. That was the part I hated—climbing into that monkey suit with the sandpaper collar. And there's no way to carry a gun in one of those things without it showing."

"Not yours, anyway," Harry Steefer said, thinking of Al Earlie's favorite sidearm—a long barreled .45 revolver that pitched a 271–grain slug.

"Say, that reminds me," Max Fane said, "did I tell you somebody took a shot at me the other day—right down here on the esplanade?"

Max's story was cut short as a thundering herd of Fuzzies galloped through the middle of the group, yeeking with delight. Hot on their heels was a group of young women who worked in the Executive Offices of the CZC. "Come back here, you little devils!" *"So—josso—aki tai washa!"* "Give me back my things!"

The Fuzzies shrieked with mock terror. *"Do—Bizzo! Fazzu! Hagga* catch us!" "Sp'it up!" "Faster!"

Apparently the Fuzzies had pulled a heist for the fun of the chase. Leading the pack in pursuit was a laughing strawberry blonde who had kicked off her shoes and was making better speed than anyone else.

The next lap around the terrace, the Fuzzies were gaining distance—and their numbers had increased by ten. The late arrivals didn't know what the chase was all about, but it looked like fun; and if there's one thing a Fuzzy can't resist it's fun—so they had joined in immediately.

The new Fuzzies were Little Fuzzy, Mamma Fuzzy, Mike, Mitzi, Ko–Ko, Cinderella, Id, Superego, Complex, and Syndrome—a clear indication to anyone who knew them that

Jack Holloway, the van Riebeeks, and Lynne Andrews had arrived.

The tenth Fuzzy—Baby Fuzzy—waddled along behind the mob for a while, but couldn't keep up. He soon lost interest and struck a course for Diamond's play area—where he could see a fascinating array of bright-colored objects and interesting junk.

The reception line was just breaking up as Holloway and his party arrived. Greetings were exchanged and congratulations conveyed to the newlyweds.

"I'm sorry we're so late," Jack said. "We had some trouble with the airboat on the way over. Lost some power on the main lift-and-drive and had to limp in on the Abbotts."

Ahmed looked past the group. "Didn't George come along?" he asked, with a note of disappointment in his voice.

Jack shook his head. "I'm afraid not, Ahmed," he said. "I tried to bully him into it, but he's off chasing some mare's nest on the Fuzzy Reservation. Said he had to re-assign all his patrol sectors and clear some equipment. I don't know why the watch commander couldn't have handled it, but George insisted he had to do it personally."

"He said to apologize for him," Gerd van Riebeek said. "Said he would toss a little shindig for you and Sandra himself when you get over to the station on Tuesday."

"Is the bungalow finished yet?" Sandra asked anxiously.

"All operational," Ruth said. "Very nearly ready to move in."

"We all dug in and scared up some furniture for you," Lynne explained. "Enough to get started with, anyway. And we all chipped in some pots and pans and dishes."

Sandra brightened. "That was very thoughtful of you. We've got some inflatables we're taking along."

"Well, you're all set, then," Ruth said. "When Gerd and I went over there, we had to sleep in the boat and mooch food off Jack until we could get into Red Hill and buy some things."

Victor Grego's kitchen had been turned into a bedlam of

portable equipment, food handlers, waiters, and busboys, with part of the caterer's entourage and supplies spilling out the service entrance and onto the penthouse's private landing stage.

Being careful not to trail his jacket cuffs through any glop, Grego wound his way through the confusion until he found Jerry Panoyian out on the landing stage, running an expert eye over a hand-held terminal—much like a general deploying troops and matériel during a battle.

Panoyian was a short man upon whose long nose perched a pair of old-fashioned spectacles. He shook his head slightly, making his crown of iron–gray hair bobble slightly, and pushed the audio pickup more tightly into his ear. "No, *no*, Melvin." he said into a voco–leader, "It's bar number *three* that's out of gin. And when you get back in here, I want you to handle the ice run. Yes, I'll have it ready to wheel."

He looked up, instantly recognizing someone not in his own livery. "Ah, Mr. Grego," he said, smiling. "How is everything going?"

"Couldn't be better, Mr. Panoyian," Grego replied. "I just wanted to let you know that we have a few late guests. You might want to refurbish the buffet a bit."

Panoyian held up a hand. "It's being attended to, sir. My headcounter spotted them as their airboat arrived. By the time they get to the salad bar, everything will be crisp, fresh, replenished. Hot roast veldbeest, chilled fruit—the works."

Briskly efficient when dealing with his own help, Panoyian's voice shifted gears when talking to a client. He thought of it as suave and smooth; most listeners found the tone oily.

"Privately, you understand," Judge Pendarvis was saying—he paused and looked about, to make sure no one could overhear—"I'm quite pleased to see Mr. Ingermann's credentials to practice before Zarathustran courts revoked. He's been a stench in the nostrils of the courts, decent men, and honest attorneys since the day he set foot on Zarathustra."

Ben Rainsford fussed with his pipe. "I'm beginning to

think there are no honest lawyers,'' he said. Then he said, ''Unnnh!'' as Gus Brannhard gave him an elbow in the ribs.

''I'm a lawyer,'' he said. ''The Judge is a lawyer. You think we're dishonest?''

Rainsford rubbed his side. *''You?* Humph. No offense, Judge.''

''None taken,'' Pendarvis replied. ''I can only speak for myself, you understand. Mr. Brannhard's reputation when he practiced on Beta Continent seemed to revolve around an astounding ability to secure aquittal for obviously guilty clients.'' The Chief Justice winked broadly at Jack Holloway.

''To say nothing,'' Jack remarked, ''of the ability to match any given three men drink for drink and still put them all under the table.''

''Welllll,'' Brannhard grumped. ''All that plea bargaining gives a man a helluva thirst.''

''I trust you gentlemen understand the confidentiality of what I just said regarding Mr. Ingermann,'' Pendarvis said. Then, in an obvious change of subject, ''What a grand party this is! Victor Grego is to be congratulated.''

''Well, the man is a very thorough manager,'' Ben Rainsford said. ''I wouldn't expect him to miss a single detail in anything.''

''Do I detect notes of grudging admiration?'' Brannhard said. ''A year ago you wanted to tie him up by his thumbs.''

''That was a year ago,'' Rainsford fiddled with his pipe some more, then looked Brannhard straight in the eye. ''The older you grow, sonny, the more you learn.''

Jack chuckled. ''I guess you can consider yourself cut down to size, Gus.''

''Never knew much about Ingermann myself,'' Rainsford said, ''but what I knew, I didn't like. I'll tell you right now that him getting disbarred is a load off my mind—for one very simple reason.''

They all looked at him expectantly.

''He'll be so damned busy trying to take vengeance on all of us, now, that he won't have time to try packing the new legislature with his own henchmen.''

"There's something to that," Pendarvis said gloomily.

"Something else that will slow him down in that department," Gus said, "is voter eligibility and candidate certification. When I say my prayers at night, I thank Ghu that none of the new immigrants pass residence requirements for either. Think what a grand opportunity *that* would be for him to logroll his own people in those seats."

"That's true," Rainsford said, wagging a finger, "*only* if they don't get that year's extension for the constitutional convention. That mess has me tearing my hair every day. And it's up to you and me, Gus, to get them off their butts. This government won't last another year without tax revenues."

"Do you think Ingermann might be behind all the stalling in the convention?" Jack asked.

"It's possible," Gus said, "but if he is, it's a cinch the connection is so tangled we'd never be able to hang it on him—much as I'd like to."

Rainsford jammed his pipe in his jacket pocket. "I been tellin' you all along—Ingermann wants to bring down the government and try to get control of the planet during the chaos. If you're hell-bent to get him deported, that charge ought to be enough to get the job done."

Gus Brannhard snorted derisively. "Ben, you can jail him; you can deport him; you can shoot him in the foot, and you can make him eat sand out of the road. But, *first* you gotta catch him; *then* you gotta make the charge stick long enough to drag him into a courtroom and slip him under a veridicator. Personally, I'd rather try to take a bone away from a bush-goblin—but, we are working at it; we are working at it."

The *hors d' oeuvres* chef had just run another dozen blue-labeled tins through the opener. As he wielded his thin-bladed knife to slice the cake and cut it into fancy shapes, he shook his head from side to side and muttered to himself.

Jerry Panoyian leaned over his shoulder. "What's the matter, Emile?" he asked.

Emile's eyebrows shot up, nearly to his hairline. "Over twenty years I have been in this business, sir," he said, "and, so help me, this is the first formal wedding reception I've ever worked where canned Extee–Three was served to the guests."

Panoyian chuckled. "You might as well get used to it, Emile. I have a feeling that Fuzzies are going to be part of the social scene in Mallorysport from now on."

Down the wide valley below Mallorysport the brilliant oranges and reds of a Zarathustran sunset were spreading low against the horizon as the sun sank slowly toward Beta. It was as though the KØ star that gave life to all things on Zarathustra was pointing back in time to Beta—Beta, where the Fuzzies had been discovered—Beta, where the murder of a Fuzzy named Goldilocks by a CZC scientist named Leonard Kellogg had set the whole question of Fuzzy sapience in motion—Beta, where the Fuzzy Institute and Holloway Station were becoming almost as pivotal to the affairs of Zarathustra as the capital at Mallorysport.

The musicians arrived and started setting up on the outdoor platform next to the portable dance floor as the terrace was washed with the red–orange light from the setting sun. Soft lighting began to come on automatically on the terraces, with brighter patches around the bars and the huge buffet table. Soon, now, it would be time to cut the wedding cake. Then, at twilight, the dancing would start with a solo waltz by the bride and groom.

Mr. Chief Justice Frederic Pendarvis puffed deeply on his panetella. It had been an enjoyable conversation with Holloway and Brannhard and Rainsford. They had come to much agreement on their respective attitudes about several things that were going on on Zarathustra at the moment. That kind of no–punches–pulled, informal shop talk was always good for everyone concerned. Cleared the air.

Pendarvis tilted his head back and blew a careful smoke ring toward the star filled sky, where Darius stood at the zenith and Xerxes was inching up from the horizon. "No, Jack," he said, adopting a more familiar term than he had ever used toward Holloway before. "It's not hard at all to be

the Chief Justice of a colonial court system—here or anywhere else. You only need keep one thing uppermost in your
mind—the law. The law is everything. It is bigger than men,
bigger than courts, bigger than governments, bigger than
armies; it decides things that are placed before it on evidence
and testimony. That's all there is to it.

"That's all there has *ever* been to it. Judges get in trouble
only when they start seeing men in front of the bench. In the
courtroom, judges are not men; they are instruments of the
legal system—officers of the court. And, judges get in trouble when they stop serving the law and start serving themselves.

"I've been serving the law for almost fifty years—started
out as a file boy. The law is my religion, and my catechism is
to apply it with fairness and impartiality. I think I have
always done that."

"You fellows are waxing pretty philosophical, considering that this is supposed to be a party and all," Brannhard
remarked.

Pendarvis smiled. "Perhaps you're right, Gus. I want
them to hurry up and cut the cake so the dancing can start. I'm
dying to get out on that floor and see if the old body is still up
to the *Shesha-slide* and the *tryex-trot*."

"Too strenuous for me," Jack said. "The last dance I
learned was the *bob-slop*. That seems like a thousand years
ago."

Rainsford fiddled with his pipe and harumphed. "It probably was, too."

A number of men had gravitated to the conversation group
around Juan Jimenez—since most of the women had gravitated there first.

A number of Fuzzies had joined the group as well—the
intellectual elements, led by Little Fuzzy and Diamond.

"That's a pretty ambitious project you and Gerd are talking about," Lieutenant Commander Pancho Ybarra said. He
was the Navy psychologist who had first cracked the problem
of Fuzzy sapience. And, he was Liaison Officer between the
Navy and the CZC Native Affairs Commission, and anyone

else who was active in issues pertaining to Fuzzies. "A permanent building for Fuzzy Institute, expanded medical research and educational programs. Where do you think you're going to get the money?"

"From the Fuzzies, if they approve of our plans," Gerd said.

Pancho snorted. "From the *Fuzzies?* Fuzzies are about as interested in money as a Khooghra is in Sunday."

"That's perfectly true," Juan said, "but you're forgetting one thing. That rich sunstone strike on the Fuzzy Reservation has been leased back to the CZC, who are paying a royalty of four hundred fifty sols per carat for the privilege of working the diggings."

"And they aren't going to piddle along cracking a ton or two of flint a day, like an independent," Gerd chimed in. "We figure that in a year the Native Affairs Commission and the ZNPF, *and* Fuzzy Institute will all be paying their own way, without any handouts from the Government."

"That must make Governor Rainsford happy," someone said.

"He's overjoyed," Gerd said. "According to the CZC staff study, we figure we'll be able to continue expanding our research into the NFMp problem and still break ground for Fuzzy Institute in a year and a half to two years from now."

"I'm still convinced that you *can't* crack the NFMp problem," Ernst Mallin said. "I've looked at the whole ton of studies, experiments, and conclusions drawn and I throw in with the camp that says NFMp production evolved in Fuzzies to meet some long since disappeared genetic requirement— and, once developed, couldn't be un–developed. It left them in a genetic dead end with a negative population growth. There's ample precedent already proven on several planets, Terra included. Fuzzies are going to become extinct, and that's that."

Little Fuzzy drew thoughtfully on the tiny pipe he liked to smoke, and frowned. At least, it looked like a frown. Juan Jimenez couldn't be sure of it, because he'd never seen a Fuzzy make that kind of face before. Diamond was doing it, too.

Partly to inject his own opinion as a mammologist against Mallin's as a psychologist, and partly to not sound so gloomy in front of the few Fuzzies present, Juan dove into the technical conversation pool. "Ernst," he said, "don't be such a doom-croaker. Your field is psychosciences, anyway."

"I still have an M.D.," Mallin chided.

"Yes, yes," Juan said. "I'm not questioning your schooling. Oh, I even used to agree with that theory. I've seen what Gerd and Ruth and Lynne have been doing since then, though. They're making steady gains on isolating the NFMp hormone and pinpointing its function in Fuzzy metabolism. When you can get that kind of information about anything produced in a mammal's body, you can find a way to chemically counteract it."

Diamond was tugging at Juan's sleeve. *"Unka Won,"* he said. "What's a *mam'a'*?"

Juan explained the taxonomic class Mammalia to him.

Diamond nodded. "Thank you," he said. He propped his chin on a tiny fist and looked serious, as though inviting Juan to continue.

"That's why I'm one hundred percent behind Gerd's plans for a real Fuzzy Institute. They've been able to accomplish wonders over at Holloway Station under much less than optimum laboratory standards. Ruth said it best: a tiny spot of light—what we really know about Fuzzies—surrounded by a twilight zone of what we think, mostly erroneous, probably. Beyond that, the dark of ignorance, full of surprises.

"There's a whole new science here, just about Fuzzies. In acquiring that body of knowledge, I'm convinced we'll also whip the NFMp problem along the way."

"I agree with you, Juan," Liana Bell said. "From what little I know, it seems that there must also be a ton of things we can teach Fuzzies."

"That's right," Juan said. "Why, within twenty years, you'll see Fuzzies graduating from Terran universities."

"Oh, piddle!" Mallin snapped.

"And why not?" Liana said, rather abruptly, surprised at herself for disagreeing with her superior. "Thorans are doing the same thing. They aren't as intelligent as Fuzzies, so far as I know. *And,* our studies indicate they have adapted very well to Terran social conventions and attitudes."

"With one exception," someone said.

Liana laughed, rather musically, Juan thought. "That's true," she said, "but it's a minor point. The Thorans believe in Great Ghu the Grandfather God the same way I believe in environment–conditioned responses."

"There's a summary tape on my desk right now," Juan said, "from the Xeno–Sciences Institute. It draws qualitative comparisons between all eight extraterrestrial races. It says Fuzzies are the most intelligent—hands down. It goes on to suggest that they may be more intelligent than we are."

That idea sharply divided everyone into two camps.

"That *can't* be true! They have no technology!"

"Maybe they don't want any."

"Right! Just because we're machine–crazy doesn't make that attribute a pre–condition of intelligence."

"They may just be at a different stage of development and evolution."

"—Or evolving at a more leisurely rate."

"The odds would favor something along those lines. In five hundred years this is the eighth sapient race we've encountered, and they are all behind us in general intelligence and development."

"From the Yggdrasil Khooghra at one end to the Thorans at the other," someone else added.

"Sure," the strawberry blonde said, picking it up. "I think it's about time we ran across a race that's more advanced than we are. Maybe they could teach me how to run a vocowriter by just thinking at it—save wearing out my voice."

Everyone laughed. The argument was over.

The musicians came back from their break. Several people drifted away from the group toward the dance floor—including Juan Jimenez and Liana Bell.

Presently, everyone was gone from around the big lawn

table except the strawberry blonde—and Diamond and Little Fuzzy, sitting on the edge of the table.

Little Fuzzy knocked out his pipe on the edge of the table, then blew air through the stem, just the way he had seen Pappy Jack do it.

The young woman was looking up at the stars. She didn't notice Little Fuzzy put the pipe away in his *shodda–bag* and walk across the table top. When he touched her hair with his tiny hand, it startled her.

He studied her with his wide, appealing eyes. "*Shu hassa*," he said. "*No hu'ttsu*. Are you a *mam'a'*, too?"

She smiled at him. "Yes, I'm a mammal, too."

Diamond joined them, with his hands clasped behind his back, and studied her intensely. "You got funny fur," he said. "A'most same as *Auntie Sand'a*. Why is?"

For a moment, she was flustered. This was her first close meeting with Fuzzies. It took a moment for her to realize Diamond was asking about her hair—almost the same color as Sandra's, but more pale. "Hair," she said. "We call it hair."

Diamond, too, reached out to feel the texture of her hair. "Fuzzies' fur all same color," he said. "Why Hagga have all different colors?"

You know, she thought, *they may be smarter than we are. There's certainly nothing wrong with their curiosity about things.* "Well, you see," she said, "it's like this. You've noticed we have different–color eyes, too?"

They both nodded solemnly.

"It depends on what color hair and eyes your parents had—and your grandparents . . ."

It was getting on into the evening. Victor Grego had long since shed his swallowtail coat and loosened his neckcloth. He was circulating among the guests in his shirtsleeves and vest, urging them to polish off anything and everything that was left to eat or drink.

He stopped short when just within earshot of the table where Diamond and Little Fuzzy were now sitting cross-legged and listening with rapt attention. Then, he spun on his heel and bustled back into the penthouse, where Ahmed and Sandra were exchanging pleasantries with some departing guests.

"Excuse me," he said. "Sandra, come over here to the terrace doors a moment."

Sandra Khadra excused herself and went to stand with him.

"You see that young lady over there?" he asked. "The one talking to Diamond and Little Fuzzy?"

Sandra nodded affirmatively.

"Does she work for the Company? I've never seen her before, but there are a lot of people who work for me who I wouldn't know now if I met them coming down the esplanada."

Sandra peered across the softly-lit terrace. "Well, I don't know her. At least, not from this distance."

Grego looked about hastily. "Where's Myra? Has she left yet? She'll know."

"Mr. Grego! What's this all about?"

Grego made a gesture of impatience. "Now that the wedding has been committed, you can call me 'Daddy,' " he said. "Would you help me look for Myra, please? I'll look on the south terrace and meet you back here."

A few moments later, he came huffing back to the terrace doors. "Not there," he said. "Oh, there you are. You found her. Good, good."

"What's the matter, Mr. Grego?" Myra echoed.

"It's some big mystery he's concocted," Sandra said.

"*Faugh!*" Grego snapped. "Myra, who's that young lady over there talking to Diamond and Little Fuzzy? Does she work for the Company?"

Myra squinted; then a look of recognition came over her face. "Why, Mr. Grego," she said. "That's the assistant I hired to help with the plans for the wedding. I was thinking about putting her on the reception desk, now. She seems to be very good with people, and—"

Grego cut her short. "Thank you, Myra. I'll explain tomorrow. Sandra, come with me, please.''

He led Sandra across the terrace—out of sight of the three at the big table. As they neared the group, he put his finger to his lips and touched his ear. Sandra was exasperated by now, but she kept quiet and listened.

'' . . . So, you see, guys, that both my parents and Sandra's parents had a recessive gene for red hair, but my parents had a dominant gene for blonde hair and hers had a dominant for either brown or black. Do you see how that works, now?''

Both Fuzzies nodded.

''And, who was it, again, who first formulated the scientific law that all genetics is based on?''

"Geggo Menda," Diamond said quickly.

''Right,'' she said. ''Mendel. First century, Pre–Atomic. Now, how long was it before any really significant research was done in genetics?'' She pointed to Little Fuzzy.

''Many–many,'' he said.

''Come on, now, Little Fuzzy,'' she chided gently. ''I explained how Hagga measure time. Now, how many years?''

Little Fuzzy screwed up his face for a moment. Number concepts were still pretty mysterious to him. *''Hundedd-fifty yiss,''* he finally said.

''Do you hear that?'' Grego whispered to Sandra. ''She's teaching them genetics.''

''So?'' Sandra said.

Grego grimaced. ''They're getting it. They're *getting* it. They understand the theory. She's explained it so it's understandable to a Fuzzy.''

He took Sandra by the hand and led her out into the light. ''Good evening,'' he said.

''Heyo, Pappy Vic,'' Diamond said enthusiastically. He jumped up and took a step toward the strawberry blonde, then put his little hand on her shoulder. ''She teach us why Fuzzy–fur always same color and Hagga–fur different colors.''

''Hair,'' she corrected.

"Yes—*heh-yeh*," Little Fuzzy said.

"Hair," she said again, attempting to correct the pronunciation.

"That's what I *said*—". Little Fuzzy blustered. *Heh-yeh*."

"She's a *Hoksu–Hagga*," Diamond said. Wonderful Big One.

"I think you're right, Diamond," Grego said. "Young woman, I understand you work for the Charterless Zarathustra Company."

She nodded.

"Do you know who I am?" he asked.

"Of course," she replied. "You're Mr. Grego, the Manager–in–Chief."

"Precisely," he said. "Mrs. Khadra, here, used to be my Fuzzy–Sitter–in–Chief—until she allowed herself to be dragged away by something as piffling as matrimony."

Sandra snorted derisively.

"However," Grego continued, "my philosphy is that in every disaster is the seed of its resolution and improvement."

The strawberry blonde frowned and pursed her lips. "I don't think I'm following you, Mr. Grego."

Grego pulled his chin back so it almost touched his collarbone. "Why, I'm appointing you new Fuzzy–Sitter–in–Chief. Ten percent raise in salary, effective this morning."

Sandra laughed. *"Very* scientific," she said.

Grego remained unruffled. "See Myra in the morning," he said. "She'll without doubt have a bunch of papers for you to fill out. Then, come straight up here. Mrs. Khadra will brief you on the job for a couple of days." He looked at Sandra. "Will 1030 tomorrow morning be all right to start?" he asked.

Sandra rolled her eyes heavenward. *"Anything*. Yes, that will be just fine. Now, will you let me get on with my wedding night?"

"Oh, of course," Grego said irritably. "By the way, in all the excitement I never did get your name."

"Stone," she said. "Christiana Stone."

XIV

It was hot for that time of the morning, windless, and the Zarathustran sun hung motionless in a hard, brassy sky. Ahmed Khadra stepped down from the airjeep and kicked at the dry, barren earth with the toe of his boot. He squinted up at the sky. "Going to be another dry year, George," he said.

"Not the first for this valley, either," George Lunt replied. He pointed off into the middle distance. "Y'see over there—where there used to be a creek winding down from that saddle, and then spreading out into a marshy area on the valley floor? See all those little hummocks? They used to be tiny islands a few meters across, covered with lush vegetation."

"Yes," Ahmed said, "you still see stalks and scorched plants, but nothing has grown down here for at least three years. What of it?"

"Why d'you suppose that is?" George asked.

Ahmed thought for a moment. "Why, I guess it's the dry weather we've been having on this part of Beta. Yes, that would be about right. The CZC started the Big Blackwater Project—drained half a million acres of swamp for farming. It cut off the moist air that caused rainfall on the Piedmont. That was about three years ago. Again, so what?"

"Well," George said, "those dry years let an abnormally high crop of land-prawns hatch out each spring. It was too dry in the uplands for them to find enough food, so they moved over the divide and down into the big woods where there was plenty of that forest moss they're fond of."

"And the Fuzzies followed the migration," Ahmed added. "What's with the guessing game, George?"

"Take it easy," George said. "I'm just giving you the data a piece at a time—the way I got it—to see if you come to the same conclusions I did."

"Sort of air—checking your own reasoning?"

"Yes."

Ahmed put his hands on his hips and looked out over the valley floor. "Nothing wrong with that. What's next? By the way, George, how did you get interested in this place to begin with?"

"Survey readouts," George said. "The data kept showing up that there's a lot of titanium in the ground up here—in several different compound forms. Didn't make sense. At first, I thought the equipment was out of whack, so I had it re-flown with different vehicles. Kept getting the same answers. Still didn't make sense. Titanium's scarce all over Zarathustra. Why should there be a concentration of it up here?"

Ahmed pointed across the valley. "Maybe it belched out of that big mountain over there. It looks like a dead volcano."

"I wondered about that at first," George said. "The way this valley's topography is laid out, the whole thing could be what's left of a very large, very old caldera. But, geology isn't my long suit, so I decided to go ahead and do all the snooping any good cop would do before I started jabbering a lot of brilliant deductions at anyone."

"So you came up here and poked around on your own," Ahmed said.

"That's why I wasn't at the wedding," George said. "Sorry about that, but it couldn't be helped. You'll see why in a few minutes."

"You're already forgiven," Ahmed said. "Lead on."

"This is about the same place where I first landed my jeep," George said, pointing to pad—marks in the loose soil, "when I first came up here."

"So you're reconstructing your movements for me," Ahmed said.

"Very good." George's square, muscular face broke into a grin. "I knew what I was doing when I appointed you Chief of Detectives for the ZNPF."

"Okay," Ahmed said. "What came next?"

"I wanted a closer look at the dried-up marsh, there, and

around that big patch of weirthorn that spreads back against the bench, there, below the saddle." George hitched up his pistol belt and started walking, the arid soil crunching under his boots. "Let me show you what I found."

Harry Steefer looked at the communication screen as he spoke, trying to read the reactions in Victor Grego's face. "Mr. Grego," he said, "I have the papers right here in front of me." He held up a thin folder, as though to prove he was telling the truth. "The fact of the matter is that we just don't know anything about the girl. She came in on the *City of Asgard* a little less than a month ago and went to work for the CZC on the twenty–first. Beyond that, there's nothing I can check unless I send her packet back to Company headquarters on Terra—and that would take a year. I can't issue a Restricted–Areas pass on this kind of information."

Victor Grego was becoming annoyed. He always became annoyed when he didn't get his own way. He compressed his mouth into a hard line. "Well, Harry," he said, "why in hell does my personal Fuzzy–Sitter have to have a Restricted–Areas pass, anyway?"

Steefer sighed. "Because *anyone* who has free access to your private residence has to have one. Mr. Grego, we decided on this almost a year ago—after we found that Herckerd and Novaes had hidden a bunch of kidnapped Fuzzies on an unfinished floor right here in Company House. To say nothing of every other Tom, Dick, and Harry in Mallorysport coming and going through the landing stages in the unused levels. I don't even like to talk about it. I'm still embarrassed by how slack I'd let things get." Chief Steefer took a deep breath and waited to see if he had sold his point to Grego. He had a hunch that he hadn't.

Grego scratched his head and lit a cigarette. "I'm certain that she's all right, Harry. Diamond is crazy about her. Fuzzies have an instinct for that sort of thing, you know. They just don't take to people who aren't on the square." He paused, waiting for Steefer to suggest a way around the regulation.

Steefer wasn't going to do it. "It's an Executive Ops

Order—S.O.P.—you signed it yourself, sir. If I make an exception for you, I'll have technicians in Computer Center wanting the same thing so Aunt Minnie can bring them their lunch, and statisticians in the Sensitive Records Section who want their girl friends to pick them up from work, and Ghu knows where it will all end.''

Grego thought for a moment. *Damn it all to Nifflheim! Who's running this company—me or the damned Operations Manual?* "Here's what you do, Harry," he said. "Issue the pass. Stamp it 'temporary,' with an expiration date that will let you get the packet to Terra and back. Attach a memo inside the packet to the effect that this personnel action is done on my personal authority, and put out a supplement to that Ops Order to the effect that exceptions will be authorized only on my personal, signed approval. When that's done, send a man up to my office with the pass and the memo for my signature. Will that serve everyone's best interests?''

"Yes, sir. That will be fine. No one is apt to ask for an exception if they have to personally justify it to you.''

"Excellent," Grego said. "I can't keep escorting her to the landing stage and meeting her there every time she comes and goes, just to get her past one of your cops. Thank you.''

Grego blanked the screen. That should get the job done, while at the same time tacitly explaining to Harry Steefer an object lesson about why people don't ordinarily resist the decisions of the Manager–in–Chief. The Company was not a god, after all. It was a machine, and there could only be room for one person in the driver's seat.

It had been Tuesday morning about 0830 when Ahmed and Sandra arrived at Holloway Station, as promised with a metric ton of luggage and gear. George Lunt had whisked Ahmed away immediately. Ruth and Lynne had dropped everything to help Sandra get situated. They had borrowed Jack's manipulator to re–arrange some logs and boulders left around the bungalow into "something more attractive." Jack didn't understand that, but he had said, "Sure. Go ahead.'' That left him without a vehicle, but he and Little Fuzzy walked across the footbridge over the creek and borrowed Gerd's airboat.

Jack wanted to get up into the Cordilleras Range right away. The patrols had reported a big mob of Fuzzies up there, so he wanted to get right up there with an armload of *shodda–bags* and steel *shoppo–diggos*, do a little trading with the natives, and persuade them to come on in to Holloway Station. Speed was indicated because in that part of Beta the hills were alive with the sound of prospectors—all trying to find enough sunstones to get rich quick. They wouldn't, of course, because they didn't know how to look for sunstones, or how to get them out of the enclosing matrix of flint if they found a vein.

A lot of these birds were pretty unsavory characters. Some of them were bound to be runaway veldbeest herders with stolen Company aircars. That kind of person would be apt to vent his frustration on a Fuzzy. A little preventive work by the Native Affairs Commissioner was indicated. The ZNPF patrol would go up there on the regular surveillance post and check them all out and jug the ones who had an aircar they couldn't prove they owned, explain the boundaries of the Fuzzy Reservation to the rest, and generally get the idea across that this was not exactly the wild frontier.

In the meantime, Jack did not want any ugly incidents involving Fuzzies. For all he cared, these guys could shoot each other up all they wanted, but Fuzzies were *his* responsibility.

Ahmed leaned down to get a better look. "I'll be damned, George. You're right. It *is* the remnants of a little irrigation ditch." He pointed along the line of the dry creek. "And it branches into three channels over there. Somebody was *cultivating* these plants before the creek dried up. But, nobody's ever settled up here. If they had we'd have found out about Fuzzies sooner than—" He stopped short. "You mean *Fuzzies* had truck gardens up here?"

George nodded.

"But, Fuzzies are hunter–gatherers. They're nowhere

near the agricultural level." Ahmed frowned and stroked his nose.

"Umm–hmm." George nodded, again. "I don't know much about anthropology, but I know hunter–gatherer societies at low Paleolithic development come a hell of a lot earlier than farmers."

"How can you be certain it was Fuzzy–farmers?" Ahmed asked.

George pointed to the ground, turning a full circle as he did so. "Why, look all around you at the dried–up tracks. Fuzzy footprints if I ever saw them."

Ahmed chuckled. "That doesn't prove anything. Fuzzies could have tramped through here by the battalion when this ground was damp—hunting prawns or something."

"Good reasoning, Captain," George said. "You're getting to be a better detective every day. And, you're right; it doesn't prove a thing. Now come over here and look at this."

He led Ahmed over to the extensive weirthorn thicket that spread along the base of the cliff. It wasn't a surprising place to find it. Wierthorn was a kind of chaparral, with long, sharp spikes every few inches along its branches. It flourished everywhere on Zarathustra. With good water, it developed a thin layer of green leaves. Without water, it went barren, dry, and brown, but it still grew—to a height of nearly two meters. When a plant died, it was simply pushed upward by the growth of a new plant under it, so that an old stand of weirthorn several layers deep might rise as much as six or eight yards, canopied over with hard, dry thorn bushes that made a little more shade to give the growing plants a little better chance. A fire would go through the stuff like a box of matches—that's how plantation operators cleared it away and kept it out of cultivated land.

George had hacked his way several meters into the thicket with a machete. He invited Ahmed to go in and have a look.

After a few moments of peering around in the dim interior of the bramble patch, Ahmed whistled softly. *"Well, I'll be damned to Nifflheim!"* he exclaimed.

The inside of the thicket was laced with pathways and runs that had been made by clearing off the random lower

branches which were in the way. There were little huts and
lean-tos, fabricated by wattle–weaving sticks and vines
among the growing weirthorn trunks, then "shingling" them
with broad, rubbery leaves from the base of the butterpaddle
plant so they would shed rainwater. The runs and structures
were all quite small—just about Fuzzy–size.

Ahmed emerged, blinking against the brighter light outside. "Well, that tears it," he said simply. "The scientific
types will go off their spool trying to make this fit in with
what they already 'know' about Fuzzies."

"It's also 'proof beyond reasonable doubt,' as we say in
the trade," George said. "Why, this would have proved the
case for Fuzzy sapience without the thing ever getting into a
court room."

"But no one had ever landed up here—or even mapped the
place thoroughly—until we began patrolling it as the Fuzzy
Reservation. At that, it couldn't be seen from the air."

"It came at just the right time," George said. "I overflew
the valley several times. When the sun is just right, you can
see regular shapes down in the thicket—but only if you look
closely and hover while you're doing it."

It was a dream of a defense against Fuzzies' natural
enemies. A Fuzzy made just about a mouthful for a harpy—a
flying predator about the size and general design of a Terran
Jurassic pterodactyl. There wasn't any way for a harpy to
make a swoop for Fuzzies who were inside the thicket. Same
for damnthings and bush–goblins. They wouldn't even try to
get at dinner if it was in a weirthorn patch.

"Okay," Ahmed said. "There's Fuzzy–signs all over the
place. Even though the creek is dried up, this place is still in
use." He pointed around the gentle slope between the thicket
and the dry creek. "See? There's several freshly-filled toilet
pits spotted around. The question is: where are the Fuzzies?
How come there are no Fuzzies?"

"Oh, there are plenty of Fuzzies," George said, "but
they're probably all hiding in the woods down at the lower
end of the valley."

Ahmed nodded. "Makes sense. They'd all be out foraging
at this time of day. They've probably never seen a Big One

before, and they probably think our vehicles are some new kind of flying appetite—like a harpy.''

"Generalizing and forming abstract concepts is what they're doing there,'' George said.

"And, if they were too far away to make it back here when they spotted our jeep, they'd take the nearest cover.''

They both stood for a moment, looking down the valley toward the woods, knowing there were pairs of wide Fuzzy-eyes looking back at them.

As they walked back toward the jeep, Ahmed asked, "Why in blazes would they stay up here, instead of going along with the migration after the land–prawns? This looks like one helluva tough place for a Fuzzy to make a living. It's a cinch the little perishers aren't getting enough to eat since the Big Blackwater Project shut off the sprinkler system.''

"That,'' George said, jumping a shallow ravine that had once fed Fuzzy Creek, "is a question we'll let the scientist types mutter about. What is your suggestion for immediate action, seein' as how you're wearing the same beret badge with the crossed *shoppo–diggos* and the 'ZNPF' on it that I am?''

Ahmed ticked off his points on the fingers of his left hand as they walked. "First, we tell Jack what we've found. Then, we come back up here with some Fuzzy interpreters and a big stock of Extee–Three so we can get this gang to come out and have a square meal while they're learning that we're their friends. Then, we do the usual trading of tools and stuff and try to persuade them to move on south, where the living is a little easier. Then, we find out what's what with the titanium concentration in Fuzzy Valley.''

"My idea, exactly,'' George said, "except for one thing.''

"Yes?''

"While all this is going on, we keep a security lid on this place that is airtight, leakproof, and lightproof. I've already drawn up a new area assignment for all the patrols, arranged so there's none of Paine's Marines covering this sector and so that only our own most trusted men will be overflying Fuzzy Valley—men who will come to us first if they see anything unusual and keep their mouths shut if we tell them to.''

"We'd better talk to Jack tonight," Ahmed said.

"That can be handled at your welcoming party," George said as he pressed the release stud on the side hatch of the jeep. "Did Gerd tell you about it? I'm tossing a little beer and pretzels fest for you and Sandra tonight. Nothing elaborate, you understand. I'm not getting rich off this job, and I imagine you're both just about champagned–out by now."

Ahmed belched affirmatively.

XV

It was comfortable and quiet in the office where the young man sat dictating a report into his VRR–augmented vocowriter. He was glad he had saved that big featherleaf tree outside the window when they assembled the Medical Center, then chose his office space from the shaded corner of the building. On a hot day—like this particular Tuesday afternoon—it made a difference. The heat pump held the temperature in the labs and other offices to an adequate level—in *his* office it was cool.

"In summary," he said into the vocowriter, "we have clearly established that the titanium which the land–prawns ingest is accumulated and stored in the middle intestine. It is not passed with other wastes, but collects in nodules on the intestine wall until a point of saturation is assumed and then disperses through all the prawn's soft tissues. The method of action and biochemical function of titanium in land–prawn metabolism is not clearly understood at this point. It is, however, clear that this property of titanium concentration is responsible for the obvious affinity displayed by Fuzzies for land–prawns as a staple item in the Fuzzy diet—even though the titanium present is not in the form of hokfusine, and thus cannot be processed into anti-NFMp by the Fuzzy metabolism.

"We have established that the hokfusine molecule present in Extee–Three emergency rations, which is present only if the farina mixture has been prepared in titanium cookers, has only five atoms of titanium; yet Fuzzies can distinguish its presence by taste alone. In short, they are fond of land–prawns, but they are crazy about Extee–Three.

"The NFMp hormone present in Fuzzy metabolism interferes with fertility and normal fetus development. The manufacture of NFMp is inhibited by any titanium–bearing organic compounds, but only at effective levels by large amounts of hokfusine. This is present theory, not conclusively established by a persuasive body of experiment, but is being actively pursued as a viable line of research which has an acceptably high probability.

"We have proven that Fuzzy metabolism does not use hokfusine directly against NFMp. The digestive process alters it, as well as a variety of other titanium–bearing compounds, into a single substance, which we presently label anti–NFMp, pending full information on its composition and properties.

"Another year or so of patient cataloging and observation should start producing a normal birth rate and acceptably low infant mortality levels among the Fuzzies who are getting enough titanium in their diet to manufacture adequate amounts of anti–NFMp in their bodies."

Jack Holloway sat down disgustedly on the outboard contragravity–field generator housing of Gerd's airboat. "Damn it!" he said aloud, in the manner of men who are accustomed to being alone. "I hope this isn't going to make me late for George's party tonight."

"*Wha' matta*', Pappy Jack?" Little Fuzzy asked as he came to the hatch and jumped down to the ground. He looked all around. "No Fuzzies *anywheh neh–yeh in–'ha* woods."

Jack smiled and scratched him between the ears. "How are you so sure of that?" he asked.

Little Fuzzy assumed a wise expression and tapped his ear with a tiny finger.

Of course. Fuzzies had keener hearing than Terrans, and across a wider frequency range. Terrans hadn't even known Fuzzies could talk until the Navy researchers discovered their normal speech range was ultrasonic, with various "yeek" sounds at its interface with human hearing. They made handy little doorbells out in the bush—they could hear a contragravity vehicle coming about ten minutes sooner than a Terran could.

"*Whassa matta*'," Little Fuzzy repeated.

Holloway shrugged. "Pappy Jack is getting forgetful.

Remember we had trouble with this thing when we took you all over to Unka Vic's house?''

Little Fuzzy nodded.

"Well, I should have pulled maintenance on it before I brought it up here, but I was in such a rush to get to the field that I forgot about it. Now we've lost more power and I can't get enough lift out of it, even with the secondaries—enough to land it safely, but not enough to fly it. Well, it's only 1600 and we've contacted five groups of Fuzzies today, anyway.''

"Wha' make do?" Little Fuzzy asked; curious, as usual.

"I think it's the energy cartridge, overdue for changing. We'll find out what the trouble is, then screen Unka Gerd and have him bring the part out to us.'' He reached inside the boat and opened the locker that held the maintenance tool kit, then stopped.

Little Fuzzy was pulling on his pants leg.

"What is it?'' he asked, as he jerked the tool kit noisily from its clamps and set it down in the hatchway.

Little Fuzzy had a finger to his lips. "Two Hagga,'' he said. "Come this way—*wahking*. I think they *tosh–ki–Hagga*—bad Big Ones.''

Jack frowned. "Why do you say that?''

Little Fuzzy cocked his head to one side and turned his ear into the wind. "One say, 'Just da old man, *by–hisse'f,* wif one of those *'itta anima'.' Ovvuh* one say, 'We come up wif ship hiding us, we drop him easy.' *Fuhst* one say, 'Ship make us good money on Omega Condinent. If we bag da Fuzzy, have good money foh him same way.' ''

The tips of Jack's mustache twitched truculently. "So that's it; kill me, kidnap you, steal the airboat. How far away are they?'' he asked as he loosened his pistol in the holster and snapped off the safety.

"No fah,'' Little Fuzzy said. "Take many—many–many sma' mahks.'' He tapped Jack's wrist watch.

Jack frowned. "How many minutes, Little Fuzzy? Think hard.''

Little Fuzzy closed his eyes tightly, trying to remember what Christiana—*Auntie K'istanna,* he called her now—had taught him about counting. Finally, he snapped one hand out in front of him with all five fingers opened. "This many," he said.

"That's enough," he said. He lifted Little Fuzzy up into the boat. "You stay until I come for you. If anybody else comes in, you run like hell. Got that?"

Little Fuzzy shook his head yes.

Jack crawled into the boat and punched out Gerd's office screen combination. The screen filled with a brilliant pattern of color that exploded into the image of Gerd van Riebeek sitting at his desk, dictating a tape. "Hi Jack," he said, turning toward the screen. "What's up?"

"No time to explain, Gerd," Jack said softly. "Leave this pickup open. My co-ordinates are J–five–seventy, S–nine–four–fiver. Got that?"

Gerd was writing on a scratch pad. "Sure, but what's—"

"A couple a fellas are working up on me that figure to bushwhack me and steal your boat. If I don't call you back in five minutes, get a patrol up here on the double. They'll either be trying to figure out why your boat won't lift or they'll be nearby, running like hell. Don't talk; just listen."

Jack thought for a minute, then reached under the control panel and pulled out the nine–millimeter automatic he knew Gerd kept there. He checked the magazine, chambered a round, and tucked it under the tool kit. Then he started whistling noisily and stopped to curse from time to time.

By the time he could hear the men's voices coming to him down the wind, he had the generator cover off and had hidden the extra pistol in among the machinery—and never let his right hand stray more than six inches away from it.

When he heard their voices stop, that meant they could hear him, now, and could be expected to deliver their calling card in about sixty seconds. He closed his hand around the automatic.

A bearded, disheveled man appeared from behind the front end of the boat. "Hi, friend," he said with a smile. So—it was going to be the stall–and–cannon play. The "stall" would take his attention, and the "cannon" would shoot him in the back.

The man was talking about something. Jack was looking at

him with his eyes, but his ears were focused about thirty
meters to his rear. When he heard the scrape of metal against
leather—a very soft sound, but a very specific one if your
whole being is focused on listening for it—he whirled on one
knee and spun himself behind the open hatch–ramp steps.
The cannon got off one shot while Jack was turning into a
firing position and judging for size and distance.

His first shot was a little high, but Jack was able to put the
second in his chest—no need to wait to see if that one did it.
He now gave the stall his undivided attention.

The automatic bucked in Jack's hand as the stall blasted off
two wild shots, kicking up a fountain of dirt around the
airboat. Jack put his second shot in the man's left chest.
When the man seemed to pause and did not drop his weapon,
Jack placed two more bullets within an inch-and-a-half of the
first. The impact snapped the man's head back and he went
over backwards in a graceful arc and lay still, his legs folded
under his body.

Jack felt a hot ache in his right side. Must have banged
himself into something as he ducked behind the steps. He
rubbed at his ribs where it hurt. The hand came back red.
"Old man Holloway is gettin' slow. That first fella creased
me a little," he said aloud.

Jack climbed back up into the airboat and peered at a
worried–looking Gerd van Riebeek in the screen. "Jack!
What the hell happened?"

Jack grinned lopsidedly. He felt hot and his ears were
ringing. "Two promising hijacking careers that will never
come to full flower. One Native Affairs Commissioner
nicked in the right side—let the other guy get off the first
shot. One Little Fuzzy safe and sound. Unnnh." He sat down
on the deck, drew his knees up to his chest and rested his
forehead on them.

Gerd was shouting from the screen. "Jack! I'll be there as
quick as I can. Try to stop the bleeding and avoid shock."

"Don't forget to call the cops at Beta–15," Jack said
softly. He felt something soft brush against his cheek and a
little arm go around his neck. He opened his eyes and smiled
at Little Fuzzy. "Everything's going to be all right," he said.

Little Fuzzy stroked Jack's arm. "You hokay, Pappy Jack? *Tosh–ki–Hagga huhtsu?*"

"Not very much, Little Fuzzy. You saved Pappy Jack's life. If you hadn't heard them, I would have been tearing into the generator and making enough noise for them to have got me."

Jack looked closely at Little Fuzzy and saw something he had never seen before. There were two small wet spots in the fur just under Little Fuzzy's eyes. Presently, another tear welled up and rolled away.

XVI

Grego whistled absently as the private lift sped toward the penthouse level. Attorney General Brannhard had organized the agenda logically and presided over the meeting smoothly. No wasted words. Grego appreciated that sort of thing. He also appreciated that no one had tried to sell the Company more than its fair share of the contribution. They sometimes did that, presumably on the theory that the Company was a bottomless pocket filled with financial assets and cash flow.

He stepped out of the lift directly into the foyer of his penthouse apartment. Christiana appeared in the living room doorway with a drink, which she handed to Grego.

"How did you manage to time this?" he asked, waving his other hand over the glass.

She grinned. "With an accomplice. Diamond can hear the lifter generator as soon as it engages at your office. There's just enough time—if everything is already laid out."

"Well," Grego said as he strolled into the living room. "You continue to amaze me, Miss Stone." He looked around the room. "Where's Diamond? He's usually climbing me like a tree as soon as I come out of the lift."

She held up one finger. "That's my fault. We have conspired to forego the usual greeting to show you something. Since it involved holding up part of dessert, I'm sure Diamond is waiting impatiently." She motioned for him to follow her into the kitchen.

"*Heyo, Pappy Vic!*" Diamond shouted. "See how I do!"

Diamond was seated at the kitchen table, in a kind of highchair. In front of him was a place setting of Fuzzy–sized silverware—actually the half-size utensils that were manufactured for very small children—fork, salad fork, soup spoon, teaspoon, knife, and butter knife. A little liqueur

glass had been pressed into service as a water goblet—
Fuzzy-scale.

Christiana set a saucer in front of Diamond and a plate on
the table. The saucer was empty; the plate contained an uncut
cake of Extee–Three. She stood back against the kitchen
counter and took a sip from her own drink.

Grego watched in rapt fascination as Diamond picked up
his knife and fork, cut off a slice of Extee–Three, and with
great dignity placed it on the saucer in front of him. He laid
down the knife and separated a single bite–sized piece from
the slice with his fork, shifted his grip, impaled the bite on the
fork and popped it into his mouth. This process was repeated,
with occasional sips from the water glass, until the saucer
was completely bare. Diamond took his napkin—a small
pocket handkerchief—from his lap, dabbed at each corner of
his mouth, folded up the napkin, and laid it to the left of his
salad fork. He turned toward them with shining eyes. ''How I
do, *Auntie K'istanna?*'' he asked.

They both set down their drinks and applauded loudly.

''Perfect, Diamond,'' Christiana said. ''You didn't miss a
thing.''

Diamond gave a whoop and bounded down to the floor. He
leaped a few steps and threw his arms around Grego's neck,
which, with its owner, had squatted down to Fuzzy–height.

After hugs and a little romping all around, Diamond
looked proudly at both his hands. *''Fingahs no weh,''* he
announced, then ran off into the Fuzzy–Room.

''What'd he say?'' Christiana asked.

'' 'Fingers not wet,' '' Grego repeated.

''Oh,'' she said, ''of course. I'm still not quite used to that
pidgin Terran. Does it have something to do with their
speaking machinery?''

Grego nodded. '' 'L' and 'R' pose quite a problem for
them. As far as we know, the sounds don't exist in *Lingua
Fuzzy.*''

They had drifted back into the living room and seated
themselves on opposite sides of the coffee table. ''You continue to astonish me, Miss Stone, and this is only Tuesday
evening of your first week. The mind boggles at what you

may accomplish by the time you have been here a fortnight.''

She laughed. ''It wasn't that difficult,'' she said. ''He had watched Hagga eat with silverware. Given the tools, scaled down to his anatomy, he practically got it the first time. The only practice he's had was with dinner, before you arrived.''

''Speaking of dinner,'' Grego replied, ''let's get that started.'' He got to his feet and went over to his private screen, punched in a combination, and lit a fresh cigarette while he waited for the dinner menu to start scrolling.

What a remarkable young woman, he thought, as she joined him to make her selection.

George Lunt's party was a little more elaborate than a ''beer and pretzels fest.'' Aside from the large cooler full of beer, there was a very respectable sideboard of cold cuts, cheeses, various sandwich makings, a tangy coleslaw of whacker–cabbage, the Zarathustran mutations of celery, radishes, carrot sticks, and pickled artichoke hearts, various kinds of crackers, salted nuts, dips, and—of course—pretzels.

George had wangled Ahmed and Sandra to let him throw the party in their new bungalow on the grounds that his quarters were certainly too small, that it would be against regulations—which he was still busily writing—to use ZNPF facilities, and, finally, that the bride and groom would inherit all the leftovers, which would ''. . . keep them both alive until one of them learns how to cook.''

The other ZNPF officers had been invited—as etiquette required on the marriage of a fellow officer. The lieutenants were starting to drift away toward their own social circle. The three off–duty captains were holding their own—Jordan Nuñez, Joseph Holderman, and Ray Pendleton—and Bruce Presley would come by to pay his respects when he closed off his shift at 2330.

Nuñez was sitting across from Jack in the group, with his tunic collar unbuttoned and one leg thrown over the arm of the big wooden armchair that had once been part of a pool–ball tree. ''Hell, Jack,'' he said, ''why'd you have to kill 'em both? If you could just have winged one of those guys, we could be sweating a thousand names out of him right now."

"That's the truth," Holderman agreed. "You know—tell him they're going to have to operate on his leg, but we won't let them put him under till he answers our questions." He winked. "And if they have to wait till the leg swells up like a banjo-bird's chest in mating season, they'll probably have to cut it off. Not that they didn't need killing—kidnap a Fuzzy and sell him on Omega, indeed—but couldn't you have been a little less *final* with one of them?"

"Wasn't time, Joe," Jack said to Holderman. "As it was, I let that first son of a Khooghra nick me. It's been a long time since that's happened. Maybe this Commissioner of Native Affairs job is just right for me. Maybe I should be flying a desk—if I'm getting so old and slow that I can't chop down two bush rats in a simple-minded ambush without getting scratched up."

"Oh, Jack," Nuñez said, "stop running yourself down. You're not quite tired old folks, yet. I'll tell you the truth— I'd hate to run up against you in a shooting scrape, and I'm about half your age."

"Thank you, Jordy," Jack said. "That honestly makes me feel better. Do we know anything about them yet?"

Nuñez fished his notebook out of his hip pocket. "Let's see," he said, leafing through the pages, "I was just going off duty when we heard the call. Your co-ordinates weren't actually inside the Fuzzy Reservation, so Colonial Constabulary had jurisdiction. But I went scooting over to Red Hill, anyway, and helped young Catlin catalog the deceaseds' possessions. They were, J.J. Roberts—we don't know what the J.J. stands for, but we think 'J.J.' is his actual first name—and one Curtis Hansson. They both had five hundred sols on them—separate from a little other money, and in each case tucked into a small white envelope. I checked in with Bruce, just before I came to the party, to see what he had gotten out of the big computer. Y'see, both these guys had a screen combination on a slip of paper tucked in those envelopes. Turns out that combination is for Hugo Ingermann's private screen in Mallorysport." He snapped the notebook shut and tucked it back in his hip pocket. "Isn't that interesting?" he said. "Both these grubby bums having fresh money on them as well as Ingermann's unlisted screen combination?"

"Anh–hanh," Holderman said. "I've been figuring that Ingermann must have some scouts out over here—ever since the sunstone claim on Fuzzy Divide was leased back to the CZC."

"Do you think it could have been a snuff job?" Jack asked.

"No," Nuñez said, "I don't think so. Ingermann doesn't see you as the big snarl in his rope. He's sunstone happy—his past actions prove that—so he's going to have a bunch of cheerful dummies over here trying to figure out bigger and better ways to steal sunstones."

"I agree with Jordy," Holderman said. "You get in a fistfight with Ingermann and bust his nose—then you can expect him to send a couple gunmen after you personally. Otherwise, he's so busy with his *real* imagined grudges that he won't have time for *fancied* imagined grudges. It is clear, though, that he paid these two slobs to do some snooping around over here." Holderman sighed. "That's why I wish you hadn't blown up both of them, Jack. It would be so much easier to just sweat a guy down than to do all this deductive reasoning."

"Oh, stow it, Joe," Nuñez said. "The important thing is that Jack's still kicking and that we know Ingermann has dumped a bunch of snoops on our turf. We'll snag a live one pretty soon now, then proceed to scare the pants off him and find out all kinds of wonderful stuff."

As soon as the last of the other guests had departed, George and Ahmed simultaneously drew up chairs across the coffee table from where Jack was sitting. With no one else there but George, the Khadras, the van Riebeeks, and Lynne Andrews, it was perfectly safe to discuss the confidential aspects of Fuzzy Valley. Jack's eyes grew large as George and Ahmed related their findings.

"So, I want to take you back up there, Jack, and let you

have a look around,'' George finished. "I want the whole thing kept strictly on the quiet, though, until we know more about what's what.''

"I'll second that,'' Jack said. "In fact, just try to keep me away.''

"Good,'' George said. "How about first thing in the morning?''

Jack nodded.

"Let's take along your microray scanner, too—find out how homogeneous the geology is and what's under the surface. You'll know more about that than I will. I could check one out from the equipment stores, but I'd rather not leave any paperwork tracks that might arouse someone's curiosity.''

"We can take Gerd along and detour over to fix his airboat on the way—then go on up there in ZNPF vehicles,'' Ahmed said.

"How about taking old Gerd all the way along?'' Gerd said. "Old Gerd is pretty curious about this thing, too.''

"He's right,'' Jack said. "Good idea not to make too much of a ZNPF parade out of all this.''

"I see what you mean,'' George said.

"We ought to take Little Fuzzy and some of the other Fuzzies along, too,'' Jack said. "If there are Fuzzies up there who are not moving south and who won't come near a Hagga, then we'll have to make contact with them via Fuzzy emissaries sooner or later. So, let's make that the 'official' reason for the trip.''

"I don't get it,'' Sandra said. "If titanium is practically non-existent in the crust of Zarathustra, why should there be one spot where it's plentiful?''

"Might be more than one spot,'' Gerd said, "but it's just that we haven't found any others yet. That *is* an area of some active vulcanism—recently active volcanoes, hot springs, geothermal areas, that sort of thing. Maybe volcanic activity encourages the formation of titanium.''

"Phooey on that,'' Jack said. "Distribution is the question. Titanium is distributed all sorts of ways, none of them very exclusive. When it gets hot, it will combine with just about anything. No, there's something definitely unusual about Fuzzy Valley."

"I still don't get it," Sandra insisted. "If titanium is so scarce in the general composition of Zarathustra, how did Fuzzies ever evolve here at all—if it's such an important component of their morphology?"

"Gerd's theory is that they're living fossils," Ruth said, "that there used to be a large order of Zarathustran primates. The rest died off. The Fuzzies have survived this far, because they're the smartest of the bunch, but NFMp is whittling them down."

Lynne had finished up some things in the kitchen and then joined the group. "The xeno–paleontologists haven't found any bones yet to hang that theory on," she said.

"Well, we've only been here a quarter century," Gerd protested. "We know nothing about the history of Fuzzies, and almost nothing about the history of the planet. The xeno–paleontologists haven't found any really ancient Fuzzy bones, either, but the existence of Fuzzies is self–evident."

Sandra stuck to her point. "I'm not attacking your theory, Gerd, but if it's correct wouldn't that mean there used to be more titanium on Zarathustra? In order for Fuzzies to develop this critical need for it in their diet? Are you saying there used to be more titanium on Zarathustra than there is now? Isn't there a rule or something about that?"

Gerd thought for a moment, smiling as he felt around for the governing principle Sandra was referring to. "Oh, no," he said. "Titanium is too heavy to be carried off as the planet developed. That wouldn't apply to Zarathustra—the gravity is almost the same as Terra." Suddenly, he realized what he was saying. *"Great galloping holy Dai–Butsu!"* he exclaimed. "I've been digging up the wrong rabbit hole all along! All the titanium ever formed on Zarathustra is still here, in its crust, and that's damned little. That point was established very early in comparative extraterrestrial planetography by—what's his name?—MacKenzie's Law."

"You mean it's constant on all planets?" Sandra asked.

"Sure it is," Jack said.

"Do you remember it, Jack?" Gerd asked. "You're the closest thing here to a geologist."

"I can't state it mathematically," Jack said, "but I know it. That tells us beforehand something of what a planet's geology is likely to be all about. Let's see now—'The rate of escape of a substance from a planetary mass will vary inversely with the gravity of that mass, varies directly with its temperature, and—" He scratched his head. "—and varies indirectly with the boiling or sublimation point of the substance in question.' That's the gist of it."

"All right, then," Sandra said. "If there's so little titanium on Zarathustra, how did Fuzzies come to have such a specific need for it in their metabolism?"

"Now, you're getting back toward my specialty," Gerd said. "That point is only *theoretically* defined in xenobiology. Remember Garrett's Theorem? It states that 'A need for an element does not arise in evolution unless the element is available in reasonable amounts and in assimilable form.' In other words—in *soluble* form." Gerd thought about that for a moment, too, then shook his head. "That doesn't get me out of the woods, either, does it? There's still the possibility that Fuzzies might not have evolved here at all."

"Pish–tush," Lynne said. "That's along the line of crackpot theories from the First Century that man was not native to Terra—none of which were ever taken seriously by the scientific community."

"That makes sense to me," George said. "How would a low Paleolithic people get to Zarathustra from another planet? Somebody take them for a joy–ride?"

"Which ones?" Ahmed asked. "The low Paleolithic Fuzzies living in the woods, or the agricultural, house-building Fuzzies that are still in the Uplands of North Beta?"

"Or," Jack chimed in, "the reading–and–writing, communication–screen–watching, machinery–operating Fuzzies that are living at Holloway Station and Mallorysport?"

XVII

"Charming," The Rev muttered as he opened the shop door. A tiny bell, suspended on a piece of spring steel so that the door would brush it into action when opened, jingled brightly. *I've never seen one of those things outside a period–piece screenplay,* he thought, *but one might expect it here.*

The white haired proprietor appeared, coming from a well-equipped back room that was many times the size of the tiny front portion of the shop. He smiled in sudden recognition. "Why, Tom," he said, "it *is* you. From the descriptions I've heard about the Junktown Rescue Mission, I rather *thought* you might be on Zarathustra."

They shook hands warmly. "It is myself, Henry. It has been a while, indeed, since I saw you. Fenris, I think—wasn't it? After a while all colony worlds begin to look alike."

"I believe it was Fenris, Tom," Henry Stenson said, "although I couldn't begin to tell you how long ago it was. I do recall it was during that squabble when the Couperin Cartel had bought up the old, original colonial company's charter—for about six–and–a–half sols and a bag of jelly beans—and tried to start running the planet. Nasty business, that one."

The Rev smiled. "I remember. The colonists and the Hunters' Co–operative; both a little unhappy about that. They captured the port authority docks and were going to blow up the *City of Malverton* on her stand if the Federation Resident–General and the new company Manager–in–Chief tried to disembark.

"I must say, Henry," The Rev continued, "You don't seem to have aged a day in the years since."

Stenson chuckled. "At my age, Tom, there's simply nothing left to wrinkle or go gray. One reaches a kind of optimum state of deterioration and stays there."

Henry Stenson was the finest instrument–maker on Zarathustra—by definition, since he was the *only* instrument–maker on Zarathustra. However, he would still have been the finest, even if the town was crawling with them. To call Henry Stenson an instrument–maker was about the same thing as calling Michelangelo Buonarroti an interior decorator.

Elderly and thin, with a tight mouth and a face that was a spider web of wrinkles, he was the last man one would think of as being a Federation agent. He was, though, and had figured pivotally in the great upheaval following the discovery of Fuzzies—the Fuzzy Flap, as local historians now called it.

He was also the only person to ever successfully bug Victor Grego's private office.

"And what brings you to my humble establishment, Tom?" Stenson asked.

The Rev produced a thin sheaf of folded papers, covered with engineering sketches. "Are you familiar with the Ballard Diagnostic Reader?"

"I am," Stenson said.

"Well, I need one," The Rev said, "and there isn't one to be had on the whole planet—and I can't afford to wait a year to get one out here from Terra."

"That's a pretty exotic piece of medical gear for a rescue mission, Tom."

The Rev shook his head. "I know, Henry, but I've got to have one. I just don't have the time or the trained workers to run medical checks on all these poor souls down here using multiple–station methods—even with good quality manual electronic sensing and metering equipment. Blood pressure here, coronary profile there, hematology somewhere else—it just takes too bloody long. Why, do you know there are people in Junktown who have never seen a doctor in their entire adult lives?"

"Shocking," Stenson said. "Shocking thing for the

Seventh Century. I thought we had excellent public health programs, here.''

"We *do*," the Rev said. "That's the hell of it. The health care is there, all right, but the people won't use it because experience has taught them that the less contact they have with the government the less trouble the government can make for them. *That's* what's shocking.''

"Well, don't make too much of it, Tom," Stenson said. "The way people are pouring into Mallorysport for the so-called great land boom, you've got to expect that most of them will be the kind that doesn't trust the government.''

"And why should they, Henry?" the Rev asked. "For the most part they're the disillusioned and disadvantaged. If a man is prosperous, he's more apt to stay home. That's what makes any immigration movement a built-in heartbreaker. Most of these people wind up broke and hungry when they find the streets aren't paved with sunstones—and where a lot of them wind up is at my mission. So, I dispense porridge and medical care, and try to patch up their souls enough for them to climb back in the ring for another round.''

"I've been watching it, too," Stenson said, "and things *are* beginning to show signs of strain.''

"That's what I'm trying to do," the Rev said, "give them a little hope, a little help, and keep them from becoming desperate.''

"It's a dangerous situation, Tom," Stenson said. "Yes, dangerous enough—even without Hugo Ingermann and his gang of thugs constantly haranguing the mob. There's an old proverb, Tom: 'A hungry man is like a wolf in the forest; he'll go where you tell him when his belly is empty.' ''

"We've both seen it before," the Rev said. "When hope goes out the airlock, men get desperate. They've got nothing left to lose, so they'll try most anything—things they would never think of doing if they didn't have their backs to the wall. They're easy marks for manipulation by people like this bastard Ingermann. I can see it coming in Junktown. Unless something happens to take the pressure off, the whole place is going to blow up one of these days.''

The little bell rang as someone entered the shop.

Henry Stenson tidied up the sheaf of papers. "Yes, I can build one of these for you, Father. The contact plate will have to be a breadboard rig, but it will sense out all the data you want. Otherwise, it will work just like any Ballard Reader in the best hospital on Terra."

Judge Frederic Pendarvis laid down the sheaf of papers, moved the ashtray a few inches to the right, and took a slender cigar out of the silver box on his desk. After he had lighted it, he leaned back in his chair and blew a smoke ring at the ceiling. Then he turned his attention to the bearded giant and the small, bristly–looking man who sat across the desk from him. "I see nothing wrong with this at all. Your assessment is quite correct, Gus. For my part, I agree that we are on solid ground with respect to the Federation Constitution *and* the body of colonial case law.

"Colonial Investigations Bureau," the Chief Justice said reflectively. He flicked a quarter-inch of ash from his panetella and smiled. "I must congratulate you both on putting this together. The very *idea* of getting all those different cops to pull together on something like this is nothing short of astounding. I've been dealing with all of the law enforcement agencies on the planet for the past fifteen years, and, I can tell you, they can be the damnedest bunch of fools—squabbling like fishwives over jurisdiction, proof of claim, interrogation priority, previous wants and warrants, perquisites and privilege—you name it. There isn't a one of them I haven't wanted to take a horsewhip to over the years, usually for clogging up the courts while they prove to one and all that *their* uniform is more righteous than the next guy's."

Ben Rainsford frowned and looked at the floor. "Only one thing I'm unhappy about," he said.

"What's that, Ben?" Judge Pendarvis asked.

"That young fella, Khadra. I wanted him to head up the CIB. Why'd he have to go and get married and run off to Beta?"

"I strongly suspect it's because he was in love," Pendarvis remarked drily.

Rainsford waved his hand impatiently and began fishing

for his pipe in the pocket of his bush jacket.

The way he throws that pipe in and out of his jacket, Pendarvis thought, *I'll bet the inside of that pocket looks as black as a Hathor wolfram-miner's lungs.*

"Will this help any," Rainsford said around his pipestem as he touched flame to the bowl, "to slow up the congestion in your criminal courts docket?"

"No," Pendarvis sighed. "It will only make it more orderly."

"Well, I can't give you the extra judgeships you asked for in either department," Rainsford said, almost defensively. "There's just no money for it. The fact of the matter is that the CZC is financing this government at the moment—until we can get a constitution out of those lame-brained delegates, elect a proper legislature, and levy taxes. And the CZC is going to expect its money back one of these days. It's a hell of a way to start out a government—in debt—but it can't be helped, I suppose. Is there anything you and Gus can come up with to reduce the load on the criminal side?" Rainsford looked anxiously at both of them in turn. "I'll go along with anything that makes sense."

Pendarvis' eyes narrowed slightly. "Not much, unless you want to do it at the expense of fair and equal justice under the law," he said evenly.

Gus knew that Rainsford had hit a sensitive spot. "I could encourage my prosecutors to be a little more open to plea-bargaining," he offered. "A lot of these criminal cases are pretty cut and dried, but they stagger on through the system with a long trial—often because the defense attorney loves to hear the pure, spellbinding eloquence of his own courtroom oratory."

"And just as often is practicing his planned future political speeches on the jury," Pendarvis added. "I would have no objection to that, Gus—as long as we veridicate the accused in open court regarding any pressure than might have been brought on him to plead guilty to a lesser charge."

"What will that get us in terms of man-days saved?" Rainsford asked, "—or whatever measure of increased efficiency is applicable."

"Not much," Pendarvis said, "but being able to get one more preliminary hearing a day on each judge's docket will do more than it sounds like."

"The civil side isn't going to get any better, though," Gus said, "and there's nothing I can do about that—out of my jurisdiction."

"Yes," Pendarvis said, almost wistfully. "There's the *real* rub. We have more criminal cases, but they are simpler than before. Our civil cases—which we also have a great deal more of—are getting more complex."

Rainsford jabbed his pipestem at the air. "It's that Ingermann s.o.b.," he said. "He's behind this caseload problem that's starting to clog up the courts. Overloading the legal system is a fine first step toward bringing down the government. It helps frustrate people. Frustration generates lack of inclination to depend on the legal systems of redress, and that generates more and more lawlessness."

"If that's his purpose," Pendarvis said, "I can see how what you suggest would suit his purpose admirably. But I question that the *soi disant* geopolitician Hugo Ingermann has an organization that is quite so efficient."

"Oh, I think he does," Gus said. "I've been studying Mr. Ingermann's operation quite closely as I remain alert for ways to rid the planet of him. As I've said, Ingermann is Out to Get Us in capital letters. The more I learn about him, the more I agree with your notion—hare-brained though it seemed at first—"

Rainsford glared at him.

Gus grinned and went on. ". . . that he's fastened himself on getting control of Zarathustra. And he's smart enough to have several scams working in that direction—on the theory that any one of them will be more apt to pay off in an atmosphere of general disruption and confusion."

A small bell chimed somewhere in Pendarvis' office, discreetly indicating that the time had come for him to go on to other matters.

Rainsford and Brannhard stood and prepared to leave.

"By the way, Governor," Pendarvis said, "I didn't request those judgeships because I thought the government could afford them, or because I expected to get them any time soon.''

"What for, then?'' Rainsford asked.

"For the record,'' Pendarvis said, "so that when we *can* afford them, I won't be completely at the end of the line for budget increases.''

XVIII

Mr. Commissioner Holloway reached up behind his own head and pushed his hat down over his forehead to shade his eyes. He chuffed on his pipe and continued to swing the microray scanner ahead of him as he crossed and re-crossed the basin of Fuzzy Valley.

Gerd had his portable lab—screwed to a contragravity lifter—programmed for inorganics and was running soil samples. The lab floated weightless at bench height, bobbing slightly each time Gerd punched a set of data into the chart storage unit.

George and Ahmed were circling the rim of the valley on a small skid, looking for other signs of Fuzzy habitation that couldn't be seen from the air.

The Fuzzies had promptly disappeared upon arrival. *"So ni–hosh shi–mosh–gashta,"* Jack had said. "You find the people like Fuzzies. Tell them Hagga love them, give good treats—give *esteefee*."

Jack set his microray scanner on the edge of Gerd's "bench," and took a long drink of water. He took off his hat and wiped his forehead with the back of his hand. "Nothing unusual about the geology, Gerd," he said. "This is all homogeneous—pretty much normal sedimentary stuff. I don't know anything now that I didn't know when I kicked my toe in the dirt and said that to begin with."

Gerd punched another test result into the chart unit and raised one eyebrow. "But now you know for sure," he said.

"True," Jack replied. "If there's anything buried in the valley, it's buried mighty deep."

"Well, there's *something* here," Gerd said, "that's putting a lot of titanium into the soil. So far, I have double, triple, and quad–ionized titanium traces, titanic acids, and titanates. The soil is rich enough to grow these plants again if it had sufficient water. The plants are sure to have picked the stuff up—and hence been tasty to Fuzzies. I'll take some plant samples back for analysis, but that's just lip service. I'm sure I'm right.''

"But, where is it *coming* from?" Jack insisted. "Can you tell that?"

"Don't know yet," Gerd said. "I'm doing a random chart, now. If that doesn't 'point a finger,' so to speak, we can lay out a point-grid, with a sample from each point on a hundred–meter checkerboard, and graph that. I did have one thought."

"Which is?"

"Does titanium ever come in meteorites?" Gerd asked.

Jack shrugged. "I don't know. I suppose it could."

"Mmmmm," Gerd said. "That's so far out of my area, I wouldn't even know how to start looking it up. If, though, there was a big titanium–rich meteorite buried up on one of these mountains, it would decompose, ever so slowly, and release compounds like this into the soil as it washes down to the valley floor."

Jack leaned on the lifter and gazed south toward the woods. "You know, we could come up here and sink a water well. I'll bet money the water table isn't very deep. Sink the well upstream," he mused, talking more to himself than to Gerd, who understood and went on with his work while only half-listening. "Wouldn't be unheard of to hit a structure that'd give us a good head of artesian flow." He jerked his thumb back over his shoulder. "Why, it's plain as day that there's a saturation layer east of that saddle where the old creek ran. All kinds of folded structures around here. With the amount of hot springs and geothermal fumaroles we've spotted, there's a good chance of hitting a pressure dome. Something's keeping those trees alive down in the woods, there. No sign of them dying back since the rainfall dropped off."

"Why would you want to?" Gerd asked.

"Want to what?"

"Bore a well, of course."

"Why to throw the switch again on the water supply,"
Jack said, "get things growing up here again. Think about it.
Live plants that are rich in titanium compounds—that could
put a whole new twist to your Fuzzy research." He laughed,
quickly and shortly. *"Fuzzy salad* might hold the key to the
whole problem."

"Hmmmph!" Gerd said.

"Son of a Khooghra!" Jack exclaimed suddenly. Without
moving his head, he fumbled behind him, making the skid
bob violently.

"What the blazes are you doing?" Gerd asked, snatching
up one of his soil samples to keep it from being spilled.

"Hand me the binos—quick!" Jack said.

Gerd placed the stereo-optic in Jack's outstretched hand.
Jack clapped it to his eyes and chuckled, talking to himself
under his breath.

"What is it?" Gerd asked.

"Here," Jack said, "see for yourself."

Gerd grabbed the binos and looked.

"So we said the Upland Fuzzies had unusual traits, did
we—traits like co-operative hunting—that woods Fuzzies
didn't bother with?" Jack said triumphantly.

Gerd gasped. Their own Fuzzies—the ambassadors—
were coming out of the woods, followed by a group of
Upland Fuzzies. Whereas woods Fuzzies just moved over the
ground in a disorderly bunch, the Upland Fuzzies—well—
they were quite a different gang—apparently.

The Upland Fuzzies were arranged in two staggered files,
several meters apart. Flankers were spaced out from the edge
of the main body, and there was a skirmish line to the front,
with three point-men moving ahead of that.

As the two groups drew closer, Jack and Gerd could see
that there was a great deal of conversation between Little
Fuzzy—who loved being the self-appointed intermediary
between the Hagga and all Fuzzydom—and another specific
Fuzzy in the Upland group. That suggested that this group of
Fuzzies had a group/headman society, which suggested entirely different things about *this* example of Fuzzy culture,

which suggested that a lot of things the Terrans had "deduced" about the evolution of Fuzzy civilization were flat wrong, which suggested that much Fuzzy research was really going nowhere on hyperdrive, which suggested et cetera.

This bunch was just as wary of the first contact with Hagga as any woods Fuzzy, but they were better organized about it. The skirmish line filled out with some members from the column. Chopper–diggers at high port, watchful eyes fixed on the aliens—in other words, the Terrans—and scouts maintaining an air–watch for harpies; very businesslike bunch of Fuzzies.

The leader advanced, with Little Fuzzy, and a rather dignified palaver took place. Jack and Gerd had to use their ultrasonic hearing aids. Upland Fuzzies still spoke in a frequency range too high for Terran hearing. As it was, they only caught about every other word, enough for them to be visually responsive but not really understand. Little Fuzzy translated—and enjoyed every minute of it.

The–by–now–rather–mythic explanation of Hagga was well received. The leader's delight with Extee–Three was ill–concealed, but handled with a certain dignity that only involved the widening of eyes and some *yeeks* of pure ecstasy. Gifts of steel *shoppo–diggo* and canvas *shodda–bags* were handled in a businesslike manner; the group came up in increments of five each, expressed approval at the trade of new for old chopper–diggers, the gift of *shodda–bag*, and *yeeks* of profound pleasure about the ration of *esteefee*.

The Fuzzy unit—no other word seemed quite as appropriate—almost spooked and ran when George and Ahmed arrived on the contragravity skid. Gerd's portable lab floating off the ground was one thing, but a thing that did that and *moved* as well, almost stretched the flee–or–fight reflex beyond its intellectual constraints. As negotiations proceeded, some of the bolder Fuzzies were persuaded to go for short rides on the skid—especially after being challenged with the example of the southern Fuzzies riding it and obviously enjoying it. Eventually, the Uplanders seemed to think it was fun—at least they still had Fuzzies' traditional attitudes about fun, which is to say they really couldn't resist it.

Ahmed picked up the microray scanner and wandered off up the slope of what they were now calling "Mount Fuzzy," taking random readings—more for something to do than anything else.

The discussion broke down on only one point, but it was a sticking-point. Jack's suggestion that they all come down to Holloway Station and get away from this grim hand to mouth existence was met with a flat refusal. The Upland Fuzzies were adamant about staying where they were. It was traditional, you know; stick close to the valley. They couldn't explain the why of it, but there was no shaking them from the fact of its necessity—another basic difference between the Uplanders and the woods Fuzzies, which suggested a whole bunch more of "and so ons" about the state of the art in Fuzzy research.

Attempts to convince them were useless.

"How are you going to persuade them?" George asked. "It's a cinch these folks are having a hard time putting beans on the table. Look at them. There isn't a one that isn't seriously underweight."

"And, as a result of malnutrition," Gerd added. "A lot of them need medical attention. I can see it from here. It would be for their own good, Jack, if we—"

"It's not my job to persuade them about anything," Jack snapped. "My job is to *protect* them. If they won't come to us, we'll have to come to them. *Your* job is to implement the Commissioner's policy and wants—namely mine. So, make some notes. You are opening a branch office of Fuzzy Institute."

Gerd started to reply, but Jack cut him off with a gesture. "Little Fuzzy, tell them we will leave all the *hoksu-fusso* we have with us, and will bring back more in less than a hand of days. Ask if there are more Fuzzies up here than this bunch."

Little Fuzzy carried on a light-speed conversation with the leader, whose face brightened when he was told about the *esteefee*. He motioned some of his troops forward. Each grabbed a blue-labeled tin of *esteefee* and tenderly hoisted it onto his shoulder.

"All Fuzzies *heh-yeh*, Pappy Jack," Little Fuzzy said.

"He say, once many–many. *Ha'hpy* make off wif some. Some no tough enough—die in cold season. Many–many go off when *zatku* move *souff*—he no know."

Jack rubbed his eyes and pinched the bridge of his nose. "Tell him they have my promise we will take care of them," he said to Little Fuzzy. He was going to say more, but there was a curious catch in his voice, so he let it go at that.

As Little Fuzzy was translating, the leader's face began to soften for the first time from the grim, hollow–eyed expression of resolve that had gripped it all through the conference. That was one way the Uplanders were like all other Fuzzies—there was something in their nature that compelled them to love the Hagga and accept their protection. Leave the valley? Not a chance. But, make the Hagga happy; that was as natural to them as eating *zatku*.

Suddenly, there was a blood–curdling shriek from up on Mount Fuzzy. *"Great Jumping Jezebel's Eyebrows!"* Ahmed bellowed at the top of his voice. *"Come here! Quick!"*

The Upland Fuzzies quite reasonably took this to be a danger warning. They scattered in every direction—making sure that all the tins of Extee–Three accompanied them—and were out of sight of the Terrans in less than a minute.

Even Holloway's Fuzzies took cover and then peeped out anxiously from under, in, and behind where they had dived when Ahmed first shouted.

Jack, Gerd, and George leaped onto the skid and George sent it skimming up the mountain slope to where they could see Ahmed jumping up and down and waving the microray scanner.

Before the skid stopped, Jack jumped off and ran a few steps to adjust his forward momentum. "Now what the hell?" he asked Ahmed.

Ahmed pointed to the bare ground. He had made some little piles of stones, and scratched lines in the loose earth with the toe of his boot. "Look at the *size* of this sonofabitch!" he said.

George had grounded the skid. "*What* sonofabitch?" he barked.

"I don't know," Ahmed barked right back, "but look at the size of it!"

Gerd still had the rangefinder he had used to chart–spot his soil sample locations. He pulled it out of his pocket and took some shots of the area Ahmed had marked out.

"The 'size of it' is about eight hundred feet long and about seven hundred feet across, shaped something very much like a regular triangle," he said drily. "At risk of sounding redundant, what is it?"

"It's—it's—it's *something*," Ahmed said, "and it's all titanium, as near as I can tell."

"Oh for—" Jack said exasperatedly. "Here, give me that." He took the microray scanner, pointed it, shaded the readout with his hand, and then made a face. He zeroed the readout, smacked the scanner smartly on its side a few times with the heel of his hand, and assumed an exasperated expression.

He handed the instrument to Gerd. "Here. See for yourself."

"Great Ghu's gallstones," Gerd said. "He's right. It's totally impossible, of course, but he's right."

George had to look next. The interruption pattern was quite clear on the readout pattern; a large triangle, with a hollow place in the middle, so that it looked much like a letter "A" on the readout screen. "Well," George said, "it's not *all* titanium. There's some other stuff there, too. I don't see why you guys are all coming unstuck. I *told* you there was a lot of titanium up here." He looked nonplussed.

"For God's sake, George . . ." Jack said. "Look. If all the titanium in the entire crust of Zarathustra was to be collected, refined, and cast into a single chunk, it *still* wouldn't be as large as this thing is. *That's* what we're excited about."

What Colonial Governor General Bennett Rainsford was

excited about was that Attorney General Gus Brannhard had emphatically informed him that the prerogatives of his office did *not* allow him to shoot a couple members of the constitutional convention out-of-hand, just to get the rest of them to take him seriously.

The idea kept running through his mind as he addressed the delegates, assembled in congress, that they would somehow more clearly understand what he was saying if he could just haul out his pistol and rap the butt of it on the lectern smartly from time to time to drive the point home.

"I have no desire to stifle debate, ladies and gentlemen," he concluded, "but if you keep on with this debate as you have, you will *legislate* representative government on Zarathustra right out of business. If a Federation High Commission were to investigate the progress of this convention over the past ten months, they would, I am most certain, declare the body politic—the *corpus comitatus*—of the people of Zarathustra Colony to be incompetent to manage its own affairs. *They*—a Federation High Commission—would then appoint a guardian government for us—a political nanny, if you will—to look after us, since we had demonstrated that we could not look after ourselves.

"I will not go that far—nor while I hold office, will I permit such a shameful occurrence. But, I'll tell you what I will do, and I'll tell you why. If you distinguished delegates do not complete the task of framing a constitution in a speedy and efficient manner, this entire colony is going to start coming down around all our ears.

"The request which you have duly filed," he continued, "for a one-year extension of the authority of this body is denied. Attorney General Brannhard will read the court order to you as soon as I have finished speaking, and furnish copies to those members who may wish to study it—*on their own time*. During the remaining two months of life which this convention now possesses, the convention will complete the task to which it was appointed—namely to write a constitution for the Colony of Zarathustra. If that task has not been completed speedily, which is to say in *less* than the allotted time, my office will apply for an *Order Nisi Quo Warranto*, which the courts will issue. Such an order will dissolve the convention on *a priori* grounds of incompetence in office and form a possible cause of action against individual members on criminal charges of malfeasance in office.''

Rainsford looked over the hall full of stunned faces before him. ''I trust you all now know how I feel,'' he said, then turned and left the platform.

XIX

"Paperwork, paperwork!" snarled the small, wiry man behind the watch captain's desk. "Damn the double-damned paperwork!"

"Are the burdens of duty weighing heavily on your scrawny frame, Captain Pendleton?" George Lunt asked quietly.

"Dammit, George," Pendleton said. He shook a sheaf of printout in the air. "What's all this crap with changing the patrol schedules—and the personnel—and the assignment areas?"

"Why, Ray," George said, "all I've done is shift the Marines from North Beta to the southern areas of the continent—essentially."

"Essentially, my Aunt Fanny," Pendleton grumped. "You've put different men on everything north of Fuzzy Divide, and changed the duty schedule for everyone else."

"Not everyone, Ray," George chided. "I've left all the lieutenants and captains right where they were on the roster schedule."

"Yeaaahhh," Pendleton said, "which means that all their sergeants and troopers are now men they've never worked with before."

"Well, that just has to be done once in a while, Ray—" George said, "—the way I want things run. I don't want people getting too comfy and routine about their work. When the ground is all so familiar that they get to screening in their report automatically, it's time to change the scenery. Keeps everybody awake."

"Sure," Pendleton said, "and makes your officers old and gray before their time."

George grinned. "But, you were old and gray when I appointed you, Ray."

"I was old and gray when I was *born*," Pendleton said. "That's how I was smart enough to live this long."

"And sweetly, too," George said. "Your disposition is the most loveable part of you. I don't know whether that's a compliment or not." He continued quickly, so as not to leave space for a rebuttal. "*I* am going off duty shift at the moment. I will be at Mr. Commissioner Holloway's residence for cocktails."

Pendleton made a face. "*I* will be here slaving over all this damned paperwork," George heard him say as the screen door slammed behind him.

"Jack," George said, "we can quarantine the whole area. I've already changed the patrol assignments all around—you should hear how the watch captains are howling about *that*—and we can keep everyone else out on the grounds that the Upland Fuzzies are just too nervous about Hagga and it will take some time for them to become accustomed to Terrans. It's all inside the Fuzzy Reservation, anyway, so the only legal niceties involved would be a written order from you. That will give us enough breathing-time to find out what the titanium thing is and decide how we're going to handle it. We don't want any curiosity for a while."

Jack nodded. "I agree, George. There are lots of questions to be answered, and the only chance we have of keeping control—short of asking for armed troops from Commodore Napier—is to stay one or two jumps ahead of everyone else with the answers."

"Questions?" George said. "There are nothing but questions, and I don't see any answers yet. To start with, why have Fuzzies built there in Fuzzy Valley and nowhere else?"

"Nowhere else that we *know* about," Ahmed corrected.

"Point well taken," Jack said. "It's the plants, of course, that pick up the titanium; that's what keeps them there. We could fly a one-item scan map of the planet from, say, fifty thousand feet, and probably depend on finding Fuzzies wherever we got a high concentration of titanium in the soil.''

"Why is there so much titanium up there, anyway?" George asked.

''I don't know,'' Jack said. "It's contrary to everything in the current body of data about extraterrestrial geology.'' He shrugged. "But, there are a lot of things on a lot of planets that are contrary data.''

"You think there could be other concentrations of titanium like this one?'' Ahmed asked.

Jack shrugged again. "Don't know.''

"Well, what do you think that big hunk of it up in Fuzzy Valley is?'' Ahmed asked.

"Don't know,'' Jack said, again.

"Could it be something the Fuzzies built a long time ago? I mean, archeological remains from their civilization?''

"Fuzzy archeology?'' George said. "That's nuts.''

"George is likely right,'' Jack said. "People who don't make any ancillary tools more refined than a low Paleolithic *coup de poing* axe and wooden *shoppo-diggo* are not too likely to have built pyramids or anything.''

"Oh, I don't know,'' Khadra said. "They could have once been a very high culture—which slowly slipped back and declined to minimum survival levels. That would answer a lot of questions about what we've found.''

"What you say is possible,'' George said, ''but it raises just as many new questions as old ones it lays to rest.''

"I know. I know,'' Jack said. "That's why I haven't been sleeping too well.''

The communication screen image shattered, shimmered, and stabilized into a replica of Jack Holloway's face.

"Jack! By Ghu, it's good to see someone who's still sane,'' Ben Rainsford said. "What can I do for you?''

"How about coming on over here to Beta tomorrow morning,'' Jack said.

Outside his bungalow on Beta, dusk was just falling. George and Ahmed were still there, but staying out of range of the screen pickup. In Mallorysport it was full night, somewhere just after the dinner hour, depending on one's eating habits.

"What the hell for?" Rainsford demanded. "I don't have the time to go tripping around visiting my friends—much as I'd like to."

Jack looked uncomfortable, hoping to convey the impression that he didn't want to discuss it on screen. "Aw, it's something scientific, Ben," he said. "We sure would like to have you over here tomorrow. It's going to be kind of special."

"Scientific, you say?" Rainsford said. "Jack, I can't go over to Beta for something that's *scientific*. I'm up to my ass in alligators over here. The only way I can get this constitutional convention moving is to make a cattle drive out of it. I can't afford the luxury of science any more. Not just now, anyway."

Jack was aggravated, and didn't make any attempt to conceal the fact. "Ben, do you remember about a year ago—when you were on your way back from a field trip— and you stopped at the Constabulary post, Beta 15, at Red Hill? George Lunt told you a story that made you think he was the biggest liar in the known galaxy. Then, when you got home, you found a message from me on your screen recorder, and beat it straight over to my camp to see for yourself?"

"Well, of course I remember it, Jack. I'm not getting senile, or anything, you know. This job is driving me nuts, but I still got all my marbles."

George Lunt came into the arc covered by the screen pickup and spoke to the Governor General. "This is just as crazy, Governor Rainsford—and it could be just as important."

"All right. I see it, now," Rainsford growled. "You fellas have turned up something that's really big. You don't want to talk about it on screen, but you want my opinion about it. That it?"

"To say nothing," Jack remarked, "of the glory of your illustrious gubernatorial presence."

"Don't lay it on too thick, Jack," Rainsford grumped. "I

got people over here in Mallorysport who do that for a *living*. What time and where shall I meet you?''

"Could your royal princeliness manage to be at Holloway Station at 0800?'' Jack asked.

"0800!'' Rainsford roared. ''That means I have to get up at 0400 in order to leave here by 0500!''

"Love will find a way,'' Holloway said. ''Seriously, Ben; this is very important.''

Ben Rainsford hopped out of his aircar, looking a bit more rumpled than usual, and strode briskly into Jack Holloway's bungalow without knocking. He confronted Jack, George, and Ahmed in the living room. ''You better have the damned coffee pot on!'' he snapped. Abruptly, he relaxed, stretched his arms over his head, and stifled a yawn.

"I would think you'd be awake by now,'' Holloway said.

"I slept all the way over,'' Rainsford said.

"And operated the aircar while unconscious?'' George asked.

Rainsford took the cup of coffee Jack handed him and blew on it. "I *am* the Governor General,'' he said. "I *am* authorized to have my own driver. *He* operated the aircar. *I* stretched out in the aft compartment and slept.''

"You slept in your clothes?'' Jack asked.

"Of course,'' Rainsford said. ''What's wrong with that?''

He didn't understand why the other three looked back and forth at each other and nodded their heads.

Ben Rainsford might have solved that one if they had not been interrupted by the chiming of the communication screen.

The image steadied down into that of Space Commodore Alex Napier. He was speaking from his office on Xerxes. In the background, they could see the harsh, angular landscape of that Zarathustran moon through the open sun–screen segments of Napier's domed office.

"Good morning, Mr. Commissioner,'' Napier said to Holloway. "I was wondering if you could tell me just what it is that you have found on North Beta.''

"No," Jack said flatly. "In the first place, we don't know. In the second place, I don't care to discuss it over a communication screen. And—" His mustache twitched like a tiger's whiskers. "—in the final place, it is entirely inside the Fuzzy Reservation, so it's really none of your affair, Commodore."

Napier knocked ash from his pipe and re-tamped the tobacco. "Only time will tell that, Mr. Holloway," he said.

"My question," Jack said, "is just how you know we 'found something,' and how in Nifflheim you came to know it this quickly."

The Commodore smiled with genuine good humor. "I don't believe TFN regulations require me to discuss my intelligence network with you, Commissioner Holloway— and if they did, I wouldn't do it via open communication screen."

"Well, it still *belongs* to the Fuzzies," Jack insisted, "because it is on Fuzzy lands."

Napier relaxed his formal manner a bit. "Come on, Jack," he said, "I'm not trying to ruffle your feathers or make any official fuss about this. May I have your permission to send three of my own people down to the site?"

"I can't think of any reason to refuse that," Holloway said, "as long as it is clear that they are not present in any official capacity and will conduct themselves under my authority."

"The Navy can live with that, I think," Napier said.

"Names, please?" Holloway said, his hand poised over a note pad.

"I have a couple of ordnance officers," Napier said, "with experience in xeno-geology and archeology— Commander Nelson Bates and Lieutenant Frank Gaperski. They both have some academic credits in those subjects, and have been interested enough to pursue them as a sideline to their Navy careers."

"Yes?" Holloway inquired.

"Also," Napier added, "I am sending down a Marine Master Gunnery Sergeant who is here to audit our readiness and weapons systems. Philip Helton is his name."

"Does he have a hobby, too?" Jack asked.

Napier chuckled. "As a matter of fact, he does. I don't think it will be of much use to you, though, on this job; his hobby is literature. However, his knowledge of his own field is nothing short of awesome. I daresay he could look at a piece of military hardware that no human creature had ever before seen, and tell you instantly what it was designed to do."

"I met a Master Gunnie on Hathor, once," Jack said, "and I'm inclined to believe what you say."

"Excellent, then," Napier said. "What are the co–ordinates?"

Holloway glowered. "Have you lost your mind, Commo-dore?" he said. "I will write down the chart co–ordinates on a slip of paper, and leave it in a sealed envelope at ZNPF Headquarters—to be released to your Master Gunnie on verification of his thumbprint only. Then, your people can join us at the site. It's hard enough to keep all these jackleg prospectors out of the Fuzzy Reservation, without having to police sightseers who happen to hear this transmission, as well."

"I see your point, Jack," Napier said. "Agreed."

"By the way, Alex," Jack said, dropping his own stiff formality, now that he felt he had some control of the conver-sation, "why in blazes is the Navy so interested in this?"

"There are—ah—anomalies in the information. My people will talk to you about it all when they arrive."

XX

Hugo Ingermann smiled and puffed his pink cheeks as he regarded the man across the desk from him. Best, really, to keep the desk between himself and such a man as Raul Laporte. Aside from the obvious fact that a certain ritual formality was necessary to mitigate against as much familiarity as might blur the distinction of who was working for whom, the truth of the matter was that Ingermann was *afraid* of Laporte. Oh, not that he considered Laporte to be any threat to the carefully constructed hierarchy of crime that he had constructed with himself at the pinnacle of control. It was more a matter of recognizing that Laporte was the kind of man whose self–control might snap at any moment. If and when it did, someone was bound to die. Ingermann preferred that the warm corpse in such a situation should not be his own.

" 'Course I'm sure of it, Mr. Ingermann," Laporte was saying. "Y'see, there's these two halfwit Marines what owe me a lot of money. I been encouraging them that I'll write off part of their debt if they bring me any useful information."

Ingermann fitted the tips of his fingers together and flexed his hands. "I see. Go on."

"Well, yesterday," Laporte said, "they come to me with this story. Seems the ZNPF has shuffled all the duty assignments around, and the platoon of Marines that's over there helping them out is soon to be joined by the rest of the company it was originally detached from."

Ingermann smiled. "And you see this minor alteration of work schedules as something of great importance," he said, flatly and without emotion.

"Well," Laporte defended, "it ain't like it was all that minor. They've pulled all the Marines off patrol duty over

127

North Beta. You gotta look at the big picture, Mr. Ingermann. Why would they all–of–a–sudden move the Marines
to patrolling the sugarplant plantations—*all* the Marines?
An' then, bring in *more* Marines?''

"Mmmmm," Ingermann murmured. "And what importance do you attach to all this, Mr. Laporte? A good deal,
apparently; otherwise you would not take the trouble to visit
my office. In short, sir, what does it mean?''

"Why, I think it means they've hit another big sunstone
strike up on the Fuzzy Reservation; that's what I think. They
move out the troops who've been patrolling that area, and
bring in *more* troops . . . Sunstones is really all that's going
on on Beta. What else could it be?''

What else, indeed? Sunstones were an obsession with
Hugo Ingermann. He pursed his lips. "And what, Mr.
Laporte, did you pay these two—persons—for this informa-
tion?''

Laporte knew what Ingermann was paying the spies he
sent over to Beta. "Five hundred sols, each, Mr. Ingermann," he said. "That's a thousand, all told. I cancelled a
thousand on their debt.''

The slight hesitation before specifying the amount told
Ingermann that Laporte was lying. "I can only see five
hundred sols' worth of information there, Mr. Laporte," he
said.

Laporte looked uncomfortable. He couldn't decide how
far to go in haggling over Ingermann's offered price of five
hundred—which was really two hundred more than he had
credited to Diehl and Spelvin.

Ingermann smiled. "However, I have some brokerage
work for you, Mr. Laporte, and I'll make you a flat offer of
three thousand for the lot.'' He reached in a desk drawer and
drew out a folio wallet, from which he extracted three pre–
counted sheaves of currency. "I want you to hire four more
operatives and send them over to Beta to prowl around and
see what this is all about—this whatever–it–is that the Navy
and the ZNPF are being so coy about keeping quiet.'' He
tossed two of the sheaves of currency across the desk and,
with a flourish, tucked the third back into the wallet. "I don't

care what your financial arrangements are with these four people, nor who they may be. However, you don't get the third thousand until I receive some definite information about what I want to know. Deal?''

"Deal," Laporte said, wistfully eyeing the wallet that had swallowed his profit into escrow.

They watched Fuzzy Divide slide under the nose of the airboat from five thousand feet, and the suddenly dry look of North Beta replace the lush forests south of the transverse mountain range.

"Listen, Gerd," Jack said, "I'm sorry I growled at you yesterday the way I did. It was just that those Upland Fuzzies were so damned pathetic. They're starving up here, but they're still determined to tough it out—come hell or high water. I'm—you well know—not an emotional man, but the look on that headman's face just got to me all of a sudden. *Ghu!*, he's a tough little guy. What was it that our gang said his name was?''

"Starwatcher," Gerd said. "Another piece of data that doesn't conform. The woods Fuzzies don't have any names beyond 'Hey, you,' but the Uplanders all have very specific handles—Starwatcher, Fireburner, Song, Dream–maker, Mark, Striker . . . It makes no sense to me, but they'll correct you in a minute if you make a mistake with a name.''

The Rev became aware that eyes were fixed upon him. He peered over the edge of the desk and encountered a fixed stare from a skinny kid of about eleven or twelve. She had stringy brown hair and wide eyes. Like a lot of the kids in Junktown, she wasn't getting enough to eat.

"You got my Uncle Charley?" she asked.

"Hi, there," the Rev said. "What's your name?"

"Lurkin," the girl replied in a monotone. "Lolita Lurkin. You got my Uncle Charley?''

"Well, I don't know," the Rev said. "What's the rest of Uncle Charley's name?''

"Walker," the kid said. "He's my Uncle Charley Walker.''

"Where are your parents?" the Rev said, making conversation while he had his data terminal run a name check for any Charley Walker that might be in the medical center or the infirmary.

"Ain't got no parents no more," the girl said. "My Ma died. My Pa kep' gettin' drunk and beatin' me up, so the judge sent me to live with Uncle Charley."

"Is he *really* your uncle?" the Rev asked as he watched the "searching" signal blink on and off on his screen.

The girl shrugged. "I dunno. He don't beat me up, though."

"Does he take good care of you?" the Rev asked.

The girl shrugged. "He does the best he can, I reckon. He ain't workin', but I get more to eat than I did with Pa." She thought for a moment. "But I gotta keep house better for Uncle Charley. Pa didn't care about that so much, but Uncle Charley likes everything to be kep' clean."

The elusive Uncle Charley was eventually located in the dispensary where he was getting medication for a persistent cough. The Rev recognized his face immediately as a parishioner.

"I hope the girl didn't bother you none, Father," he said. "I told her to meet me here after school. She ain't been in the way, has she?"

"Not at all," the Rev assured. "We've had a nice chat."

"I got a job now," Uncle Charley said, abruptly changing the subject and anxious to let the Rev know he was employed.

"That's wonderful, Charley," the Rev said. "What kind of job is it?"

Uncle Charley frowned slightly. "I don't just exactly know, but Mr. Laporte gave me some money in advance. That shows he trusts me to report for work."

"Raul Laporte?" the Rev asked.

"That's right," Uncle Charley said. "You know him, hunh?"

"Heard of him," the Rev said.

"He hired a whole bunch of men yesterday—and I was one of 'em," Uncle Charley said. "Things are a–lookin' up down here in Junktown. Lotsa guys got jobs now that didn't

have none before—'' He paused. ''—before you came here,
Father. You've been good luck for Junktown, an' I want you
to know that I appreciate what you done for us.''

"That's what I'm here for, Charley,'' the Rev said, "to
help people.''

Uncle Charley bid his farewell and the Rev watched from
his office door as Uncle Charley and the Lurkin girl went out
the front door. Uncle Charley stopped to slip five sols into the
poor box before he opened the front door onto the esplanade.

Poor bugger, the Rev thought. *He's so bad off he's got to
go to work for Laporte—and con himself into believing it's a
good deal.* The Rev smacked his right fist into his left palm
with frustration. *It's not right, God. Dammit, it's not right!*

By late afternoon the newly-arrived remainder of Captain
Casagra's company of Marines had worked out a wide trench
around the big titanium "it" on the side of Mount Fuzzy,
using manipulators and power shovels.

The entire scene in Fuzzy Valley looked more like a
country market fair than a serious attempt to uncover an
ancient artifact—or meteorite—or metallic concentration—
or whatever.

There were so many aircars grounded on the valley floor
that several Marines had been detailed as traffic cops to keep
the vehicles neatly parked in rows and make screen contact
with incoming and outgoing traffic to keep people from
running into each other.

Combat cars drifted overhead at four hundred feet, with
orders to fire on any vehicle that did not acknowledge screen
contact and obey orders to sheer away from the area and
reamin outside the air space above Fuzzy Reservation.

This was all too much for the Upland Fuzzies. They had
conferred briefly with Commissioner Holloway, expressed
gratitude for the additional supply of Extee-Three he gave
them, and disappeared when the traffic began to get thick.

Little Fuzzy had flatly stated that the Uplanders would be
back around sundown for a romp with Holloway's Fuzzies.

"How can you be sure?'' Jack asked him.

Little Fuzzy tilted his head and blew a plume of smoke

from his tiny smoking–pipe. He pointed to his own chest.
"Fuzzy," he said. He reversed the hand so it pointed toward
the woods at the south end of the valley. "Fuzzies," he said.
"Be back when sun go down." He pointed to Mount Fuzzy.
"When shadow come dis far—" He drew a line in the dirt
with his *shoppo–diggo*. "—Fuzzies come back; see how you
make do."

Before lunch–time the power shovels had skinned off the
surface soil from an area about the size of two football
fields—some one thousand feet on each side—bigger than a
square containing four city blocks.

Commander Bates and Lieutenant Gaperski in their khaki
duty–uniforms, Sergeant Helton in Marine field greens and
ankle boots; they were already on a first–name basis with
Holloway's group by the time the Marines grounded their
vehicles and began to line up for lunch at the field kitchen
scow.

Bates pointed to the excavation and moved his finger
around its perimeter to describe the area. "You see what
they've opened up there," he said. "There was a rockfall
from up the mountain slope—oh, several hundred years ago,
judging by the depth of sedimentary material that's washed
down over it. Also, we can see the same rock specimens on
the upper slopes."

"I judge," Gaperski interjected, "from the appearance of
recently broken faces, there on the scarp, compared with the
rockfall that's been protected from weathering by silt deposits, and those compared with the weathered rock faces on
the east slope, that the rockfall—a big one, too—must have
come down about seven hundred years ago give or take a
century."

"That's reasonable," Bates agreed. "We don't know
what the weather has been like, except for the past quarter-
century."

Phil Helton grinned at Jack—when Bates and Gaperski
weren't looking—and winked. Jack caught it and winked
back. These Navy guys had never cracked rock with a vibrohammer, but they sure knew their geology. Jack had been

earning his living with geology for longer than Gaperski had been alive, and here they were—with a crease in their pants—"explaining" it all to him.

Jack decided that he and Helton were going to get along.

The excavation went fast enough until the trench began to grow very close to the titanium "it." There was a lot of geothermal heat in the ground on Mount Fuzzy. That was fine as long as the Marines were sitting in the engineer's air-conditioned cab of a power-shovel, and the rest of the Marines were working on the surface. The slight breeze carried away the heat. But when it came time to get down in the trench with shovels and clear away the dirt and rock from "it" by hand—tossing it back to where the heavy equipment could pick it up without risk of damage—then the work became slow and unpleasant. It was hot and sticky down in the hole where the air didn't circulate well.

Painstakingly, the diggers uncovered a long object, shaped rather like a capital letter "A" that had laid over on its face. As its shape was slowly revealed, there also emerged a spherical object that occupied the space between the legs of the "A."

"That mustard-colored stuff all over it is the same sort of thing as rust," Bates said.

"Except that it's titanium 'rust,' " Gaperski explained.

"I think you're right," Holloway said. "From here—and without my glasses—I'd say the stuff is mostly composed of the sesqueoxide—Ti_2O_3—and the sulfate—$Ti_2(SO_4)_3$."

Gaperski gawked for a moment, then realized he was not talking to a layman.

Holloway eyed the two Navy officers for a moment. "The sulfate is a by-product of local volcanic activity," he said without expression.

Out of their range of vision, behind them, Helton was consumed with paroxysms of soundless mirth.

"My soil analyses show doubly, triply, and quad-ionized titanium, together with titanic acid and titanates, leaching down into the valley soil as the runoff water from the mountain percolated through the loose rock and soil covering the thing," Gerd said to Rainsford. "That explains the organic molecule, very much like hokfusine, that we found in the plant samples from the valley."

"I can see that," Rainsford said solemnly. "I have a degree in Xeno–Sciences, you know."

Gerd wasn't certain what that meant, but knowing Ben, it could mean he was either stating the obvious or making fun of the Navy ordnance officers.

As it sank toward the horizon, the sun turned more reddish, touching off the spectacular Zarathustran sunset and sending out long, pastel shadows across the valley floor, shadows that slowly crept over the vehicle park and foretold a comfortable evening after the oppressively hot day that was almost past.

"I think," Commander Bates said, "that we should knock off for the day. We ought to scan the thing thoroughly in the morning, before any additional excavating is done. There is no abnormal radioactivity, but we should proceed cautiously from here on."

In the slanting, orangish light, Phil Helton suddenly exclaimed something that no one heard clearly. He bounded down the "steps," left as the power shovels had reduced the size of the excavation with each successive layer of soil and rock removed, into the large hole, which was by this time several storeys deep.

The others followed curiously—and more slowly.

Helton walked up to the titanium thing, almost as though it might be alive. He ran his hands over the flaking, oxide–encrusted surface, sort of talking to himself. He picked up a square–point shovel that had been left by one of Casagra's Marines when the work had stopped for the day and scaled off a patch of the titanium "rust" until he had exposed a seam in the metallic layer underneath. He banged at it a couple of times with the shovel, then cursed loudly and quite clearly enough for anyone to understand.

He turned to the group standing on the level above. "Toss down a geologist's hammer, someone, will you?" he said. It was not so much a request as a command.

Soon, the specified tool landed in the fresh dirt a few meters from where he stood.

Helton waved, then bent and picked up the hammer. He measured off a distance from the seam with his fingers and then gave the surface a couple of smart, loud *whacks*.

No one had the slightest idea what he was doing—except Master Gunnery Sergeant of Fleet Marines Philip Helton, who knew *exactly* what he was doing.

Helton retrieved his shovel and forced it into the seam. Then he drove it in like a wedge, using the hammer. He pried a little, to open the seam. Then he drove the shovel point a bit farther in and repeated the process. Finally, he pried a lot. The others could see the shovel handle bend under the strain of force applied by Helton.

Laboriously, he forced open a small "hatch," a little over two feet square in the surface of "it." He threw down his tools and stuck his head inside.

Presently, his head popped out. There was a strange smile on his face. "Throw me a light!" he shouted. When he had the light, he stuck his head back inside, wriggled his shoulders into the "hatch," and was still for not more than two minutes. It seemed like an eternity to the watchers.

Helton pulled back out into the light, brushed some dust off his face, and sneezed twice. He stood back, almost reverently, his eyes fixed on the scaly titanium surface of "it."

Finally, he turned his face up to the group on the step. There was still a strange smile on his face. "I know what it is," he said clearly and evenly.

The silence was thick and heavy. A trickle of sweat wandered down Helton's cheek, ran along the line of his jaw, and dripped off his chin onto his shirt. He took several steps closer to the dirt parapet where Holloway's group and the two Navy officers stood. Instinctively, they drew back, as though the glitter in Helton's eyes and the strange smile on his face were both some kind of contamination he had acquired when his head and shoulders had been poked inside the "it."

"I know what it is," he repeated.

Holloway wanted to scream *"What?"* but he was as spellbound as the others by the scene at the bottom of the dig—washed by the eerie sunset shadows of Zarathustra.

Finally, Helton stopped, seemed to regain control of himself, and took a deep breath. He looked up at the group again.

"It's a hyperdrive star ship," he said. Then, his voice broke and wavered a little. "Somewhere," Helton said, "there is another star–traveling race."

FUZZY BONES

XXI

The Mess Sergeant re–located his cigar at the exact mathematical center of his mouth. ''I don't care if they're all Grand High Poo–Bahs of Shesha,'' he said. ''They ain't military. I can't feed 'em. I gotta justify everything on my head–count sheet. If they ain't military, there's no square on the form for me to tally their meals.''

Helton grimaced, more out of embarrassment than anything else. He had sort of attached himself to this battalion—and ''adopted'' it while he was kicking around on Xerxes. Of course, he knew all the principal NCOs and the officers and trusted most of them to know their jobs.

''*Vee*–dahl, dammit,'' Helton said. ''If you look very closely at TFMC Reg 30-1, you will notice that it provides for the feeding of officials of the civilian government at a field mess facility, and that they are to be accorded treatment at a level equivalent to full colonel or above.''

Vidal Beltrán glared at Helton. ''Well, then, why in hell isn't there a space on the form?'' he exploded.

Lesser Sergeants Major quailed before the authority of a Master Gunnie. Fleet Admirals and Force Generals were uneasy about his opinions of their operation. Field grade officers deferred to his judgement. If there was anyone in the armed forces who would *never* be cowed by a Master Gunnie, it was certain to be a Mess Sergeant. Like the captain of a man–o'–war, his kitchen was his quarterdeck. He held the only authorized command power within the walls of his chow hall—it was written that way in the regulations.

Helton smiled at him. There was nothing so elegantly elemental as a Mess Sergeant in the full flower of a temper tantrum.

"Because," Helton said, "there are perhaps two times per decade when such a notation would be necessary on your Form 3033. There's a supplemental and you foot it out on the 3033. Reg says you can attach a D.F. signed by the commander of the mess—that's you."

Beltrán jerked the cigar out of his mouth. "Well, how the hell do *you* know so much about it, Phil?"

Helton held up the first two fingers of his right hand and ticked off each one of them with his left hand. "Because," he said, "I've audited enough mess halls to cover this planet." His face softened abruptly. "And I ran one for two years; that's how I got my seven," he finished.

"You—?" Beltrán said.

"That's right," Helton interrupted. "There's hope for you yet."

"Well, hell," Beltrán said deferentially, "them guys got their own camp set up over there. Why they need to eat with us, anyway?"

Helton held up the same two fingers. "Common courtesy, for one thing. There's something in the hymn about Marines being kind to civilians. For another, if we've found what I think we've found, we're going to have to violate some of their territorial rights; and a man who's sat at your table is easier to talk to about that kind of thing."

Beltrán nodded affirmatively. "Yeah, I get you, Phil. You think I should lay on something special?"

"Not a chance," Helton said. "You just run the menu and make sure it's cooked right. Those are a bunch of smart old ducks. If they think we're trying to butter them up we could get a lot of political blowback. Just be nice and don't 'sir' them to death."

Beltrán clenched his cigar back in his teeth. "Got it," he said. "No D.R.O.s. Let 'em go through the line."

"Now you're cooking, Sarge," Helton said. "I have to go

collect my two tame officers and join the governor and his friends at their airboat for cocktails. We'll be wandering back over here around 1800, so start one of your veldbeest roasts a little late.''

As the senior officer, Commander Bates proferred the casual invitation after they were all comfortably situated and starting to chat. "By the way, gentlemen; since you will likely be staying over tonight, we would be honored if you could join us in the mess for dinner.''

"Why that's very kind of you, Commander," Ben Rainsford said. "I was just thinking about that. I've got to get back to Mallorysport, but there's no point in my starting out this late in the day. Better to arrive early tomorrow.''

"We won't know a great deal about this until we get reports from Helton, Bates, and Gaperski," Pancho Ybarra said.

There was a pause of silence, during which the soft clicking sounds of the sunscreens which kept direct radiation out of Space Commodore Alex Napier's domed office could be heard.

"Our own satellite readouts show that they've dug up something pretty big. It's made of titanium, mostly. But we have no idea yet as to what it is. We'll probably get reports tonight that contain estimates of the situation.'' Lieutenant Commander Ybarra was keen on his job—*Liaison Officer: Extraterrestrial Life–Forms*. He had originally been stuck with deciding for the Navy if Fuzzies were sapient; now he had a chance to get some of the "glory" back from that ghastly job—ghastly because it could have been a career–buster for him if he had made the wrong decision.

Captain Conrad Greibenfeld, the Exec, sighed. "Well, I hope we get something out of it. We have a company of Marines and a heavy equipment section tied up in it.''

"Bosh, Connie," Napier said. "There's nothing on the property book about it. As for Casagra's company, that comes under 'Friendly Natives, Policing Safety Of.' ''

"What about this Marine enlisted man?'' Greibenfeld

said. "Bit unusual to put him in charge of auditing the dig, isn't it?"

"Master Gunnies *are* a bit unusual," Napier remarked drily. "Their job requires abilities of inductive reasoning and intuition that would crack the skull of the best Intelligence officer in The Fleet."

"Steve Aelborg wouldn't be glad to hear that," Greibenfeld remarked.

Ybarra cleared his throat. He sensed one of those little senior officer tiffs coming and felt obliged to try and head it off lest he get hit with a wild shot. "I think what the Captain means, sir, has to do with credibility, or credentials, or experience, or something like that." He looked expectantly at Greibenfeld.

"Yes, Alex," Greibenfeld said. "Is this guy really as good as they say he is?"

Napier carefully knocked the heel out of his pipe and stared into the air for a moment. "He is," he said. "I knew him on Baldur when I was a boot lieutenant and he was a master sergeant. He pulled my butt out of the fire; probably saved my career in the bargain."

Greibenfeld raised his eyebrows. He had the notion that enlisted men had to be watched all the time and that the officer corps was something like a mother hen who had to keep the ratings from injuring themselves. "How in Nifflheim could a Master Sergeant—" he began.

Napier cut him off. "It had to do with some foolishness over a woman, as such matters often do," he said. "Let's leave it at that."

Phil Helton sloshed the inch or so of tepid highball in his glass and stared at it for a moment. "Something like us they are, but not quite the same," he said. "People, though, that we have not met—or at least they were when this thing went down, here. They may have died out while we were trying to land some plumber's nightmare we called a space vehicle on Mars. This thing has been here as long as *Homo s. terra* has been in space—probably longer."

"On the other hand," Holloway added, "they may *not*

have died out. We may have just been missing connections with them. Space—there's an awful lot of it."

"Oh, poppycock," Ben Rainsford snorted. "We've had the Dillingham Drive and been in hyperspace for nearly five centuries. If there was another star-traveling race, we would have met them by now."

"Not necessarily," Commander Bates remarked. "There was an early theory about that which the textbooks call 'Fogleberg's Folly.' "

"Wasn't he the guy who said 'You can't make an omelette without breaking eggs'?" Gerd van Riebeek said.

"I thought that was Lenin," Ahmed Khadra said.

"I thought it was Abraham Lincoln," George Lunt said.

"I don't know if he said it or not," Bates said exasperatedly.

Holloway jumped in and broke up the digression. "What was his theory?" he asked. "I'm not familiar with it."

"Most people aren't," Bates said, "—outside the military, that is. Brigadier General Jerome H. Fogleberg, TFMC, had a theory about the distribution of intelligent races throughout the galaxy, which is known as 'Fogleberg's Folly,' a name which, by marking his peculiar position in history, might indicate that Fogleberg was somewhat off the mark in his concept.

"Fogleberg was known affectionately to his troops as 'Ol' Fogey,' and his unusual theory is thought to have arisen from his preoccupation with the reading of romantic literature having to do with the *noblesse oblige* of the mercenary soldier's trade. His contemporaries often said of him that he thought morale was something that came out of a bass drum."

"Sounds rarified, all right," Rainsford said. "I've never heard of it."

"You're not an astrogator," Bates said. "It falls in the category of don't-let-this-happen-to-you information.

"Fogleberg," he continued, "assumed that the distribution of stars by spectral class was uniform in space—not a bad idea when you're dealing with small volumes of galactic space. *But,* he also assumed they were evenly distributed in temporal terms—that is, in terms of when the novae popped which created them.

"He set out with a two-ship expedition to chart a new volume of space for star distribution. If his distribution theory was correct, then subsequent exploration should turn up a given number of intelligent races."

"Did it work?" Gerd asked.

Bates shook his head. "Fogey was so busy looking for active stars that he missed a black hole."

"What happened?" Jack asked.

"No one knows for sure," Bates replied. "His companion ship saw his ship wink off the screen and they never found a trace. Since the event horizon of a black hole is quite different at hyperspeed, Fogey may now be a coat of paint on the body, or his ship may have dispersed into free atoms floating around space, or himself, ship, and crew may be wandering around in an alternate universe trying to figure out what happened."

"I get it," George Lunt said. " 'Fogleberg's Folly' was that he became the victim of his own thinking."

"You got it," Bates said.

Ben Rainsford jerked his pipe out of his pocket and started to fill it. "What does that have to do with my assertion about random encounter with other star-travelers?" he asked, with faint irritation. "You comparing me to this Fogleberg fella?"

"Heavens, no!" Commander Bates said.

"Great Ghu's ghost, Ben," Jack said. "Simmer down."

Lieutenant Gaperski slipped smoothly into the fray. "I think what Nels was leading up to was the current Navy Doctrine on such a random encounter, Governor. It's no secret or anything. It's just not widely publicized in the civilian sector."

"We *have* to have some very specific and uniform idea about it, though," Bates said, "in order to meet our own responsibilities to the Federation."

A look of realization flashed on Jack Holloway's face. "Oh, I know what you mean. It's fairly new, isn't it?"

"Yes," Bates replied, "and it proceeds from Fogleberg's theories, but along less—ah—presumptive lines."

"Somebody's Estimate," Jack said.

"McKettrig's Estimate. You brief them on it, Frank. I don't have my data terminal with me and I can't remember all the numbers."

Gaperski pulled his hand held data terminal from his hip pocket and punched up a code. He read the data as it scrolled.

"We're pretty sure there are eleven or twelve billion stars in this galaxy that are very much like our own," he said. "I won't bore you with the probability reductions, but they are very comprehensive.

"Given: a galactic volume of 5.3×10^{11} cubic light years.

"Given: probabilities indication of 1,580 star–traveling races or races with enough technology to have a star–drive if they want it.

"Given: normalized distribution of stars and star–travelers across several drifts and age patterns that draw to a median expression.

"Then: each star–traveling race with have to itself a volume of space which is 3.34×10^8 cubic light years. Expressed as a sphere, its diameter would be 858 light years.

"If: during the course of normal voyages of discovery, charting, and colonial business such as trade and military traffic, a brand new star and its—perhaps—solar system of planets is examined closely each year,

"Then: in order for us or any other star–traveling race to examine the 'home sphere' and an equal–sized volume of space adjacent to the home sphere—at the rate of one star per year—the time to so examine our own territory and the territory next door will be close on to *33,000 years*.

"Expressed as a probability, the odds of a purely random encounter with other star–travelers is thus about 1 chance in 1.7 million."

There was a long silence.

Gaperski paused, still holding his data terminal, in case there were questions. "So, while you're waiting to accidentally meet the star–traveling aliens," he said, trying to break the tension of the moment, "don't give up sex or breathing."

"Are you sure that's right?" Rainsford asked.

"If the galaxy is put together more or less the way we think it is, and if the best minds in the business haven't made any mistakes in theory—although I'll admit there was certainly a lot of argument over the past couple centuries as they cross–checked their own and earlier work—then it's right. It wouldn't be in the manual otherwise.''

"It's an interesting perspective," Holloway said reflectively. "We've been industriously working away, colonizing hyperspace, and we've managed to push out a whole one hundred light years per century. Yet here we are, still in our own back yard.''

"We may not even be in the yard yet," Bates said. "We may just be pushing open the screen door.''

Gerd frowned. "I don't follow you.''

"Well," Gaperski said, "scientists are given to differences of opinion when matters are still in the half–theory, half–observation stages.''

"Like cops," muttered George Lunt.

"An early theorist—Smith, Smitt, Schmidt; something like that—came up with one notion radically different from McKettrig's Estimate. Without pulling out all the data for you; he calculated a 'home sphere' diameter of 2,400 light years and a one–star–per–year time to examine it of *120 million years*.

Ben Rainsford chuffed on his pipe. "Then why do you use this McKettrig fella's arithmetic in your technical manual?''

"Good point," Gaperski replied. "We use it because it is the most ambitious and optimistic set of probabilities.''

"That's like what we used to call 'Cheerful Charley Chemistry' when I was in school," Gerd said. "Coming up with experiment results that offered the least amount of thorny problems and alternates that had to be solved out.''

"Oh, there are still plenty of variables," Bates said. "For example, the probability of encounter is higher in a long search than in a short one. Another factor is the number growth of colony planets. As they get into the exploration act, the number of stars explored during a standard galactic year will grow steadily—even exponentially among colonies that are more curious about neighboring stars, or which are prone to just plain wanderlust.''

"That's not what I asked you," Rainsford said. "Why do you use McKettrig as the official Navy doctrine?"

"McKettrig offers us the soonest possibility of random contact with other star–travellers," Gaperski said, "and, therefore, should such a random encounter occur, the least possible chance for the Navy to get caught with its pants down."

"Ummph," Rainsford grunted. "Now it makes sense."

Helton pondered. "He's right, of course, but that's not the main consideration."

"I agree," Rainsford said expansively. "The important thing is to direct ourselves toward shortening the odds and try to make such a contact as quickly as we can manage it."

Helton smiled and shook his head. "Wrong. They may not be friendly."

The sun was down. The daylight was slowly failing. At the edge of the excavation two small figures stood together and regarded the huge object at the bottom, while the others were finishing a get–acquainted romp back and forth across the valley near the weirthorn thicket.

"What is?" Starwatcher asked.

Little Fuzzy stood with his hands clasped behind his back. "Greensuit Hagga say is ship—same as Hagga come this place in."

"How can be?" Starwatcher asked.

"No know." Little Fuzzy shrugged and dug his smoking pipe out of his *shodda–bag*. He began to tamp tobacco into it thoughtfully. "When some gashta—we all Fuzzies, now—on that place,"—He pointed to Xerxes, about 30 degrees above the horizon—"see round thing many, many times bigger than things Hagga fly here in." He pointed to the ground at his feet.

"Can be this one?" Starwatcher asked.

Little Fuzzy shrugged, again. "Hagga know many things—much as want. I ask Pappy Jack when he no busy."

The crew of Marines working nearby were preoccupied with their onerous task—onerous as all after–duty–hours tasks are—of setting up floodlights on skids so the dig could be tidied up after chow. They paid no attention to the Fuzzies talking. They were talking *Lingua Fuzzy*, anyway, so only an occasional *yeek* was audible to Terran ears.

"I would think it'll be days before we can safely get inside," Bates said. "What do you think, Phil?"

The group was walking across the dry creek to where the field mess was set up.

"Sounds right to me," Helton said. "We might have to stabilize after we date it and take samples. The whole thing might be ready to crumble. We have no idea how much of a beating it took in the landing."

"We'll transmit preliminary reports to Xerxes at 1930, and go on from there," Gaperski added.

"You're still convinced that this is a hyperdrive vessel of some kind?" Rainsford asked.

"Yes, sir," Helton said. He slowed his pace a moment and looked up at the sky, half whispering to himself, " ' . . . there is a country/far beyond the stars/where stands a wingèd sentry/all skilful in the wars.' " Then he jumped briskly across a little erosion gully and caught up with the others.

XXII

"Let's see," Holloway was saying as the five of them walked back toward their own vehicles. "Gerd's airboat will sleep four, and with the ZNPF car and Ben's luxurious transportation of office—"

Rainsford snorted.

"—all of us and the two drivers can sleep inside. We won't have to pitch tents."

"I've got to call my office," George Lunt said as they climbed into the boat.

"I've got to call my wife," Ahmed said. "Tell her I won't be home tonight."

Rainsford yawned. "I don't have to call anybody. I just have to get up at 0400. Why call your office, George? You afraid the duty captain has gone to sleep? You worry too much."

George frowned. "I need to get more men up here." He looked at the readout. "Pendleton is on at this hour. Oh, boy. He'll fly into a fury about the paperwork."

"Why do you want more men, George?" Jack asked. "Things seem well in hand to me."

"Security," George replied. "This is my jurisdiction. I don't care how snappy a job the Marines are doing. It's up to me to watch the watchers, so to speak. I don't want any more of this leaking out than can be helped until we know where we stand with the Navy."

"That's sound," Jack said. "You're the ZNPF commander, not me."

Phil Helton flipped the key on the familiar, sturdy, green enameled piece of equipment. The high pitched wavering

147

whine and the readouts showed his report now being transmitted at sixty speed on scramble–8 to Xerxes.

Presently the operator came back on screen. "The Commodore has asked that you screen him back in one standard
hour, Gunnie, and he suggests that it would be desirable for
Governor Rainsford and Commissioner Holloway to be present, as well."

Helton acknowledged and quickly ended the transmission.
He muttered under his breath, "—if they haven't gone to
sleep, yet—" and grabbed a passing corporal to carry the
message.

At 2030 the three of them were in the communications
center, with Rainsford bristling because he had been de-
prived of yet another hour's sleep.

Gaperski and Bates were hovering, a little to one side,
should the Commodore have instructions for them.

Alex Napier's image on the communication screen,
dressed in gold–braided Navy black, was concluding his
remarks. "So I expect to have the rest of Lieutenant Colonel
O'Bannon's battalion down there sometime tomorrow. I
want to set up surveillance over a couple hundred square
miles and have it carefully scanned for any more objects of
this nature. The battalion will be prepared to remain for some
time—until we have this thing totally evaluated."

"Now, just a minute, Commodore!" Ben Rainsford said
vehemently, almost before Napier got the "evaluated" out.
"As Governor General of Zarathustra, I most strenuously
recommend that you get my personal approval before you
start drawing boundary lines and occupying territory on the
planetary surface."

Holloway dove in, as well. "Approval or no approval; this
is Fuzzy land. Anything on the Fuzzy Reservation *belongs* to
the Fuzzies. The Commissioner of Native Affairs—namely
me—will not tolerate any high–handed violations of Fuzzy
territory."

Rainsford barked: "I *appointed* you Commissioner!"

Jack's mustache was twitching. "And you can un–appoint
me any time you don't like the way I'm doing the job. I've

told you that before, Ben.''

"Gentlemen, gentlemen," Napier said. "I appointed Governor General Rainsford, so let's not anyone get too big for his pants.

"I'm trying to help your government hang onto control of things, not set you to quarreling with each other—or with me," Napier added with just the correct note of ominousness. "The Navy is not interested in running anyone's planetary government—but we are quite competent and capable, if the need arises. My point is that one wild rumor about all this business could cause the very kind of crisis as the question of Fuzzy sapience did. Now, then, can we have some consensus and co-operation, please?"

Holloway and Rainsford looked at each other for a moment, both thinking, *if we don't hang together, he can hang each of us separately any time he wants to*.

Holloway turned back to the screen. "If you allow my ZNPF men free access to all parts of the site, I'll go along with you for a few days. If the whole business disturbs the Fuzzies or anyone bothers them, the deal is off."

"That sounds fair, but I want to be copied with all reports," Rainsford said.

"I think the Navy will manage, gentlemen," Napier said. "Now, I desire that Master Gunnery Sergeant Helton be in charge of the dig proper. He has more knowledge of vessels and equipment than all of us put together. Lieutenant Colonel O'Bannon will be in charge of the security and scanning operations. Lieutenant Gaperski and Commander Bates will act as liaison between the two and report directly to me, as well."

Everyone looked at each other and nodded agreement.

"And, one other thing," Napier said. "Sooner or later, you're going to have people from the press all over you, so I'm sending down Major Max Telemann to act as Information Officer on the project and keep the media out from under your feet."

From five thousand feet the camp in Fuzzy Valley was a tiny blur of light, with a bright, starlike point to one side of it.

With powerful onboard stereo–optics the site of the dig could be made out clearly enough in the glaring floodlights to see its major features. Dust drifted upward through the beams of the lights and a slight shimmer from the geothermally heated ground of the mountainside shined nacreously.

"Dammit, Charley," Raul Laporte said. "Keep this thing in a steady circle or you'll make me muddy the readings on the infraslides."

"I'm doin' the best I can, Mr. Laporte," Charley Walker said uneasily. Like most people, he was instinctively afraid of Laporte.

"See that you do," Laporte growled. "We've only got two passes—at the most—to get this before the combat cars get us on their screens and challenge."

This is nuts, Laporte thought—*hanging myself out in the open this way. Cheaper than hiring it, though, and I can beat Ingermann at his own game. Three thousand—the cheapskate!*

"Okay. I got it. Make tracks, Charley," he said.

Charley started breathing again, straightened out the airboat and eased the velocity up.

Laporte brooded.

Hugo Ingermann often worked late at night. It was a matter of convenience more than habit. The kind of people he frequently dealt with were creatures of the night. It was their natural environment, since that side of human nature is a being of the darkness.

Spread out on the desk before him were scanner readings and infraslides delivered to him earlier by one of Laporte's men. It was disgusting. All that information and not one scrap of it corroborated his theory. Therefore, the information must be somehow in error. And now, Laporte was coming to collect, if he could believe the screen call he had just had from *The Bitter End*—and there was no reason not to.

There was a rap on the office door.

Laporte entered, smiling and amiable; yet menace oozed from every pore of his body. "Good evening, Mr. Ingermann,'' he said, and sat down on the opposite side of the desk.

"Good evening, Raul,'' Ingermann replied. Just the right amount of deference, to show who worked for whom. Ingermann puffed out his round, pink cheeks and spread his hands in mock helplessness. "Raul, these data just don't show a damned thing about the sunstone strike.''

"That's because there *is* no sunstone strike, Mr. Ingermann. I've had men over there on the ground and I've had overflights made at night—like this one. There is only a big hole in the ground where they're digging something up.''

"I can see that!'' Ingermann snapped. "What do you think the thing in the hole is?'' he asked in a more even tone.

Laporte's voice dropped about three tones. "I don't know what it is. It looks to be just what my people say has leaked out about it—the buried wreck of some kind of spaceship. It's been there a long time. So far, no word about any sunstones.''

Ingermann laughed, shrilly and high-pitched. There was a rather odd look on his face that Laporte did not like at all. He decided it was time to start cleaning his fingernails.

"All that digging?'' Ingermann said. "All those people? Coded messages flying back and forth, like featherleaf pods in a high wind? And all you can tell me is that crackbrained rumor about a buried spaceship?'' He laughed again. "I thought you had better sense, Raul.''

Laporte shurugged and went on cleaning his fingernails with a huge clasp knife.

"These idiots in the Colonial Government,'' Ingermann chuckled. "The richest deposit of sunstones yet is practically within spitting distance of this spot.'' He pounded a pudgy finger on one of the infraslides. "And all they can come up with is a cover story about a—a *spaceship wreck!*'' He spat out the words.

"I came for the other thousand sols you owe me,'' Laporte said in a very quiet voice.

Ingermann wiped tears of mirth from his eyes. "Oh, Raul, you're going to have to do better than this before that thousand ever sees daylight.''

"The deal was 'definite information,' '' Laporte said.
You have your definite information. Now, I'll have my
money.''

"Not until you find the sunstone strike, you won't!''
Ingermann leaned forward suddenly, slapping the palms of
both hands flat on the desk.

In the absolute silence that followed, Laporte raised his
head from the preoccupation with fingernails and looked
Ingermann in the face.

When he sprang from the chair, he landed on his knees, on
top of the desk, with a knee on each of Ingermann's hands.
Printout stacks and infraslides cascaded off onto the floor.
With a snatching motion of his left hand, he grabbed Ingermann by the neckcloth, pulling him a little closer.

Slowly, Laporte placed the point of the knife against
Ingermann's left carotid artery, just below the jawbone.
Ingermann's round, pink cheeks turned chalky white. "The
money,'' Laporte said.

Ingermann inclined his eyes to indicate the appropriate
desk drawer.

Laporte lifted his left knee. "You get it,'' he said. Ingermann opened the drawer with the released hand, opened the
wallet, and shook out the sheaf of currency.

When Laporte was again standing on the floor and some of
the color was returning to Ingermann's face, Laporte said, "I
don't think you have the nerve, sir, to try anything what
wouldn't be smart. Y'see, there's one of my men out in the
hall with a submachine gun. If I don't come out of here with a
smile on my face, his orders is to come in here and turn you
into dog meat.''

Ingermann cleared his throat and adjusted his neckcloth.
"I understand,'' he said.

Laporte nodded. "Good. I hope this don't have any bad
effect on our business dealings in the future, Mr. Ingermann,
but we are gonna have to be more specific about what the deal
is.''

Outside Ingermann's office, Laporte closed the door quietly, put away his knife, and walked off down the empty corridor.

XXIII

An austere but rather shaggy gentleman of middle years peered out of the screen. "Surely you jest, Governor," he said. "Why, we've been a fixture in Mallorysport—to say nothing of bringing a tiny scrap of culture to the rest of the planet—for almost ten years, now. *You* are going to *dissolve* it; just like that? Preposterous!"

Ben Rainsford glowered into the pickup at his end of the conversation. "I didn't say I was going to *dissolve* it, Mr. Wachinski. I said there's no money for it."

Holger Wachinski was the director of the Mallorysport Civic Opera Association, an annoying—to Ben Rainsford— leftover from Nick Emmert's administration as Resident General, before the CZC charter had been revoked. He was quite naturally in high dudgeon to discover that his budget had been chopped off.

"I must say, that's pretty mundane of you, Governor. As bread feeds the body, art feeds the soul, even if you—" Wachinski stopped, realizing he was not helping his case.

Rainsford chuffed on his pipe. "It don't make a damn whether I like opera or not, Mr. Wachinski. I'm in a position of having to make bricks without straw, here. If it comes down to a choice between opera and having citizens robbed on the esplanade, I have to can the opera and hire more cops—except I've not got enough money for that, either."

"You realize," Wachinski said, with what he hoped was an oracular tone, "that you're just contributing to the un-employment problem?"

Better yours than mine, Rainsford thought, but he decided not to say it. He rubbed his eyes. "Look, Wachinski; how much of your budget do you raise by private subscription?"

Wachinski looked at the ceiling for a moment. "About

half—enough to cover the opera company. But that's useless without the symphony."

"I'll tell you what I'll do, Wachinski," Rainsford said. "You get off your butt and raise enough more to pay for half the symphony, and the Colonial Government will match-fund you on that part for the rest of the season. If the opera company caves in, you'll still have the orchestra. Deal?"

Deal, Wachinski thought, *a decree*. "Under the circumstances," he said, "we'll try to make do."

The Navy cruiser, at that altitude, looked about the size of a pool-ball fruit from the ground when it began to turn out its cargo of men and vehicles.

There is a certain precision and grace in the sight of a line battalion turning out of a ship. It is as much of an aerial ballet as a convoy movement from ship to ground. An enormous quantity of vehicles are involved for several hundred men—or so it seems. All of these particular vehicles were of a squatty, ungainly appearance, built to withstand incredible punishment and still operate. The center was an almost solid skirt of service equipment for ordnance, maintenance, vehicle recovery, field kitchens, supply boats, communication centers, and operations centers. Ranged around these were squad buses in neat platoon lines, with the four companies positioned port, starboard, aloft, and below. Casagra's men were already on the ground, sweating and cursing with the dig. Spiraling gracefully away from the main body, the scout cars skimmed and darted like airborne sheepdogs.

Holloway and his group were still at the site; in fact had been waiting for the battalion to arrive. There were a few things Holloway wanted to get clearly understood with the battalion commander before he went back to Holloway Station, and George Lunt had a few points he wanted to pick over, as well. Rainsford had departed well before dawn, ranting and raving about the exigencies of being Governor General.

As the battalion vehicles encamped, the commander's car grounded about a hundred meters from the waiting group of officials.

Lieutenant Colonel James O'Bannon and his exec., Major Richard Stagwell, dismounted and crunched across the dry soil of Fuzzy Valley toward them. Ordinarily, it would have been the other way around, but officials of the civil government were in the waiting party, so deference was being observed.

Introductions were exchanged all around, which took an inordinate amount of time, since ten people were involved.

Holloway looked over O'Bannon and Stagwell, figuring out the best way to handle them.

O'Bannon was a little shorter than average, and was one of those men who could spend three weeks in the field and never put a wrinkle in his impeccable field greens. He had a handsome, almost boyish face, contradicted by the tinge of gray in the regimental beard and mustache which framed his jaw. His eyes were slightly hooded, like a cobra's, of an indeterminate color, and never betrayed expression, even though he smiled obligingly from time to time.

Stagwell was tall, raw-boned, and agile-looking. He grinned a lot, and had the look about him of a man who could run five miles with a machine gun under each arm and not even be breathing hard.

"One thing I want to get straight," O'Bannon said, "while there's just us here—including the civilians. Helton, you're in charge of the dig. I'm giving you Casagra's company to handle that, but you work through him. Don't go off on any vast projects without clearing with him. Somebody gets injured down there; he's the commander and he'll have to answer for it—not you."

"Yes, sir," Helton said.

"Another thing, Gunnie," O'Bannon continued, "if you mess into my security and scanning operations without my say–so, I'll fry you. Do we see eye–to–eye?"

"Yes, sir," Helton repeated.

O'Bannon turned to the civilians. "I want Commissioner Holloway to brief my staff and commanders on matters regarding the Fuzzies. I want Major Lunt to do the same with respect to ZNPF operations. As to what we may have found here, the fewer people having specific knowledge of that, the happier I'll be about it. That means I want Casagra's men to continue to camp and mess away from the rest of the battalion and have minimum contact.'' He sighed and paused for a moment. '' . . . Not that it will do much good, the way Marines gossip, but we can try.

"Questions? Okay. There will be Officers Call in twenty minutes.'' He pointed back over his shoulder, without looking, to where tents were already blossoming from the ground. "I'll see you all then.'' He turned and left.

"Gruff little fella, isn't he?'' Gerd asked.

'' 'Businesslike' is the word I'd use,'' George Lunt remarked.

"I've noticed,'' Holloway said to Helton, "that you don't 'sir' very many people, Phil.''

"Only the ones I respect a lot—sir,'' Helton said.

After the briefing, Helton took Major Telemann over to Casagra's company area, where it had been decided he should be assigned, since they were handling the most sensitive part of the operation. They went in Telemann's aircar, fitted out for Public Information Operation, which is to say crammed with electronic gear to monitor news agencies' activities.

Telemann was the only Marine on site in khakis instead of field greens. Best foot forward with the public, and all.

Vidal Beltrán watched from the back hatch of his kitchen scow as they set up. He knew instinctively what it all meant.

"Another damned mouth to feed,'' he said disgustedly.

An entire corner of Victor Grego's private office was occupied by one of his most cherished possessions—a large globe of Zarathustra, suspended on its own contragravity unit, with the moons Xerxes and Darius, to scale, circling it as it rotated; the entire affair illuminated by a fixed orange spotlight representing the KØ star that gave life to the planet. At mid-morning in Mallorysport, the terminator line had crossed the coast of Beta.

"Victor?'' the voice from the communications screen said. "Are you listening?'' It was a bold thing for a lesser big wheel to say, even if he was the lesser big wheel that was in charge of Company Science Center.

"Uh?" Grego said, looking back at the screen. "I was just checking something on the map, Juan. It's early morning on Beta, now. Where is your archeologist?"

"He says he just spent the night in the best hotel in Red Hill, but that it was still ghastly. Wants to know if he should come home, or what. I thought we might have him hang around over there a day or so and see what the gossip is."

Grego frowned. "I'm not gainsaying your staff, Juan, but I don't recall that we have an archeologist on the payroll. What would the Company have wanted with an archeologist on an uninhabited planet?"

"He's not really an archeologist," Juan said. "He's an analytical geologist with a master's in archeology. It's the closest we could come to the real thing."

Grego lit a cigarette and absently scratched his Adam's apple as he took the first puff. "So, we have a 'routine archeological dig' on a planet where there *is* no archeology, and they won't let the CZC archeologist on the site. What do you make of it, Juan?"

"Just that," Juan said, "plus the fact that the place is swarming with Marines. Apparently Napier has sent down a large patrol force and they've cordoned off a large area of the Fuzzy Reservation."

Grego frowned. "Well, then, it must be something pretty big. Old Man Holloway wouldn't sit still for that otherwise. Yes, Juan, I like your suggestion. Tell our man to hang around town a couple days. Tell him too bad about the crummy hotel, but that it's above and beyond the call of duty, or something. In the meantime, I'll get hold of Harry Steefer and see what he can come up with. When your man gets back from Beta, I want to see him instantly."

"I'll keep you posted, Victor."

They broke connection.

Grego leaned back in his chair and looked at the ceiling. He wasn't thinking about archeology, though. In fact it was difficult for him to concentrate, so he decided to clear the block from his mind.

What a remarkable young woman, he thought, as he punched out a screen combination.

A mass of bright colors swirled across the communication screen and exploded into the image of Christiana Stone.

"Yes?" she said. "Oh. Mr. Grego."

"Good morning, Christiana," he said. "I have a suggestion. Tell me what you think of it." Without waiting for an answer, he continued. "When you bring Diamond back from Government House, you could stop off at your place and change into a dinner dress. Then we'll take Diamond out to dinner at—oh—say, *Alfredo's*. He can show off his table manners in public. Be good for him, don't you think?"

"Oh, he'd love it, Mr. Grego," she said.

"That wouldn't interfere with your plans, any, would it?" Grego asked.

"Not a bit," Christiana replied. "I think it would be delightful."

"Good," Grego said. "We'll want to get there early, though, so we don't keep him up later than he's accustomed. I'll meet you at the penthouse about six."

About 0600 at Holloway Station the group that had gone to North Beta were sitting around the Khadra's living room with Sandra, Ruth, and Lynne Andrews.

"I think," Ruth van Riebeek said to her husband, "that to say this thing they've found up there has 'vast implications' ought to insure your place in history, Gerd—not as a scientist, but as making the understatement of the century."

"Hmph!" Gerd said.

"But they're not certain that it's the remains of a hyperdrive ship, are they?" Lynne Andrews asked.

"No," Jack said, "but given the judgement of a man like Phil Helton, I'd say it's about a ninety percent shot."

Ruth looked at the other two women. "Well, I suppose it's our turn to raise *your* eyebrows, now. Gerd was right about the titanium content of the plants from Fuzzy Valley. They differ in content and amount from one kind of plant to another, of course.''

"That's not so eyebrow–raising," Gerd said. "What did you find out?''

"The titanium compounds are all similiar to hokfusine," Ruth said. "Given something to compare hokfusine with, it won't be so much of a job; to finger its functions in Fuzzy metabolism will be much easier.''

"All these compounds," Lynne said, ticking off imaginary numbers on her fingers, "for example, have degradation fractions that are *piperidine.*''

"Hmmm," Gerd said. "That's an organic compound already known on Terra. So, with enough vitamins *like* hokfusine, that can inhibit NFMp production, the Fuzzy birthrate can work itself back to normal—if the work we've done so far is right.''

"You mean it might not be right?" Jack said.

"I mean," Gerd said, "that there are many and varied times when I *wish* it wasn't right.''

"I don't follow you," Jack said. "If you can solve the NFMp/anti-NFMp problem in Fuzzy metabolism, what's wrong with that?''

"Well," Gerd said, exhaling noisily, "the irritating aspect of what we might rather grandiosely call 'The van Riebeek Theory,' is that the observations and deductions involved in its formulation keep coming back to Garrett's Theorem—that the need for an element does not arise in evolution unless the element is readily available. If you admit the applicability of Garrett's Theorem to Fuzzy biochemistry—which, by the way, I never tumbled to until Sandra raised the question—you keep landing back on square one, where resides that alarming idea that *Fuzzies did not evolve on Zarathustra.* It just doesn't make sense, but it keeps haunting the data we've developed.''

"Maybe they came on that hypership you guys claim is being dug up on North Beta," Ruth said.

"Oh, for Ghu's sake, Ruth!'' Gerd exploded. "That's the

confoundedest nonsense I've heard all week—and I've been hearing some pretty weird ideas.''

"Well!" Ruth sniffed. "I was just trying to make you feel better.''

Ahmed waved his hand. "You can fight later. Dinner's almost ready.''

XXIV

"You're falling for him, aren't you?" The Rev leaned back in his chair and ran the heel of his hand over the graying hair at his temple.

Christiana's eyes blinked once, then grew large. "Oh, Father Gordon!" she said, flustered. "It's just that he's—well—he's a very nice man, and I—I—"

The Rev leaned forward again. ". . . And you've never had a man be nice to you before, without he was expecting to get something for it." He finished the sentence for her.

She frowned and thought hard for a moment. "I guess you're right about that part." A short, choking laugh escaped from her. "All my life. With Daddy it was good treatment for good behavior; bad treatment for bad behavior—except that it was a shell game. I never knew which number was coming up. Then there were all the boys in school when I was growing up. . ."

Still a lot of that to be done, The Rev thought to himself.

The Rev pushed the box of tissues across the desk. She jerked out two of them and blew her nose.

"So, now you've got a pretty nifty job uptown, working for the CZC," The Rev said, "and you think you need my advice about whether you should move to a better address?"

She squinted at him. "Well, I'm not sure about that."

"You know you're going to have to do it," he said. "You just told me that you're changing for this—ahh—dinner date *before* you pick up Diamond because you don't want Diamond to know you live in a cheap hotel in Junktown. What you're saying, of course, is you're afraid Diamond will tell Grego and Grego will start wondering why."

"You see what I mean?" she said, with a note of anguish

in her voice. "I'm not sure I can cut it. I've tried running with those fine-haired dogs at the top of the pile and they've walked all over me. I don't know if I can take another round of that."

The Rev fitted the ends of his fingers together and studied the pattern they made. "Have you had a payday, yet?" he asked.

"Tomorrow," she sniffed.

"You take your pile of money and put down the rent on a nice little apartment—preferably within spitting distance of Company House," he said, "even if you have to sleep on the floor until *next* payday. I told you before, you don't belong down here—you like people too much."

"Well, what are *you* doing down here?" she asked. "You like people."

The Rev grinned at her. "My job is to help people. That's why I'm down here. It don't make a damn whether I like them or not."

"If you think that's the thing to do," she said, "I'll try it. I just had to have someone else's opinion. I—I'm kind of confused right now."

"Course you are, m'dear," The Rev said. "That's because you're falling for him. Didn't I just tell you that?"

"What make do?"

Sergeant Beltrán looked up suddenly from his cubbyhole desk in a back corner of the kitchen scow. Four Fuzzies were peeping bashfully around the edge of the open back hatch.

"What make do?" Little Fuzzy repeated.

Beltrán had never seen a Fuzzy up close. He was fascinated. Like many men who were extremely tough, he turned to goo at the sight of those wide, appealing eyes. "Why—ah—I'm planning tomorrow's menu for a bunch of unappreciative slobs," he said.

Little Fuzzy and the three Upland Fuzzies stepped through the hatch into the back of the kitchen, sensing that Beltrán was an all-right Hagga.

"S'ob?" Little Fuzzy said. *"What's a s'ob?"*

"Marines," Beltrán said.

"Greensuit Hagga?" Little Fuzzy asked.

Beltrán nodded affirmatively.

"Greensuit Hagga—*Mahreen*—*s'ob*? All same thing?"
Little Fuzzy asked with his usual intent stare of inquisitive-
ness.

Beltrán thought for a moment. "Pretty much—yes," he
said, "but some of them might not understand if you called
them 'slob'."

Little Fuzzy turned to his companions and *yeeked* to them
in *Lingua Fuzzy* for a few moments, then turned back to
Beltrán. "They no speak Hagga, yet, but I say them what you
say."

The Mess Sergeant leaned down from his stool to get a
closer look at these little people. The Upland Fuzzies drew
back a bit, nervously fingering their brand–new steel
chopper–diggers.

Little Fuzzy threw out his chest and pulled his chin back.
He reached out a tiny hand and fingered the texture of
Beltrán's uniform sleeve. "Cook food this place?" he asked,
sniffing curiously. "Give to greensuit Hagga?"

"Every damned day," Beltrán sighed. Then he added,
"Would you guys like something to eat?"

Little Fuzzy nodded.

"What do you want?" Beltrán asked.

A light came into Little Fuzzy's eyes. "*Esteefee?*" he
asked. "You give *esteefee?*"

Beltrán scratched his head. "S.T. Fee," he said. "What's
that?"

"All Hagga have *esteefee*," Little Fuzzy said. "I show."
He shouldered Beltrán aside—at about kneecap level—and
began looking up and down the stowage shelves. Finally, he
spotted a group of the familiar, blue–labeled tins. He pointed
with his chopper–digger. "*Esteefee*," he said triumphantly.

Beltrán looked, then looked again. "You mean you want
to eat *that?*" he exclaimed.

Little Fuzzy nodded. "*Esteefee—big t'heet*," he said.
"You make do?"

Sergeant Beltrán shook his head, wiped his hands on the
seat of his pants, relocated the cigar in his mouth, and dug a

can of the emergency rations off the shelf. He blew the dust off it and ran it through the opener. He got a metal plate from the drying rack and divided the slightly oily, slightly rancid—smelling, gingerbread—colored cake into eight portions—two (ugh!) helpings each for the Fuzzies.

As the Fuzzies were digging into the Extee—Three, yeeking with delight, Beltrán continued to shake his head in disbelief. Then he rummaged around in a drawer and dug out four of his one hundred milliliter measuring cups—about right for a Fuzzy—and set them down, filled with water from the ionization tanks that serviced the kitchen.

At the time *Alfredo's* opened its doors in Mallorysport—some twelve years earlier—it had been the most rigidly elegant spot to dine on the planet. At the time it opened it had been the only *remotely* elegant place to dine on the planet. *Alfredo's* had maintained its standards, growing in status and reputation as Zarathustra itself grew. The staff was impeccable. The cuisine was excellent. The management showed an uncanny ability to obtain rare delicacies near and dear to the Terran palate—delicacies that could not be had anywhere else on the planet. When, for example, a shipment of frozen oysters would arrive from Terra, the gourmets of Mallorysport would cheerfully stand in line during a driving rainstorm for the privilege of paying an astronomical price for a taste of home.

The interior was a symphony of red sylkon drapery, crimson carpeting, and raised paneling of native woods. Elegance—ah—the elegance of a fine, quiet old restaurant back on Terra. Colonists became uncontrollably hungry for such an environment from time to time, so why not assuage two hungers at the same time?

The maître—d' did not turn a hair at the sight of a Fuzzy in the company of a heavy—set gentleman and a good looking strawberry blonde. His establishment had been graced by the presence of non—Terran diners before, and its resources were available to the task of dealing with any requirements any of them might have. So was the maître—d'. He was a huge African who had more the look about him of a bouncer in a

Junktown dive, but was so at ease in his tuxedo and so in place with his environment that he seemed not at all out of place in this luxurious dining room.

He picked up three scarlet menus and stepped from behind his station. "Your reservation, please, sir," he said. "Mr. Grego, I believe."

"Good evening, Walter," Grego said. He extinguished his cigarette in the stand next to the velvet roped archway. "We will be three for dinner."

Walter cleared his throat deferentially. "There is one problem, Mr. Grego," he said.

Grego's eyebrows shot up. "If you mean the Fuzzy—" he began.

Walter held up a placating hand. "That, sir, is not a problem at all. *Alfredo's* is accustomed to an occasional non–Terran—and we have no prejudice in the matter at all."

"Then what's the difficulty?" Grego asked.

"Well, Mr. Grego," Walter said, "the rules of the house are totally inflexible in one respect."

"And that is—?" Grego began to bristle.

Diamond sidled up to Christiana and she placed a protecting hand down over his back.

Walter looked uncomfortable. "During the entire history of this room, Mr. Grego, no male creature has ever been seated unless he was wearing a neckcloth. Your guest does not have one."

"Well, for Ghu's sake!" Grego exploded. "I'm sure you keep a couple around in the checkroom to avoid this kind of embarrassment to people who are not aware of the rule."

Diamond tugged at Grego's trouser leg, a sad look upon his face. "Pappy Vic," he said. "We go home?"

"Indeed we do, sir," Walter said, "but I cannot see how a neckcloth designed for a Terran will be of any service to a being who is only sixty or so centimeters tall."

Grego tapped his foot impatiently. He was not a man who was accustomed to problems he could not dissolve with his own mental assets.

Diamond again tugged at Grego's trouser leg, his face sadder than before.

"Just a minute," Christiana said quietly.

She picked up Diamond and seated him on the counter at the maître-d's station. She placed her index finger under his chin and lifted it up. "Now, hold still, Diamond," she said. She reached behind her head and pulled loose the black velvet ribbon that was holding her hair. As her strawberry blonde hair fell loose about her shoulders, she shook it free and unfurled the ribbon. Then, stooping slightly, she pulled the ribbon around Diamond's neck, snugged it down, and tied it into a bow knot. "There;" she said, "not only a neckcloth, but a very formal one, at that."

She picked Diamond up and set him on his feet on top of the counter. "Take a look, Diamond," she said, as she turned him around to face the mirror behind the counter.

Victor Grego and Walter exchanged glances.

Diamond looked at himself in the mirror, registered broad approval, and then took each end of the little bow tie between a tiny thumb and index finger, snugging down the knot. *"Hoksu,"* he said simply. Then he turned and hugged Christiana, although his little arms only went about half way around her.

Walter raised his hand, displaying the appropriate number of fingers to indicate the waiter's station. A young man in gray semi-formals began bustling toward them.

What a remarkable young woman, Grego was thinking.

The two Marines were dirty and dusty. Sweat streaks stained the front of their shirts and spread down along their backs, as well as under their arms.

"Are you absolutely sure?" Phil Helton said intently.

One of them puffed noisily on the cigarette he had just lighted. "We're sure," he said. "And, we've got chips in the pola-pack to prove it."

The other Marine spread out the photo images on the table in front of Helton. A mild breeze flapped the tent they were sitting under.

Helton looked, then stroked his chin. He thought for a moment, then looked back at the two technicians. "Okay," he said, "you guys go get something to eat, right now. Tell

Beltrán I said so. Grab some sleep. I'll wake you up at midnight, we'll have some breakfast—then you're coming with me. We'll leave for Holloway Station at 0100.''

XXV

Jack Holloway rolled over in bed and cuddled the nine–millimeter automatic into his fist.

"Now what the hell—" he grumbled.

There was a furious thrumming of fists on the front door of his bungalow. Jack looked out the window at the brightening sky. It was just about dawn. "They better have a warrant," he muttered to himself as he rubbed the sleep out of his eyes.

He crept through the darkened house to where he could see the front door. There were three Marines there. That made no sense to him, until he recognized Phil Helton.

Holloway opened the door, the pistol still hanging in one hand. He yawned. "Morning, Phil," he said.

Helton was excited. He motioned for the two Marines to wait outside, then stepped into Holloway's living room as Jack waved him inside with the pistol.

"Now, what's this all about?" Holloway asked as he shambled into the kitchen and moved the coffee pot control to IM. "Coffee'll be out in a minute," he said. "Want some?"

That all happened so fast that Helton had no chance to reply. "Put your pants on, Jack," he said, "while I wake up whoever you want to take with you. We need some Fuzzyologists—and fast."

Holloway was bemused. "Why, you could have given me a call on the screen, Phil. I'd be glad to send a couple of people up there. What's all this bugle–blowing about?"

"I couldn't put it on screen," Helton said. "We've been going through the interior of the ship, and we've found—remains. They're about a meter tall. To my uneducated eyes they look like mummified Fuzzies—except for the fact that they're a little bit too big."

Holloway was suddenly wide awake. "Did you say *inside* the ship?" he snapped.

"I did," Helton replied.

"How in hell did they get in there?" Jack asked as he poured two cups of coffee. ". . . Wander in and get trapped when the avalanche buried the ship?"

Helton accepted one of the coffee mugs. He shrugged. "I don't know, Jack. Hardware is my business. That's why we need some Fuzzyologists."

Holloway picked up his mug and went toward the communication screen. "I'll wake up Gerd and Ruth. They'll be the ones to figure it out."

"No." Helton held up a hand. "No transmissions—especially not on civilian screens. O'Bannon will have my ass if word of this gets out before we know what it's all about. We're on total scramble for communications. You tell me where their bungalow is; I'll go get them up."

Holloway looked at Helton curiously. "It doesn't seem to me that all this security is necessary, Phil," he said.

Phil Helton gave Holloway a flat stare. "Better to use it and not need it than to need it and not have used it," he said. "Now, where's the van Riebeek bungalow?"

Holloway was a little startled to see that the two Marines with Helton were parked outside the front door of his bungalow, at parade rest, and at sling arms.

He pointed across Holloway's Run toward Fuzzy Institute. "You go across the footbridge, there, and—you see the bungalow just to the left of the big building—behind the featherleaf tree?"

Helton nodded. "Okay. Remember, Jack—no screen calls," he said. "Heusted, you come with me. Strauss, you stay here."

Heusted fell into step behind Helton.

"Say, Phil," Holloway called after him. "Is it okay if I give this guy a cup of coffee?"

Helton grinned back over his shoulder. "Sure," he said. "He won't bite."

The face of a serious young man looked intently from the communications screen. *"Serious charges were leveled at*

the Colonial Government today in a statement from the
Federated Sunstone Co-operative—''

''That's one of Ingermann's gangs,'' Leslie Coombes said
to Grego.

Grego nodded.

''—*that the cloak of secrecy dropped over the Beta excavations form part of a conspiracy between the Colonial
Governor's office and the Navy to strip Zarathustra of much
of its native wealth, in the form of a huge sunstone deposit
which has been uncovered on Northern Beta Continent.
Spokesmen for the Co-operative stated that a decision is yet
to be made as to filing legal actions on behalf of the citizens of
Zarathustra, but insisted that the Co-op will 'look after its
own interests' and not stand for any more—to use the words
of its president—'neo-fascist invasions of Zarathustran surface territory by Terran Federation Marines.'*

''*Governor Rainsford's office could not be reached for
commentary, but a news conference is scheduled for tomorrow afternoon, and insiders suspect that this topic will be the
dominant one.*

''*This has been Dawson Foley, with today's update on that
story, returning you now to All-Planet News Central.*''

Grego chuckled. ''I bet Ben Rainsford is cleaning his
pistol right now.''

''If he heard this 'cast, he is,'' Coombes acknowledged.

''Turn over to the ZNS,'' Grego said. ''Planetwide Publi-
cations is going to interview this public relations guy the
Marines sent down to Beta to keep the press shooed away
from the entire operation.''

''. . . *and now here to introduce today's guest is analyst
Franklin Young. Frank. . .*''

''Thank you, Ed,'' said a young man—extraordinarily
young to be a news analyst, Victor Grego thought.

Franklin Young rearranged his gangly frame in the chair as
he checked which pickup was on. ''Our guest today is Major
Max Telemann, TFMC, who is the Public Information Officer for the North Beta excavations.''

Telemann had a youthful exuberance about him, with an

open and affable face that smiled easily. He was perfectly at ease, relaxed and jovial, and, one suspected, extremely competent in his job—which was to act in the best interests of the Terran Federation Marine Corps.

"Now, then, Major," Young said, "what exactly is it that has been found on Northern Beta?"

Telemann laughed amiably. "We don't know yet." He paused for the remark to soak in. "We think it's an old wrecked space ship—one which has been there a long, long time."

Young snorted. "How can that be, Major? We've only been on Zarathustra for a bit over a quarter-century. If there's a hypership buried on Beta for—as you put it—'a long, long time,' then *it* would have been the first to land on Zarathustra, and Zarathustra would not have been discovered so recently as 629 A.E. Could you elaborate on that?"

"Gladly, Mr. Young, gladly," Telemann said. "You must understand that there is still an enormous amount of analytical data to be accumulated and interpreted, but the main points of the matter are these: it might be an early hypership of some old merchant design—one of which we are at the moment not familiar—or it might be some ancient sub–hyperspeed probe that coasted this far and then crashed here."

Young leaned forward eagerly, sensing an advantage. "Crashed? Crashed, did you say?"

"It could have happened," Telemann said with a nonplussed look. "Those old ion–drive vessels, for example, were known to travel enormous distances on very little thrust—and with no crew; only automatic programming."

The interviewer pressed a stud in the console next to his chair and a tape replay flashed into life on the huge screen behind the center of the set. It showed an aerial view of the Beta site. It was a bit fuzzy, indicating that it had been taken from a very high altitude and then enhanced.

"Our own overflights of the area," Young said, "show this object to be in one piece and in reasonably good condition. If this 'vessel,' as you call it, had crashed, there would be a huge pile of scrap there, instead of what we see in this tape. How do you explain that, Major?''

Telemann shrugged. ''It could have been programmed to make an automatic landing on the first planet encountered that was of a specific type.''

This kid has done his homework, Telemann thought. *He's getting ready to go in for the kill.*

''Your replies seem quite vague, Major,'' Young said. ''Does this represent the best information you have on this—ah—situation?''

Telemann leaned back in his chair, using body language to delude Mr. Young into believing that he held the advantage. ''It's not so much a matter of information, Mr. Young,'' the Major said. ''The question is more one of accurately interpreting the information we have. For example, one idea that has been advanced is that this vessel might be the lost portion of the Fogleberg Expedition.''

''The Fogleberg Expedition?'' Young said hesitantly.

''Heavens, yes,'' Telemann said. ''I thought everyone knew about the Fogleberg Expedition! One of the vessels was lost. No trace has ever been found. Let me think, now—what year was that?''

''Why—uh—yes. Of course I'm familiar with it,'' Young said.

''It's one of the possibilities we're looking into,'' Telemann said. *Now that I've dragged you onto unfamiliar ground, maybe you'll shut up on that line of questioning,* Telemann thought.

''But why, Major,'' Young asked, ''why the heavy security procedures and the exclusion of the press from the site?''

''Exclusion?'' Telemann said, slightly aghast. ''Goodness, no. We're not excluding anyone. For the moment, though, precautions must be taken. We're conducting a scientific excavation. We can't have a lot of non–essential people trampling around the place, muddying up the archeological evidence. Haven't you been getting our information sheets? We put out a fact sheet and an update broadcast every day.''

Young was growing impatient—a certain way to lose

control of the interview. "Malarkey," he said. "It's censorship. That's what it is."

Telemann looked hurt. "But, Mr. Young," he said, "we're freely sharing information with the news media. Less than that *would* be a form of censorship; and we don't practice censorship. I can't tell you anything we don't know, however, much as you might wish me to be able to—or much as I might wish to be able to."

"You're still not allowing the press free access," grumped Young.

Telemann spread his hands innocently. "Now, surely you must know there's ample precedent in cases like this. You're aware, I'm sure, Mr. Young, that there was a recent archeological dig on Thor. It was of a very delicate and important nature, and required a good deal of interpretation before non–scientists could be allowed in—leaving footprints all about. That took *five years* to open up to the press." He paused a moment, waiting for Young to start a reply, so he could step on it. *"But,* in the meantime, all the news people were kept informed with information and screen 'casts of the progress."

"Is that the reason for all the Marines?" Young asked. "Marines who have orders to shoot?"

Telemann chuckled good–naturedly. "How do you know they have orders to shoot?" he asked.

"We know," Young said.

"Have your reporters been crowding too close to the patrol limits?" Telemann asked amiably.

Young made a sour face. "Let's get serious, Major," he said. "If this is as simple as you say, why all the Marines, with or without orders to shoot?"

Telemann composed himself into a grave and wise figure, dropped his voice about two tones and looked soulfully past Franklin Young, directly into the lighted pickup. "Under the Federation Constitution, the Navy and the Marine Corps are charged with the protection of the public and Federation citizens. Likewise, it is our responsibility to police the safety of friendly sapient races. *Whatever* is on North Beta, we have the legal obligation to make certain there is no danger about it—'' He shrugged. ''—such as contamination, radiation leakage; that is, nothing that might threaten the safety of any person. Fuzzies are persons, too, you know.''

Young broke in. ''This all seems a bit melodramatic, Major. Do you mean to tell me that the public welfare comes before the Navy's interests in this matter?''

Telemann spread his hands, as though to show there was nothing concealed in them. ''The briefest reading of the Federation Constitution will show that, Mr. Young.'' Abruptly, he leaned forward. ''Besides that, this object is on the Fuzzy Reservation. The Marines are there at the express request of Commissioner of Native Affairs Holloway, and on the concurrance of Governor General Rainsford. It's quite normal procedure—policing the safety of friendly natives. I can't quote the regulation to you, but I'll be glad to furnish a copy so you may pass it on to your viewers.''

Young settled in for the ''heavy shot'' that would round out the interview. *Climb back in the ring and hope for a technical knockout,* he thought.

''As you may be aware, Major Telemann,'' he said, ''there have been many speculations about this affair, some of them involving stories from fairly reliable sources, to the effect that this entire—ahh—scenario which you have recited is only an elaborate coverup for something else.''

''Do you mean that balderdash about a sunstone strike?'' Telemann said, as he leaned back relaxedly in his chair.

''For one,'' Young said. ''Are you prepared to comment on that?''

''I don't have to be prepared to comment on it,'' Telemann said, ''because it's nonsense. It's true there are some remarkable sunstone deposits on the Fuzzy Reservation, and I can see quite easily that some people might connect mining rumors with our archeological dig. If you stop to think, though, the Navy has no interest—*and no authority*—to engage in mining operations.''

Young broke in quickly. ''How about 'policing the safety of friendly natives,' upon whose reservation territory such a sunstone strike might have been made?''

Telemann laughed with genuine amusement. ''I don't

know, Mr. Young, whether or not you are acquainted with
Mr. Commissioner Holloway. If not, then I'm certain you've
heard of the bulldog tenacity with which he guards the rights
and interest of the Fuzzies.'' He paused for a reply.

Young nodded agreement.

''Well then, there you are,'' Telemann said, again spreading his hands. ''That's the purpose of this interview; to
inform the public of the facts as we know them. There is a
need to restrain public reaction to these unfounded rumors
about the activity on North Beta. Why, I heard a story just the
other day that this is all tied in with an impending invasion by
aliens in battle cruisers. Have you heard that one yet?''

''Yes,'' Young said, ''yes, I'm afraid I have.''

''Well, then,'' Telemann said, ''it's plain that we both have
the same kind of ridiculous rumors to deal with—and they
spread faster than we can get the truth to the people.''

''I certainly agree with that,'' Young said gloomily.
''Well, our time is just about up. Thank you for being with
us, Major. Our guest today on *Your News* has been Major
Max Telemann, TFMC, Public Information Officer for the
North Beta Excavations, as they are coming to be called. This
is Franklin Young for Zarathustra News Service. . .''

Victor Grego stubbed out his cigarette as he shut off the
screen. ''If they want to 'inform the public,' as they so
grandiosely refer to what they're doing, why in blazes do
they run this program at the mid–morning coffee–klatch
hour, when no one is watching but insomniac night–shift
workers and indolent household help?''

Leslie Coombes assumed a look of mock astonishment.
''Why, Victor,'' he said. ''The news services are fulfilling
their responsibilities to present all sides of any given story—
but, of course, in such a way that they can keep it best stirred
up in the public mind. Now, they have run this very fair
representation of the Navy's side of things. It's 'unfortunate'
that the only time available for the 'cast happened to be at this
rather inopportune hour—in terms of wide audience. But, be
of good cheer; they'll run some roaring nonsense—designed

to foment riots, if possible—around 1900 tonight when everyone on the planet will be watching.''

"I'm sad to say you're probably in close proximity to the truth, Leslie," Grego said. He yawned. "Well, I have a company to run, and you have a legal department to run. We've loafed away the biggest end of an hour, here, and I must say I'm not any closer to sniffing out the trail than I was to begin with.''

Coombes rose to leave Grego's office.

Grego held up one hand, with the index finger pointing toward the ceiling. "There's *something*, though— dammit—something I can't put my finger on.'' He looked up at Coombes. "Tell you what, Leslie,'' he said. "Drop 'round my place about 1730 for cocktails. I'll either have it figured by then—or—maybe you can jog this old brain a bit.''

"I'll see you then,'' Coombes said.

XXVI

"Results! You dolts! *I want results!*" Hugo Ingermann angrily slapped the *off* switch on his communications screen just as Franklin Young was signing off on the Telemann interview.

He hurled himself back in his office chair and propped his chin on one fist. "Biggest sunstone strike since the planet was opened, and you bungling louts can't find out anything about it beyond this—this—" He waved his other hand petulantly. "—this *cover story* about them digging up some damned old spaceship."

He looked around the room, eyes glittering. "More men!" He leaped to his feet. "That's the ticket! We must send more men to Beta and spy this thing out!"

Hugo Ingermann was alone in his office.

The hard-backed ridge between the upland plateau of North Beta and the Piedmont and woods of South Beta was already beginning to show up on new maps as "Fuzzy Divide."

The sun that warmed Zarathustra was creeping up over the Cordilleras, filling the Marine command car with shafts of orange light and shifting shadows as Fuzzy Divide slid under its nose five thousand feet below.

Gerd van Riebeek yawned. "It's barbaric, is what it is. It's kidnapping—drag a man out of his bed at dawn."

"What it is, is fame," Holloway remarked, his smile making the points of his mustache turn upwards. "Whether you know it or not, you and Ruth are likely the foremost Fuzzyologists on the planet."

"Hmmph," Gerd said. "What about Juan Jimenez?"

Holloway wagged his hand, with the fingers spread.

"Good point, but I wouldn't give you six to five one way or the other."

"Immaterial," Helton said.

"Why so?" Ruth asked.

"Jimenez is a CZC Company man. That's the last thing I want around this place—for a while, anyway." Helton smiled. "You people are involved with the Native Affairs Commission. That means you're under a certain amount of government control in your research—and in the way you release information about it."

"Intimidating, isn't he?" Gerd sniffed as he sipped at his coffee.

"Businesslike, is the word I'd use," Jack said. "We don't know what kind of interest the CZC might have in this—or, for that matter, just what it's about. When we know that, there'll be plenty of time to share data with them."

"On our terms," Ruth remarked.

Gerd sipped at his coffee, again. "Mummified Fuzzies," he said to no one in particular. "Are you sure?"

Helton shrugged. "Weapons systems are what I'm sure of. I can't say."

"How long can they have been there?" Gerd asked, again of no one in particular.

"Might have been a very long time," Helton said.

Gerd chuckled. "Thought you couldn't say."

Helton gave him a level look. "That's what I said," he remarked. "I didn't say I had no opinion."

Jack laughed out loud. "There for you, Dr. Fuzzyologist."

Gerd waved a hand to indicate that he yielded the point and was ready to listen.

"How do you think they got in there?" Holloway asked.

Helton shrugged. "Like I said before—weapons systems and hardware are my specialty. What I can tell you is that we have mapped the entire ship. A lot of it was caved in by the landing, but we have precise locations for you of the remains. You won't have to spend much time inside, and it's safe—as long as you don't start tearing out bulkheads."

Gerd was tapping his nose with his index finger. "How

closely can we date the ship with the remains? We might have something very interesting, there.''

"We've done that,'' Helton said. "The remains are younger than the ship is.''

"Which doesn't prove a damned thing,'' Holloway said.

"That's my thought,'' Helton said.

Gerd took on an irritable look. "That's not what I mean,'' he said. "How *old* are they?''

Helton's face brightened. He saw what Gerd meant immediately. "The remains are ten to twelve centuries old—'' Then he held up a cautioning finger. "—unless there are hydrocarbon accelerations we know nothing about. That's why I dragged you good people out of bed at such an ungenteel hour.''

"What about the ship?'' Ruth asked. "How old is it?''

Helton looked down at the deck under his feet for a moment. "We can't say anything definite about that. Maybe less than two thousand years old—maybe more. We have to do a long rundown on the oxides to get anything close to a guess.''

"You realize, of course,'' Gerd said, "that trying to accurately date the remains while they're still inside the ship is pretty unreliable.''

Helton nodded. "Yes, and I also realize that we have no one at the site with anything resembling the skill to do a proper job of removing them and making a thorough analysis—which, I suppose, explains O'Bannon's instant approval of my idea to import some Fuzzyologists and do the job correctly.''

"Colonel O'Bannon is an intelligent man,'' Gerd said, nodding affirmatively.

"For a Marine,'' Helton said.

After the general laughter had subsided, Jack Holloway chuffed thoughtfully on his pipe for a moment, then looked seriously at Helton. "Phil;'' he said, "remember what I said about you not 'sirring' very many people?''

"Yes, sir,'' Helton replied with a broad grin.

"Aside from the fact that he's obviously a competent

man," Holloway said, "why do you show him that kind of respect?"

Helton's face took an immediate change of expression. "Because he's not in awe of me," Helton said. "Captains jump when I growl. Senior officers solicit my opinion before they proceed. O'Bannon always knows exactly what he's doing. He's not about to be dazzled by the mystique of the omnipotent Master Gunnie. So, I defer to him—unless I think he's wrong."

Victor Grego had slogged his way through a luncheon meeting in the Board Room with several of his division managers, solving problems and making decisions in areas they should have been able to manage without his advice. That was, he thought, why they were called "managers."

Now he sat behind the large desk in his own office, leaned back in his chair, and lit a cigarette. It might just be time to shake up the leadership in a few departments—a wonderful way to convey the idea to everyone that the Manager-in-Chief was not just sitting on his duff, reading reports.

Of course, this thing on North Beta had everyone up in the air—rumors and rumors of rumors. Harry Steefer's over-flight readouts on the excavation and the "object" indicated that it was likely made of titanium, but none of the spies from the CZC Police who had been shunted over to Beta had come up with anything positive on just what the thing *was*.

Grego blew smoke at the ceiling and watched his lazily turning globe of Zarathustra. It would be just about morning coffee-break time at the North Beta Excavations. He formed a mental picture of dusty Marines lining up to get their coffee and pastry. A whole battalion of Marines. . .

Suddenly, he sprang forward in his chair and tapped the switch on his private communication screen. After the swirling burst of color dissolved, Myra Fallada's face appeared in it. He could tell he had interrupted her at some task. "Myra!" he said. "Get me Juan Jimenez at Science Center—instantly."

Myra frowned. "Yes, Mr. Grego," she said.

Grego stubbed out the cigarette. In less than a minute, Juan Jimenez appeared as Myra switched in the channel. "What is it, Victor?" Jimenez asked.

"Juan," Grego said, "isn't there a scientific principle which states an organism does not evolve a need for any element that isn't fairly plentiful in the environment?"

Jimenez stroked his chin. "Yes—yes, Victor, there is. I can't recall it at the moment though—I mean to name or state it. I can find out for you. How soon do you need the data?"

"Yesterday," Grego said vigorously. "Can you have it by five—I mean *everything* about it." It was not a question.

Jimenez looked bemused. "Why—uh—I expect so. It's likely stored in with the xenobiology bank. I'll put someone right on it."

Grego frowned. "No, no, no, Juan. Do it yourself. Don't let anyone know what you're pulling out of the computer. And don't discuss it with anyone."

"This must be pretty damned big," Jimenez said. His face took on an aggravated look. "I mean, for common scientific data that's available to anyone who wants to look it up."

"That's not the point," Grego said briskly. "Dig up everything you can and bring hard copies to my apartment at 1730. Then, if we have what I think we have, I'll explain it all to you."

Jimenez frowned and pursed his lips.

"—Honest," Grego said.

"You mean you want a barracks cover in a child's size," the supply sergeant said.

"No, no, Sam," Vidal Beltrán said exasperatedly. "When I say this big—" He held out both hands with thumbs and forefingers circled. "—I mean *Fuzzy* size."

The supply sergeant reared back in mock surprise. "Oh, well—why didn't you say so? We don't have those in regular issue. To get one *that* small you'll have to go to officer's supply."

Beltrán gnawed his cigar. "What I want you to do, Sam, is take one and cut it down to fit a Fuzzy."

"Which Fuzzy?" Sam asked.

"The one that's the drillmaster for the Fuzzies that live up here in this valley," Beltrán said.

"Kind of like a badge of office, you mean," Sam said.

Beltrán gnawed his cigar—more happily this time. "Yeah," he said. "He oughta have a hat."

Sam leaned on the edge of his console. "Hmmmmm," he said. "I can cut down the frame and the sweatband—and the cover. The visor, though; that'll have to be completely re-designed. Hmmmmm."

"Come on, Sam," Beltrán said. "You can do it from a component pattern."

"Hmmmm," Sam said, shifting his weight to the other elbow.

"Look, Sam," Beltrán said, "I'll get your section some goodies from the mess."

Sam straightened, suddenly more interested. "What kind of goodies?" he asked.

As Juan Jimenez stepped out of the lift at the penthouse level, he was not thinking of the packet of data printout which was under his arm. He was not thinking of why Victor Grego was in such a hell of a rush to get the information.

He was thinking about the inconvenience of shuffling around his cocktail date with Liana Bell. Probably better to push it up to dinner, anyway. There would be much more time to talk with her that way. He could demonstrate his *savoir-faire* with the wine list. Perhaps it would be appropriate to dine at *Alfredo's*. It couldn't hurt to start things off with a bit of a splash.

Now, if I can just break loose from this meeting by—oh— 1930 or so. . .

Jimenez was startled out of his ruminations by the sudden opening of the portal and the appearance of Leslie Coombes' slender and suavely elegant self on the other side of the doorway.

"Come in, Juan," Coombes said. "Victor's in the kitchen, just fixing cocktails. Would you care for one?"

"Yes, Leslie; yes I would," Jimenez said. "I had to juggle around a cocktail date to get this stuff over here." He wanted to get that one in. He hadn't been Director of Science Center all that long and it showed a certain devotion to the Company.

When they were comfortably situated in the living room, Jimenez opened the packet and read over the main points which he had already highlighted on the printout that afternoon in his office. He laid down the sheaf of paper on the coffee table. "That's all the data we have on it at Science Center," he said. "I think I see what you're driving at, Victor. The postulates of Garrett's Theorem indicate the disturbing notion that Fuzzies may not be native to Zarathustra. There's utterly no evidence to support such an idea, though. . ."

"I knew it!" Grego interrupted. He smacked the table with his fist, hard enough to make the nibblements bowl jump about a centimeter off the surface.

Leslie Coombes pursed his lips. "Knew what?" he asked in an irritated tone.

Grego beamed. "Don't you get the drift? All this crap about the North Beta Excavations . . . If the wrecked spaceship story is true, and *if* Garrett's Theorem is true, and *if* Fuzzies aren't native to Zarathustra, then *that wrecked ship* might be how they got here."

Jimenez sipped at his drink. "That's all a little preposterous, Victor," he said.

Grego pierced him with a gaze. "So was hyperdrive—five hundred years ago," he said evenly.

"Now, now, chaps," Coombes remarked. "We're not arguing a court case or anything."

"I'm glad you brought that up, Leslie," Grego said, "because I was just about to. Leslie; do you know if Garrett's Theorem has ever been used as evidence in a court case?"

Coombes chuckled. "I doubt it, Victor. It's only a theory."

Grego was deadly serious. "Just the same," he said, "I want you to check it out thoroughly in case law. Find out if it's ever been raised as any kind of evidence in a court case."

Leslie Coombes averted his eyes. "I'll look into it first thing tomorrow," he said.

Jimenez took another sip of his drink and fetched some

nibblements for himself. He had never seen Victor Grego in such a state. "Victor," he said hesitantly, "this is only a matter of speculation on the part of an obscure scientist. Why all the excitement?"

Grego sloshed the brandy in his snifter irritably. "If we can mount a legal action which cites case law involving Garrett's Theorem," he said, "we may stand a chance of getting the Company's charter back. Don't you see?" He looked around the table, seeking a glimmer that the other two men seemed to follow his line of reasoning.

Leslie Coombes was nervous. "Victor," he said, "even if there is case law precedent on—ah—Garrett's Theorem, we haven't got anything resembling a chance of winning such a suit. There just isn't enough evidence that we can prove."

Grego frowned deeply. "We don't have to *prove* a confounded thing, Leslie," he said. "All we have to do is—I believe the phrase in your business is—'raise a reasonable doubt' in the minds of a jury. The case will stay in the courts for years, anyway. In the meantime, maybe we can get some of the Company's assets unfrozen and start showing a profit again."

"I can see that," Jimenez said thoughtfully. "Why, the expert testimony alone will eat up hundreds of hours."

"You see?" Grego asked triumphantly. "It will buy us some time. While it's all churning around in the legal system, new information may come to light which will help us. On the other hand, it may hurt us. But, at least we'll be doing something. We can say that we've *done* something—and sooner or later we'll have to be able to say that, because sooner or later somebody from the Board of Directors is going to come out here with a tar–bucket and a feather pillow and want to know why we've been carrying the Colonial Government with Company funds."

"And sitting on our hands while we do it," Jimenez added.

"Precisely," Grego said.

Coombes stroked his long, aristocratic jaw. "Hmmmmm," he said. "There're good points to what you say. But after I've done the check on case law in my computer, I'd like to talk to Fred Pendarvis and see how he would feel about such a case.''

''No!'' Grego said emphatically. ''Judge Pendarvis is exactly the man I want to try the case. The law is his religion. If anyone talks to him about it before we file, he'll disqualify himself from sitting. After it's on the docket—and it will be on *his* docket—we can confer in chambers. *That's* the time to find out how he feels.''

Jimenez was looking at his watch.

A smile flickered over Grego's face. ''Got a date, Juan?'' he asked.

Jimenez looked up quickly.

Coombes turned his thin features in Grego's direction, with the half–amused expression he always wore. ''He said something about that when he got here,'' he said.

Jimenez looked pained. He was being teased about Liana and he knew it, but he knew it was only teasing.

''Well, no matter,'' Grego said. ''I think we've done about all there is to be done for the moment. We'll get back on this as soon as Harry Steefer's people come up with something we can put some weight behind about this hyper-ship thing.''

Grego glanced up at the readout on the wall. ''Besides,'' he said, ''Christiana will be bringing Diamond home from Government House any time now.'' He got to his feet. ''Anyone for a refill before we break up?''

''I've got to be going,'' Jimenez said.

''I'll have just a splash with you,'' Coombes said, ''until Miss Stone arrives.''

No sooner were they comfortably situated in the living room than Christiana did arrive with Diamond. Grego leaped to his feet and took her wrap.

Leslie Coombes was bemused. This was the only occasion he could recall when he had ever seen Victor Grego rise to greet one of his own employees.

As the screen cleared, a young man in gray semi–formals looked out of it at Ivan Bowlby. For a moment, Bowlby did not recognize him. Then he said, "Good evening, Anthony."

"Hello, Mr. Bowlby," Anthony said. "I thought I'd give you a call before the dinner–hour rush started."

Bowlby concealed his irritation. "What is it, Anthony?"

"Well," Anthony said, "when you helped me out of that bind over the chuckleweed last year, I told you I'd keep my eyes open for you. I think I may have something that would interest you. I don't know."

"Yes?" Bowlby said.

"You remember that prostie you put out of business in Junktown?" Then he added quickly, "The one I helped you out on?"

"Yes." Bowlby said.

"She was in here a couple nights ago for dinner—with Victor Grego." Anthony paused to let the remark soak in.

Bowlby sat straight up in his chair. "Are you sure?" he asked sharply.

"Sure I'm sure," Anthony said. "They sat on my station—and there was a Fuzzy with them. They was all very friendly."

"How do you think she's connected with Grego?" Bowlby asked.

"I don't know," he said. "I gotta go now. Walter's looking at me with the bad eye." Anthony broke the connection.

Ivan Bowlby sat back in his chair and peered at the ceiling. *Whatever it is,* he thought, *she's connected with Grego. Ingermann has been foaming at the mouth to get an information source inside the CZC, and I think—if she's trying to turn straight—that it shouldn't be too big a job to persuade her to help out. Hmmmm. I think I can turn this one into ready cash.*

Phil Helton jumped down from the edge of the ramp about two feet from the bottom. He had two pair of coveralls slung over his arm. "Here," he said to the van Riebeeks. "Slip these on. It's pretty dirty and dusty in there."

"What if we get lost?" Ruth asked as they both started shucking on the coveralls.

Helton smiled. "Can't happen," he said. "We've strung engineer's tape to the locations of the remains. Just follow it in and follow it out."

Ruth and Gerd climbed the steps up the portable scaffolding and picked up two power–lights from the pile of equipment there. They took a look around the rim of the excavation, where Marine guards were posted to restrict access to the wreck, looked down at Helton and Holloway, then bent down and crawled into the aft hatch of the whatever–it–was.

"What kind of drive system did this thing have, Phil?" Holloway asked. "Any idea yet?"

"I can't say for sure," Helton replied. "What we do know is that it was housed in the sphere part, there, that's aft and between the legs of the rear–extending nacelles. It's going to be a puzzle, because it's just about all melted together into one big lump."

"And that's what forced the ship to land here." Holloway said. "Am I right?"

"Likely," Helton said. "It used to be larger than what we see now. The ship may have been *intending* to land and what melted down the drive was the cause of it crashing on the mountainside. From examining the lower decks, I'd say she was in trouble and making an emergency set–down—this isn't the ideal spot to land something that big."

"So you think the lift drive—or whatever their equivalent was—finally quit, maybe a hundred meters up," Holloway suggested.

Helton nodded. "Yep," he said. "The helmsman was a good one, though. He brought her in on forward momentum toward the valley floor and used the mountain slope as a ramp to brake mass–velocity against gravity. Kept her pretty much in one piece."

"Do you think you can ever figure out what kind of drive it was?" Holloway asked. "If it didn't operate on the same principle as the Dillingham, we could learn a lot from it."

Helton shrugged. "We can but try," he said. "We'll dope out as much as we can by taking the drive apart as far as possible—until we get to the fused parts. Then we'll do test borings of the melted areas and map the core samples. Maybe we can work out a crude plan of what the guts of the thing used to look like.''

Light was reflecting off the inside surface of the open hatch. The van Riebeeks emerged and stood up on the scaffold platform. Even from the distance Holloway could tell they were shaken.

Once back on the ground, Gerd turned to Helton. ''We're going to have to get some equipment and technicians up here,'' he said.

Helton nodded. ''I can authorize that. What do you think?''

''We can't be positive,'' Ruth said, ''until we move the skeletons and remains back to Holloway Station, take measurements, and make comparisons with our own Fuzzy data under laboratory conditions . . .''

She paused and Gerd finished the sentence for her. ''It looks like we have found some Fuzzy bones.''

XXVII

Lieutenant Colonel James O'Bannon stroked his beard and looked at Major Max Telemann in a way that not even that expert reader of human character could fathom. "I watched your 'screen interview in Mallorysport with that young news analyst," he said.

Telemann's face brightened into a warm smile. "And how did you like it, Colonel?"

"You ought to be ashamed of yourself, Max—lying to that kid on the air—even if it is in our best interests at the moment."

Telemann put on his astonished look. "Lie? *Me lie?* Of course I didn't lie!"

O'Bannon leaned forward slightly. "It sounded that way from *my* end," he said.

"Oh, heavens, no," Telemann said. "Of course not. Every word I said was a perfectly truthful example of some line of speculation that we're working on. The interviewer merely assumed that I was talking about exclusively *Terran* vessels." Telemann shrugged. "It's not my fault if his attention is so preoccupied with the Federation that he never thought of the notion there might be another race with hyperdrive." He shrugged again.

A faint smile played over O'Bannon's face. He was silent for a moment as he flicked an imaginary speck of dust from the toe of his boot. "Telemann," he said finally, "If I'm ever stupid enough to stand for public office, will you be my press agent?"

"Why, certainly, sir," Telemann said, "but I can't imagine why a man of your intelligence would want to run for elected office."

Ben Rainsford stormed back and forth in his office, chuffing madly on his pipe. "Why can't they run this like a proper dig?" he demanded. "Regardless of what they've got—or think they've got. Archeology is an exact science. You don't go in and conduct a dig with manipulators and power shovels, for Ghu's sake!"

Gus Brannhard was excited about exactly nothing. He rested his huge frame in an easy chair. Only his eyes followed Rainsford as he paced. "Be realistic, Ben," he said. "You know as well as I do that there isn't a really trained archeologist on the whole planet."

Rainsford jabbed his index finger toward the ceiling. "It's an affront to science and the scientific method! That's what it is!"

"And there isn't time," Brannhard added quietly.

"If you don't have time to do it right the first time," Rainsford said as he noisily knocked out his pipe in the ashtray, "when will you have time to do it correctly?"

Brannhard chuckled, which made Rainsford even madder. "Be practical, Ben," he said. "The TFMC helped out the ZNPF when they were short-handed. Then they found this whatsis up in Fuzzy Valley. The Navy became very interested and wanted to know all about it and damned quick, so they butted into the situation. Now, you know as well as I do that when the Navy thinks it's important to find out something, archeology, or any other science, is going to be sucking hind tit."

"Oh, Nifflheim with it!" Rainsford said as he hurled himself into the chair behind the desk. "Now then, what the blazes are we going to do about this range war on Delta Continent? Who do we indict and how do we catch them?"

"Sir," Helton said, "the scanner crew's report from yesterday has a very interesting item in it."

Scanner crews had been combing Fuzzy Valley, looking for more buried titanium. They had found some, and dug it up, but it was mostly scraps—presumably debris from the wreck. Not very interesting.

O'Bannon rubbed the first two fingers of his right hand

back and forth across his expressionless forehead. "Go on," he said.

"It seems there is a large cavern behind the rockfall on the mountainside," Helton said. "There are several good–sized titanium objects inside."

"Mmmmmm," O'Bannon said. "What's your recommendation?"

"I think we should tunnel in and find out about it," Helton said flatly.

"How does Casagra feel about this idea?" O'Bannon asked.

"He concurs," Helton replied.

"Then why isn't he here to say so?" O'Bannon asked.

Helton grimaced. "He's re–deploying some of the guard detachment. Asks that you excuse him, and says he'll talk to you about it after Officers Call."

"I see," O'Bannon said. "How would you go about boring this tunnel?"

Helton shrugged. "The best way available. I mean, when I have a readout on what equipment of that nature is available on Xerxes, then I can pick the best method from what we have at hand."

O'Bannon got to his feet. "Okay, Gunnie. Get your shopping list and pick out what you think is the best shovel. I'll talk to Casagra and get back to you."

The airboat bobbed slightly as it eased slowly down the canyon, close to the ground, taking advantage of whatever cover there was.

"Take it easy, Alex," Jimmy said.

Alex looked pained. "This is very delicate," he said. "It makes me nervous."

"Not as nervous as you'll be if you scratch up Ingermann's airboat," chimed in a third man.

Alex half–turned from the controls. "Oh, be quiet, Morrie," he said to the third man. "It just makes me more nervous."

A large beefy man in the rear of the boat suddenly jumped to his feet. "Look out!" he shouted.

Alex jerked around in time to see that he was heading straight for a rock outcropping. He swerved to miss it and barely regained control after the evasion.

The beefy man came forward toward the pilot's station. "Listen, Alex," he said, "if you can't handle this thing maybe I ought to take over."

"You can have it, Squint," Alex said. "I don't know what I'm doing driving this thing, anyway. I don't have any experience working this close. I'm scared to death."

"All right, then," Squint said. "Why didn't you say so to begin with?"

The fifth man was topside, sitting in a stowage sling, with about half his body sticking out of the open top hatch. His job was to watch the sky for Marine patrols. His name was Dave. "Listen, you guys," he said. "Not so fast. Look up there to the left, just above that bench."

Jimmy stooped down and looked out the front of the boat, while everyone else scrambled for a look.

"What do you make of it?" Dave asked.

"Looks like fresh blasting in the rock to me," Morrie said.

"Either that," Dave said, "or a big crack opened up by an earthquake." He jumped down to the deck, swinging his weight on the cargo straps. "Take it on up to the ledge, Alex. Let's see what's what."

Above the sandstone ledge, layers of flint and conglomerate were laying vertically at an angle. Apparently an earthquake had cracked these apart, making a fissured passage-way without disturbing the sandstone bench.

Dave stroked his chin. "Ledge ain't wide enough to set down the boat. I sure would like to see what's in there."

"You think somebody's been diggin' for sunstones in there?" Squint asked.

"That's what we're supposed to be lookin' for," Jimmy said.

"But we can't set the boat down," Alex whined. "Let's just forget it."

"No," Dave said. "No, I want to see what's in there."

Morrie had been peering at the ledge, which couldn't be more than several meters wide. "Look," he said, "Alex can ease the boat over so the side hatch is above the ledge and let down the hatch while he keeps it locked on hover. The four of us will jump out and go in for a look.''

Alex looked anguished. ''I can't hold it on hover that close all the time you're in there.''

Squint glared at him. ''You don't have to, stupid,'' he said. ''After we're out, shut the hatch and hide this thing someplace on the canyon floor—but someplace where you can see the ledge. When we come out, we'll give you the high sign and you can bring her back up and get us.''

Dave and Jimmy were already gathering up some light-packs and a couple of vibrohammers.

Once inside, the four found themselves in a long, fissured chamber that came together at the top in an acute angle.

As he shined his light around, Jimmy whistled in amazement. ''Wow,'' he said. ''You don't think this thing could fall in on us, do you?''

''Of course not,'' Squint snapped. ''Can't you see the rocks is leanin' together at the top? They're holding each other up.''

''Come on,'' Dave said. ''Let's see what's up ahead.''

About a hundred meters into the mountain, the slowly narrowing fissure had pinched down to the point that a man could go no farther. Frustrated, they began to shine their lights around.

''Boy it sure is hot in here,'' Morrie said. ''It's hard to breathe.''

''Great Ghu!'' Jimmy said, suddenly alarmed. ''You don't think we're inside a volcano, do you?''

Everyone looked uncomfortable for a moment.

''Naw,'' Squint said. Proud of his deductive powers, he added, ''We didn't see no volcanoes from up above did we?''

''It could be dormant,'' Jimmy said. ''What if—''

Before the argument could start, Morrie let out a shout of surprise. ''Hey! Hey, you guys—lookit this.''

Squint turned his light to the same spot on the sandy floor as Morrie's was. ''So what,'' he said. ''You found some shiny pebbles.''

Morrie bent down and snatched up two of the shiny bean-shaped pebbles. He rubbed them between his palms, then slowly opened his hands. There was a slight glow coming from within his cupped palms.

"Jeez," Dave said. "They *are* sunstones!"

"Aw, come on," Jimmy said. "You don't find sunstones just laying around. They have to be cracked out of solid flint. Everybody knows that."

Dave frowned. "Well, then, somebody *has* been digging sunstones in here."

"No, no." Morrie shook his head. "It's too hard to get them out of the flint. When a guy finally gets one, he puts it in a little bag. Nobody would be careless enough to drop a half–dozen of them on the floor, unless—" He shined his light down the fissure. "—Unless somebody was stashing a whole bunch of them away, down there. *Then* some could get dropped without anybody noticing."

"A man can't get through there," Dave announced with authority. "It isn't wide enough."

"A Fuzzy could have though—stupid," Squint said. "A Fuzzy could be trained to do that."

"Jeez," Dave said. "There could be enough sunstones back there to make us all rich for life. What are we waiting for? Let's take the vibrohammers and open up this narrow spot—see what we find."

"What about Ingermann?" Jimmy asked.

"The hell with him," Squint said. "We'll take a handful back to him and keep the rest."

"Just enough to get him excited," Morrie said.

"Right," Squint said, "and while he's scheming how to get over here and steal, we all get the hell off the planet as fast as we can."

Morrie picked up one vibrohammer. "That's assuming we find anything."

"Only one way to find out," Squint said, picking up the other one. "We'll spell each other on these. You two guys go back to the opening and get some fresh air. We'll call you when it's your turn."

The communications sergeant came hurrying toward Phil

Helton and Captain Casagra, peering at a sheet of printout in his hand as he walked briskly along.

"What have they got on Xerxes that we can use?" Helton asked rhetorically as the sergeant gave him the sheet. Helton held it over to one side so Casagra could see the list.

The sergeant sidled around so he could look over Helton's shoulder.

"Hmmmmm," Helton said. "Collapsium cutter. That's no good. Heading drill, 1.5 meter. Do the job, but we have to shore up behind it, and it could still get the whole slide moving—cover up the wreck all over again." He snorted derisively. "Power shovel, Mark X. Terrific. We have those, but I don't think we want to make a life's work out of taking the slide apart. Ahhhh. M–79 terrene. That gives us a two–meter headwall and it glasses up the tunnel behind itself. What do you think, Captain?"

Casagra cleared his throat. "Sounds good to me. They use it to bore passageways on Xerxes. It wouldn't set up any stresses in the rockpile."

"Good," Helton said. "Check it off. Wait. I have to sign for it, too."

After Helton had signed the inventory sheet for the piece of equipment, Captain Casagra did the same. "Okay," Helton said as he handed the printout back to the communications sergeant. "Hop this over to Colonel O'Bannon, get his approval, and transmit it back to Xerxes. Don't forget to tell them we want their own operations and maintenance people to come down with it. I sure don't know how to run the thing; only seen one once before."

The sergeant gulped. "Colonel O'Bannon? Himself?"

Helton smiled. "Sure. He won't bite your head off. He just looks like he might."

As Helton and Casagra walked away, their boots crunching in the dry soil of Fuzzy Valley, Casagra spoke. "Did the Fuzzy Institute people get everything they wanted?"

"Indeed," Helton replied. "They're all back at Holloway Station, now, with their Fuzzy bones—furiously analyzing everything, I imagine."

"How soon do they think they'll have something for us," Casagra asked.

"They think a couple of days; either confirmation or denial of authenticity. Gerd van Riebeek is coming up sometime tomorrow. He's going to interview the two Marine technicians who made the find, take some tapes of the wreck—that sort of thing."

Casagra looked alarmed. "Tapes? Visual records? Does O'Bannon know about this?"

Helton nodded. "He wasn't too thrilled about it at first, but when Gerd offered to let him review the tapes before they left the site and censor out anything he wanted, there wasn't much he could object to."

The stalwart five on the other side of the mountain were having their difficulties. They would chip away enough rock from the sides of the fissure to allow a man through, only to find the passage narrowed again less than a dozen meters further. They labored in shifts; one could only stand about a half–hour's work in the close, oppressive heat of the passage.

But they kept at it, because every time they broke through a narrow place they would find a few more sunstones. All of them had the fever by now. Sunstone fever.

"Listen," Dave said. "We better quit till morning. It's almost dark outside."

Squint leaned back, gasping for breath. "So what? It's dark in here all the time. We can keep working with the lights."

"That's not what he means," Morrie said. "The lights in here will show out through the mouth of the fissure."

Dave nodded. "Marine patrol be on us within an hour unless we shut down."

"Aw," Squint said. "We're a good hundred–fifty meters inside the mountain by now."

Dave frowned. "Yeah," he said, "and you can see a lighted match or a cigarette coal for two kilometers— especially out here where it's *really* dark, with no city lights or anything."

They made a dark camp in the airboat, squabbled endlessly over how to divide up the sunstones already found, and had an uninspiring dinner of Extee–Three.

As each man fell asleep, exhausted, he curled his hand around the pistol he had sneaked under his pillow.

XXVIII

It was that indeterminate time when it is neither night nor dawn. There was only enough light to discern that light was coming. The dark, gray, humpbacked shapes of Marine vehicles and inflatable tentage were just visible in the paler gray light that was slowly brightening in the east. Lights were on in the kitchen scow, where the mess sergeant and his crew had already been working for about an hour. Lights were on in the communications center, where the duty NCO stood in the aft hatchway, watching the light grow, and scratching himself. Then he yawned and stretched, turned, and went back to his monitor screens.

O'Bannon was pulling on his left sock when his communication screen chimed softly, indicating a routine transmission.

It's starting already, O'Bannon thought. He reached over and tapped the key. When the image cleared, he said, very simply, "O'Bannon."

The face in the screen was that of an anxious young man. He was wearing field greens, a single bar, and a worried look. "Sir," he said nervously. "Lieutenant Crocker reporting."

There was a pause.

O'Bannon rubbed his hand across his forehead. "Well, then, Crocker," he said. "Report."

"Yes, sir," Crocker said. "The intruder we logged yesterday morning still hasn't turned up. I think they've gone to ground someplace inside the reservation."

O'Bannon grimaced. "Well, then, they'd be sitting still, wouldn't they? If you're on the move and they're sitting still, it shouldn't be too hard to spot them, should it, Lieutenant?"

Lieutenant Crocker looked uncomfortable. "No, sir—no,

199

sir; it shouldn't. I'm certain we'll turn them up. In any case, I've taken steps to make sure they don't get out of the area."

"I think that's an excellent approach, Crocker," O'Bannon said, with just the right tone of cynicism in his voice, "because if they do, I think we can find you a somewhat less sensitive job—on Nifflheim, or, perhaps, Yggsdrasil."

The muscles around Crocker's eyes were beginning to tighten. "I understand, Colonel," he said.

"Have you run an inbound spiral search?" O'Bannon asked.

"Uh—no, sir," Crocker said. "We've been doing standard grid."

O'Bannon softened his expression. *Already scared the kid to death,* he thought. *Time now to prop him up a bit.* "Try running an inbound spiral. Five cars. Slideback formation. That should flush 'em if they're down in the brush someplace."

"Yes, sir. Thank you, sir," Crocker said.

"Okay, son," O'Bannon replied. "Report back before evening chow."

Jack Holloway and Gerd van Riebeek missed breakfast by a mile, but they arrived at Fuzzy Valley in time for the mid–morning coffee–break.

Sergeant Beltrán motioned them aside. "You guys don't look like you ate yet today," he said. "Huh?"

They both shook their heads.

Beltrán nodded in approval of his own sagacity. "Come on over to the kitchen scow. I'll fix you something up. You can't get by till lunch on coffee and pastry."

When they emerged from the kitchen scow, well–fed and still marveling at the meal which Beltrán had whipped up on the spur of the moment—using odds and ends—an enormous closed cargo scow was just settling out of the sky. Its landing point was midway between the excavated wreck and the rockslide over the cave–mouth.

Phil Helton was on the ground, talking the lander chief

down to the right spot. O'Bannon, Stagwell, and Casagra were off to one side, observing the operation.

"Come on, Gerd," Jack said. "Let's see what this is all about."

By the time they had walked to the site the scow had settled to the ground and lurched off contragravity.

After greetings had been exchanged, the flight crew had already secured the scow, the equipment crew had grounded the hatch–ramp, and a man wearing field greens and an orange cap was crunching across the ground toward them.

As the man drew closer, Holloway could see a black stencil on his left shirt pocket; an engineer's hammer, framed by the inverted "V" of a mason's square at the bottom and a spread divider compass at the top. "TFN" was stenciled below the design.

The man stopped, saluted the officers, and said, "Master Chief Construction Mate Lyman Byers reporting, sir. The difficult we do immediately; the impossible may take a whole shift."

O'Bannon returned the salute and looked slightly bilious. *These guys from the construction battalion even have their own compliments on the load–list,* he thought. He inclined his head toward Helton.

Chief Byers' face brightened as he ambled his lanky frame over to where Helton was standing with Jack and Gerd. "Whatcha' need, Gunnie? Gotta bore a big hole in something, huh?"

Gear was already coming out of the scow, to where the equipment crew was laying it out in precise rows on the ground.

Helton outlined his requirements as Byers listened attentively—with a concentration that was far different from his previous country–boy attitude.

"Take your own soundings," Helton said. "I want the shortest, straightest tunnel you can manage, *but* I want you to pull out when the headwall is about six inches short of breaking into the cavern. Can you cut it that fine?"

"No problem, Gunnie," Byers said seriously. "If the

inside face of the rockfall was perfectly vertical, my operator could cut it fine enough to leave you a windowpane, if'n you wanted one.''

Helton smiled. "Okay, get to it, then."

By now the terrene itself had come out of the scow, on its own contragravity skid. It had the look of a short, fat torpedo with a snubbed-off nose. Directly behind it came the control cabin, a collapsium-hulled affair of smaller diameter than the terrene head. It housed all the sensors, controls, and pickups, as well as the operator. To the rear of it, it carried a collapsium counterweight, so that when the entire affair was on contragravity and working, the weight of the terrene to the front was balanced to level by the counterweight at the rear.

As Byers loped off across the dry soil, his crew was already swarming over the equipment at the complicated task of mating the terrene with its control cabin.

"Your men are pretty flamboyant—with those blinding orange caps, aren't they?" Gerd asked of no one in particular.

"Oh, there's a reason for it," Helton said. "That's a damned dangerous piece of gear, especially when it's hot. They wear those gaudy caps so they can tell the players from the spectators. Anyone not wearing a loud orange cap gets within a hundred meters of that thing, the crew chief goes out and runs him off, be he captain, corporal, or general."

Holloway's itch of curiosity was getting the best of him. "Y'know, Phil, I've heard about those things, but I've never really seen one."

"That's not surprising," Helton said. "There are only six of them in the entire Federation Navy."

"Well, how does the damned thing work, is what I want to know," Holloway said. "All I've ever heard is that it bores holes in solid rock—which makes no sense to me of itself."

"In a nutshell," Helton continued, "there's a nuclear reactor inside the terrene itself. There are little bitty ones in the twenty centimeter models they use to bore drainage lines and air vents. There's a one-meter model. It makes a tube big enough for a man to crawl around in and string commo lines and fiber optic bundles along the walls. Then, there's this monster; two–meter tube. Makes nifty lift shafts and lateral drive tunnels to connect up underground complexes on places like Xerxes, where no–one can live on the surface."

"But how does it *work?*" Holloway insisted.

"I'm getting to that part," Helton said. "As the reactor heats up, a series of heat baffles raises the temperature of the outer skin until it's hot enough to vaporize rock—hotter for granite than for sandstone, for example. As the terrene proceeds through the rock, controlled by the operator in the collapsium cabin—who has to be a pretty brave guy, by the way—it also melts the rock around the periphery of the tunnel to a depth of several centimeters. So, you see, it cases the tube as it goes, in a kind of crackle–finish glass—sometimes in very pretty colors, too."

"Hmmmm," Holloway said. "I see. What's the skin made of? Can't be collapsium. Collapsium's a lousy heat conductor. Whatever it is, it must be wild stuff to take those temperatures."

"The answer to that is such a complicated secret that even I don't know it," Helton said. He laughed. "And even if I did, I probably couldn't explain it. In any case, it must cost like crazy to build the things. Otherwise we'd have more of them."

"How do they operate the little ones?" Gerd asked. "They'd be too small to have a control cabin with a man in it."

"Remotely," Helton said. "The control signals are input through a cable bundle that the terrene drags down the hole behind it. The operator works from a stationary console. But, the M–79 is so big and has so much mass that it has to be run with a tighter set of reins."

Mr. Throckmorton inhaled deeply before delivering the last point of Colonial case law noted in his brief. "The point, your Honor, is even more clearly stated in the case of *The People of Yggsdrasil Colony* versus *The Federation Resident–General, The Chartered Yggsdrasil Company, et al.*

As Throckmorton droned on, Attorney General Gus

Brannhard was the picture of serenity on the outside, eyes half closed, not a muscle of his huge frame moving. Inside, though, he was dancing with glee as he awaited the conclusion of Mr. Throckmorton's precedents in this absurd matter of *The Federated Sunstone Co-operative* versus *The Colonial Government of Zarathustra*—so he could rip the fool's shoddy case to pieces. Hugo Ingermann hadn't chosen very well. Now that he was barred from practicing law before Zarathustran courts, he had chosen The Honorable Eustis Throckmorton as his own personal shyster. Perhaps Mr. Throckmorton had come cheaply. Ingermann's penchant as a centisol-pincher was well known.

Throckmorton finally wound down and finished his argument.

Justice Pendarvis nodded toward him, then turned his gaze toward Brannhard. "How say you, Mr. Attorney General?" he asked.

Brannhard cleared his throat with a rumble. "I say that Mr. Throckmorton's case is no case at all, and, in any event, cannot at present be heard by this court."

"And why is that, Mr. Brannhard?" Justice Pendarvis asked, although he knew the answer as well as Gus did.

"The element of conspiracy has been cited in the plantiff's causes of action. It is a widely known point in Colonial Law that a colonial government—or any of its agencies—cannot be made the defendant in any complaint which cites conspiracy among the causes of action—uh—without the specific permission of that government for the plaintiff to pursue his case."

"Are you suggesting, then, Mr. Brannhard," Justice Pendarvis said, "that Mr. Throckmorton's case cannot be tried in this court?"

"Not at all, your Honor," Gus replied. "Merely that it cannot be tried as the issues are presently framed unless Mr. Throckmorton petition the Colonial Government and obtain its permission for trial. I, for one, would not be friendly to such a petition, having the acquaintance that I do with Mr. Throckmorton's employer."

Throckmorton's eyes were getting wider and wider.

"Object!" Throckmorton said hastily. "The present Colonial Government of Zarathustra is not one duly elected under the Federation Constitution. It is merely a fiat government, set up by Commodore Napier to govern *pro tempore* during the period between those decisions which bear your Honor's name and such time as proper elections can be held."

Justice Pendarvis leaned forward on his elbows. "Overruled, Mr. Throckmorton," he said quietly. "An appointed colonial government has all the force of authority as an elected one, save on one point. It cannot levy taxes."

"I—I forgot," Throckmorton said.

Brannhard fluffed his gray-brown beard. "I suggest," he said to no one in particular, "that Mr. Throckmorton was hoping that the Court had forgotten."

"There is an alternative, Mr. Throckmorton," Justice Pendarvis said.

Throckmorton's face took on a glow of anticipation. Perhaps there was a way to salvage this mess, after all.

"You may take your case to a Terran Federation Supreme Court on the home planet. They, having superior jurisdiction over this Colonial Supreme Court, will be pleased to hear your case, although I might suggest that the calling of witnesses might occupy a few years—considering travel times involved—and amount to no small expense to your client."

Throckmorton's face fell.

Justice Pendarvis rapped his gavel lightly. "This case to be continued for a period of thirty days, in order to allow Mr. Throckmorton to prepare the petition in question. If such petition has not been secured by then, the case will be removed from the docket.

"Next case, please," Pendarvis said to the crier, as Throckmorton gathered up his brief and slunk out of the courtroom.

Great, noxious clouds of vapor and steam poured out of the tunnel as the terrene bored steadily into the rockfall. The remainder of the crew had cordoned off an area several hundred meters on a side with orange engineer's tape. Part of the men patrolled the perimeter, more for something to do than anything else. The rest, wearing breathing gear, were jockeying huge air–changers, each on its own contragravity sled, and blowing the fumes away with the prevailing breeze. Periodically, Byers, who was standing with his hands on his hips, talking to the operator over a commo attached to his earphones, would motion for the two work parties to switch off on their respective chores.

"That's very eerie," Holloway said, as he stood and watched with Gerd and Phil. "I thought it would make more noise."

Helton shrugged. "Mighty engines must not always make a mighty noise. In this case, just the hiss of vaporizing stone and the noise of some of the glassed–up wall fracturing." He smiled. "You know what we call the three sizes of these things?"

Jack and Gerd both shook their heads.

"The little one," Helton said, "we call 'snap.' It doesn't make any more noise than a teakettle. The mid–size one we call 'crackle,' because it seems to cause more fracturing of the tunnel lining. Now, what do you suppose we call this one, the grandpappy of them all?"

Jack hesitated for a moment. "Pop?" he said tentatively.

Helton winked and made a single, decisive gesture with his index finger. "You got it," he said.

The vapor clouds began to die away into wisps.

"Looks like they're in at the six–inch wall," Helton said. "Time for me to go to work."

He walked briskly off toward Chief Byers.

"What did he mean by that?" Gerd asked.

"I don't know," Jack said, "but if we watch, we'll probably find out."

Helton motioned for Chief Byers to move one side of his headphones so he could hear. "Are you down to the mark?" he asked.

"On the button," Byers said. "We're backin' her out now."

"How long will it take you to blow down the temperature enough for me to go in there in a heat suit?" Helton asked.

" 'Bout twenty minutes, if I use the air changers," Byers answered without hesitation.

"Good," Helton said. "I'll go draw the gear."

Sweating and gasping for breath, Squint and Dave finally knocked off the last confining outcropping and were able to squeeze into the cavern. They were astonished at what they saw. Morrie and Jimmy heard the vibrohammers stop and came down the fissure on the run.

"Ghu! It's hot in here," Morrie said, then stopped short.

"What shall we do?" Jimmy said.

Squint growled and wiped the sweat from his face. "Why, get as many sunstones as we can carry, before we all die of suffocation—stupid."

"Yeah, yeah!" Jimmy said excitedly. "And we'll keep this a secret and come back later, with breathing gear."

"Wait a minute," Dave said loudly. "Shut up, you guys. What's that noise?"

"What noise?" Squint asked.

"Listen!" Dave said.

They all fell silent.

"*That* noise," Dave said. "That popping and snapping noise. Sounds like it's coming from that rockfall over there."

"Great Ghu!" Morrie wailed. "The mountain's gonna cave in on us."

"Maybe," Squint said, "but I'm gonna get some sunstones first. Let's get busy."

Tendrils of vapor trailed from the top of the tunnel opening and the walls still popped and crackled from the rapid cool-down as Phil Helton disappeared into the tunnel mouth, wearing a hot suit and carrying a snooper-phone in a heat-shielding container.

"Now what's he doing that for?" Gerd said. The little hillock where they stood was a grandstand seat from which to watch the entire affair.

The terrene crew had moved that massive piece of equipment to one side, where it bobbed on contragravity, a few feet off the ground, and were re-stringing their orange engineer's

tape to make a cordon about sixty meters away from the
machine.

O'Bannon, Stagwell, and Casagra were still to one side, in
a close little group, talking quietly among themselves.

"Well, Gerd," Holloway drawled, "if you were planning
to bust into a strange place like that, wouldn't you want to
listen to the inside of it a little bit before you charged ahead?"

"Yeah," Gerd said. "Yeah, I guess I would."

It was still a little uncomfortable, even in the hot suit, as
Helton placed the snooperphone on a special collar so the
pickup wouldn't melt against the glassed–up surface of the
headwall.

He cranked the gain and listened.

Now, that's damned strange, he thought. *A cavern, closed
by a rockfall hundreds of years ago . . . And there's
somebody–or some thing–in there, using vibrohammers.* He
pulled the audio pickup out of his ear, turned, and trotted
back toward the light at the end of the tunnel.

Ingermann's face was a pale maroon, and his neck bulged
out over his shirt collar. "Throckmorton!" he shouted.
"You blockhead! Why did you have to stick in that damned
conspiracy in the causes of action? Why didn't you draw the
complaint just as I told you? Can't you follow simple instructions, you nitwit?"

Throckmorton was quivering in his chair. "I—I thought it
would make a solider case, sir," he said in a small voice.

"Solider case?" Ingermann screamed. "Solider case?
How in Nifflheim did you ever pass the bar to practice law on
this planet—" He paused to suck in another gasping breath
before continuing. "—or any other colony world, without
knowing you have to have the government's permission to
sue them for conspiracy."

"Well, sir," Throckmorton began.

"You numbskull!" Ingermann raged. "*Out!* Get out of
my sight!"

Throckmorton gratefully rose to take his departure.

"Just a minute!" Ingermann said. "Who was the presiding judge?"

"Why, uh, Justice Pendarvis," Throckmorton replied.

"I thought so!" Ingermann shrieked triumphantly. "He's been trying to get me ever since I set foot on Zarathustra. Oh, don't kid yourself. He and Brannhard have been working behind my back for years. Well, I'll get him. I'll get him if it's the last thing I ever do. Him and his sanctimonious mouth; I'll send him to *Nifflheim*, so help me."

Ingermann had been talking to the top of his desk, his eyes glazed, his breath coming in short rasps. Suddenly, he looked up and saw Throckmorton. "I told you to get out, didn't I?"

Throckmorton nodded.

"Well, then, get out!" He strode around the desk as Throckmorton made a terrified retreat into the corridor. Ingermann slammed the door as hard as he could, then staggered back to the desk and leaned upon it, breathing heavily, for several minutes.

Chief Byers helped with the fastenings as Helton shucked off the hot suit. As soon as his head was free, Helton asked, "Chief—how soon can you have that cold enough for men in body armor and breathing gear to go in? Huh, Chief; how long?"

"Take at least forty–five minutes to an hour, Gunnie," Byers replied. "Still be pretty warm, at that, an' it'll crackle up the walls somthin' fierce."

"It won't make them unstable, will it?" Helton asked as he peeled off the last vels from the over–boots.

"Oh, nothin' like that," Byers said. "Some little–bitty pieces might fall out, but you'll be as safe in there as a pit in a prune."

O'Bannon frowned deeply. "Vibrohammers? Vibrohammers, did you say?"

"Yes, sir," Helton replied. He had joined the little knot of officers on the knoll.

O'Bannon pursed his lips. "I imagine, Helton, that you have already formulated some ideas about how to handle this."

Helton smiled. "As a matter of fact, Colonel . . ."

"Get on with it," O'Bannon said as he rubbed the first two fingers of his right hand across his forehead. "What's your idea?"

"Fan out a cordon of scouts and combat cars all around the mountain in a pattern, say, six kilometers in diameter, together with an aloft surveillance in case they try to make a break for it. Slowly pull the purse string tight, looking for civilians or aircars in the area, concealed or trying to keep concealed. Arrest anyone who's not one of us—no matter how good their story. It'll be an hour before the tunnel is cool enough. Then, I'll take six men, blow the headwall, and go in."

O'Bannon thought for a few seconds. "Couple things you overlooked, but basically I like it. I'll lead, with the scout platoon and elements of 'A' Company. Dick," he said to Stagwell, "you lead the aloft cover. Use a waffle–iron pattern." He turned to Casagra. "Glen, you dig in some crew–served automatic weapons about two hundred meters from the tunnel opening so they have good crossfire—and another one up here where we're standing, with some rockets, too. If Helton and his guys don't come out of there first, Ghu knows what we'll be up against. We should be able to make lift in fifteen minutes. Now, let's see if we all have the same time."

Four hands extended as each man checked his watch.

As Casagra and Helton trotted away to their respective tasks, O'Bannon was on his belt commo. "Bushmeyer," he barked at his driver, "put down whatever kind of trash you're reading and get my car over here on the double." Pause. "That's right. I'm on the little knoll, in plain sight."

"Get me Sergeant Chin," Helton said into his commo. "Have him meet me at the tunnel. Right now."

Sergeant John Chirgantha Chin was a cocky little three–striper with a body like a coiled spring. He always looked as though he were about to burst out laughing about something.

"Is there anyone in your company who's tougher and more reliable than you are?" Helton asked him.

"Of course not," he replied. "Nobody in the whole Corps—except maybe you, Gunnie." He grinned.

"Okay," Helton said. "I'm flattered already. I need you and five men for a little chore, here. Who do you recommend?"

Chin ticked off on his fingers as he named them. "Henshaw, Cooper, Bradley, McDermott, and Holden."

Helton squinted at him. "Aren't all those men in your squad?"

"Of course," Chin said, "That's why they're so tough."

"Are they all available?" Helton asked.

"Sure, Gunnie. We're off duty today."

"Okay," Helton said. "Have them draw body armor and assault rifles. Three sleep–gas grenades per man. Breathing gear. Draw a set for me, and draw six Pattycake mines. We're going in through the headwall of that tunnel, but I don't know what's on the other side. There's something there, but I don't know what it is."

"Sounds like fun," Chin said. "When do we jump off?"

"Sixty minutes after the Old Man lifts off with the patrols," Helton said.

"Okay," Chin said with a jaunty wave of his hand. "I'll be back with the bodies and the stuff in a little while."

By the time Sergeant Chin had left to gather his men, Gerd and Jack had walked over to the tunnel site.

Helton sat down on a rock and lighted a cigarette.

"What in blazes is going on?" Gerd asked.

Helton told them about the patrol cordon while he was making up his mind whether to tell them the rest.

"Aren't you afraid whoever they're after will get away?" Gerd asked.

Holloway nudged him in the ribs. "They won't get away from these guys," he said.

"For that vote of confidence," Helton said, "we will not charge you the customary admission fee to watch Marines doing what they're supposed to do when it comes to the bottom line."

After a few more expressions of astonishment and a flock of questions from Gerd, Sergeant Chin arrived, with Helton's gear slung over one arm and his men in a neat file close behind him.

"Now, what's this bunch outfitted for?" Gerd asked.

Holloway laughed. "You tell him, Phil. I've already figured it out."

Helton spoke as Chin helped him into the body armor. "There's something or other inside the cavern, using vibrohammers. After O'Bannon gets the perimeter pulled in nice and tight, we're going in."

"Then what's with the crew-served weapons out here?" Gerd asked.

Helton smiled. "Oh, those. Well, those are in case we don't come back out first."

"Great Ghu's galluses!" Gerd said. "Just like that! Aren't you scared?"

"Are you scared when you examine an alien organism for the first time and don't know whether it may give you some unknown, some fatal disease?"

"Well, of course I am," Gerd said. "But we take precautions. Sterile procedures; that sort of thing."

Helton pulled the magazine from the assault rifle, inspected it, inspected the weapon, then slammed the magazine home and chambered a round. "We take precautions, too, but they don't have to be sterile. We wear 'em, carry 'em, and fly in 'em." He leaned close to Gerd and Jack. "Confidentially, I'm scared to death. In my trade—as, I imagine, in yours—it has a good effect on my ability to survive."

Chin and the other Marines had already lain down on the ground to rest, arranged in a circle, so that each man's stomach made a pillow for the next man's head.

"Look at that," Gerd said. "They're getting ready to blow the headwall and go up against an unknown quantity and they're taking a nap."

Helton sat back down on his rock and lighted another cigarette.

Forty minutes later, he got up and went over to the other Marines. He lightly kicked the sole of Sergeant Chin's boot. "Time to go," he said simply.

Helton walked back to Gerd and Jack and shook hands with them in turn. He stared off into the middle distance for a few seconds. "Reminds me of a verse," he said.

"The Milky Way is tracks in time
  where we have danced,
Unwitting that the deadly tide of life
    on us advanced,
To dissolve us into formal counterparts
And make us slaves and patrons of the arts."

"Who wrote that?" Jack asked.

"Can't remember the name," Helton said. "Have other things on my mind at the moment—such as my own mortality. But, he was a First Century novelist who was also given to writing sentimental poetry."

Helton turned back to the other Marines. "Okay, you guys; mask up. Let's go." With that he pulled on his own breathing gear, cleared it, and led the other men toward the mouth of the tunnel.

XXIX

Christiana squinted at the man across the table from her. "Just who *is* your employer?" she asked.

The man, who had never introduced himself, had a pale complexion. His eyes were colorless, hypnotic; he wore an old-fashioned hat.

"That, dear lady," he said, "I am not at liberty to reveal. As stated, though, he is willing to be quite generous with you in exchange for anything of interest regarding the plans of the CZC. Inside information, one might call it, if one cared to use a slangy phrase. This—ah—generosity will not take so much the form of financial reward, although that is a consideration, as the continued opportunity for you to pursue your quite promising future—unencumbered by a past that might prove less than palatable to Mr. Victor Grego."

They were sitting at a back table in *La Rondo*, a bistro and sandwich shop that was neither in Junktown or in the new city, but in the fringe area between them.

Christiana's mind was racing. How could they know of her affection for Grego? No, no. That didn't have to be it. They just knew she had a good, honest job—one that was close to the pivots of power in the CZC. *That's* what they were blackmailing her about. She didn't dare let them know how she felt about Grego; then they'd have a real stranglehold on her.

"I'll have to think about this," she said. It was all happening too fast. Only a few hours from the time she found a note shoved under her door until this—this, from this ever-so-polite gangster, bag-man—whatever he was.

The man in the hat leaned back in his chair. "Take all the time you like, dear lady," he said. "The entire balance of my day is at your disposal."

"I—I mean I need a few days to think it over," she said.

"Regrettably, time is a luxury we cannot afford in the matter," he said. "You must make up your mind now."

Christiana chewed at her lower lip. She certainly didn't want Grego to know about her short, disastrous career on Zarathustra as a prostitute, and she could tell by this man's eyes that he would really spill it if she didn't co-operate. The only thing to do was agree to the proposition and try to find a way out later. Possibly through the man in the hat she could get at who he was working for and find some way to shut him up for good. She was astonished to find herself thinking like that, but Victor Grego had become worth that much to her. He was beginning to become everything to her.

She took a deep breath, put her elbow on the table, and hoped she had a convincingly tough look on her face. "Okay," she said, "you got a deal. How do we pass the information?"

"Right here," the man in the hat said. "Tuesdays and Fridays at 1600. I will meet you at this table and we will have a pleasant chat about matters of interest to my employer."

"What if I get tied up, or something," she said, "and can't make it?"

The man in the hat made a noncommital motion of his hand. "You have only to screen this establishment and explain matters to the proprietor, who is an aquaintance of mine. Your story will be checked by one of our—um—observers. If you have lied, our relationship will terminate and Mr. Grego will receive some distressing news."

Christiana got to her feet. "See you Friday," she said.

The man rose as she did, and doffed his hat. "It will be a pleasure to see one so lovely as yourself again at that time," he said.

She turned and left, anxious to get out on the esplanade, into the sunlight, and into the fresh air.

Helton and Sergeant Chin had just placed the last of the shaped-charge Pattycake mines, neatly arranged at sixty-degree intervals around the periphery of the headwall.

"Give 'em thirty seconds," Helton said, as he prepared to

set fuse timers. "Two–second decension. We'll start on the top two. Go."

They each quickly set the fuses—30—28—26—on three of the six mines, figuring two seconds to move to the next one and set it, so all six would go off at once. Then they jumped up and sprinted back down the tunnel. All seven of them flopped down on the tunnel floor and pressed the heels of their hands over their ears.

With a deafening roar, the entire headwall of the tunnel blew inward. The Marines were already up and running toward it.

Helton, in the lead, was thinking, *I sure hope the inside mouth of the tunnel isn't five feet off the deck of the cavern, or something. A guy could break his leg that way.*

Through the smoke and dust, Dave could see the ghostly figures charging at them just before the first one leaped into the cavern. "Stand and fight!" he shouted. "It's our only chance."

Squint didn't even listen. His pockets laden with sunstones, he was squeezing through the narrow opening of the fissure. "*You* stay!" he shouted as he waddled heavily down the passage.

The three crouched and opened up with their pistols. One Marine went down. They might have a chance, after all. They began dodging around, to find a little cover and not be stationary targets. Jimmy drew down on the last Marine to jump into the cavern. The shot caught him and spun him around. He dropped his rifle, flopped on his belly, and lobbed a sleep–gas grenade with his good arm.

All the other Marines were spread out on the cavern floor, lying prone, propped on their elbows, and drenching the far corner of the cavern with automatic fire.

Dave was the last one they got, because he was the smartest and the quickest. As he broke cover to get to a better position, a burst stitched him up the right side. The impact threw him against the cavern wall, with his arms spread wide. His pistol flew out of his hand and skittered across the floor as he sagged down into a sitting position. As he died, he smiled at the Marine who had come up close to look at him.

Those outside heard the gunfire and shouts. It seemed like a year, but it was actually less than three minutes from the time the headwall blew until Helton came walking back out through the wisps of sleep–gas that were beginning to drift from the tunnel mouth. His men were close behind. One had his rifle at sling arms and with one hand was holding pressure on the wound in his other arm. Another had a knotted tourniquet on one leg and was hopping on the other, with his arms across the shoulders of the man on each side of him.

Helton stripped off his breathing gear. "You guys get over to the battalion surgeon," he said to the two wounded men and the two that were helping. "The other two; take an air–scrubber in there and start it up. Then you get over to the doc, too. Have him check you over."

"What happened?" Holloway put the inevitable question.

Helton looked down at the front of his body armor. With his thumb and index finger, he extracted a bullet from the chest area, held it up to the sunlight, smiled, and put it in his pants pocket. "Three tried to put up a fight," he said. "The other one made a run for it."

In the far distance there was the *pop–pop–pop–pop–pop* of automatic weapons fire, followed by a muffled explosion.

"I see they found the transportation and someone there tried to get away," Holloway said drily.

Helton smiled and nodded. "Might be our lost sheep. Maybe he had someone waiting for him. We may still have to flush him out."

Helton posted two guards at the tunnel mouth. "Nobody, but *nobody* has access to this place except myself and Commissioner Holloway. That includes the Captain and the Colonel and the Corporal of the Guard. I'm in charge of the dig, and this is part of the dig."

"What about Colonel O'Bannon?" one of the guards asked timidly.

"It includes Colonel O'Bannon, too. *Nobody.* Understand?"

They both looked unhappy and nodded.

Helton motioned to Holloway to follow him. "Come on,

Jack. I want your opinion about something.''

Gerd began to follow. Helton turned. ''Nobody but Jack or myself, I said. Sorry, Gerd.''

Gerd protested.

''Put it in writing,'' Helton said. ''What I said stands until I say different.''

Inside, the cavern was warm and large, with a high roof structure. It was also light inside—all the time. The roof and walls were studded with sunstones, excited to thermofluorescence by the geothermal heat of the mountain.

Jack's mouth fell open. ''There must be *millions* of them,'' he said as he slowly looked at the glowing lights. ''I see it, but I can't believe it. You did the right thing to clap the lid on this, Phil. If word of this gets out, it won't just start a Sunstone Rush—it'll start a Sunstone *War*.''

''Well, Ingermann's boys won't be telling anyone. That's probably who they were working for,'' Helton said. ''How would you go about explaining this place geologically?''

''For one thing,'' Holloway said, ''it's the answer to my speculations about 'the dying–place of the jellyfish,' and why the sunstone deposits get richer close to Fuzzy Divide.''

Jack kicked his toe in the rock powder on the cavern floor. ''This was the *original* dying–place of the jellyfish. If I were going to speculate, I'd say a bunch of the jellyfish died here, for whatever reason, and sank into what used to be a mud layer.'' He pointed to the roof of the cavern. ''Apparently North Beta and South Beta were once separate continents and this place was a shallow sea between them. As the tectonic plates drifted together, they pushed up this formation while the mud layer was still hardening into flint. Ground water slowly dissolved the limestone layer beneath the flint and made this cavern.'' He reached down and picked up a handful of the rock dust. ''That's what this stuff looks like to me— decomposed limestone.

''You did the right thing to put the lid on this, Phil,'' he repeated.

''That's not the real reason, though,'' Helton said. ''Come over here.''

Against one wall of the cavern was a row of instrument

racks, like computer consoles, perhaps, but totally alien–looking. There were pieces of furniture, desks and chairs—all about Fuzzy size. There were some Fuzzies there, as well, mummified by the warm, dry air of the cave and much better preserved than the remains that had been found in the wrecked starship. A recent earthquake had apparently opened the fissure through which Ingermann's stooges had entered the cavern, and the outside air was making the mummies start to deteriorate.

"Great Ghu," Jack said softly as he looked over the scene. "More Fuzzy bones."

XXX

"This is incredible!" Holloway said. "They must have been here at a time close to the crashing of the ship—at least before the rockslide that buried it. Why would they drag all this stuff up here from the wreck? Just to have something to play with?"

"Perhaps," Helton said. "The ones in here were trapped by the rockslide that closed the cavern. We'll have to date it out and see if both events were caused by the same rockslide."

"That might explain the Fuzzy bones in the ship. Gerd and Ruth will be able to date the remains. That will help tell you if there were two separate rockslides."

"Or," Helton said, "the survivors of the wreck may have been long–since picked up when the Fuzzies found it, and all this gear was left behind. The Fuzzies who died inside the wreck could have wandered in there and been killed by radiation leakage."

"Too easy," Jack said. "If there was all that much radiation leakage, it would have contaminated the whole area, and Fuzzies would have abandoned the place—not dragged all this electronic gear into the cave."

"Maybe they did," Helton said, "then came back later—much later. It's all too much for me. I'm going to have this stuff impounded and taken to Xerxes where it can be gone over properly."

Jack's mustache twitched. *"Just a minute!"* he said gruffly. "This stuff is on a legally established Fuzzy Reservation! It's *their* property, and, as Commissioner of Native Affairs, I intend to see they have some say–so about what's done with it."

Helton smiled. "Eventually, I suppose you will. In the meantime, I'm impounding it under Priority One. All perfectly legal. You'll get a copy of the inventory, and Governor

Rainsford will co-sign the order for its removal from the planetary surface. There are records and scientific apparatus here, not built by Terrans, and obviously never intended for use by Terrans. Under Federation Law, the Navy has the first priority for the examination of—let's see, the code states it . . . Oh, yes. 'Artifacts of unknown or unestablished origin.' ''

Holloway was silent for a moment, trying to think of a loophole in Priority One. He couldn't think of any. If anyone could, he should be the man. He'd been skating on the edge of the law on more planets than he could remember. ''Dammit,'' he said, ''you *are* within the law.''

''I guess Napier had a hunch about that when he put me in charge of the dig,'' Helton said. ''I will guarantee you one thing, though.''

''Which is?'' Holloway said.

''Tight security,'' Helton said. ''I'll have the battalion surgeon put those six guys in quarantine. They, and only they will pack this stuff up for transfer to Xerxes, and I'll have the chief psychologist there put them on ice. I'll also have Byers' boys drive a hatchway in the tunnel, keyed to yours and my thumbprints only.''

''And blast shut the tunnel that Ingermann's stooges came through,'' Holloway said.

Helton nodded.

''And what about the bodies?'' Holloway asked.

''I'll have the same six that blasted in here with me pack those up according to Dr. van Riebeek's specifications and cart them outside, where they will be turned over to him for further research and comparison.'' Helton waited for Jack's reply.

''Sounds airtight to me,'' Jack said.

Helton grinned. ''No such thing as totally airtight security, Jack, because it's handled by people. All the works of man are flawed by human nature in some way.''

''Well,'' Holloway said with a chuckle, ''I'll settle for what you've outlined. You're right—as usual. Xerxes is the only place around that has any chance of deciphering what's here.''

"Thank you," Helton said.

"Besides," Holloway continued, "we're going to have quite enough to do to keep the news of 'something big' out here from being all over the planet by sundown. I don't relish the size of the task."

"Do you want to be in here when I make the inventory?" Helton asked.

Holloway shrugged. "Not necessarily. I trust you."

"Well, you *could* help out," Helton said. "It'll go a lot faster if you measure and I write than if I do it all myself."

While Helton was expressing his displeasure to Chief Byers over the fact that a two–meter security hatchway could not be freighted from Xerxes and installed in the tunnel before morning, Colonial Governor Ben Rainsford and Attorney General Gus Brannhard were unraveling puzzles in Mallorysport.

"Now, what in Nifflheim did Ingermann hope to accomplish by sending his tame lawyer into court with a case like that?" Rainsford demanded. "Surely he knew Pendarvis wouldn't admit it on the issues framed in the complaint."

Gus Brannhard sloshed the whiskey in his glass. "Of course he did. He just wanted to tie things up for a while. If Pendarvis had scheduled the case for a preliminary hearing, that would have given the plaintiff certain 'Rights of Discovery,' the authority to subpoena records, take depositions, that sort of thing."

"Federated Sunstone Co–operative, indeed!" Rainsford jerked his pipe out of his pocket and began to tamp tobacco into the bowl. "Isn't a *real* prospector in the whole shebang!"

"The best he could have hoped for might be an injunction against the CZC and the colonial government entering into or pursuing *any* kind of joint ventures or leasing agreements." Brannhard rumbled, like a volcano preparing to erupt. He was chuckling. "Then, young Throckmorton had to 'beef up' the case by trying to sue the government for conspiracy. I bet Ingermann roasted him alive over that one."

"In the meantime," Rainsford grumped, "the press is

roasting me alive—especially the news analysts. I could throttle that young squirt at ZNS. Do you know he infiltrated my own staff? *My own staff*, by Ghu! They didn't have any useful information for him, though. They don't know any more about what's *really* going on over on North Beta than I do, which is precisely zero.''

Brannhard chuckled, again. ''Why, Ben, all you have to do is take a run over there and ask Jack. He'd tell you what's going on. I'm sure he would.''

''Well, *isn't that just fine!*'' Rainsford exploded. ''Take a run over to North Beta, the man says!'' Rainsford took his pipe out of his mouth and ticked off his points on the fingers of his other hand. ''The Constitutional Convention is coming to a fast boil. There are crazy rumors all over town. I've been going on screen every night to try and pacify people. 'There, there—nothing to worry about, folks; just digging up a little old spaceship wreck over there. Everything's gonna be just fine.' For every yard of wool I get knit together, Ingermann and his gang come along behind me and unravel it before I can get home to watch myself on the screen. People are going nuts in the streets. Junktown is like a combat zone: the only thing that's holding it together is that priest fella down there with his soup kitchen. That reminds me, I want to talk to him.'' Rainsford made a quick note into his stenomemophone. ''Haven't had a good night's sleep in Ghu knows how long. And you want me to drop everything and take a little junket over to North Beta. Don't you go losing your marbles on me, too, Gus. Do you have any idea how foolish a man feels, standing up there shooting his mouth off just like he knew what he was talking about?''

Brannhard shrugged and refurbished his drink. ''It was only a suggestion, Ben.''

''Sure,'' Rainsford said. ''Easy for you to say. I'm the one that has to stand in front of that pickup and try to sound like I know what's what, when I have no idea how it's going to come out. You try *that,* some time and see how ridiculous it makes you feel.''

''I do,'' Brannhard said quietly.

''*When?*'' Rainsford demanded.

"Every time I take a case to trial," Brannhard replied.

"Hmmmph!" Rainsford grunted as he re-lighted his pipe. "And the CZC," Rainsford said, jabbing the air with his pipestem. "That's another thing. They're about as much help as a zebralope in heat, lately."

Brannhard looked genuinely alarmed for the first time in the conversation. "They're not holding back on the support Grego promised the government, are they?"

"No, no; nothing like that," Rainsford said. "Victor just doesn't seem to have his mind on what he's doing some of the time. It's that Fuzzy-sitter of his; that's what it is."

"Christiana Stone?" Brannhard asked.

"That's the one," Rainsford said. He leaned forward in his chair. "Do you know," he whispered, "I was over there the other evening, and I saw them holding hands in the kitchen."

Brannhard grinned, showing white teeth through his gray-brown beard. "Why, you old snoop," he said.

"I was *not* snooping!" Rainsford declared. "I just happened to see it. That's all."

The midnight to 0400 shift had just gone on guard at the tunnel mouth as Helton left the cavern after thoroughly taping its contents. The tape would stay on his person until he had transmitted it to Commodore Napier—then it would be erased.

"Remember, guys," Helton said to the two Marines, "nobody goes in there except Commissioner Holloway or myself. Got that clear?"

They nodded. "Right, Gunnie," one of them said.

As soon as Helton was out of sight, one of the sentries whispered to his buddy. "Jim?"

"Whattaya want, Ev?" the other one said.

"Why would they leave the lights on in there?" Everett Diehl asked.

"How do you know the lights are on?" Jim Spelvin said. "There's a tarp over the far end of the tunnel."

Diehl smirked. "I sneaked a peek when the Gunnie came

out. He had his back to me while he pulled the tarp—and he left the lights on.''

"Aw, don't worry about it," Spelvin said.

"Well, it seems damned funny; that's all," Diehl said.

"Maybe he's drying fruit in there!" Spelvin said exasperatedly. "How should I know why he left the lights on? Bad enough we should get the mid–watch. We're the rankers in the guard mount. How come the privates draw the easy hours?''

"Akor said he wanted NCOs on the mid–watch," Diehl said.

"Malarkey!" Spelvin said. "He put us on the mid–watch because he doesn't like us. He never has liked us. We're the rankers and he gives us the dirty jobs.''

Perhaps a half–hour passed with neither of them saying anything.

"Jim?"

Spelvin started. "Now whattaya want? Do you know how hard it is to sleep standing up?''

"I'm going in and take a look," Diehl said.

"That's crazy," Spelvin said. "Why bother? We won't have to turn this drill again. I heard they're going to set a security hatch in the tunnel tomorrow morning.''

"That's what I mean," Diehl said. "If we don't look now, we'll never get another chance.''

Spelvin was silent for a moment. "What if we get caught?''

"Aw, there won't be anybody around to check on us for at least another hour," Diehl said. "Besides, if you see anybody coming, you can throw a pebble down the tunnel. I can beat it back out here before they're close enough to see I'm gone.''

Spelvin was thinking, a feat which required every ounce of his attention. Presently, he said, "Okay. You go first, but then I get to go look, too.''

"That's fair," Diehl said.

Only a few meters inside the tunnel, there was no light at all. Diehl turned around and looked back the way he had come, as though reassuring himself that the tunnel mouth was still there. Then he proceeded slowly, with his arms out-stretched to the sides to keep himself in the middle of the tunnel. Periodically, he would sweep one hand in front of himself, but soon he began to see a dim corona of light seeping around the edges of the tarp.

He took a deep breath, then slipped between the tarp and the rocks at the lip of the tunnel entrance.

Corporal Diehl's mouth fell open. He tried to voice some profane expression of astonishment, but discovered that he couldn't make a sound. He blinked in the comparatively bright light. He staggered forward to the center of the cavern. His rifle sling slipped off his shoulder and the weapon fell to the cave floor, but he didn't notice. He stopped and turned around and around, looking at the polychromatic glow above him.

Finally, he realized that he couldn't remember how long he had been there, except that he felt slightly dizzy. He took out his pocket knife and went over to one of the sidewalls, intent on prying loose a couple of sunstones to take with him.

He didn't notice the bloodstains on the wall, but was happy to put away his knife when he saw a handful of sunstones scattered loose on the floor. He scooped up a half dozen or so, retrieved his rifle, and hurried back the way he had come.

"Jeez!" hissed Spelvin. "What took you so long? I was beginning to get worried."

"G—g—go see for yourself," Diehl stammered. He still couldn't talk straight.

If Mr. Justice Pendarvis was harried by the chaos that reigned in both the legal system and the proceedings of the Constitutional Convention, he showed no outward signs of it.

The Chairman, a chubby Ph.D. with a beard, had called the convention to order at 1000 hours, and announced that he had requested Judge Pendarvis to make a few remarks of an advisory nature.

The delegates immediately began to whisper and mutter comments between themselves.

A hush fell over the convention as Pendarvis walked across

the platform. He was tall, slender, and walked with a slow and measured step. It was rumored that he could turn an attorney to stone with a single baleful gaze.

"Esteemed delegates," he began. "It is with both pleasure and humility that I have accepted Dr. Pine's invitation to address this convention. I have devoted most of my life to the law, and so it comes about that my sincerest hope in this situation is to be of help to this body in framing and adopting a constitution for the planet of Zarathustra." He paused, looking over the delegates, and was pleased to notice that he had them hanging on his every word. It had been a couple of decades since he had pleaded a case. It was satisfying to see that he had not lost his touch. "It is with interest that I have noted your proceedings, ladies and gentlemen. While it is not without weight that there are a multitude of issues to be settled before such a document can be properly drawn, it is, I'm sure you must agree, also true that many of these issues are somewhat extraneous to the task at hand. This in no way diminishes their importance; it just makes for tough going. As some of you must know," he continued, "the court dockets are bulging. However, I will entertain some suits in equity, affidavits, and veridicated depositions designed to clarify those issues that do not directly bear on adopting a constitution and set aside matters that are clouding the points of law which this Constitution must soon decide. The law is the rock upon which any government must be built. Such has been the case for as long as I have been on Zarathustra, and so long as I am alive, it will continue to be the case.

"Now, then, who has some questions for me?"

At mid-morning in Fuzzy Valley, Sergeant Beltrán heard a familiar voice at the back hatch of his kitchen scow.

"What make do?" Little Fuzzy asked.

"Yeh, *Sahdge,*" Starwatcher echoed. "What make do?"

The Upland Fuzzies had picked up the ability to speak within Terran hearing range in record time. They had caught on to the habit of mid-morning coffee-break even more quickly—except that for them it was *estee-fee* break.

"Hi, kids," Beltrán said, chewing on his eternal cigar.

"You like *estee–fee?*"

Loud noises of approval from Little Fuzzy, Starwatcher, and the four Upland Fuzzies who accompanied them. It had become a ritual between them, much like the Terran habit of shaking hands in greeting.

Beltrán pulled one of the blue–labeled tins off the stowage shelf and blew the dust off of it. The supply of Extee–Three was beginning to run a bit low. Have to do something about that. He'd never be able to convince ration supply that someone was actually *eating* the stuff. Well, a little trading around could get that straightened out. That's how NCOs make a living, isn't it—trading stuff around among themselves?

After the Fuzzies had finished off their treat, they made solemn introductions between Beltrán and the four new Fuzzies, with Beltrán squatting on his haunches and seriously shaking each one's tiny hand in turn.

The Fuzzies crowded around him. "What make do, *Unka Vida'?*"

"Yeh, *Sahge;* what make do?"

Beltrán pulled down a bag from above his desk. "Ahem," he said. "Inasmuch as Starwatcher, here, is the leader of the Upland Fuzzies, and inasmuch as he has graciously allowed us to camp within his territory, the men of the First Battalion would like to present this badge of office to him."

He drew out the tiny barracks cover, expertly cut down to fit a Fuzzy, with a handmade twelve–pointed star for an insignia badge, and ceremoniously placed it on Starwatcher's head.

The Fuzzies were delighted. They whooped and howled, and some of them lapsed into loud yeeks within their own speech range.

"Lemme think," Beltrán said absently. "Mirror. Mirror. Where's a mirror?" Ah, there was a mirror over the lavatory where the cooks washed their hands. But, it was screwed to the bulkhead. Well, no matter.

He picked up Starwatcher and held him up in front of the mirror. Let's see, that was too high, and standing him on the edge of the lavatory was too low. He hoisted the Fuzzy up on his shoulder and steadied him with one hand. Starwatcher sat back and regarded his own reflection very seriously. Then he looked sidewise at Beltrán. Then he reached up with tiny hands and cocked the barracks cover over to one side and snugged the little visor down above his right eye. He contemplated this for a moment before nodding approval. Then he threw his arms around Beltrán's neck and hugged it vigorously.

Beltrán's cigar fell into the sink, but he didn't care. He had made a Fuzzy very happy.

Hugo Ingermann's eyes lighted up with unconcealed glee. "An inside man at the CZC you say? One with a direct pipeline to Grego, himself?"

Ivan Bowlby preened himself, like the proud little bird he was. "Yes, Mr. Ingermann, and I don't think the information we'll be getting will be too outrageously expensive—considering."

"Well, who, man," Ingermann asked eagerly, "who?"

Bowlby wagged a finger. "Now, now," he said. "It's my contact. You'll have to be content to work through me on this matter."

Ingermann's neck began to swell. The expression of joy on his face was replaced with one of rising anger. "Why, you son of a Khooghra! You're trying to put the squeeze on me, aren't you?"

Bowlby took the hankie from his jacket pocket and sniffed at it. "Sticks and stones, Mr. Ingermann," he said. "Sticks and stones. If I'm forced to put this information out to the highest bidder, you'll see how utterly reasonable I'm being in my offer of it to you exclusively."

Ingermann's face began to redden.

"And no rough stuff, either," Bowlby cautioned. "There is another go-between below my level. If something happens to me, then you'll be forced to deal with him, and he may not feel the generosity toward you that I have come to know during our long and profitable association together."

"All right!" Ingermann said suddenly. "I'll give your 'inside man' a try for two weeks. Two weeks—no more. If I'm not satisfied, then you can both go to Nifflheim!"

"Done," Bowlby said quietly and extended his hand.

XXXI

"Helton!" O'Bannon roared from inside his tent. "Is that yourself?" Actually, it wasn't a roar, but the tone of voice was pretty tense for the unflappable Lieutenant Colonel James O'Bannon.

Helton raised his eyebrows. An observance of the niceties of protocol seemed indicated. "Yes, sir!" Helton barked. "Permission to enter—*sir!*"

"Come in!" O'Bannon barked back at him.

Helton stepped through the tent portal and snapped to an attention brace with a deafening clack of boot-heels.

O'Bannon was in his sock feet and seated at his field console. "Sit down," he said simply, with a wave toward the other field chair.

Helton sat.

O'Bannon fixed him with a cold look. "Exactly *why* does Commodore Napier want to see us?" he asked. "Have you gone and put my tail in a crack?"

"His indication to me, Colonel," Helton said, "was that he desired to de-brief us on the contents of the cavern."

O'Bannon waved his hand as if at some triviality. "Well, then," he said, "there's no need for me to go along. I haven't the least notion of what's in the cavern." He glared at Helton. "Because they won't let me in the damned place!" He paused. "My own damned troops, and they won't let me in the place! Perhaps you might be able to explain that in some way that I can understand."

Helton pursed his lips and inhaled.

"Well?" O'Bannon snapped.

"It's part of the dig, sir. You put me in charge of the dig. That is a part of the dig, and I have declared it off-limits to everyone. I have this tape—"

"Lest you lose track of things, Gunnie," O'Bannon

hissed, "I am in *command* of this operation. *Nothing* is off–limits to me!"

"I felt the Colonel should look at this tape before I take him into the cavern," Helton said, deftly switching to the more formal third–person form of address. "I have to destroy the tape after the Colonel has looked at it."

"Helton," O'Bannon said, "I looked your record over pretty thoroughly before I put this kind of responsibility on you—Master Gunnie or no Master Gunnie. But, by Ghu's guts, you have overstepped yourself!"

Helton looked at O'Bannon directly. "Would the Colonel like to rant and rave some more, or would he prefer to see the tape at this time?" he asked evenly.

O'Bannon had been looking at his own feet. Without moving his head, he lifted his gaze and peered at Helton through his eyebrows.

Commodore Alex Napier closed the folio in front of him and arranged it in the exact center of his desk. There was no sound in his domed office, except an occasional double click as photo cells acted to close one segment of the sunscreen and open another.

He tapped the heel from his pipe, blew through the stem, and carefully refilled the bowl with tobacco. After lighting the pipe, he puffed lightly on it and stared at the floor for several minutes. Then, he leaned forward and punched out a combination on his communications screen. The burst of colors solidified into the face of a smooth–cheeked young ensign, the duty officer in the Operations Center.

"Yes, sir," the ensign responded.

"Get me your boss, Mister," Napier said.

"Commander Johnsen?" the ensign asked.

"He *is* the Ops Officer, isn't he?" Napier said.

The ensign swallowed. "Yes, sir," he said.

"Thank you," Napier said.

Momentarily, a man with iron–gray hair, wearing the insignia of a full commander appeared. "Yes, Commodore," he said.

"Carl," Napier said, "is the *Ranger* still our fastest corvette?"

"Yes, sir," Johnsen said, "she is. She's fitted and provisioned for emergency launch right now."

"How soon can she be provisioned with Class–A rations and fully manned?" Napier asked.

"Six to twelve hours, Commodore," Johnsen said. "She's on half–crew liberty."

"Mmmm," Napier said. "Well, Carl, there's no dreadful rush about it, but I'll have a courier mission for her in the next few days—week at the most."

"I'll put her on standby alert," Johnsen said.

"Thank you, Carl," Napier said. He blanked the screen and punched out another combination—this time to the private office screen of his Executive Officer, Captain Conrad Greibenfeld.

Greibenfeld was just sitting down behind his desk when the screen cleared. Apparently he had been out of his office. "Yes, Alex?" he said, using the first–name address, since there were no junior officers or enlisted men within earshot.

"Connie," Napier said, "I need a good Class–A agent—one with an impeccable security record."

"Sure, Alex," Greibenfeld said. "How long will you need him?"

"Might be quite a while," Napier said. "I want him attached to my personal staff."

Greibenfeld looked slightly uncomfortable. He liked to be in on everything, and here was "something" he was obviously not in on. "Very good, sir," he said. "I'll send you a selection to choose from. Say, three of them?"

Napier smiled. "That won't be necessary, Connie," he said. "Just pick the one with the most spotless record and highest fitness rating from the qualified Class–A agents on the station."

"Yes, sir," Greibenfeld said. "I'll get right on it, personally."

Napier chuckled. "Don't look so pained, Connie. You'll find out all about it at the meeting."

"What meeting?" Greibenfeld asked suddenly.

"The one you'll get about an hour's notice on," Napier said, and blanked the screen.

Everett Diehl rolled over in his bunk, rubbed the sleep out of his eyes, and stretched. That was the only good part about drawing the mid-watch; you could sleep until noon that morning, if you wanted to. Then, Diehl remembered what had happened in the cavern the night before. It seemed like a dream, now. Quickly, he reached down and scrambled one hand into his right boot, pulling out the sock he had wadded up in it. Carefully, he opened the sock and was relieved to see the half-dozen shiny pebbles inside. He warmed them between his hands. They started to glow softly. It wasn't a dream. What he had seen was true; maybe an acre of cavern roof and walls, thickly embedded with sunstones.

"Jim?" he said. "You awake?"

Spelvin's head emerged from under the pillow in the next bunk. "I am now," he said. "What time is it?"

"1030," Diehl said.

"1030?" Spelvin grumped. "Why the Nifflheim did you wake me up if it's only 1030?"

"I can't sleep," Diehl said simply. "Jim? Did you pick some up, too?"

"Some what?" Spelvin asked sleepily.

"Sunstones," Diehl said.

Spelvin sat bolt upright in his bunk. "Shhhh!" he hissed, looking over his shoulder.

"It's all right," Diehl said. "There's nobody in the barracks but us. Did you pick some up, too?"

"Yeah," Spelvin said, scratching himself. "A few," he lied. He had nearly half a sock full of the precious gems. The time that Diehl had spent gaping in wonderment, Spelvin had spent gathering up loose sunstones—some undoubtedly spilled from the pockets of the late Mr. Squint—right up to the place where a cataclysmite charge had collapsed the fissure at the rear of the cavern.

"Y'know, Jim," Diehl said, "I been thinkin'. We could sell a couple of these apiece and pay off Laporte, once and for all."

"Sure," Spelvin said scornfully. "Right away he'll start wondering where we got that much money all at once. It oughta take about ten minutes for him to find out that we had sold some sunstones to get the money."

"So?" Diehl said.

"So Raul Laporte is the kind of guy that would beat us to a pulp and pull out our fingernails one at a time till we told him what we know," Spelvin said. "In the end of it, we'll be out our sunstones, *and* the information."

"Well, what're we gonna do then?" Diehl whined.

Dense as he was, there was a reason for Spelvin being a junior sergeant while Diehl was a corporal. "We'll tell him what we know in exchange for him wiping out our debt. I think the information is worth that much. *Dumb*–bell," Spelvin said.

"So what're gonna do with the sunstones?" Diehl asked.

"Nothing," Spelvin said. "If we try to sell 'em on Zarathustra, somebody is going to get nosy about how come two Marines got hold of some sunstones—especially two Marines from this particular battalion."

"You mean we could *still* wind up gettin' our fingernails pulled out," Diehl said.

"Now you got it," Spelvin said. "We just put 'em away until we get transferred to some other planet. They'll bring at least three times as much anyplace but Zarathustra, anyway. We sell 'em off one or two at a time and put the money away, see?"

"Yeah," Diehl said dreamily. "It would work out to a whole bunch of sols, all right."

"Then, maybe we can get out of these green suits," Spelvin said, "and start living like human beings. Maybe buy a little business someplace, maybe a little restaurant and tavern."

"Maybe our own little whorehouse, too," Diehl said dreamily.

Gerd van Riebeek laid the binocular loupe and went back into his office. His own observations jibed with the report abstract, but it all seemed a bit odd to him. Well, it would all hinge on whether there was one rockslide or two. He still felt uneasy about the test results. There was something—something he couldn't put his finger on.

"Yet," he said out loud in his empty office. "Not yet we got it. Eventually, though, we will." He thumbed the intercom on his communications screen.

A thin, middle-aged face materialized before him. "Haskins, here," said an efficient-looking man in a white lab coat.

"Bill, how are you doing on the sides analysis of those rock samples?" Gerd asked.

"I've cross-typed and done weathering comparisons with freshly-broken faces," Haskins said. "I've still a little double-checking to do, but it looks to me as if it was all one rock-slide. The tape records are quite clear. There's absolutely no overlap of weather aging or solar radiation absorbtion in sample belt 'B'. It all came down at the same time. I'll have a final for you this afternoon or early tomorrow."

"Thank you, Bill," Gerd said and blanked the screen.

He was still drumming his fingers on the console and staring out the window at his pet featherleaf tree when Ruth came in the office with a sheaf of printout in her hand.

"Gerd—" she began.

"Have you seen the datings on the two sets of Fuzzy bones?" he asked her abruptly.

"Why, yes," Ruth said. "I did some of the fractioning analyses myself. Why?"

"Anything strike you as odd about the comparisons?" Gerd asked her.

"Not chemically," she said. "Not until—"

"There's something odd there," he interrupted, "but I can't quite put my finger on it."

She sat down and laid the printout on his desk. It was obvious she wasn't going to get a word in about it until Gerd got around to what he was pondering over. "Well," she said, "what is it?"

Gerd leaned back in his chair and laced his fingers together on top of his head. "The Fuzzy bones in the starship are about three hundred years older than the Fuzzy bones from the cave," he said simply. "It doesn't make sense."

"You mean it doesn't make sense to *you*," Ruth said. "What's so odd about it?"

"That's just it," Gerd said. "I can't put my finger on it. Something to do with Fuzzies burying their dead. The ones that were trapped in the cave; that I can understand. They couldn't get at them to bury them. But what about the ones in the ship? Why were they left there?"

"Radiation?" Ruth suggested.

"Did you find any radiation abnormalities in the remains?" Gerd asked her.

"No," she said, "but it could have been short–life radiation. Fuzzies don't know anything about nuclear hazards. If some of them got into the ship and died, the rest would studiously avoid the place, I would think."

"Mmmmm," Gerd said. "I guess that will have to wait for engineering data. After the Navy is through tearing everything apart, they may be able to decipher what the ship's drive was and tell us something about potentials for radiation leakage."

"And types," she said.

"And types," Gerd agreed. He leaned forward in his chair and began riffling through the stack of printout. "What's this?" he asked.

"This," Ruth said, "is what I came in here about in the first place."

"Which is?" Gerd asked.

"Which is," Ruth said, "what I've been trying to get a word in edgewise about since I got here. Namely, my readouts show that there was a much higher concentration of anti–NFMp in the Fuzzy bones in the wreck than in the Fuzzy bones in the cave."

Gerd carefully and deliberately shook a cigarette out of the pack on his desk, lighted it, and leaned back in his chair once again. "Questions, questions, questions," he said, staring at the ceiling. "Why do we always have more questions than answers?"

"Send him in, Myra," Victor Grego said to the image in the intercom screen.

The uniformed man who entered Grego's office shut the door behind himself. That figured. Anything important enough to bring Harry Steefer over in person must be pretty confidential. The Company Police Chief was not a messenger boy.

"Afternoon, Harry," Grego said, motioning him to a chair. "What is it?"

Steefer could not conceal the fact that he was pleased about something. "We've finally done it, Victor. We have penetrated the ZNPF. Our man has managed to wangle himself an assignment to the liaison patrol up there in Fuzzy Valley where all those Marines are milling about."

"What has he found out?" Grego asked.

"Precious little, so far," Steefer replied, handing over a slender folder, "but there's more there than meets the eye."

Grego lighted a cigarette, flipped open the folder, and absently scratched his Adam's apple as he looked over the report.

"The very fact that he can't find out anything means there's plenty worth finding out," Grego said. "Uh—the Colonial Investigations Bureau doesn't know about him, do they?"

Steefer grinned. "Course not. Then it wouldn't be a secret anymore, would it?"

Steefer was no sooner out the door than Grego's private screen chimed. He keyed it on. "Why, hello, Christiana," he said. "You're looking lovely this afternoon."

"Thank you, Mr. Grego," she said, slightly flustered. It was her normal reaction to a compliment—especially one from Victor Grego. Then she frowned slightly. "I was wondering, Mr. Grego, if I could have the afternoon off. I—I have some things to attend to."

"Where's Diamond?" Grego asked.

She brightened. "Oh, he's over at Company House, playing with Flora and Fauna. I'll be back in time to get him."

Grego held up a hand. "No need, my dear. I'm going over there, myself, as soon as I can break away from here. I'll bring him back home. You take as long as you like."

"Thank you, Mr. Grego," she said.

"Christiana," Grego said. "Are you all right? I mean, is anything wrong?"

"Oh, no," she said. "I—I guess I just have my mind on my errands."

"Dinner?" he asked.

"I don't know how long I'll be," she said. "I'll screen you, either at Governor Rainsford's or at home."

"Okay," he said and blanked the screen.

It was a dingy, gray afternoon, with a misting rain coming from the overcast sky and slanting across Mallorysport. The esplanade was practically deserted. Christiana held up the collar of her coat against the rain and the chilly wind that was driving it.

What was she going to do? Sooner or later the man in the hat was going to wise up that she was giving him pretty innocuous information, with just enough important nuggets in it to keep the charade going. She couldn't betray Grego, and yet she couldn't go on like this. It made her feel dirty. She couldn't risk letting him find out about her past. She might lose him. That made her feel dirty, too.

The rain started coming down harder as she ducked in through the door of the *La Rondo*.

XXXII

The entry door chimed. Ben Rainsford came out of his kitchen, drying his hands on a towel he had pulled through the belt of his bush–jacket. He had tried having someone else cook and wash up for him, but they just never got things quite the way he wanted them, and they were never around when he was trying to find something for himself. The fits of temper he got into trying to find where the cook had hidden his favorite paring knife just weren't worth whatever the convenience was supposed to be.

Rainsford opened the door, then extended his hand. "Victor," he said. "How nice to see you."

"Yes," Grego said, shaking hands. "I might say the same, Bennett. We ought to get together more often."

Rainsford's face took on a mournful look. "If we ever get a minute to ourselves," he said. "I imagine you have just as many chucklewits running to you these days as I do; dithering over some problem they could solve themselves if they'd just stop and think it out."

"Amen to that," Grego said, stepping into the foyer. He reached down and tugged lightly at the towel. "Doing a little surgery, are you?" he asked.

"Just tidying up in the kitchen," Rainsford said as he pulled the towel free and draped it over one shoulder.

Grego's eyebrows went up. "How do you find the time to do your own housekeeping?" he asked.

Rainsford explained the entropy factor of it, then added, "I have a woman come in to clean and dust once a week. We have an understanding. She doesn't touch my desk or anything in the kitchen except the floor, and I give her money."

Rainsford was about to say something else when they were suddenly overrun by Fuzzies. Even when there were only three of them it sometimes seemed like a hundred Fuzzies.

"Heyo, Pappy Vic," Diamond whooped joyously. "What make do?" He braced himself and slid the last several feet on the foyer's highly–polished floor, then clamped his tiny arms around Grego's leg to regain his balance.

Flora and Fauna were in hot pursuit, howling noisily. "Heyo, Unka Vic. Heyo! Heyo, Pappy Ben. You no say Unka Vic come."

Rainsford gathered them both in his arms and picked them up. "Pappy Ben forgot," he said. "Pappy Ben, Unka Vic have Big One talk to make. How about Extee–Three? *So–siggo esteefee?*"

"*Hoksu fusso,*" they shrieked in delight. "*Bizzo–asho. Esteefee! Nozzo so–siggo esteefee.*" With that, they both leaped from Rainsford's arms, tumbled end over end on the floor a couple of times until they got their footing, and all three scampered into the kitchen.

Grego winced. At first it looked as though they were going to break their necks.

"How about you, Victor?" Rainsford said, as he turned toward the kitchen. "You care for some *tosh–ki waji?* It's a good half hour before my guest arrives."

"At this point," Grego said, "I think a cocktail is a wonderful idea."

Since they weren't in the habit of running everywhere they went, it took Rainsford and Grego a bit longer to reach the kitchen. The Fuzzies were hopping up and down in eager anticipation. Rainsford had taught them early–on not to climb on things in the house without permission.

"Where's Christiana?" Rainsford asked as he opened a cupboard and rummaged around for one of the familiar blue–labeled tins.

"Yes," Diamond demanded. "Why no Auntie Ki'stanna?"

"She had some errands to run," Grego said, half to Rainsford and half to Diamond, "and, since I was coming over anyway, there wasn't any reason for both of us to make the trip." Diamond's face took on a pouting look. "We'll likely see her later this evening," he said to Diamond. "Now have your esteefee treat."

Rainsford set the tin on the counter with a plate, and a knife for dividing it.

"Bizzo so," Flora and Fauna clamored, waving their arms for Diamond to hurry. In what was obviously a well—rehearsed drill, Flora and Fauna laced their fingers together into a stirrup, so Diamond could get a leg up and climb onto the counter top.

He expertly ran the can through the opener and sliced it into manageable portions almost faster than the eye could follow. And why not? A table knife is not so much different from a steel *shoppo—diggo*. Diamond handed the plate down to Flora and Fauna, picked up the empty tin and its lid, walked to the end of the counter, and dropped it in the trash. He glanced at the two Terran humans and made a slight but decisive movement of his head—as if to say, "See what good house manners I have?" He picked up three tiny plastic tumblers, which used to be two—ounce measuring cups, nested them together, and tossed them down to Fauna. He jumped off the counter with a squeal of glee, landed lightly on the floor, and all three of them went pelting back out onto the south lawn, where they would fill the water cups at the fountain and make Fuzzy—talk while Ben and Vic made Big—One talk.

"Why in Nifflheim do they want to go out in this drizzle?" Grego asked.

"Mmmmmm?" Rainsford said absently as he finished mixing a four—portion jug full of cocktails and poked the stopper into it. "Oh, they won't get wet. They'll all sit in Flora and Fauna's pup—tent, which the Marines—ah—liberated for me, watch it rain, eat their Extee—Three, and have a grand time." Rainsford paused with his hand on the cupboard door. "Did you ever have a tree—house when you were a kid, Victor?" he asked, his hand still poised on the knob of the cupboard door.

"No," Grego said. "No, I didn't have a tree—house, but one place we lived had a lilac thicket next to the house. I was about nine, I guess. I hollowed out that lilac thicket—carefully, a little bit at a time, so no one would know. If you knew where the entrance was, you could get in; if you didn't, it was just a big lilac bush.'' He shrugged. ''Must've been about six feet tall—a lot taller than I was, anyway. On hot summer days, I'd crawl in there and read. It was absolutely perfect. Quite enough light, and it was cool and smelled so good I can't begin to describe it.''

Both men stared into the distance, not really seeing each other, but looking into the past.

''I had a tree–house,'' Rainsford said. ''I worked like a slave getting the roof weather–tight. I liked to go up there when it rained. When there was an electrical storm, I'd go up there and spend the night. Damned wonder I wasn't struck by lightning.'' Suddenly, Rainsford jerked open the cupboard door and took down two glasses. ''Well, let's go in the living room, shall we? There are a couple of mutual goals I want to chat with you about before my guest arrives.''

When they were comfortably situated, Rainsford filled his pipe and lighted it. ''When are you going to file a suit to regain the CZC charter?'' he asked. That was one thing about Ben; he always got right to the point.

Grego blinked with surprise he couldn't conceal, then recovered. ''Why, Bennett,'' he said, ''what possible causes of action could we use to frame such a complaint?''

Rainsford leaned back in his chair and laughed heartily, making his bristly red whiskers shake with mirth. ''Oh, Victor,'' he chuckled. ''It's no wonder you're Manager–in–Chief. You're as smooth as a tilbra's belly.''

''I *think* that's a compliment,'' Grego said, ''but I repeat—how could we hope to get such a case into court, much less think of winning it?''

Rainsford wiped his eyes and leaned forward, suddenly serious. ''You know, Victor, just because I spent a lot of time over on Beta, counting tree–rings and banding birds, a lot of people think I'm an eccentric old fud who has staffed the government with roughnecks and has about as much business being Governor General as a khooghra does being an archbishop.''

''You're nothing like Nick Emmert. That's for sure,'' Grego said. ''A few people have found some difficulty getting used to that.''

"Well, Victor," Rainsford said, "the point is this—just so we can stop being coy. You think I don't know about Garrett's Theorem? I'm a xeno–naturalist, and not one that just popped out of college with a diploma stuck in my ear. I've been keeping touch with van Riebeek's research on this NFMp hormone thing. It's no secret, either, that the Company Science Center is drilling a few holes along this line of reasoning. Now, whatever the Navy is onto over on North Beta, there's more to it than some anonymous starship. Yes, yes," he interjected, "I was there when they dug it out and saw it with my own eyes."

"What makes you *think* there's more to it than that?" Grego asked.

Rainsford smiled. "The simple fact that Alex Napier won't tell the Governor General—me—anything more about it. The information I was getting from him just levelled out and stopped at that point."

"If *you* can't get anything out of him, what can the Company do?" Grego asked.

"Why, file a lawsuit in Central Courts, alleging that there are no sapient beings on Zarathustra who are *native to the planet*. Therefore, the Company's charter was unlawfully voided—or voided by mistake if you want to put it more politely. As a principal party in such an action, that will give the Company certain Rights of Discovery to make legal establishment of information that now has its legal existence on the basis of 'to the best of knowledge and belief.' You'll be able to take veridicated depositions, and they'll have to open records for your examination which you wouldn't otherwise be able to get your hands on."

"Sounds like you've been talking to Gus Brannhard," Grego said.

Rainsford snorted. "You bet your boots I have! What's the good of an Attorney General if he isn't the slipperiest lawyer on the planet? Gus says there's precedent in colonial law for this sort of thing. The Chartered Yggsdrasil Company took a whack at it after the Yggsdrasil Khooghra was declared sapient. They lost, of course, because they didn't have much of a case. Maybe they had the wrong lawyer. Gus could probably have gotten them at least a draw—and tied up the courts with the case long enough for the Company to bail out its investment."

Grego decided then and there not to tell Rainsford anything remotely connected with his spy in the ZNPF or the fact that he had Leslie Coombes digging through colonial case law, looking for applications of Garrett's Theorem. He sipped his drink and smiled. *The old boy's been doing his homework,* Grego thought. *Everyone thinks he just fusses with that ghastly pipe—when he's not arguing with someone or throwing a temper tantrum.* "Why are you being so good to me, Bennett?" he asked.

Rainsford fussed with his pipe for a moment. "Aw, hell, Victor," he said, slightly embarrassed. "I've been worried about you. You've been mooning around over that girl like a lovesick banjo–bird. And I—well—let's just say I know how that sort of thing can distort a man's perspective."

"I didn't know it showed," Grego said, unruffled.

"Not to everyone, maybe," Rainsford said, "but to me, it shows."

"You think my judgement is out the airlock?" Grego asked.

Rainsford squirmed a bit. "Now, I didn't say that, Victor," he said. "I just said I've been concerned."

"And you want me to try and get the Company's charter back," Grego said, "so I can resume my role as 'the petty despot of Zarathustra.' You once called me that several times, you know."

"Well, dammit," Rainsford said irritably, "you'd better make an effort at it. You've got a Board of Directors to answer to. They'll be standing in your hip pockets before long. I expect a gaggle of them to show up every time a ship docks on Darius."

"That's not their way," Grego said quietly. "They'll send out some spies, first. Just to see if they need to bring a rope with them when they do come."

"But are you *doing* anything about it, confound it," Rainsford said.

"The Company is looking after its interests," Grego replied. "You realize, of course, that if we do get the charter back, you'll be out of a job."

Rainsford chuffed on his pipe. "No; I'll be out of *this* job—" He lifted his eyes toward the ceiling. "—something I have been devoutly hoping for ever since Alex Napier shoehorned me into it."

Grego stubbed out his cigarette and held out his glass for the refill Rainsford proferred from the now unstoppered jug. Rainsford set the jug back on the coffee table. Both men looked at each other for a moment.

"The Company," Grego said, "in such an eventuality, would petition that you be retained as Resident–General."

"I don't *want* to be Resident–General," Rainsford insisted, "*or* Governor General. I want to go back over to Beta and help out at Fuzzy Institute."

"Well," Grego said, "there's no blinding rush to come to a decision at this point. I just wanted you to know that I think you've been doing pretty good, and—"

The chiming of the entry door interrupted.

Rainsford leaped to his feet. "Ah!" he said. "That will be—mmmmm—" He rummaged around in his pocket, took out a slip of paper, and read from it. "The Right Reverend Father Thomas Aquinas Gordon. We will now see what's what with this so-called whiskey priest who's supposed to be holding Junktown together with his fingernails. I want your opinion about his young fella, Victor. That's the main reason I asked you over here." He straightened his bush jacket and started for the door.

Outside, The Rev put the palm of his hand in front of his face, blew at it and quickly inhaled through his nose—for perhaps the twentieth time since leaving the mission. It wouldn't make a good first impression for his breath to betray the fact that he'd had a couple of bracers beforehand. Meetings with Colonial Governors General were not occurrences that happened to him frequently. He was nervous, but his head was quite clear. That was the trouble; his head was always clear. Perhaps the true loss of innocence occurred when one reached the point of being able to see through every sham, con–game, deliberate lie, and frailty to which the human spirit was subject.

"And they wonder why I drink," he muttered to himself, just as the door was opened by a rumpled little man with bristly red whiskers, who looked like he had just come out of the deep woods.

"Father Gordon," Rainsford said cheerfully, shaking hands with his visitor, "do come in. I've been looking forward to meeting you." Rainsford ushered him into the living room. "I've been hearing lots of good things about you, and I wanted to meet you. I'd like your opinion on something."

As the introductions were being made, Grego thought, *Says he isn't qualified to be Governor General. Faugh! I haven't heard such a smooth line of patter since the last time I talked to someone I wanted to get on my side.*

"We were just about to have another drink, Father," Rainsford said. "Will you join us?"

"I'd be delighted," The Rev said.

"Anything in particular you'd like?" Rainsford asked.

The Rev chuckled engagingly and nodded his head. "If you pour it, Governor, I'll drink it."

"Fine," Rainsford said. "Just fine. Well, I'll be back in a moment. You and Mr. Grego can be getting acquainted."

This is rich, The Rev thought. *Here's a chance to look over this guy Christiana's all out of shape about–and he doesn't even know she's been pouring her heart out to me about him.*

No sooner had Rainsford returned from the kitchen than the Fuzzies came rushing in with an empty plate and hopeful looks on their faces. The Rev was momentarily startled. He had heard a lot about Fuzzies, but never really seen one in person.

Grego handled the introductions.

"They certainly seem trusting," The Rev said to Grego and Rainsford.

He was startled again when Diamond spoke. "We know good Hagga from bad Hagga," he said. " 'Sides, you come

see Pappy Vic and Unka Ben. That make you hokay, too."
He scratched his head. "*Unka Wev*," he said thoughtfully.
"Not know name like *Unka Wev*."

"Come on, now, Diamond," Grego said. "It's *Rev,* with
an 'R.' *Auntie K'istanna* has been teaching you about 'R.'
Now try to say Unka *Rev*."

Diamond screwed up his tiny face. "*Ehr–hev*," he managed. "*Eh–rhev*." He took a deep breath. "*Unka Rrrrrev*,"
he said. It still gargled a bit, but the pronunciation was
coming through. Diamond looked pleased.

The Rev took a long sip at his drink and studied Diamond.
Diamond studied him back, with his little head cocked over
to one side.

"Remarkable," The Rev said. "I used to think people
were exaggerating the humanity of Fuzzies." He made a
quick, noncommital gesture. "But, then, I've always
throught they exaggerated the humanity of Terrans, too."

"Everyone thinks that—until they meet a Fuzzy," Grego
said. "I used to think it. In fact, I blush to think what I used to
think about Fuzzies."

"They're little people—just like us—" The Rev said,
"—except they're covered with soft, golden fur."

"Not *exactly* like us," Rainsford said. "Nature never
makes exact duplications—even in character. However,
Fuzzies are a totally sane race. And, they cannot be driven
insane. They know the difference between right and wrong,
good and bad—and their ethical system is highly developed,
more highly developed than ours, I'm bound to think. For
example, they have no concept at all of crime or doing hurt to
another in any premeditated way."

Diamond made a sweeping gesture to include everyone in
the room—Terrans and Fuzzies. "Make friend, make help,
have fun; is only way be good. *Hagga*—" He made a pointing gesture, with his fingers spread, toward the Terrans.
"—Big Ones—make good place for Fuzzies, keep Fuzzies
from hurt. Big Ones make dead dem things hurt Fuzzies;
make dead the *hah'pie,* the *dam'ting,* and make dead Bad Big
Ones. Fuzzies love *Hagga*. So much—many–many—for

Hagga to teach Fuzzies.''

"You see what I mean about ethical systems, Father Gordon?'' Rainsford said.

The Rev abruptly turned his attention from Diamond, at whom he had been staring in rapt attention. ''Oh,'' he said absently. ''Please call me Rev. Every time someone says 'Father Gordon' I get the uncomfortable feeling that my dowdy old bishop has come around to check up on me.''

Rainsford chuckled, around his pipestem. ''Very well,'' he said. ''Rev it is.''

"I may be jumping to conclusions,'' The Rev said, ''but it seems to me that Fuzzies are totally innocent creatures.''

"There's much to that idea,'' Grego said. ''They learn anything that arouses their curiosity faster than hyperspeed. They've been around Terran humans, now, for a bit over a year and already they seem to have developed some instinct—I call it an instinct because I don't know what else to call it at this point—that lets them instantly distinguish between good guys and bad guys. They won't have anything to do with bad guys.''

"It's strange,'' The Rev said reflectively. ''Beings that are totally good; the Vision finally realized. And we had to come this far through space and time to find it.''

"I don't know much about theology,'' Rainsford said, ''but I think Fuzzies are the most extraordinary discovery ever made by *homo s. terra*.''

The Rev laughed. ''I don't know much about theology, either, Governor. At least that's what they kept telling me at university. I just try to help people who can't help themselves—feed 'em, keep them well, heal them when they're sick, get 'em going again when they want to give up. Theology never cured a kid of malnutrition. Theology won't make a man able to do a day's work when his belly is empty.''

"The Fuzzies must sense that in you,'' Grego said.

The Rev leaned forward. ''I don't like to pry, but why is Diamond wearing a bow tie?''

"You're a lot like a Fuzzy, at that,'' Grego said. He told The Rev about that evening at *Alfredo's* when Christiana made a bow tie for Diamond from her hair ribbon. "He insisted on wearing it all the time, after that," Grego said, "so I had some made up in Fuzzy–size—pastels for daytime, black for evening, and a white one for formal affairs."

"He's a sentimental old fool," Rainsford said, half–apologetically, as he fussed with his pipe.

"*Me*, sentimental?" Grego snapped. "I happen to know your Fuzzies sleep on the bed with you."

Rainsford blanched. "How did you—" he began.

Grego grinned. "Flora and Fauna told Diamond, and Diamond told me," Grego said with satisfaction.

"*That's* the hell of it," Rainsford said. "With Fuzzies around, nobody has any secrets."

"With Fuzzies around," Grego said, "nobody *needs* to have any secrets."

"I'm not sure I understand," The Rev said, taking another sip of his drink.

"You will," Grego said, "after you've been around Fuzzies for a while." He paused a moment, choosing his words. "Fuzzies show us what we are capable of being. We sometimes lose track of that, as we scramble to earn a sol or two here and there. That's because Fuzzies freely give us what we all yearn for more than anything else—love. Love with no strings attached."

Mmmmmmm, The Rev thought, *Christiana picked a pretty good guy, here. No wonder she's getting a little frantic to hang on to him.*

Diamond rushed over and hugged Grego's leg. "Fuzzies make *Hagga* happy," he said. "That make Fuzzies happy. Everybody make friend, have fun, make help, be good."

XXXIII

"You say why to me, *plis.*"

"*Not* say why to you!"

Two tiny figures were silhouetted against the star–filled sky, and lighted faintly by Xerxes, which was at about the half–full phase. One of them had a khaki barracks cover cocked on the back of his head. The other was quietly smoking a little tobacco pipe. They were sitting on a rock outcropping above Fuzzy Valley.

"*So noho–aki dovov heeva aki. Aki gashta, shi so,*" Little Fuzzy said intensely, lapsing into *Lingua Fuzzy* to make his point. "You tell me how no say to me. Me Fuzzy, like you."

"Is secret duty," Starwatcher said, speaking slowly as he worked through the unfamiliar Terran words for an abstract concept. "Come down from old one to me—to me when old one say I now *Haigun* of these Fuzzies. He told by old one who make *him* the *Haigun*. That how duty pass from old one to young one—many–many times. So many–many no one know when start; just that *is, so.*"

"Me see—*is, so*—but must know *why,*" Little Fuzzy said.

"Me no *have* say you," Starwatcher replied tersely. "Me *Haigun*. Not have to make answer—no to *gashta,* no to Hagga."

"Hagga only want help Fuzzies," Little Fuzzy said.

Starwatcher fingered the visor of his barracks cover. "Me know," he said quietly.

"You, *Haigun,*" Little Fuzzy said, "but, see." He took the two–inch silver disc that hung on a chain about his neck and showed it again to Starwatcher. The dim light glinted faintly on it, not enough to read the lettering, but enough to see it was there: the numeral *1*. Below that was LITTLE

250

FUZZY, and below that, *Jack Holloway, Cold Creek Valley, Beta Continent*.

"You see—" Little Fuzzy paused. "—*idee–disko*. You, *Haigun;* me, *Numba'–One Fuzzy*. Big job, be *Numba'–One Fuzzy*. What if Pappy Jack ask Little Fuzzy why Starwatcher all the time look at stars and moons? If Little Fuzzy have to say, 'Me not know, Pappy Jack; he won't say to me,' so–then Pappy Jack maybe think Little Fuzzy not much of a *Numba'–One Fuzzy*. Not know easy fact, so–such. Maybe Pappy Jack say, 'You Fuzzy; dem Fuzzies. Why you not know? You *Numba'–One Fuzzy*—and dem Fuzzies no trust you?' Make Little Fuzzy feel bad—let Pappy Jack down. Not help Pappy Jack is bad thing to do. Must be good to Pappy Jack. Pappy Jack find Fuzzies—help Fuzzies—*save* Fuzzies."

Little Fuzzy paused again, to let the importance of his remarks gain weight, knowing the silence would help to generate a reply from Starwatcher. Little Fuzzy hadn't failed to learn some diplomacy from watching the tactics of persuasion that Terrans used to convince each other.

"Me know," Starwatcher repeated slowly. "Fuzzies not have food. Pappy Jack give *hosku–fusso*." He moved his hand in a semi–circle to include all of Fuzzy Valley. "Old ones die, but new young ones not come. Starwatcher not know why. Is *Haigun*—so–such must know why, but not. Pappy Jack give *hoksu–fusso* to eat. Greensuit Hagga good, too, but Pappy Jack make them come this place. Pappy Jack Best Big One."

"If Pappy Jack ask," Little Fuzzy said, "so–then you say to him, 'Me *Haigun*. Me no have say you why look at stars and moons.' You so–say Pappy Jack?"

"No," Starwatcher said softly. "No so–say Pappy Jack."

"Then say me," Little Fuzzy said. "I Pappy Jack's *Numba'–One Fuzzy*, but no say him why. He ask, then I say, but not say any time else."

Starwatcher took a deep breath. "Old *Haigun* make me *Haigun*, but not say me what duty is—most, but not sum of it." Starwatcher pointed toward the sky. "Blue star go about white star three hands, before old *Haigun* die. Then, he so–say me, 'It be said, when lights come in sky, *gashta* go to far place. When lights come in sky, *gashta* be saved and taken up this place. You watch. You *Haigun*.' Then, he die.''

Little Fuzzy digested this for a moment. *"Prrrr—prrrophesy,"* he said, working hard over the unfamiliar ''R'' sound.

''What that mean?'' Starwatcher asked.

''Is when you so–say thing happen before it happen,'' Little Fuzzy replied. ''But, *why* old *Haigun* so–say you? *Why* watch for lights?''

''He no say,'' Starwatcher said. ''He not know. Only know to watch. Only know stay in valley and watch. Rest is forgotten.''

Little Fuzzy knocked out his pipe on a stone, blew through the stem, and thought for a moment. Then, he began to refill the pipe from his little tobacco pouch. This was going to be a two–pipe problem.

Xerxes was several degrees higher in the night sky before Little Fuzzy spoke again. ''See lights in sky?'' he inquired.

Starwatcher held up two fingers. ''Two times,'' he said. ''Old *Haigun* not dead then. He see, too.''

''What he say?'' Little Fuzzy asked.

''He so–say, not lights we watch to see,'' Starwatcher said. ''I ask him how he know, but he no say me how.''

''When last time you see?'' Little Fuzzy asked.

''Star turn hand–of–hands since,'' Starwatcher said, opening and closing his fist five times.

''You see on that place?'' Little Fuzzy asked, pointing at Xerxes with his pipe stem.

Starwatcher nodded.

''That when *gashta–Hagga*—Big Ones—come this place,'' Little Fuzzy said. ''Big Ones save Fuzzies. *Prrrrrophesy* now *is, so*. Fuzzies go to place where you see lights.'' He tapped his chest with his pipestem. *''Me* one of dem Fuzzies. Hagga teach many things to Fuzzies there.''

Starwatcher jabbed his finger toward the ground. ''But, *we* not go. We here, yet. So I watch.''

The intercom chimed. Alex Napier thumbed the switch. "Yes?" he said.

"Lieutenant Moshe Gilbert is here to report," the yeoman replied.

"Send him in," Napier said. He broke the connection, laid his pipe in the large ashtray, and tugged the bottom of his tunic to smooth the front of it.

Napier could see nothing amiss in Lieutenant Gilbert's grasp of protocol. He reported properly and with briskness, but he looked awfully green to be a Class–A Agent. His two front teeth were markedly larger than they should be, which made him look younger than he was, and he had that well–scrubbed, just–out–of–the–Academy look about him, which is to say that innocence oozed from every pore. The only thing missing that Napier could think of was freckles. It taxed the mind to believe that this young man was a graduate of the Navy's Advanced Protection and Escort School, yet there it was in his records, along with a string of commendations for successfully completed assignments. But, then, Napier reflected, the most efficient and ruthless agent he had ever seen was a sweet young thing who looked like a cheerleader.

Napier toyed with the records jacket. "When did you go to APES?" he asked, although the date was plainly entered on Gilbert's personnel form.

"Five years ago, sir," Gilbert replied. "Spring class of 650."

"I see," Napier said. "At ease, Lieutenant, and have a seat." He motioned him to a chair.

"Thank you, sir," Gilbert said.

Napier filled his pipe and leaned back in his chair while he lighted it. "Relax, son," he said, talking around the pipe-stem, between puffs. "No need to *sit* at attention, too."

"Yes, sir," Gilbert said.

"Did Captain Greibenfeld tell you anything about the nature of this assignment?" Napier asked.

"Only that I would be assigned directly to your staff, sir—for an indefinite period," Gilbert said.

Napier smiled. "If you have any hot dates planned for the

next year," he said, "I suggest you cancel them." That would be enough to tell him, for the moment, Napier decided. Then, if any scuttlebutt got back to him about the duration of the mission, he would know that Gilbert wasn't the man he wanted. "I'll brief you on the final phase when the time comes," he continued. "In the meantime, your direct responsibility will be to create first-generation copies of several tapes and documents—as I furnish them to you. I consider this to be very sensitive information, Lieutenant. You are responsible to no one on this station, now, except myself. You will wear a sidearm at all times, whether you are engaged in building the duplicate file or not. If, any any time, *based on your own judgement,* any compromise of security has occurred, you are to arrest the parties concerned and bring them to me under guard."

"And if they refuse?" Gilbert said.

"You will shoot them dead on the spot," Napier said evenly, "and inform me at once."

Without replying, Gilbert took his Class–A Agent's identity plaque from his pocket and pinned it to the breast pocket of his blouse. "I take it you mean I start immediately, sir," he said.

Napier was pleased. "You take it correctly, Mister," he said.

Gilbert leaned forward slightly in his chair and reached behind his back. From under his blouse he withdrew a nine-millimeter automatic. Pointing its muzzle toward the ceiling, he stripped a round into battery and thumbed the hammer back down to the double-action safety position.

"Personal?" Napier inquired.

Gilbert nodded.

"Inventoried when you came on station?" Napier asked.

"No, sir," Gilbert said, smiling. "You know Regulations don't require that of a Class–A."

"Then, why are you making this show?" Napier asked, puffing slowly on his pipe.

"So you'll know I have it and where I carry it," Gilbert said. "You're my direct boss, now. I'm on assignment. I owe you the courtesy."

Napier nodded thoughtfully.

Class–A Agents were distributed throughout the military services and were assigned to normal duty—from which they could be detached to perform Class–A functions. Most often it was just a matter of being present in the pay room when personnel were paid in cash, but there was also the matter of transporting payrolls and acting as couriers for diplomatic level and high–security documents. In their Class–A functions they were required by regulations to be armed. Most of them habitually carried a personal weapon, since it was often more expedient and efficient than digging up a Master–At–Arms to draw an issue sidearm. They were not required to surrender it on boarding any station, vessel, or civilian carrier—or even acknowledge that they possessed it.

Napier got to his feet. "I think we understand each other, Mister, on the importance I attach to this matter." He lifted the front of his tunic to reveal a pistol tucked in the front of his waistband.

"Are you expecting trouble, sir?" Gilbert asked. "I mean, is there an agency of active intent to compromise this set of security?"

"I doubt it, Lieutenant," Napier said, "but I'm a great believer in prevention. Hell; at the moment, only a few people are even aware of this situation. There will be more, of course, as their Need to Know comes into the picture."

"Is that the reason for the beat–to–quarters–and–man–guns treatment the Commodore is applying, here?" Gilbert asked deferentially.

Napier sat down. "The reason," he said gruffly, "is the potential of Federation–wide importance. You'll see that as we work along on building the duplicate folio. At the moment, your capacity is basically that of an armed copy–boy."

"Yes, sir," Gilbert said. That seemed clear enough. The Old Man was telling him to keep his nose clean and curb his curiosity.

"Take the rest of the day to clean up any loose ends on your regular duty job, Lieutenant," Napier said. "You start here at 0800 tomorrow. I'll have desk space rigged for you in the outer office. For now, that is all."

Gilbert got to his feet, saluted smartly, and said, "Yes, sir. Thank you, sir."

As soon as Gilbert had departed, Napier punched out the combination for the Communications Center. As the screen cleared, he said to the yeoman, "Get me First Battalion commo on Zarathustra. I wish to speak with Lieutenant Colonel O'Bannon, Sergeant Helton, and Commissioner Holloway, either in that order or as a group."

"I'll signal you when I have them on screen, sir," the yeoman said.

"Put it on scramble–8—and thank you," Napier said.

"What do you mean, he's not here?" Christiana said apprehensively.

"I mean, he's not here," the sexton replied. "He had an appointment with the Governor General at Government House, but I expect him back—"

Christiana clenched her fist as her hand flew to her mouth, and she bit the knuckles to keep from crying out. "Governor Rainsford?" she said. "He had an appointment with Governor Rainsford?"

"Why, yes, Miss," the man said, "but he'll be back—"

"That's all right," she said, cutting him off, again. "I'll see him some other time." She turned and hurried out of the mission, onto the darkened esplanade.

Christiana was accustomed to being double–crossed, used, and taken advantage of. It was something she had allowed to happen to her all her life. She had grown to mistrust people—until she met Victor Grego—so it was natural, in her mind, to assume that The Rev's visit to Ben Rainsford might also involve some breach of the confidence into which she had taken him.

It had stopped raining as the wind turned warmer. Both Xerxes and Darius peered through the remaining ragged clouds, intermittently flooding the poorly–lighted esplanade with shifting patches of pale illumination.

Christiana almost didn't hear her name being called.

"Chris. *Chris!*" the voice said. "Over here!"

She turned toward the sound, trying to orient herself with

her surroundings. She hadn't been aware of walking so far, but here she was, in front of *The Bitter End*. Recognition flashed across her face. "Gwennie!" she said, hurrying toward the short blonde with the unmistakeable cascade of curly hair falling across her forehead and spilling down around her shoulders.

They hugged each other.

"What are you doing down here?" "I thought you'd be Uptown by now." "I'm moving up the street, at least." "You're looking great." They both talked at once for a moment, and then paused for breath.

"Gwen," Christiana said, "what are you doing out here without a wrap? Here, take my coat."

Gwen's face was flushed, and two rivulets of sweat trickled along her collarbone before they joined and disappeared down the front of her dress. She exhaled cigarette smoke through her nose. "I'm all right," she said. "It's hot enough to bake Ghu's gizzard in there. I had to get some fresh air."

"Busy weekend coming up, huh?" Christiana said.

Gwen nodded. "Marines are starting to drift in already. And, how's *your* love-life?"

Christiana shook her head. "I don't know," she said. "That's the hell of it."

Gwen squinted through the cigarette smoke as she used both hands to pinch the fabric of her dress and tug the damp garment away from her body. She moved her hands back and forth with a quick, fanning motion to make the air circulate inside her clothes. "Honey," Gwen said, "one *never* knows; that's the *real* hell of it."

"I just can't get anything out of him," Christiana said. "I mean, he's attentive enough—but really formal about it—but I don't know where I stand with him."

"Yeah," Gwen said thoughtfully, "Jim is the shy type, too. 'Course I haven't really picked between the two of them, yet. I think I like Jim better, though. Ev's always shooting his mouth off about how great he is—never how great *I* am."

"I thought you and Laporte—" Christiana said, "—were—uh— I mean, I thought that's why you moved the act over here from *Pandora's Box*."

Gwen made a disdainful gesture. "Laporte? No, that's just to keep the animals off me while I'm working. Laporte? I'd sooner go out with a khooghra; the conversation would be better."

Christiana nodded understanding. "I'm just paralyzed, Gwen. I've got to make a move with this guy, but I'm afraid to *do* anything for fear I'll lose him."

Gwen put her hand on Christiana's arm. "Look; let's go inside and talk a while. We got time for a drink before I go back on."

In a few minutes, Christiana poured out the story of what a wonderful man Victor Grego was, how he was attentive without pawing over her, how he always treated her like a real lady, how kind and considerate he was—both toward her and Diamond—to say nothing of the good manners he had.

"Sounds like a hell of a find to me," Gwen said. "Why don't you just snap him up?"

Christiana frowned and looked down at the table. "He—" she faltered. "He doesn't know what I did before. I'm afraid to tell him. I mean, he's a high–class guy. He might not be able to handle it. I keep thinking we could go away someplace, but I know he'll never leave the Company."

"What makes you think he wouldn't understand?" Gwen asked. "If he's *that* high–class, he should be able to understand."

Christiana snorted. "*Rodney* was that high–class—I knew he'd understand—the *bastard*. When I told him what Daddy was doing and begged him to help, all *he* did was fling me out of his life."

"You're going to have to tell him, Chris," Gwen said. "Sooner or later. Guys like Victor Grego have a way of figuring things out for themselves. Otherwise they wouldn't be where they are. If my Jim could figure *anything* out, he'd be a Master Sergeant by now."

"Oh, I don't know, Gwennie," Christiana sighed. "I thought I had a way to go, and now I've got this guy putting the screws to me for information; and threatening to tell Victor about me if I don't come across."

Gwen nodded. "*He* sounds like somebody that's working

for Laporte—or maybe Bowlby. He could be an independent, but *those* bums wouldn't let him keep breathing if he was. Remember what Bowlby did to you.''

"I know, I know," Christiana said. "I can't betray Victor, and I can't keep feeding useless malarkey to this guy in the hat. Sooner or later he's going to get wise that what I'm giving him isn't that useful.''

Gwen leaned forward and put her hand on Christiana's arm. "Listen, honey," she said, "let me snoop around a little and see if I can find out who the guy is working for. Would that help?''

"I guess," Christiana said. "I'll just have to figure it out as I go along, I guess.''

"Good," Gwen said. "How can I get in touch with you?''

XXXIV

The orange sun was just setting behind the ridge as Jack Holloway grounded the airjeep among the lengthening shadows in front of his bungalow.

The instant it lurched off contragravity, Little Fuzzy was out the side hatch like a shot and streaking for the Fuzzy-sized door next to the front door of Jack's house. There were so many things to tell his family, and Mike and Mitzi, and Ko–Ko, and Cinderella.

Jack ambled after him, let himself in the house, and dropped his gear on the big desk–table. He deposited his rifle on top of the pile of gear, unbuckled his pistol belt and laid it on the table, too. Then, he took a good, long yawn and stretch—and scratched himself here and there.

A few minutes later, he emerged from the kitchen with a highball and sat down at the communications screen. He would think about dinner while he played back his messages, he decided, and then screen Gerd and Ruth at their place.

Lieutenant Colonel James O'Bannon sat down on his bunk, after his guests were comfortably situated and provided with drinks and ashtrays. He reached down and began to unlace his boots. "Dick," he said to Major Stagwell, "you'll be in charge, of course, while I'm gone. I want you to bust loose with some liberty for the men. See that Casagra's bunch gets the biggest end of it. They've worked the hardest and the longest. Not much left for them to do, anyway."

Stagwell puffed his pipe and nodded. "You want to maintain current patrol density, Jim?"

"You bet I do!" O'Bannon said. "I don't want a banjo-bird to get within a hundred kilometers of this place without our knowing about it—certainly not until I'm shut of the responsibility. . . .Come down here to shoo a few news-people away from a hypership wreck, and now we've got a damnthing by the tail.''

Stagwell nodded again and took a sip of his drink.

O'Bannon peered at him. ''Y'know, I think I'll have one of those, myself,'' he said as he tugged his boots off. He ambled over to his field chest and began to fix himself a drink. ''I'm sorry I can't tell you more about this, just now, Dick,'' he said, while his back was still turned, ''but the whole thing is just too damned hot. Maybe after Phil and I have talked to Napier and come back down from Xerxes . . .'' He turned to Helton. ''Will you have everything case–packed and ready to go by the arrival time of the *Ranger?*'' he asked.

''Easily, Colonel,'' Helton said. ''We've plenty of inflata-bles, so we can cover it all completely and cushion the gear enough to not disturb so much as a speck of dust.''

''Good,'' O'Bannon said. ''What about your quarantine cases?''

Helton smiled and took a slug from his glass. ''They're the ones that'll do the packing,'' he said.

O'Bannon nodded. ''Good thinking,'' he said as he walked back to his bunk and sat down. ''Let's see; that will be 0900 on Saturday. I'd better screen McGraw tomorrow and tell him we're coming. Wouldn't look good if he were off chasing skirts when we arrive.''

''I just arrived,'' Holloway said to the image in the screen. ''Got to talk to you about some things. How about after dinner?''

Ruth van Riebeek moved into the pickup range, alongside Gerd. ''Why don't you just come over here for dinner, Jack?'' she said. ''You probably don't feel like cooking, anyway, after coming all the way down from Fuzzy Valley.''

Jack was about to accept when he saw two more women in the background, setting the big table in one end of the van Riebeek living room; Lynne Andrews, slender and blonde, and a tall brunette that he couldn't recall having seen before. Confound it! This was confidential stuff. He started to make an excuse. "Well—uh—" he began. "I don't want to impose . . ."

"Nonsense," Ruth said. "We're doing a whacking big veldbeest roast. There's plenty—even if you'd brought a platoon of Marines with you."

That did it. No graceful way to back out, now. Just have to see how it works out. We don't have to be there until day after tomorrow, anyway. "Okay," he said. "Let me clean up my screen messages, here, and say hello to the kids. Then I'll be along—say twenty or thirty minutes?"

Ivan Bowlby raised his handkerchief to his nose, as if to protest the acrid smell of stale tobacco smoke that filled *The Bitter End,* and sniffed. "I have to have better information than this, Joseph," Bowlby said, "or I can't go on paying you to act as go-between."

The man in the hat smiled cryptically. "Mr. Weisberg, if you please, Mr. Bowlby. I prefer Mr. Weisberg to the familiar. We are both gentlemen doing business together, are we not?"

Bowlby looked uncomfortable. "Whatever you like," he said. "The point is that my client will not pay for this sort of information. It's no better than office gossip, really."

Joseph Weisberg smiled again and spread his hands. "It's what she is telling me, Mr. Bowlby, and that is what you hired me for—to get the information from the girl and pass it on to you. As I remember, your reasons had to do with your own anonymity and my being new on Zarathustra. I recall nothing in our arrangement regarding the—ah—quality of what I bring to you, which consideration, I'm sure you will admit, is a highly subjective matter at the best."

"Very well," Bowlby conceded. "We'll let it slide as it is for a few more weeks. If I don't get some highly confidential data, we'll just have to terminate our deal."

"Perhaps," Weisberg said, "if I could speak with your buyer, he could give me a better notion of what he's after. Some specifics would be of great assistance."

Bowlby made a quick, irritable movement of his head.

"Out of the question!" he snapped. "My buyer—as you put it—requires even more anonymity than myself in this."

Weisberg shrugged. "There are ways to preserve it," he said. "I don't have to be *introduced* to him to discuss the matter."

Neither of them had noticed the short blonde with the cascading curly hair who had slowly eased her way along the bar to a point from which she could overhear the conversation while appearing to fiddle with her drink and watch the crowd in the front of *The Bitter End*. Bowlby she recognized easily enough. His entertainment agency handled all her bookings. But she could not recall having ever seen the man in the hat before.

Jack Holloway could not recall having seen the tall brunette before, even after he had been introduced to her.

"Miss Bell is a sociologist from Company Science Center," Gerd was saying. "She's doing a comparison study on Fuzzies."

All Jack could think of was that he had to talk to Gerd and Ruth privately, and he couldn't think of any unobtrusive way to handle it, so far.

"I'm afraid I've just scratched the surface, here," Liana Bell was saying. "Fuzzy social structures are, I feel, far more complex than we might have thought."

"How so, Miss Bell?" Jack asked. "We've been around Fuzzies for something over a year, now. I would think we'd have a pretty clear idea about such things."

They were sitting in a relaxed group around a gigantic wooden slab, sliced whole from the bole of a pool-ball tree, that served as a coffee table in the van Riebeek living room. Dinner had made Jack feel alive again; he hadn't realized how tired he was until he walked across Holloway's Run from his bungalow to the van Riebeeks'. He got out his pipe and began to fill it.

"Oh, Commissioner," Liana Bell said engagingly, "please call me Liana. Dr. Mallin is always addressing me as 'Dr. Bell.' It makes me feel like I should be wearing flat-heeled shoes and have my hair up in a bun.''

Jack looked down at her feet, as if to punctuate the fact that she was wearing sturdy boots.

She giggled in an attractive way. ''Field work is different,'' she said.

Confound it! Jack lighted his pipe, interested in what Liana had to say, but with his mind still on the problem of telling Gerd and Ruth to clean up their work and pack for a short trip to Xerxes. Commodore Napier had been very insistent about having a couple of Fuzzyologists along to help his own people evaluate the equipment from Fuzzy Cavern.

''I wish I could spend a month over here, studying the Fuzzies,'' Liana said.

Oh, Ghu! Jack thought.

''But I can't, of course,'' she said. ''It's out of the question at this point. Dr. Mallin would never stand for it. Juan should be in about the middle of the morning to take me back to Mallorysport.''

Ah! Jack thought. *That tall brunette!* He had met her at Ahmed and Sandra's wedding reception. Word was that Juan had been squiring her around Mallorysport ever since. It must be for real; it wasn't like Juan to date one of his own employees, even if Ernst Mallin was her *immediate* superior.

Liana had been busily explaining to everyone what a fine and magnificent person Juan Jimenez was, but Jack had only been listening with one ear as he finally connected on where he had seen her before.

''Do you mean, Miss Bell—'' Jack started to say.

''Liana,'' she corrected.

''Do you mean, Liana, that you've been able to draw conclusions about Fuzzy society in a few days that have eluded qualified xeno-naturalists for more than a year?''

''Oh, Commissioner Holloway—'' she began.

''Jack,'' he corrected.

''Yes,'' she said, ''Jack. No, I don't mean that at all. It's only a matter of specialization. I look for things that are within a very narrow spectrum, really. And I haven't drawn any conclusions; I've only found a number of fascinating things about Fuzzies that raise unique questions in sociology.

They're an other human race, and yet the patterns in Fuzzy social systems are not at all what we might suspect by application of our own history as a comparison.''

"The other human race," Gerd said, drawing reflectively on his cigarette. "Good phrase."

"You see," Liana continued, "we've always applied Terran ethnology to other intelligent species which were at different levels of development. Eight times, now, we've been pretty much right. This time, I'm not so sure. I don't think we can stretch those comparisons far enough to make room for Fuzzies. They just don't want to fit into our orderly explanations for our own behavior. That's what's so exciting about it. With Fuzzies, we may have to start from scratch in order to unravel their sociology."

Jack nodded agreement. "What brings you to this idea— and so quickly?" he asked. With his pipe, he motioned for her to continue.

"Contradictions," she said simply. She paused. "Let me see, now, how to put this non-technically.

"Fuzzies appear to be a paleolithic society," she said, "that is, according to the way we're used to measuring such things. In a paleolithic civilization there are tradition structures which we normally expect to find and from which we can identify the development level of the culture. These have nothing to do with weapons, tool-making abilities, and those sorts of things. I mean, nuts and bolts are not in my speciality. A lot of these expected traditions are totally absent in Fuzzy society. They just don't fit with our established definition of an intelligent species that is in a primitive state of civilization."

Gerd nodded. "I've got to give you that," he said, "and I've been wondering about it from the beginning. Fuzzies have about as much concept of magic and religion, for example, as they do of nuclear physics and electronics. Yet, Little Fuzzy's catechism for explaining why something exists often operates on the grounds that it is so 'because Pappy Jack says it's so.' "

"And that certainly doesn't fit," Ruth said. "I've worked with extraterrestrials on Loki and Thor and Shesha. Every-

thing functions as a result of how the gods feel that day to
those people. Great Ghu, the Grandfather God of the Thorans, has so many helpers and minor gods keeping track of
everything for him that—the last I heard—we still haven't
completely cataloged the pantheon which the Thorans credit
with running the planet—not to mention the rest of the
universe.''

"Exactly,'' Liana said. "And Fuzzies are supposed to be a
primitive society; without any of the traditional nature gods
and spirits that such peoples invent to explain natural
phenomena.''

"I've worked with the Khooghras on Yggsdrasil,'' Gerd
said. "They have a vocabulary that consists of the grand total
of eighty–two words, but they still have room for one,
arooshta, that means supernatural. They use it quite a lot,
since their level of sapience is so low that almost every
mundane occurrence is quite mysterious to them.''

Jack leaned forward in his chair. "By gum!'' he said,
"you know, you're right. I've been on a lot of those planets,
myself—plus a lot more—but I'd never looked at it quite that
way. The Fuzzies *are* unique in those respects. Say on,
Liana, say on. What other trees have we overlooked as a
result of standing in the middle of the forest?''

Liana beamed. Jack Holloway was beginning to warm up
to her. Without being fully aware of it, she wanted his
approval because Juan Jimenez took a great deal of stock in
Jack's opinions about things and people.

"Well,'' she said, "there are a lot of things that derive—
or, in this case, fail to derive—from the primitive's attribu-
tion of natural occurrences to supernatural causes, and the
vacancy seems uniform among Fuzzies.'' She ticked off
several points on the long, slender fingers of her left hand.
"They have no perceivable ritual practices, except for burying their own dead, and that could merely involve sanitation
and the desirability of making it harder for predators to trail
them. They have no Creation myths that I've been able to
find. There is no stereotyping of sex roles; females hunt
alongside males, and males assist with child–rearing. They

don't fight over territory or resources—like watering spots, for example. There is no tribal structure, unless you call temporary banding together in groups of five or six tribal. I don't. I can't find any concept of a hierarchy; no hereditary chiefs or medicine–men. I think, by the way, that Little Fuzzy's obvious leadership role is a very isolated occurrence.

"And," she continued, "Fuzzies don't measure time in any sort of record–keeping way. Numbers and counting just don't seem to interest them. You all know about that, of course, but for a society composed of people with Fuzzy–level intelligence, such practices are completely unheard of."

"But not impossible," Jack said.

Liana frowned prettily. "I don't follow you," she said.

"What I mean," Jack said, "is that a primitive intelligence doesn't learn things which have no practical benefit to apply. It doesn't mean that the primitive is not *able* to learn, say, to tell time—only that he is not interested, because he can't see any use for it."

"That's one of the things that makes this business of measuring intelligence and charting social systems so tricky," Liana said. "We have the stubborn habit of applying our own yardsticks to totally alien creatures, and singing ourselves a lullaby that it's all right because they are anthropomorphic and *look* something like us."

"You're right, of course," Jack said. "We never had the least notion that Fuzzies could count beyond twenty–five—using the fingers of one hand to count with and those of the other hand to keep tally. Christiana Stone, though, taught Little Fuzzy to tell time by counting the digit marks on a watch. As soon as he saw it was useful to us, he picked it right up—and without any repeat lessons, either. Then, there's Starwatcher. He counts time by star and planet movements, although he still uses the old hand–and–fingers method."

"Starwatcher?" Liana said. "I don't recall him."

Gerd shifted uncomfortably in his chair.

Jack squirmed a little, as well. Damn! Old Man Holloway is getting forgetful. I don't think we want someone from

Company Science Center to know much about Upland Fuzzies just yet—at least not till we're ready to start releasing our data.

"He's another Fuzzy I know," Jack said smoothly. "I imagine you'll meet him sooner or later—that is, if you continue your Fuzzy project."

Liana's face became eager. "Yes," she said, "I'm dying to continue. There's so much to be learned."

Lynne Andrews had been quiet during most of the conversation, but now she suddenly spoke up. "What about contamination?" she asked. "Won't all this exposure of Fuzzies to Terrans change their society and contaminate the study experiments? Their language has so many Terran words in it now that it's either a distinct dialect or even a new language—sub-Fuzzy."

Contamination. Lynne's M.D. was in pediatrics, so it was natural for her to think in terms of infection versus immunology.

Liana pursed her lips. "I don't think contamination is really the right word," she said reflectively. "Influence would be better, that is, as far as future development is concerned. Terrans have branched into Fuzzy social systems at year 654 A.E. with resulting interaction and influence—us on them and them on us—but we can never tamper with the *origins* that shaped the social systems. It was what it was when we first viewed it in time, and nothing can change what happened before the moment when Jack discovered Little Fuzzy hiding in the shower stall."

"You mean it's a natural system," Gerd said.

"What?" Liana asked.

"As differentiated from an artificial, or created system," Gerd replied. "It's a term xeno-naturalists use a lot. The computer guys and the environmental engineers talk about systems all the time. They mean something man-made. When we talk about systems, we're often talking about ecology, or food chains, or breeding habits, so we use the term natural systems to avoid blurring the two ideas."

"Oh, sure," Liana said. "I see what you mean. Yes, it's a natural system. All the Fuzzy culture that existed before that first contact between Fuzzy and Terran is already imprinted. Nothing can change it. But, we have to analyze it if we hope to understand the nature of events which produced it, and which made Fuzzies what they are.''

Jack leaned back and stared thoughtfully at the ceiling. "How can you get around their alien thinking?" he asked. "They think as well as we do—maybe better—but their processes of thinking are different; their thinking patterns are alien, by definition.''

"Custom," she said. "Ingrained custom forms the fabric of social systems, so we study that. Once established, such practices do not undergo essential change. Look at us; wherever Terrans go, the first thing they plant is coffee and tobacco, so they can have coffee and cigarettes in the morning. The next local product is some source for ethyl alcohol, so we can have a cocktail hour at the end of the day. The natives on planets like Loki and Gimli and Thor—and even Shesha and Uller—think it's a religious observance.''

"Maybe it is," Jack said.

"The Fuzzies would think that, if they had any notions about religion," Ruth said. "They understand the cocktail hour is very important to Terrans, so they always go to great pains not to interrupt it.''

"Big Ones drink *tosh–ki waji*. Make Big One talk," Gerd said.

Liana spread her hands. "Social systems," she said. "I think what Gerd said about natural systems is likely a more revealing way to put it. We never really escape from a social system, *because* it's a natural system. All the impact of technology on human culture hasn't made the slightest dent in those kind of systems; they've been with us longer than the wheel.''

"Something could, though, couldn't it?" Lynne asked. "Surely there must be something that would have such a profound effect on our civilization that it would alter society itself.''

Liana shrugged. "Nothing big enough has come along yet," she said. "If the Atomic Wars, contragravity, the Dillingham Drive, and interstellar colonization weren't big enough, I can't think of anything that would be. That's why we use social system establishment as a common denominator.

"The idea of a 'clean break with the past' is a romantic notion easily poked full of holes by reality. Our social systems are what shape us and define us. We are essentially nothing, except in relation to them. We cannot deal out the deck again.

"The same holds true for Fuzzies. At least that's the way I would approach examining the matter."

Jack smiled. "Is there anything you're *not* sure of, Liana?"

She missed the edge on his remark. "Yes," she said. "Yes, there is. I can't say yet whether they have a nuclear family. Mating appears to be on a random and transient basis. We don't have a long enough observation chain to be certain what happens to these pairings if a viable birth results."

"Hell," Gerd said, stubbing out his cigarette, "we don't even know how long it takes a Fuzzy to reach adulthood—and probably won't until we've watched Baby Fuzzy grow up, however long that might take."

Liana Bell's eyes fairly sparkled. "That's why I envy all of you," she said. "Here you are, right at the beginning of the most important body of knowledge in Terran history—to a sociologist, anyway. I've just hit the high spots. It'll take years to get a rough idea of the true operations of Fuzzy culture. There's a whole career here for a *half–dozen* sociologists."

Lynne Andrews suddenly spoke up. "Why don't you ask Dr. Mallin to loan you out to Fuzzy Institute?" she asked.

Liana's eyes widened. "Is that an invitation?" she said excitedly.

Ruth and Gerd looked at each other for a moment. "It certainly is," Ruth said. "We've all got, as you say, a lifetime of work all mapped out. You certainly won't be encroaching on any of our programs."

"You could stay with me," Lynne said. "I have a whole bungalow to myself."

"Oh," Liana said, her mouth making an "O" as she said

it, "that would be too good to be true." She frowned. "Dr. Mallin wouldn't hear of it, I'm afraid."

"Ask him," Jack said flatly. "He can't put you in jail, and he can't shoot you in the foot; all he can do is say no. And," he added, "I imagine Juan Jimenez might be persuaded to put in a word for you."

Liana's eyes narrowed slightly. "I'll talk to him about it tomorrow," she said.

Fait accompli, Jack thought. Looks like we're just before seeing a lot more of Juan over here. It will be interesting, to say nothing of how she might be able to explain why the Upland Fuzzies have a lot of habits that are different from the woods Fuzzies. Well, all in good time, one supposes.

He leaned forward and knocked out his pipe. "I don't know about the rest of you," he said, "but I'm for getting a good night's sleep in my own bed—for a change."

Gerd got to his feet as Jack did. "I'll walk across the Run with you, Jack," he said. "I've been sitting all day."

At last, Jack thought. "Sure, Gerd," he said. "Why not have a nightcap at my place? The women are probably dying to talk about a dozen things without us around, anyway."

XXXV

"What make do, Cobra–Eyes?"

O'Bannon's head jerked around instinctively, his face already formed into a scowl. He was standing in his tent, in his undershirt and sock feet, and had just finished fastening the spiral–nebula–and–anchor insignia to a fresh field–green shirt that hung from one of the ridge rings.

There was no one there—not at eye–level, anyway. He looked down and located his visitor; a Fuzzy with a khaki barracks cover cocked on the back of his head, who had one foot crossed over the other and was leaning on his steel *shoppo–diggo*.

"What make do, Cobra–Eyes?" Starwatcher repeated.

The scowl vanished as O'Bannon squatted down and extended his hand to the Fuzzy. "What's all this stuff about 'Cobra–Eyes?' " he said, although he knew the answer perfectly well. "Where'd you get that one, Starwatcher?"

Starwatcher extended a tiny hand in greeting. "That what all Greensuit Hagga call you," he said. "Must be your front name. Is so?"

O'Bannon knew full well that the men of the First Battalion referred to him as "Cobra–Eyes," behind his back. As a matter of fact, he took a good deal of secret pride in it, but for morale purposes he had to pretend offense when someone let the term slip in his presence. As a matter of fact, the nick–name was spreading. Spies informed him that Colonel Tom McGraw, the commander of the Marine brigade stationed on Xerxes—and his immediate superior—so identified him with such regularity that it was becoming common for officers on Alex Napier's staff to routinely refer to him as "old Cobra–Eyes."

"It's not a front name," O'Bannon said. "It's a nickname."

Starwatcher wrinkled his nose. *"Nich–name?"* he said, his vocal machinery clicking a bit over the unfamiliar word.

"Right," O'Bannon said, "except they all think I don't know about it."

Starwatcher's face brightened. "Oh," he said. "Is same as *Unka Vida'* so–say other Greensuit Hagga be 'S.O.B.' Is so?"

O'Bannon suppressed the desire to laugh. "Yes," he said soberly. "Is so."

Starwatcher nodded decisively. "I know, you know; but I not supposed to act so you know." He shrugged. "Hagga do many–many that make no sense to Fuzzies. Many–many things for Fuzzies to learn. Now," he said, pointing at the shirt with his *shoppo–diggo,* "what make do?"

"Changing clothes," O'Bannon said, as he shucked on the field–green shirt and buttoned it. "I'm going on a trip. Would you like to come along?"

"T'ip?" Starwatcher said. "What mean—*'t'ip?'* "

"Well, you just take a trip down to Investigations and straighten them out, if there's no one in the division who can handle the job." Victor Grego ground out his cigarette with just the proper display of irritation to drive the point home.

Chief Steefer's image in the communication screen looked uncomfortable. "Mr. Grego," he said, "do you know how long it would take to run security verification on every employee in the Company, even if I had everyone in the Detective Division drop the work at hand and start immediately?"

"Nonsense," Grego snapped. "Every cop we have has waived veridication privacy as a condition of employment. We'll start with you and me—and make damned sure everyone in the Company knows about it. Then, you veridicate all your captains and lieutenants, and they—well, so on down the line. Once that's done, you ask for voluntary compliance from everyone else. I'll back you on it."

"Mr. Grego!" Steefer protested. "It will still take better than six months!"

Good. Harry wasn't using first names. That meant he took this all seriously. And it meant that Victor Grego was in complete control of the conversation.

"Nonsense, again, Harry," Grego said. "By the time we've done all the senior people and you've put a detective task force on the rest of the job, our security leak will flush from cover and take wing. There might be a half-dozen people involved. You won't have to veridicate more than— say—a couple hundred people before someone starts to crack."

Steefer had his own cop's idea of the problem. Never should have let Grego talk him into bending the rules about that Stone woman. Grego was developing a bad blind spot about her lately. No point in bringing *that* up, but it couldn't hurt to put a tail on her—strictly on the quiet. Stubby Butler would be the man to trust for that job.

"Isn't this pretty extreme?" Steefer asked. "Just because someone beat us to the punch on a land deal doesn't mean the Company is riddled with spies."

"Oh, faugh!" Grego said. "The land deal isn't the important point, Harry. The point is that no one knew we had decided to aquire that parcel and develop it. Don Duncan and I had finalized the project plans that afternoon in my office. Next morning, someone had opened an escrow on it."

"It could be co-incidence," Steefer ventured.

Grego drew his mouth into a tight line. "Like the co-incidence of the Navy knowing everything that was said in my office when Henry Stenson had it bugged—with a bug no one could find."

Steefer winced.

Looks like I hit a nerve with that one, Grego thought. "It's not your fault, Harry," he said. "No one could have found that bug. The land deal, though, is *still* not the point." He lighted a cigarette while he waited for Steefer to see the obvious. Steefer didn't. "Look at it this way," Grego said.

"Do you recall the file you brought over and showed me several days ago?"

"Yes," Steefer said. "Yes, I do." He remembered how pleased Grego had been when told that the Company Police had finally infiltrated an undercover man into the ZNPF on Beta.

'If this little land deal can find its way out of a confidential conversation through some leak in the Company, then the contents of that file can escape through the same hole, no matter how tiny it might be."

Recognition flooded across Steefer's face. "Ghu!" he exclaimed. "I never thought of that. I apologize—profusely. I'll get on it immediately."

"Good," Grego said. "Keep me posted. I'll make myself available for veridication at your convenience. Might have a better impact if we both did it at the same time."

"That's right," O'Bannon said to his private communication screen. "We haven't been able to find anything wrong with them, but I want you to put them in quarantine as soon as we arrive on Xerxes. Run a complete psychophysical profile on all six. How long will that take?"

The image of Lieutenant Joseph diCenzo smiled back at O'Bannon from the screen. "About three standard weeks, Jim," he said. "What if I don't find anything unusual? Stamp 'em 'fit for duty' and ship them back to the unit?"

O'Bannon looked irritated. "No, Joe," he said. "If you don't find anything wrong with them, check back with me. I may want you to repeat the tests."

Joe diCenzo shook his head. "Oh, Jim," he said, and made that clucking sound of disapproval that doctors love to make. "Using the Chief Psychologist as a jailer to buy time in a security isolation situation. Shame on you."

"That's *not* what I'm doing—" O'Bannon said stiffly. "—exactly."

"It's all right," diCenzo said. "Really it is. Take my word for it; this sort of thing is done all the time."

"We're all agreed, then," Gerd said to Jack. "Ruth says she'd rather go on up there this evening and get a good night's sleep in the airboat before the *Ranger* picks us all up in the morning."

"Suits me," Jack agreed, "even though I haven't spent a hand of nights at home since this thing in Fuzzy Valley started. Not that it would make much difference, anyway; we'd have to start out well before dawn if we left in the morning."

"When do you want to jump off, then?" Gerd asked.

"Any time you want," Jack said. "I can't even begin to put a dent in the work that's piled up here—not today, at least. I'm at your disposal, Dr. Fuzzyologist."

Gerd mused. "Let's see. I can get things cleaned up here and lay out enough work for a week or so by, say, 1630. We could be in the air by 1730."

"That would put us at the camp before 2300," Jack said. "Sounds okay to me."

"I'll have Ruth pack a lunch," Gerd suggested. "We won't want to take time to sit down to dinner."

"If you like," Jack said. "No need, really, though. I know the Headquarters Company Mess Sergeant. We could have a hot snack of some kind when we get in."

"Hmmmm," Gerd said. "Beltrán *is* a treasure that way. We should take along some *tosh–ki waji,* in that case. But, will he be up that late?"

Jack laughed. "As far as I can tell, he never sleeps."

"I'll see you, then, after I break away here," Gerd said.

"Fine," Jack replied. "I'll get all packed up and meet you at your bungalow at 1630."

"1630 it is," Gerd said, and blanked the screen.

"No, I *can't* wait for him," Ben Rainsford said to his communication screen. "I'm leaving here not later than 1630."

O'Bannon rubbed the first two fingers of his right hand across his forehead. "I must have your signature on these authorizations. Will you be in quarters after you leave your office?"

"No," Rainsford replied, rather testily, "I will not. I'm going straight to Justice Pendarvis' home for a very crucial reception—something essentially political, rather than social. If your man misses me here, have him bring the stuff over there. I'd like to have the Judge look it over, anyway. My secretary will give you the address. Anything else, Colonel?"

"No," O'Bannon replied. "That will be fine, sir. Thank you very much, Governor."

"No trouble at all," Rainsford said, as he pressed the key that would bring the receptionist back on the channel. "Glad to be of help."

After Miss Werner took over the call and blanked Rainsford's pickup, he chuffed furiously on his pipe for a moment. "Confound the Navy," he said to his empty office. "Confound everybody," he said to the stack of papers on his desk. "And especially confound everybody who makes these damned scientific discoveries when I'm stuck here trying to hold the government together with spit and glue. Only the greatest set of artifacts discovered this century—maybe *any* century—and I'm not out there in the thick of it where I belong. *Damn it all to Nifflheim, anyway!*"

Gwen dropped two full lines of lyrics from "Senchant Star" when she saw Diehl and Spelvin come into the smoky main room of *The Bitter End*. The musicians bridged it over nicely, and no one else noticed. The Friday night after–work crowd was already starting to build up. It would drop off a bit as the office workers and tradespeople drifted away to home or dinner, but by 2100 or so the joint would be packed and people would be standing three–deep around the tables in the casino room.

She discreetly returned Jim Spelvin's wave in her direction as he and Everett Diehl hurried toward the bar across the back of the main room. Ghu! Why doesn't he get hold of himself? He could amount to something if he'd quit making a life's work out of being a Marine bum. They're all alike. Damned Marines! Healthy and dumb. Always dead broke by the end of payday liberty. . .

She watched—only half paying attention to the rest of the song—as the two of them elbowed through the crowd at the bar, then said something to the bartender. Soon there was a whispered conversation with Raul Laporte, who had abruptly come from the gambling room, then all three of them headed toward Laporte's office. Now, that was strange. Laporte did not often invite anyone into his office—certainly not a couple of Marines whose main worthiness involved being in debt to him.

O'Bannon rubbed the first two fingers of his right hand across his forehead as he flipped open the folio and began going over the paperwork inside.

Inventory and certification; in order. He thumbed the page back. Receipt for his copy of inventory, signed by Commissioner Holloway; in order. Form DRO-10 for removal of "artifacts of unknown or unestablished origin" from the planetary surface, signed by Commissioner Holloway, and with signature blocks for Governor Rainsford and himself.

O'Bannon smiled as he signed the copies in the space provided for himself. Below his space—as Officer–In–Charge—was another for NCO–In–Charge. It bore the name and signature of Philip Helton, Master Gunnery Sergeant of Fleet Marines. "Sergeant–Major Miller will be glad to hear that," he said to himself. He initialed the attachments of authentication, which cited the Federation Constitution and TFN Regulations governing such matters under Priority One.

He moved his attention to the papers in the left wing of the folio—those of a purely military nature. Travel authorization, with names of involved vessels, roster of personnel, travel itinerary—all in order. He signed in the appropriate places, then looked up at Helton. "NCOIC, you say?" he said.

Helton shrugged. "Only of the dig. That's specified on the DRO-10. Besides, I out–rank Miller."

"I know you do," O'Bannon said. "I talked to Governor Rainsford while you were bringing this stuff over. If you should miss him at his office—he's leaving there early—you'll be able to get him at Judge Pendarvis' home." He handed Helton a slip with the information. "What time do you think you'll be back?"

"It's right there on the itinerary, Colonel," Helton said.

O'Bannon gave him a dead pan look. "Officers have an itinerary," he said flatly. "You have a schedule."

"I see your point," Helton said.

"Hmmmmm," O'Bannon replied.

Helton turned to leave.

"Phil," O'Bannon said quickly.

Helton turned back toward him, hitching the folio under his left arm. He expected mild disapproval of his not departing formally, but wasn't in the mood for it. "Yes, sir?"

"I'll stay up until Holloway and his party get here—make sure they're settled—that sort of thing. No reason for you to bother with that. You'll be tired after the trip, I imagine." O'Bannon spoke slowly, as though choosing his words.

"That will be fine, sir," Helton said. "Anything else?"

"Yes," O'Bannon said. "Take my command car. Bushmeyer will be quite rested, as usual. And, I want you to take a couple of men with you for security. I don't like the noises I've been hearing from Mallorysport lately. There's trouble brewing up over there. I can smell it—even from here."

"You mean more civil disorder?" Helton asked.

"Something like that," O'Bannon said. "If it goes to Martial Law again, I hope they send in the Second Battalion this time; they haven't been kissed yet."

Helton nodded.

"Watch yourself, Phil," O'Bannon said. "And let me know when you're back—even if I've gone to bed."

XXXVI

"Do you think you can persuade Starwatcher to come to Xerxes with us?" Holloway asked.

Little Fuzzy threw out his chest and pointed at it with his own thumb. "Sure, Pappy Jack," he said. "Easy make do. Me *Numba'-One Fuzzy.*"

Orangish light from the afternoon sun shifted in patterns through the interior of the airboat as Gerd brought it up to altitude and set his course for Fuzzy Valley.

"What do you think, Little Fuzzy?" Ruth asked. "Do you have any ideas about the ship and the dead Fuzzies we found in it and in the cave?"

Little Fuzzy shrugged. "Me no know," he said. "Starwatcher say his people have story that Fuzzies come from someplace else—someday go back that place. Many things yet for Little Fuzzy to learn."

Jack nodded. "Many–many things for Hagga to learn," he said. "The Fuzzy remains in the ship aren't woods Fuzzies and they aren't Upland Fuzzies. Do these new Fuzzies have anything to do with the remains we found, or do they just occupy the same geography? What does the Fuzzyologist say, Gerd?"

Gerd grimaced. "Damned questions. Every time we find the answer to one question, it brings up two more questions. We're getting nowhere at hyperspeed—even though we know an enormously larger amount of information about Fuzzies than we did a year ago."

"We know that the decomposing titanium ship hull caused the soil in Fuzzy Valley to become richer in several different kinds of titanium compounds," Ruth said. "Oxides and nitrates of titanium, sodium tritanate, titanic acids—that sort of thing—not to mention other nitrate compounds from rainwater leaching down into the valley. That's why the Fuzzies cultivated plants there—until the drought dried up the vegetable patch. The plants picked up titanium from the soil.''

Jack thoughtfully packed tobacco into his pipe. Little Fuzzy promptly dug into his *shodda–bag* and began doing the same. ''Then why,'' Jack said, ''when the woods Fuzzies began their southward *volkerwanderung,* following the land–prawns, did the Upland Fuzzies stay? They knew it was going to be a hard life.''

Gerd shrugged. ''Maybe they thought the rain would come back and things would pick up again. After all, they had no way of knowing that the Company's draining Big Blackwater was causing a permanent climate change.''

Jack held his index finger in the air. ''Let us,'' he said, ''ask a definitive eyewitness source. How about it, Little Fuzzy? Why did one group stay and the other group migrate?''

Little Fuzzy delayed his answer until he had finished lighting his pipe. He blew out a plume of smoke. ''They— what you call Up'end Fuzzies are the *Haigunsha.* We, you so–say woods Fuzzies, are *Kampushi–sha.* We, both us, *Gashta.* No fight; not good. Make friend, make help, have fun.'' He screwed up his tiny face for a moment, forming the words for the concept. ''We just—not same—even though same—*Gashta.''* He shrugged. ''We go—they stay.''

''Does anyone know about that, Little Fuzzy?'' Gerd asked.

''No,'' Little Fuzzy said simply. ''Too much time ago. Many–many.''

''Maybe the Fuzzies came on the ship,'' Jack said. ''*Somebody* came on the ship. Maybe they brought the Fuzzies with them.''

''So what happened to them?'' Ruth asked. ''Dead? Rescued? What was their relationship to the Fuzzies?''

''Damned questions,'' Gerd muttered.

''Two tribes of Fuzzies,'' Ruth said, half to herself.

''What is *t'ibe?''* Little Fuzzy asked quickly.

While Ruth explained it to him, Jack moved up into the control seat next to Gerd's. ''You know,'' he said. ''We ought to push a little bit—not too hard—to borrow that sociologist—what's–her–name—Liana Bell. She could have a field day with this, and just might come up with some answers that will help us out.''

''Well,'' Gerd mused, ''let's wait until we see what Napier can come up with. In any case, we'll be gone about a week, and we can't do much about it until we get back.''

''That reminds me, Gerd,'' Jack said, ''is it okay with you if I borrow your airboat and go back down to the Station while you and Ruth and Little Fuzzy are gone?''

Gerd looked at him. ''Aren't you going along?''

Jack waved his pipe noncommitally, ''Oh, I'm not going to be much use up there, and I've *got* to catch up on the work that's piled up for me. Besides, I think I can depend on you and Ruth to look out for Fuzzy interests. There's really nothing we can get crabby about, anyway, what with Napier invoking Priority One.''

''Sure,'' Gerd said. ''That's all right with me. We'll keep you posted by screen—at least as much as the Navy allows us to.''

''You know, Gerd,'' Jack pondered. ''I've sort of been rolling a little theory around in my head. Tell me what you think of it.''

''Go on,'' Gerd said.

''If someone crashed that ship here—and *someone* certainly did—they could have had Fuzzies on the ship with them. They were on their way *from* somewhere *to* somewhere and just had some problems—like the time I borrowed your airboat to go up the Cordilleras, lost power, and had to set her down in the woods.''

''And damned near got killed by those two woods tramps,'' Gerd said.

''Yeah,'' Jack said, running his hand over the scar on the right side of his ribs. ''They could have died off, but there is a disturbing lack of remains. Or, they were rescued. If they were rescued, that disturbing lack of remains would indicate one hundred percent survival.''

''Which is not statistically persuasive,'' Gerd said.

''No,'' Jack replied, ''but it's possible. It would also indicate a speedy rescue. So, they were rescued and left some of the Fuzzies behind.'' Jack held up his hand. ''I know what you're going to say. That's not a practice in keeping with logical procedure and ethics of a star–traveling race. But, suppose this. Suppose some of the Fuzzies ran off into the woods, couldn't be found by the rescuers, and were abandoned out of necessity. That would form the original group of ancestors for the *Zarathustran* Fuzzy. Cut off from the parent gene pool, there would be some random genetic drifts that developed them into an essentially different species. *That* would account for the difference in stature between the Fuzzy bones in the wreck and the Fuzzy bones in the cave.''

''The ones in the cave, too?'' Gerd said.

Jack nodded.

Gerd shook his head. ''The ones in the cave are three hundred years newer than the ones in the wreck.''

Jack snorted. ''Well, they wouldn't change much in that length of time.''

''Yeah,'' Gerd said gloomily. ''I have to admit that.''

''It might go a long way to explain why Fuzzies need titanium when they couldn't have evolved the need for it,'' Jack said. ''What do you think?''

Gerd nodded. ''It's worth pursuing. I'll give you that. Damn Garrett's Theorem, anyway,'' he growled. ''I don't know why xeno–naturalists can't draw an easy problem once in a while.''

Jack leaned back in the chair and puffed his pipe. ''That, Dr. van Riebeek, is one of the reasons I never had the desire to take up science as a trade.''

''Profession,'' Gerd corrected.

While Gerd van Riebeek's airboat was still in the air, a Marine command car grounded on the landing stage at the level just below the residential suite occupied by Justice and Mrs. Frederic Pendarvis.

Helton spoke to the two men with him. ''Karnowski, you and Ash hop out and make a show of guarding this thing as soon as I clear myself with that local cop over there.'' He leaned forward and tapped Bushmeyer on the shoulder. ''And you stay awake, son. I don't want you lifting off into the overhead. Makes paperwork.''

In answer to the door chime, and in the temporary absence
of the butler he had furnished for the occasion, the caterer
opened the door. He was a bit startled to see a Marine outside
in the corridor.

''I have paperwork for Governor Rainsford to sign and
thumbprint. I understand he is here,'' Helton said.

Jerry Panoyian smiled deferentially. ''You are correct,''
he said. ''If you will be good enough to step into the foyer and
wait a moment, I will tell him you are here, Sergeant.''

As Panoyian turned to go, Helton put a hand on his shoulder. Panoyian turned, slightly surprised. No one ever
touched him except to shake hands.

''Just a minute,'' Helton said. ''Who's that over there—
with the good-looking girl and the Fuzzy wearing a bow
tie?''

Panoyian's eyebrows shot up into his hairline. ''Why,
that's Mr. Victor Grego, the Manager-in-Chief of the Chartered Zarathustra Company,'' he said with a slight look of
disdain.

''Oh,'' Helton said. ''Thanks. Thank you very much.''

Jerry Panoyian tugged at the jacket of his formals, as if to
say, ''Some crust for a Marine,'' and turned to fetch Ben
Rainsford.

Helton finally caught Christiana's eye at the same time he
saw Rainsford—whom he recognized—working through the
crowd, followed by a tall, slender gentlemen whom he did
not recognize. Helton winked at her, as if to say ''Nice
going.'' She hesitated a moment until she recognized him,
then frowned and squinted worriedly as she realized Helton
was the only person in the room full of highly-placed officials and powerful men who knew of her previously avowed
trade. But she sensed he had no intention of meddling in her
life, smiled happily at him, and turned back to the conversation.

Judge Pendarvis caught the exchange between them,
watching it over the top of Ben Rainsford's head. He hadn't
spent a lifetime in the theater of the courtroom without
learning to spot minute subtleties of human reaction.

As they drew closer to the foyer, Helton heard Rainsford

say back over his shoulder, "Some poppycock about removing artifacts from the planetary surface. I want you to see if it's legal before I sign anything."

Helton and Judge Pendarvis were introduced.

"Ah," Helton said, shaking hands, "the man who changed the history of Zarathustra," he said. "Your name looms large on the lips of law professors in Terran universities these days. An honor to meet you, sir."

"I was only following the law as I saw it, Sergeant Helton," Pendarvis said. He waved his hand toward a door. "Shall we step into my study?"

Once inside the comfortable, booklined room, Pendarvis stopped short. "How rude of me," he said. "Would you like a drink, Sergeant?"

"No, thank you, Judge," Helton said. "My day isn't over yet. I have to get back to Beta tonight."

"Of course," Pendarvis replied. "I understand." He took the folio which Helton handed him and sat down at his desk.

While Pendarvis and Rainsford were going over the paperwork, with occasional pointing at paragraphs by Rainsford, accompanied by the question, "Is that legal?" Helton stood and looked at the books. One didn't often see old books anymore, made of paper, with pages that had to be turned manually. They took up too much space when compared with chips designed to be put through a readout screen. Helton loved the smell of them. He moved slowly down the shelves, stopping occasionally to look at the titles, with his hands clasped behind his back, and rocked up and down slightly on the balls of his feet. It must have cost a fortune to ship these things out here, unless some Zarathustran antiquarian was actually running a printing plant on the planet.

"This is all in order, Ben," Pendarvis said. "Ink it in the spots indicated. I've extracted your copies." He got to his feet and picked up the slender panetella from his ashtray. "Do you like books, Sergeant?" he asked Helton.

Helton started slightly, then turned abruptly with a grin. "Very much, Judge. Very much.

'There is no frigate like a book
To take us lands away,

Nor any corsairs like a page
Of prancing poetry.' ''

"Well said," Pendarvis replied. He sighed. "Would that more people thought so." He walked over to where Helton stood, and ran his hand over one of the shelves. "I rather thought you did, from the meticulous way you had prepared and arranged the papers in the folio. Only one misplaced comma, which I corrected."

Rainsford joined them and handed the folio back to Helton, who opened it, went briefly through the papers, pausing for a moment to note the Judge's correction.

"I believe you're right, sir," Helton said. "It could go either way, but I think this usage makes better sense."

Rainsford jerked his pipe from his bush jacket pocket and fired it up. "What is this?" he demanded. "Federation business or a grammar class?"

Pendarvis smiled benignly at him. "Ben," he said, "did I ever tell you 'The Pendarvis Theory of Technology?' ''

Rainsford shook his head while he began to produce huge clouds of smoke from the pipe.

"You'll likely enjoy this, too, Sergeant," Pendarvis said to Helton. "Simply put, it is my theory that everything wrong with everything is the fault of language teachers."

Helton leaned forward attentively.

"If a child is taught," Pendarvis said, "that it's all right if you mis-spell a word occasionally, or don't always punctuate exactly correctly, then you are teaching that child that small mistakes are okay, as long as people know pretty much what is meant. I feel this is a dangerous attitude to foster in a highly technological society, because it encourages people to think 'Well, after all, the readout is only a *little bit* over into the red zone. Maybe it will return to normal while I'm trying to remember which way to adjust the control. Let's see, now, was that to the left or to the right . . .' Do you agree?"

Helton nodded. "Absolutely, Judge. The commonest criticism of my evaluations revolve around my being too particular about details, but I say *almost* on target is no better than missing it by a million miles.''

"Where *will* the scientific method turn up next?" Rainsford snorted.

Pendarvis shook hands warmly with Helton. "Well, I know you have a great deal left to do tonight, Sergeant. I don't want to keep you from it, and I must get back to my guests. However, next time you are in Mallorysport, will you do us the honor of paying a call on Mrs. Pendarvis and myself? We have a good deal to talk about, I suspect.''

"I'd be honored, sir," Helton said. "I'll screen ahead." He turned and shook hands with Rainsford. "Thank you for your time, Governor.''

Rainsford waved his pipe vaguely. "No trouble at all," he said as Pendarvis ushered them from his study to the foyer.

After another round of goodbyes, Helton caught a second glimpse of Christiana, sitting on an ottoman, talking and laughing with four Fuzzies. Lovely girl, really. This is certainly a better environment for her than Junktown. She was never cut out for that kind of life, anyway.

After Helton had departed, Pendarvis closed the door and beckoned Rainsford to follow him back to the study. He went to the sideboard and poured them both a small brandy. He handed one to Rainsford and stood, silent, for a moment, staring into the distance and reflectively sluicing the brandy around in the snifter with a slow circular motion of his hand. Finally, he turned to Rainsford. "Who would have thought it, Ben," he said. Then, more musing to himself than talking to Rainsford; "An educated man and a gentleman—in Marine field greens." He took a small sip of his brandy and fixed his gaze on a painting over the fireplace. "And wearing stripes on his sleeve," he continued. Pendarvis frowned. "Not an officer at all," he said. Still staring at the painting: "What do you make of it, Ben? It's another inexplicable paradox of the human spirit—one that had never crossed my mind until just now.''

"I'll admit it's at least unusual," Rainsford said, "to find a career Marine and an educated man both living inside the same skin, but I don't know that I would call it a paradox. The factual universe is largely made up of paradoxes.''

Pendarvis sighed and set his glass down on the sideboard. "I suppose you're right," he said, "but it's still quite a revelation—to me, at least. Well, let's get back into the bull-pen."

"That's more like it," Rainsford said enthustiastically. "I've just about got old man Buchanan whipped into shape so he thinks he's made up his mind to take a position and stick it out."

Outside in the corridor, Helton waited for the lift that would take him back down to the landing stage. He looked up and down, to make sure no one was watching, then danced a little jig and sang to himself:

> When I was a young man I lived all alone,
> And never saw a lady I wanted to own.

Spelvin and Diehl were all smiles when they came out of Raul Laporte's office—a contrast to their usual appearance after the usual fierce tongue-lashing from Laporte.

From the stage, Gwen saw them come out into the main room. Each had a piece of paper—about receipt size—in his hand. They compared them for a moment, smiled some more, shook hands, and folded up the receipts and put them in a pocket.

Strange, she thought. What business could those two have had with Laporte? They certainly didn't have enough sols together to pay off their gaming debts, but they sure are acting like it.

Laporte emerged from his office, said a few hurried words to his bar manager, then pushed hastily through the crowd, toward the back door.

"Take a long break," Gwen said to the lead musician. She darted toward the rear of *The Bitter End*, threw on a wrap, and was soon out the door—just in time to see Laporte disappear around the corner on foot. There's only one place he can be going this time of night without an aircar. The only place that close is Hugo Ingermann's office, and Ingermann is always there at night.

XXXVII

It had been a long and exhausting evening.

Victor Grego loosened his neckcloth as he crossed the landing stage, with Diamond tagging along with him. His private aircar would take Christiana on to her place. He was just too tired to see her home.

She understood that perfectly well, and had suggested it. What a marvel she had been tonight. So many ruffled feathers to be smoothed down; she pitched right in and just charmed the pants off those old bull zebralopes who were swinging the biggest hammers in the Constitutional Convention. And Bill Zeckendorf; he had bought up a large chunk of Mortgageville from the banks that had foreclosed all those one and two-mile–square parcels when the last immigration boom had fallen apart. Let's see—when was that—must be about nine years ago, now. He was itching to develop the place, huffing and puffing about unfair competition from the Company, and was making ugly noises about a Restraint–of–Trade suit. Could turn nasty. Christiana had him eating out of her hand like a tame tilbra in less than thirty minutes.

What a remarkable young woman.

Grego let himself in the back door of his penthouse and turned to close it. "Do you want anything before the sleep–time, Diamond?" he asked.

Diamond stretched and yawned, then patted his little belly. "No, Pappy Vic," he said. "Diamond *too'fu* now." Yes, supper at *Alfredo's* after the reception had been a rather exceptional affair, too. Walter seemed to have outdone himself again.

"You run along, then, Diamond," Grego said. "Pappy Vic has some thinking to do."

Grego stopped in the kitchen and poured a generous helping of brandy into the snifter. He paused for a moment, thinking of the racing wheels that spun inside his brain, decided it would take a bit more to put him to sleep, and sloshed in some more brandy. No point in going to bed— even at this point of fatigue—if your mind refuses to stop running scenarios, making lists, and cross-indexing information. Tossing and turning for hours is worse than staying up.

He brushed the switch as he entered the living room, bringing the lights around the ceiling-edges to a soft glow. Comfortably situated in his favorite chair, he absently reached into the bowl of nibblements he kept on the coffee table and his mind went back to the first time he had seen Diamond. There had been a Fuzzy loose in Company House—one who had escaped from the group Herckard and Novaes kidnapped on Beta—who had gradually worked his way up to Grego's penthouse and eaten all the salted snacks out of the nibblements bowl.

Then Diamond looked about for a soft, warm place to go to sleep and that's where Grego had found him—curled up on his own bed. At first he had been outraged; Fuzzies were the enemy; Fuzzies had cost the Company its charter. But no one who is sane can dislike a Fuzzy. In the abstract perhaps it is possible, but in person there is no Terran human who wouldn't want a little friend like that.

Grego turned on the communications screen. Perhaps something to take his mind off all the things he was responsible for, all the things he alone could keep control of, was in order.

The swirls of colored light dissolved into an image as the audio came up.

" . . . *And it is this grasping conspiracy between the criminal lunatics running the colonial government, the banking cartels, and the blackest lot of thieves among all of them*—The Zarathustra Company—*that seeks to rob you; yes, you, the common people of this planet of your birthright. Not a birthright made in a series of shady deals on Terra and in the lofty salons of exploiters located at the top of Company House, but the birthright earned by the farmers, the frontiersmen, the colonists who have made this planet what it is today, who have shaped it from the mud made by its soil and your own sweat*—that *is your rightful share of all the good and glorious things of Zarathustra. Your blood has fallen on this soil! You have bought and paid for it!"* Ingermann thumped his fist on the lectern in front of him. *"It is . . ."* His voice dropped to a whisper. *"Zarathustra is . . .* YOURS!" He spread his arms wide in benediction.

The announcer's smooth voice segued over the fading picture. *"The preceding was recorded at an earlier time for broadcast at this hour."*

Grego wiped his forehead. "Ghu!" he said. "Just what I need to calm me down!" He inhaled deeply from the snifter and leaned forward to change the channel. "Surely there must be some mindless, nonsensical screenplay I can watch."

George Lunt took his feet off his desk and turned toward his Chief of Detectives. "Ahmed," he said, "you realize that we're going to have to turn him loose."

Ahmed Khadra nodded. "Let me bake him and baste him for a while. We can hold him seventy–two hours while we verify his identity and check for wants and warrants."

A grin crept over George Lunt's square face. "You're sure there's nothing personal about this?"

Ahmed snorted. "Well, the discovery that the CZC has planted a man right under our nose in the ZNPF *does* rub me the wrong way *just a bit.*"

"How did you turn him?" George asked.

"Bardini was in Red Hill and overheard the guy making a screen call to Harry Steefer in Mallorysport," Ahmed said.

"Did he hear any of the conversation?" George asked.

"No," Ahmed replied, "but they weren't talking about the ball game."

George frowned. "Has this guy had duty on anything but routine patrol?" He frowned more deeply. "I mean, has he ever been assigned to the detachment in Fuzzy Valley?"

Ahmed nodded affirmatively.

George let his hand fall on the desk. "That tears it," he said. "Okay, put him on the griddle and see what he really knows. We may not have been compromised too badly. We still have to turn him loose, though. He hasn't committed a crime he can be charged with.''

"Industrial espionage—'' Ahmed began.

"—is not against the law—unfortunately,'' George finished.

"Could we hang him with fraudulent enlistment?'' Ahmed inquired thoughtfully.

George's mouth drew down into a hard line. "I haven't written the regulation covering that, yet,'' he said.

"Hmmmm,'' Ahmed said. "Well, there isn't much more we can do tonight.'' He looked at the wall readout. "The mess is closed down by now. Why don't you take pot luck with Sandra and me?''

"I don't know,'' George said. "You sure she won't mind?''

"I'll give her a screen call right now,'' he said. "Besides, if I don't go home right away, I might as well not go at all.''

Grego leaned back in his chair and took a sip of brandy.

An austere, rather shaggy gentleman of middle years peered soulfully from the screen. *"This is your host, again, Holger Wachinski,"* he said sonorously, *"inviting you to join us for this, our last selection in tonight's concert by the Mallorysport Symphony Orchestra. The* Spellbound Concerto *is notable as one of the earliest pieces of serious music to utilize an electronic instrument in the solo capacity. Distilled from the sound track music of the screenplay of the same name, composer Miklos Rozsa performed a masterful fusing of the delicate tonal quality of the Theremin with the richness of the then–traditional orchestra.*

"Co–inciding almost exactly with the beginning of the Atomic Era, this exquisite concerto immediately received many awards, and remains a durable and lasting piece of work on its own merits—" Wachinski turned. *"Ah! Soloist John Kvassny has just come on stage to enthusiastic applause. And now, Maestro Cascora is approaching the podium . . . Ladies and gentlemen—Spellbound."*

Grego was beginning to relax, now. He was, after all, accustomed to the public slanders of Hugo Ingermann, but not after a fourteen–hour day of bargaining and dealing to get this cattle drive of a Constitutional Convention going the direction he wanted. What with the Company loaning vast sums to the Colonial Government to keep it on its feet until a Legislature was seated in accordance with a soon–to–be–adopted–it–was–fervently–hoped Constitution, Grego couldn't afford to sit around and let the new government pay him back with money it taxed away from the Company. The Company had to get some breaks in the tax laws, and the best way to do that was for the Company to have its fingers into writing those tax laws. A majority of the stalwart old pioneers on the convention would also be sitting in the Legislature. Now was the time to get them on the Company's side—while it wasn't too obvious to them that the Company had an axe to grind. If Jimenez and his eggheads could raise just one reasonable doubt about Fuzzies being native to Zarathustra, then they could take it all to court and possibly get the Company Charter back—or a reasonable facsimile of it. Might have to live with a duplex version—a re-chartered Company *and* a Colonial Legislature. In any case, it couldn't do any harm to make some influential friends for the Company while the opportunity presented itself.

Grego took a deep breath and let it out slowly at the first soaring notes of the *Spellbound Concerto*. Spellbound. He was going to have to do something about Christiana, too. She was on his mind more and more these days, and not in her capacity as Chief Fuzzy–Sitter either. Things were going on inside him that he didn't even want to identify, much less actually deal with. But he was going to have to deal with them, and he knew it.

Gwennie's eyes were the size of saucers as she listened outside Hugo Ingermann's office door. She was certain that the thumping of her heart could be heard all over the building.

She could only catch a phrase once in a while as Laporte and Ingermann talked, but it was still the most astonishing conversation she had ever heard. An entire cave, full of sunstones! That's the news that Ev and Jim brought to Laporte, which sent him streaking to Ingermann's office. It couldn't be true. It was just—impossible. Surely those two jarheads knew better than to tell a lie to Raul Laporte, just to get out from under their gambling debts. He'd cut their throats and leave them in the street for that. Maybe they were getting ready to ship out and hadn't told her. No, that made no sense. If their unit was leaving Zarathustra, they could just run out on the gambling debts—without risking the wrath of Laporte. So, it must be true; yet it was unbelievable.

She started as she heard a chair scrape on the floor in the office. Did she have time to get down the corridor and out of sight—before Laporte came out? She tugged at the doors on a couple of offices. Locked. She tugged at another one. It swung toward her. It was a janitor's closet. She darted inside and pulled the door almost shut behind her, peeping out through the narrow crack, into the corridor—like a mouse hiding in its hole.

Presently, Laporte came out of Ingermann's office, looked up and down the corridor, and sauntered away with his hands in his pockets.

Gwennie jumped out of the closet as soon as Laporte was out of sight around the corner of the corridor. The problem now, was to beat him back to *The Bitter End* so he wouldn't miss her when he returned. Somewhere along the way, she'd stop and give Chris a screen call.

Hugo Ingermann was just buttoning his jacket over the automatic pistol he had tucked in his waistband as he came out of his office. He stood there a moment, looking at the back of the short blonde who was scurrying away down the corridor. Now, that was odd. There was never anyone in the building at this hour except himself, his callers, and the cleaning help—and he had never seen the cleaning help move that fast. He frowned, then his eyebrows shot up. He quickly locked his office door and moved off after Gwennie with a speed that was surprising for a man of his bulk.

Gwennie hurried down the esplanade, figuring to go back into *The Bitter End* by the front door, as was her habit after a fresh-air break outdoors. That would be faster than the twisting route Laporte would have to follow down the back alleys. Besides, Laporte wasn't in a hurry—she hoped.

There was a public screen up ahead, under the light. She stopped there, cleared a channel with her card and punched out a call–number combination. She didn't bother to pull the hush–hood. This part of the esplanade was deserted, with the single exception of a grimy old man who was sitting on a bench and swigging reflectively from a bottle.

No answer. She punched it out again. Still no answer. Chris wasn't at home. She must be at Grego's penthouse, then. Gwennie hesitated a moment, feeling a little awkward, then punched out that combination.

The music and the brandy were unwinding Victor Grego very nicely from the crushing tension of the thousand things he had been thinking about. Naturally, he grimaced irritably and cursed profanely under his breath when his private communications screen chimed softly.

He savagely punched the access key. The colors swirled and burst, dissolving into the image of a short blonde with touseled, cascading curly hair. "What is it?" he asked brusquely.

Gwen was still out of breath from half–running for several hundred meters along the esplanade. "Is Chris there?" she asked.

"Chris?" Grego said querulously. The only person he called Chris was Dr. Jan Christiaan Hoenveld, and he could not for the life of him even begin to speculate why this rather disheveled and breathless young woman should expect the Company's chief biochemist to be at his residence at this time. "Chris?" he repeated. "Are you sure you have the right screen combination?"

Gwen saw that he did not understand. "Yes, Chris," she said. "Chris Stone. You don't know me; I'm her friend, Gwen."

"Oh," Grego said, suddenly catching on. "Christiana. No," he said abruptly, still irritated by the interruption. "No, she is not."

"Mr. Grego," Gwen said, "I apologize for calling you at this hour, but I *have* to get hold of Chris at once."

Grego looked at the readout above the screen. Why, it was past 2200 hours. But there was a wildness in Gwen's eyes that was unmistakeable. He softened his voice. "Have you tried her apartment?" he asked.

"Yes, *yes*," Gwen said. "She's not there. That's why I thought she might still be at your place."

Not there? Grego thought. *She must have stopped to pick up some things on the way home.* "Well," he said, "I just had my driver take her home a short time ago. Why don't you try again in a little while."

"*I don't* have *a little while*," Gwen pleaded. "I don't *know* when I'll get another chance to call. Look, will you do something for me?"

Grego hesitated.

"It's *very* important," Gwen said intensely.

"What is it?" Grego asked.

"Try to get hold of Chris and tell her I've got to talk to her—*tonight*. It's about the sunstones on Beta."

Grego's ears pricked up instantly. Sunstones on Beta? "What about the sunstones on Beta?" he asked.

"Oh, no," Gwen said, a look of sick terror coming over her face. "No, please. Please. Please don't—"

Grego was momentarily confused. Then he saw that Gwen was looking at something beyond the angle of the screen's pickup range. There was the sound of two gunshots. Gwen spun off to one side, out of the pickup's transmission frame.

"*Gwen!*" Grego barked. "Gwen! Are you all right?"

She reappeared on Grego's screen, leaning against the left wing of the Kiosk, with her arms folded across her chest. Her face was contorted with pain.

"Gwen!" Grego said again. There was no point in asking if she was all right. The grayness of her face and the gasping, labored breathing made it plain she was not. "Where are you?" Grego asked. "I'll get an ambulance car there at once. What happened?"

Her eyes rolled back and she began to slowly slide down the kiosk's baffle panel.

"Gwen!" Grego said, loudly and sharply. "Don't pass out on me! Tell me where you are!" He felt so damned helpless, but he knew he had to keep her attention focused on his voice.

She reached out with her right hand and, with a snatching motion, grabbed the hush–hood bar on the other wing of the kiosk. Blood was soaking through her dress just above the right breast. She pulled herself back into a full standing position and braced herself between the two wings of the kiosk. Her face was contorted with pain, and then she coughed uncontrollably for a moment. She shook her head, as if to clear her vision, spat something at her feet, and leaned close to the pickup. "Ingermann," she rasped hoarsely, *"it's INGERMANN!"* Then her grip on the hush–hood bar loosened and she slid down out of the pickup's range.

"Gwen!" Grego shouted. "Gwen!" No answer, no sound of movement. His mind was racing. As long as the circuit was open, he could have the call traced. He sprang to his feet to do just that, then stopped.

From one side of the pickup area, a hand reached into the transmission frame. The screen went blank.

XXXVIII

It was quiet in the conference room that adjoined Alex Napier's office. It was quiet because Commodore Napier liked it that way. He liked for everything to be quiet. He did not always get his way.

Regardless of what time it was anywhere else in the cosmology, it was 2000 hours on Xerxes. Xerxes ran on Fleet Standard Time, which was the same as Galactic Standard Time, in universal use by all mariners.

Colonel Tom McGraw was the last officer to come in from the passageway. He shut the hatch behind him and folded his lanky frame into his chair. He was tall, rail–thin, with close–cut gray hair, and commanded the Marine brigade that was attached to Xerxes Base. There was a small spot on his chin where a lipstick smudge had not been totally scrubbed off—hardly noticeable. Alex Napier noticed it.

Napier spoke from the head of the long oval table. "Gentlemen, you have probably been hearing some scuttlebutt to the effect that electronic gear of presently unknown origin has been found on Northern Beta Continent in conjunction with the wrecked hypership we are excavating there. For once, the scuttlebutt is correct."

Everyone chuckled obligingly.

"This material," Napier went on, "has been impounded under Priority One and is being brought to Xerxes by Jim O'Bannon and Master Gunnie Helton on *The Ranger*. That vessel will arrive early tomorrow afternoon, our time. Accompanying them will be Dr. van Riebeek and his wife— uh—the other Dr. van Riebeek, who have been studying the Fuzzies for something over a year now. Pancho Ybarra is coming up from Mallorysport and is due to arrive tomorrow morning. There will also be a couple of Fuzzies in the van Riebeek party. Liaison Officer—Commander Ybarra—the

Navy's only MOS—official Fuzzy Watcher, as some say—
will divide the escort duties for the civilians and the Fuzzies
between himself and my special aide, Lieutenant Gilbert.''
He waved his hand to identify Moshe Gilbert in the event
someone might not know who he was.

"You will notice," Napier continued, "that several staff
officers are not here. That is because the work to be done has
nothing to do with their sections. I want the entire matter kept
as quiet as possible until we know pretty well what we have,
here. I'm not imposing any security restrictions on this, but
neither do I expect any one of you, or your subordinates, to
engage in social conversation on the subject until I pass the
word. Captain Greibenfeld will conduct the balance of the
briefing. Connie. . .''

The Exec picked up a file folder and a yellow, ruled note
pad and got to his feet. He moved to the lectern in one corner
of the room. Moshe Gilbert sat down at the projection console in the corner facing him and threw a map of North Beta
onto the screen. Greibenfeld *harrumphed* politely and began.

Grego paused for just a second. The shock of what he had
just seen soaked in as his mind rapidly catalogued the information that could be useful. He lunged forward at the communications screen and punched out a combination—playing the call board with his whole hand, instead of his
usual one–digit–at–a–time–with–the–index–finger method.

The screen cleared to reveal a Company police sergeant
with his feet up on his desk—who was nothing if not astonished to see the purposeful–looking face of the Company
Manager–in–Chief glaring out of his comm screen. He jerked
his feet off the desk as though it were hot and cinched up his
neckcloth's knot. "Yes, *sir*, Mr. Grego," he said.

"Who's your watch captain?" Grego snapped.

"Uh—Captain Lansky, sir," the sergeant said.

"Put me through to him—instantly," Grego said.

"Yes, *sir*," the sergeant replied briskly.

The screen image switched to that of Captain Lansky.

"Morgan," Grego said, "where's Chief Steefer? Right this minute?"

Lansky was almost as astonished as the sergeant. "Why, I imagine he's at home, Mr. Grego. Why?"

"Look on your locator log, man," Grego said. "This is important."

Lansky peered at something on his desk. "Yes, sir," he said, "he's at home. Checked in from there at 2100 hours."

"Thank you, Morgan," Grego said. "No time to explain now. We'll be getting back to you."

An equally bewildered Chief Steefer appeared to be in the middle of getting ready for bed when Grego screened him.

"Listen carefully, Harry," Grego said. "I only have time to go over this once." He launched the information he had about Gwen; her first name, her physical description.

As Grego talked, Steefer was thinking, *Ghu; what's all this fuss about some Junktown floozie? Mallorysport P.D. sweeps up a couple of them a week, drilled by person or persons unknown. Nifflheim, it's not even my jurisdiction.* But he continued to dutifully make notes on the yellow pad in front of him.

"Okay?" Grego said.

Steefer nodded.

"Two things make this important, Harry. She was desperate to get in touch with Christiana. And, the last thing she said, when whoever it was shot her was—now get this— 'Ingermann. It's Ingermann.' "

It took Steefer about two seconds to get it. "I—think I see what you mean, Mr. Grego. He may have really stepped in it this time."

"Ghu, I hope so," Grego said. "I fervently hope so."

"I'll make some calls from here and get the ball rolling right away," Steefer said.

"Right," Grego said. "Then, you pull your pants back on and get down to fifteenth level. I want you to run this personally. Have the entire detective bureau drop what they're doing and stay on it till we find her—if it means looking behind every grimy door in Junktown. She may still be alive. At least that's what I'm hoping for."

"I'm on the way, Mr. Grego," Steefer said. "Anything else?"

"Yes," Grego said, "two things. I want you to have a detective go to Christiana's apartment and determine if she's there, and, if so, that she's all right. If she's not there; find her. They may be trying to get her, too. We won't know until we can piece some more of this together. If she is there, have a man watch the place, but don't let her know about it. Your man is to report directly to me from the public screen in that building as soon as he has anything."

Steefer nodded and drew a line under something on his note pad.

"The other thing, Harry," Grego said; "I know Gwen was calling from a public screen. I could see the esplanade in the background. I think it was *Pequod Plaza,* but I'm not sure. In any case, it's a good place to start looking. Questions?"

"No, Mr. Grego," Steefer said.

"Good," Grego replied. "I'm going to call Gus Brannhard now and have him put the City Police on it, so you should be hearing from Al Earlie by the time you get to your office. Now, you guys squabble out who's in charge of the operation any way you want to, but be prepared to set up a command post in Junktown if you don't turn her up right away and start calling in off–duty detectives."

"Yes, sir," Steefer said.

Grego could see a perplexed–looking Mrs. Steefer in the background of the screen pickup. Don't worry about it, Mrs. Steefer; you married a cop, not an accountant. "Remember, Harry . . ." Grego said.

"Yes, sir?" Steefer inquired.

"Find that girl!"

Grego was mildly stunned at the sight of Gustavus Adolphus Brannhard in his pajamas. Then he realized that he had always supposed Gus slept naked in the crotch of a tree, with a bottle of whiskey cradled in the crook of his arm.

"Oh. Victor." Gus said and yawned. "It's you. What's up?"

"Sorry to wake you, Gus," Grego said.

"That's all right," Gus said. "I had to get up to answer the screen anyway." His shaggy chest hair was curling out of the pajama collar and wisps of it protruded from the spaces between the buttons.

"Look, Gus," Grego said. "We're onto something very important, here. Why don't you have a jolt to get your heart started and I'll tell you about it. You'll be fascinated; guarantee it."

"Good idea," Gus said. "Be right back."

"I'll hang on," Grego said.

When Gus Brannhard returned to the pickup area of his screen he had a half–glass of amber fluid in his hand and a sparkle in his eye. "Shoot," he said.

Grego narrated the events of the past half hour. When he got to the "Ingermann. It's Ingermann" part, Gus leaned forward attentively. Trying to find a charge he could make stick to Hugo Ingermann was Gus's hobby. "Ohhhhhhh," he said. "Ahhhhhhh. I think we have a tiny match here with which we can burn down Ingermann's house."

"I do, too," Grego said, "but only if the girl is still alive and we can find her before someone realizes they've blundered and try to make sure she's shut up for good."

Gus set down the glass and rubbed his palms together gleefully. "I'll get Al Earlie right on it," he said, "and I'll have Colonel Ferguson put the Colonial Constabulary on alert and seal off the city. Let's see—I better wake up Max Fane. We'll probably need some warrants before this is done with. Besides, he'd never forgive me if he wasn't on it from the beginning."

"Good," Grego said. "Keep me posted. I'll be right here and I'm staying up until we have something definite—one way or the other."

Alex Napier turned off the lights in his cabin and climbed into his bunk. As he pulled the sheet up under his chin he was thinking that a lot more people knew what might be up, now, but he was pleased with the way the briefing had gone this evening. Sharp young lad, that Gilbert, too; sharpest he'd seen in some time. When the question was put to him while

they were having a nightcap, he had already figured out what
the rest of his mission was to be after all the scientific findings
were in, the duplicate folio built up, and the "armed copy
boy" phase of his assignment completed. Yes, have to keep
an eye on young Gilbert. He might be going places in this
man's Navy.

He slept.

Having done everything he could do, for the moment,
Victor Grego opened the terrace doors, picked up his brandy
snifter, and went outside. He liked to sit there, in the quiet of
the night, and listen to the city. Sometimes Mallorysport
would speak to him by the distant hum of human activity that
drifted up to the top of Company House. Sounds from far
away were all blended together at that altitude and the result
was that the *character* of the city at that moment would
effulgently come to his ears.

Tonight, there seemed to be a suspiring murmur of discon-
tent bordering on misery. And small wonder; Mallorysport
was still digesting an enormous helping of immigrants. The
poor, the poor; why are the poor always with us? We have
conquered the very stars, and with all our science and all our
pluck and all our will to cross the endless gulfs of space, we
have not been able to lift the human spirit high enough to
erase poverty and its children—the broken, the pitiful, the
helpless. . .

His ruminations were cut short by the soft chiming of his
private screen. He rushed back inside and opened the key. It
was Harry Steefer. "Yes, Harry," Grego said matter-of-
factly.

Steefer was obviously pleased with himself. It was now
less than an hour since Grego had put him to work. "We've
got her, Mr. Grego," he said. "Her name's Gwen Ramsey."

"Is she . . . ?" Grego ventured.

"Yes," Steefer said, "she's still alive. She's in Mallory
Memorial with two slugs in her. They're going to dig 'em out
as soon as they can get her stabilized. They won't let anybody
talk to her till after that. She's out, anyway, so there's no
point to try until she comes out of post-op."

"You have a forensics man there with an envelope—*in the operating room*—so he can positively testify that those are the bullets that came out of her. If we get lucky enough to bag Ingermann with a gun on him, I bet you a five-sol that they'll match it."

"Been taken care of," Steefer said.

"What kind of odds are we looking at?" Grego asked.

"Not too bad," Steefer said. "The next twelve hours are crucial. If she makes it through that, the doc says she has an excellent chance."

"I want two cops on this around the clock, Harry," Grego said. "One of ours and one from the city. I want them so close to that girl they can hear her breathing."

"Been taken care of," Steefer said.

"*Nobody* talks to her but you, Al Earlie, Gus, or myself until we get a veridicated statement from her. When they find out she's still with us, somebody will try to get in and finish up the job they botched."

"Wouldn't do 'em any good," Steefer said smugly. "We have an eyewitness."

"An eyewitness! That sounds too good to be true," Grego exclaimed.

"Yes, sir," Steefer said. "The first thing my people did was to check in with all their informants. Old J.B. was sitting on a bench and saw the whole thing. Of course, he dived behind the bench when the first round went off, but he has already picked Ingermann's face out of the book. Old J.B. tells us interesting things from time to time and we give him a few sols from time to time. He was the one that called the ambulance."

"Wonderful," Grego said. "You guard him like he was the Company sunstone vault—and get a veridicated deposition."

"It's being done right now," Steefer said.

"Anything else happen tonight that might bear on this?" Grego asked.

"Well—" Steefer hesitated. "I don't know if it's tied in or not. Al Earlie's boys picked up a couple of drunk Marines tonight for disturbing the peace. They told the interrogator a fascinating yarn about a mountain of sunstones on North Beta. The hell of it is they had some sunstones on them and their story holds up under veridication. They might have told Ingermann the same thing. You know how sunstone–happy he is. Something like that could tip him over the edge and make him do something foolish—the something foolish that he did.''

Several things came together in Grego's mind and a picture started to form. ''Very interesting,'' he said. ''Have Al hold them for a day or so. I'd like to talk to them in the morning. We've got a leasehold—at very high royalties, I might add—on a rich deposit over there on the Fuzzy Reservation. Don't let them bail out until I talk to them. If somebody shows up with a *habeus corpus* order, we'll have something to dig at. Anything else?''

Steefer's face became serious—almost grave. ''I don't like to be the one to tell you this, and you may be mad at me, but I had a hunch about something, so I had Christiana Stone followed for a few days.''

''Yes?'' Grego said frostily.

''I put Stubby Butler on it. Remember him?''

Grego paused. ''Oh, yes. The guy who always works alone. Lorenzo Butler. Go on.''

''Well,'' Steefer continued, ''she's been meeting some guy at the *Rondo* every Friday afternoon. Usually gives him a packet of papers. Could be our information leak.''

Grego was silent. Finally, he murmured, ''Stay on it, Harry. We'll see where it takes us.'' Suddenly, Grego was tired—bone tired. He wanted to lay down and go to sleep and never get up again. ''I'm going to bed now, Harry,'' he said, ''but you call me if there are any startling developments.''

''Yes, sir,'' Steefer said. ''Like I said, Mr. Grego, I hate it to Nifflheim to have to tell you that, but—''

''It's all right, Harry,'' Grego said. ''I've never been mad at a man for doing a good job of what I told him to do.''

George Lunt pushed himself back from the table. ''Why,

you're just a marvel of a cook, Sandra," he said. "I would never have thought anyone as pretty as you would be a good cook, too."

"Boy, George," Sandra said, "are you full of it. And this after that crack you made about leaving the party snacks after the George Lunt Memorial Beer Bust, so Ahmed could 'stay alive until I learned to cook.' "

Ahmed guffawed. "What'd you think, George—that I married her for her brains?"

Sandra said something indelicate and took the empty plates into the kitchen.

"Gentler sex, indeed," George said.

Ahmed looked at his watch. "As soon as I'm sure our CZC man is asleep, I'll go back over to detention and rattle him up a bit. We'll have to let him go day after tomorrow, but I want him to think his employers are going to let him rot there."

"Do we have anything new?" George asked.

"Yes," Ahmed said. "I talked to Holderman before dinner and we have the stuff back from our friend at the bank. CZC has been depositing the guy's pay into his account right on schedule."

George turned serious. "Well, then, we've got the goods on him on that one. Get printouts of it. We will, of course, lodge the stiffest possible complaint with the Company."

Christiana chewed her lip and squinted at the comm screen. "So that's where it stands at the moment, Miss Stone," the doctor was saying. "She's been asking for you, so I thought I should let you know."

"I'll be right over," Christiana said.

The doctor held up his hand. "No, there's no use to that, Miss Stone. You couldn't talk to her until after she comes out of the recovery room, and, in any case, the police have put a hold on all visitors."

Christiana caught her voice and took a deep breath. "So what do you think?" she asked.

The doctor shrugged. "It looks pretty good. She's stabilizing nicely, and neither bullet hit anything terribly irreplaceable. One went through her right lung, but it didn't collapse and we're holding pressure on it without too much leakage. You get a good night's sleep, now, and I'll screen you again after I make rounds in the morning.''

"Okay," Christiana said softly. "Okay. Thank you very much." She blanked the screen and slumped down in the chair, sobbing quietly.

After a few minutes, she got up, went into the tiny kitchen of her apartment, and started throwing dishes against the wall. When the cabinet was empty, she stood there in the middle of the room and clenched her fists. "That's enough!" she shouted at the broken crockery. "Dammit! *That's enough! By God, that's enough!*"

She went back to the communications screen and punched a call-number for an air cab.

Victor Grego was awakened by the insistent chiming of his front door. Groggy, he got out of bed and tugged into his robe. "Now, what in blazes—" he said, rubbing his eyes as he entered the foyer. Probably some cop with the latest blast, hot off the relay. He opened the door, intending on a vigorous admonishment toward whoever it was—for not merely giving him a screen-call.

"Christiana!" he blurted out.

She looked small and frightened and vulnerable. There were tear-streaks on her face and a puffy redness around her eyes.

"Why didn't you just use your key to the landing-stage door?" he asked.

"After what I've got to tell you," she said, "you may want it back. Can I come in?"

"Of course," Grego said. "Please."

Her knees started to give way, but she threw out her hand and caught herself on the door-jamb.

"Here, let me help you," Grego said.

She pulled away from him. "I'm all right," she said. "I'm just—all right." She threw her shoulders back and walked stiffly into the living room.

Grego shut the door and followed. "You look awfully shaky, my dear," he said. "Can I get you a brandy?"

"I think it's going to be a necessity," she said. Her legs started to buckle again and she sat abruptly on the couch in an attempt to conceal the fact.

Grego disappeared behind the pullman bar, then reappeared—almost instantly—with a small snifter glass and his own unfinished drink. He handed her the small snifter and put a box of tissues on the coffee table. Then he sat down in his chair and waited.

Christiana took a healthy swallow of the brandy and a deep breath. She started to say something, but her voice quavered and stuck. She set down the snifter, jerked two tissues from the box and blew her nose. Then she picked up the snifter glass, got to her feet and began pacing nervously. "When I came to Zarathustra," she began, "I was running—and I kept on running. After I knew I was falling in love with you, I still kept running—running and making a mess of everything I left my tracks on. Well, I'm sick of running, now, and sick of being scared all the time. I picked a peculiar way of taking revenge, though it made some weird kind of sense at the time." She stopped and leaned against the open terrace door. She took two deep breaths and another swallow of brandy, then turned to pace back across the room in the opposite direction. "One would have thought it the easiest and most natural proposition imaginable to become a—" She drew her mouth into a line, making little parentheses dimples at either corner. "—a whore. After all, I had been compromising all my life, grabbing at crumbs, letting people use me as a—convenience. But I couldn't even do that right. Though one would think it quite simple, I managed to muff it."

Grego listened attentively, silently, except for lighting an occasional cigarette. Once, he refilled Christiana's brandy.

By now, most of the tissues were not in the box, but in a pile on the coffee table. " . . . and that's why I let that horrible man blackmail me," she concluded. "And now I'm here, in the middle of the night." She paused. "I didn't tell him anything very important, but I would have done anything—*anything*—just to hang on a little longer." She hesitated, at first turning to pace some more, then stopping and turning away, looking in the other direction, her back to

Grego. She suddenly shuddered, as though from a hard chill
that quickly passed.

Victor Grego was not a man to be understanding toward a
Company employee who disaffected, but suddenly this
woman was more important to him than the Company. That
frightened him, because he had drained his very life into the
Company for nearly twenty years. Every last scrap of energy,
loyalty, and cunning that he possessed had been willingly and
eagerly yielded up to the Company. Now, here was
something—a mere Terran human creature, assailable by the
frailties and failure of the zeal that renders the human spirit
brittle and fragile—which, at least for the moment, meant
more to him than all the grinding labor he had poured out to
make the monolith of the Company impregnable. His entire
body ached with the sensation of it, and it ached with the pain
he knew Christiana must be going through at the telling of
these things to him—unbidden and somehow unashamed.

Grego stubbed out his cigarette and got to his feet. He
brushed at his eyelid with one hand. There seemed to be
something in his eye.

"And now, it's come to this," she said. "If Gwen hadn't
been trying to help me, she wouldn't have gotten herself
shot." She turned back and looked at Grego; an anguished, a
tormented look. "Oh, Victor," she whispered. "What have
I done? What have I done—just because I want you—just
because I was so terrified of losing you, without even knowing how you feel. Gwennie is the only and closest friend I
have on Zarathustra," she said. "Can you imagine how I'll
feel if she—if she doesn't pull through?"

She stared at Grego, and he stared back at her. They both
knew there was something that should be said, but neither of
them could think what it was. Finally, Grego held out both
his arms. "Not the only friend," he said. "Not the only
one."

She rushed into his embrace and buried her face against his
shoulder, shuddering and sobbing.

He folded his arms around her, rather clumsily at first, then
with more assurance, and a warm, wonderful feeling of
rightness. He patted the small of her back, and ran the flat of

his hand up and down her spine until she stopped shaking.

He stroked her hair, gently brushing it back from her ears, then ran his fingers over one ear. It felt hot and feverish to his touch. "My love," he said softly, "if I know everything there is to know about you, then there's *nothing* they can blackmail you with—nothing they can put between us. Besides," he said, "I love you for what you are now; I don't despise you for something you might have been in the past—a past that's over and done with and gone, now. You are who you are right now. That's the person I love."

She reached up and stroked his cheek with the back of her hand, then hid her face against his shoulder again. "I love you," she mumbled into the left lapel of his robe.

He lifted her head and looked at her. "How's that again?" he asked.

"I love you," she said, and made an enormous sniffing sound.

He brushed the fresh tears out of her eyes with his index finger. "And I love you," he said. He looked down at the floor and flexed his bare toes into the carpet. "I've just been trying to figure out some way to tell you without sounding like an old fool."

She smiled at him, rather wanly. "Oh, Victor," she said, "you could never be a fool. You're the finest man I've ever known."

They looked at each other for a long time, each studying every detail of the other's face. Finally, he kissed her, gently at first, and then with increasing conviction.

She kissed him back, fiercely pressing her entire body against his, her arms locked around his neck. No one had ever forgiven her for anything before, and now here was the poignant deliverance from guilt and fear coming from the only man she had ever desired to forgive her her blind and foolish terror and just accept her for herself.

Grego turned, with his arm about her waist. She turned, with her arm around his waist, and took a step forward. She began to walk, never taking her gaze from his face, smiling, adoring him.

Very slowly, they left the living room and Grego turned off the lights.

In the hours before dawn, a gentle breeze comes up the valley below Mallorysport, blowing in from the sea. This night it was warm and moist and came in through the still-open terrace doors, making the curtains ripple and furl into the room. A little gust puffed in from the south terrace, caught the pile of tissues on the coffee table, and blew them off onto the floor.

IXL

Alex Napier's slumber was troubled.

He awakened in the middle of the night and could not get back to sleep. He lay on his right side and thought; then he lay on his left side and thought, but sleep did not come to Commodore Alex Napier. He thought that in his heart he must have divined what the answers were going to be within the xenology workup that would begin tomorrow. He thought that this extraction and decording of the alien equipment was going to be much like the extraction of a tooth, so far as the Federation itself would be concerned. No more smug immunity from decay; no more snug assurances of the superiority of Terran civilization—that idea of mastering the galaxy, which Terran humans could pull on like a comfortable pair of warm gloves.

And he was going to be the one who would carry the news to the home planet. He was going to be the one who pointed out that the emperor was *not* wearing clothes at all. It wasn't fair. Someone senior should have to carry that load.

He rolled over on his back and smiled, thinking of what he had told Pancho Ybarra. The then–Chief Psychologist had protested that he was only a lieutenant and it was a preposterous presumption for him to have to decide whether or not Fuzzies were sapient, when the best psychological brains in the Federation—

Napier had cut him off, pointing out that those best psychological brains in the Federation "Aren't on Zarathustra, Pancho. They're on Terra, five hundred light–years away, six months' ship voyage each way."

Now here *he* was, gored by his own ox, whatever that meant. There *wasn't* anybody senior to *him* within five hundred light–years, and it was time to pay the rent on that large, comfortable office with the built–in wet bar and the genuine wood paneling on the bulkheads, and the spacious private cabin.

Napier sat up and looked at the faintly lighted readout on the bulkhead of his cabin. 0238. This was getting nowhere at hyperspeed. He reached over and turned on the bedside light, got up, and shrugged on his robe—dark blue with white piping. As he was scuffing into his slippers, he took a sidelong look at the nine–millimeter service automatic on the lamp table. Why in Nifflheim had he taken to packing a pistol around his own ship? Was he expecting a mutiny—a surprise strike attack by alien battle cruisers—a bloodthirsty boarding party? No; none of those. For the past week or so it just made him feel better to be armed. He made a noncommital movement of his head. If it makes you feel better, do it, and worry about why later on. He dropped the pistol into his robe pocket and opened the hatch into the passageway. Once before, he had been unable to sleep; and insurrection erupted the next day.

Go with your instincts, Napier, he told himself. They haven't steered you off course yet, a dim voice from the past told him. He stepped into the eerie red–lighted passageway.

. . . *break, break, net. PC, this is white scout five. I have eyeball contact with planetary surface. Dropping down for a closer look. . .*

Napier stepped into the lift. His hand played over the control and it started to descend.

. . . *four kliks and closing. Steady. Steady. Keep the slideback straight . . . Whip 'em with the daisy chain on my mark———Mark!*

He didn't know exactly why—instinct was as good a term of description as any—but he felt he was going to have to intervene—again—in the civil government's affairs on Zarathustra. Dammit! He didn't want to intervene. No Space Navy C.O. did. It was against Service Doctrine, and it had to be impartially justified after the fact; that always meant a Board of Inquiry.

. . . *stand by, killer; I got a little situation to fix here. Get back to you when—Look out, Red! Three on you in a draw spread. Take a rack heading; I'll flank for you . . .*

Napier stepped out of the red–lighted lift into another passageway. He strolled down it to the Communications Center and let himself in.

. . . you fellers are as safe as a pit in a prune; they near missed Luna with that one . . .

"What's the commo traffic?" he asked the Petty Officer who came hurrying up to him. It didn't happen very often, but when Napier couldn't sleep he always shambled up and down the passageways in his robe and slippers and eventually went down to the Commo Center. His question was always the same. "What's the commo traffic?" he repeated.

. . . SORRY TO GET YOU UP, BUT I KNEW YOU'D WANT TO SIGN THIS WARRANT YOURSELF. . .

The P.O. was Leonard Dickey, sharp as they made them, and Napier knew he could rely on his situation estimate. "It's pretty quiet, sir," Dickey said.

Napier had his hands clasped behind his back and was looking at the opposite bulkhead, covered with communications screens in groups of twenty, each group monitored by a yeoman who played the sound in and out on all of them constantly and absorbed, by some process of osmosis that Napier didn't understand, what was going on on all twenty at once.

. . . AND ASK YOURSELF, WHERE WILL YOU SPEND ETERNITY?. . .

"Go on, son," Napier said. "I'm listening."

"Except for Mallorysport, Commodore. Sounds like they're getting ready for a war or somethin' down there."

"Which bay is that on?" Napier asked.

"Five and part of six, sir," Dickey replied.

"How so?" Napier asked. "You mean there's an unusual flurry of traffic?"

"Yes, sir." Dickey said.

Napier had drifted over to stand behind the yeoman's station on bay five. Almost all the screens had active transmissions instead of the usual static scenic views from pickups on top of the tallest buildings that prevailed at this time of night. "How do you sense this out, Dickey?" Napier asked.

. . . *ZEBRA FIVE—CHECKING WANTS AND WARRANTS, WE JUST FILED ONE FOR SUSPICION OF ASSAULTING AN OFFICER. SUBJECT CONSIDERED ARMED AND DANGEROUS. GO IN AND PICK HIM UP. YOUR BACKUP IS IN THE AIR AND CLOSING ON YOUR LOCATION.* . .

"Well, sir," Dickey said. "There was a shooting along toward the end of the Evening Watch, before I came on. Somebody plugged a girl down in Junktown. Ordinarily, this wouldn't amount to a hoot on Nifflheim. It's nothing unusual in that part of Mallorysport. But this time! The whole damned town blew up. Both police chiefs went down to their offices in the middle of the night—and they're still there. The Attorney General jumped out of bed, woke up the Colonel Marshal, and started cranking out warrants. The Colonial Constabulary surrounded the city and are checking papers on everyone that tries to leave. I never saw anything like it, Commodore."

"Hmmmmm," Napier said. "Anything specific on the shooting?"

"Yes, sir," Dickey replied. "They found the girl and she's still alive. They put out an attempted murder want on—uh—" Dickey peered over the yeoman's shoulder at a log sheet. "Hugo Ingermann. Some kind of fat cat in the local underworld."

"Hmmmmmm," Napier said again. "I think I'll sit in on this station for a while and get the feel of this. Where's your commo chief, by the way?"

"Uhhhh, I think he went down to the Chief's messroom for a sandwich, sir." Dickey said. "Shall I go check?"

"Please do," Napier said, as he tapped the yeoman on the shoulder and slid into the control chair at the console. With some effort, Napier kept a straight face. He knew perfectly well where the commo chief was. He was in the time-honored location occupied by commo chiefs on the Midwatch for as long as there had been modern navies. He was

asleep on his bunk with his clothes on, his senior Petty
Officer instructed to wake him if anything developed that
looked like it might shake the foundations of the universe—
or draw a senior officer to the Communications Center.

Napier began playing the keyboard. Dickey was right, all
right. It sounded like every cop in Mallorysport was busier
than a Fuzzy with the trots and a dull chopper–digger. They
were rounding up shady characters by the platoon, and scour-
ing the city for this Ingermann guy. Of course, from what
Napier had been able to gather, they had been after Ingermann's pelt for years, now, and they finally had him on an
airtight charge. But the whole Mallorysport underworld,
headquartered in Junktown, was starting to blow up and leak
radiation all over the place. The ratcatchers were looking for
business; the rats were all scurrying to find a hole to hide
in.

Presently, Chief Petty Officer Dave Thoss arrived, and
seemed thoroughly conversant with the situation—as indeed
he was, because Dickey had briefed him on it while he
washed his face, combed his hair, and slipped his shoes on.

"Screwy, isn't it?" Chief Thoss said. "What do you make
of it, Commodore?"

"I don't like it, Chief," Napier said. "Don't like it a bit.
This is more like a combat zone than a normal, rowdy
honky–tonk part of town where the principal commerce is the
separation of military personnel from their pay."

An open communications screen, previously silent,
erupted into activity. *COLCON CAR FORTY–EIGHT—
COME TO NEW VECTOR HEADING TWO–SEVEN–
NINER—DEPRESS TWELVE DEGREES—PUT A SHOT
ACROSS THAT GUY'S BOW—GREEN AIRBOAT,
NUMBER ONE–SEVEN–ZERO–ONE STROKE PAUL VIC-
TOR. FAILURE TO ACKNOWLEDGE HAIL.*

"They really mean business," Dickey said.

"Seems to me they're trying to keep the town buttoned up
tight," Chief Thoss said. "The *City of Houston* just dropped
out of hyperspace. She's due to dock on Darius at 1100, and I
imagine they're afraid their man might slip on board and get
away."

"Hmmmmm," Napier said. "What's our vessel on standby status tonight?"

"Just a moment, sir," Chief Thoss said. He consulted a clipboard hanging on the bulkhead behind them, then turned and stepped back over to the station. "It's the *San Pablo,* sir," he said. "Light cruiser, she is. Commander Akerblad commanding."

"Good man, Akerblad," Napier said. "Put her on full alert right now—and load a company of Marines right after morning chow—full combat gear. I'll talk to Tom McGraw a little later on." *After he's spirited whichever female ensign he's currently fooling around with out of his quarters,* he added silently. "But you go ahead and send the order down through channels to the brigade operations officer at 0730, and log the action on my V.O.C.O."

"Yes, sir," Chief Thoss said. "Sounds like you're expecting trouble, Commodore."

Napier leaned back in the control chair and laced his fingers together across the back of his head. "Not necessarily, Chief, not necessarily. I just have a dreadful dislike of the idea that trouble might come calling and find me with my britches down around my ankles."

Victor Grego stood in his robe on the south terrace of his penthouse apartment on the roof of Company House, sipped from a mug of hot coffee, and wiggled his bare toes in the grass—real grass, not artificial. He was fond of saying that he lived on his own real turf. He made a mental note to get after the gardener about more frequent feeding and watering of the terrace lawn. It still hadn't come back up to snuff from the mobs of people marching around on it during Ahmed and Sandra's wedding reception.

Ghu! but he felt rested. He hadn't slept so well in years. The timer chimed on his public 'screen and he turned from the early morning sunlight and brisk, invigorating fresh air to go inside and watch the news 'cast.

He made a detour through the kitchen, where he stopped, nuzzled under the ear of the strawberry blonde, and patted her bottom.

"Victor!" she said. "Stop that. You'll make me cut my-self."

"Well, my goodness, Christiana," he said, shaking a fresh cigarette out of the pack on the counter and lighting it, "we can't have that. Wouldn't do to damage that splendid carcass."

She stopped what she was doing and turned toward him. "Don't you think," she said, "under the circumstances, that you could start calling me 'Chris,' like everyone else does?"

"Nope," Grego said airily. "I dislike diminutives. I am, however, fond of nicknames, and shall proceed to think about one for you." He swept out of the kitchen. "Something appropriate," he said. " 'Punkin,' perhaps."

"Punkin!" she shrilled, and hurled a mushroom at his receding back.

Now, then—he opened the key on the communications screen—to see just what the newshounds have sniffed out about this shooting business.

". . . and so, today, local police agencies are seeking the arrest of Hugo Ingermann on a charge of attempted murder. Now, for a live report, we switch to news director Franklin Young at the scene of the crime."

". . . Thank you, Hal. With me this morning here at Pequod Plaza *is police Public Information Officer, Lieutenant Grisha Kodoulian. We are standing directly in front of a public screen kiosk where a young woman was gunned down late last night. Lieutenant Kodoulian, how can the police be certain that this crime was actually committed by Hugo Ingermann?"*

"We have," said a rather rumpled–looking young man in plain clothes, *"a statement from the victim, who is alive, but still in critical condition, and we have an eyewitness to the actual shooting itself."*

"And who might that be?" Young asked, although he knew perfectly well what the answer would be.

"I'm not in a position to comment on that at this time, Frank," Kodoulian said. *"We have the witness in protective custody at the present time, and a police guard on the victim until she's out of danger."*

"Then you're certain of a conviction?" Young said.

Kodoulian smiled. *"Assuming we can arrest Mr. Ingermann, yes, I think the Colonial Attorney General expects he can get a conviction."*

"Thank you Lieutenant Kodoulian," Young said. *"We have been talking with police lieutenant Grisha Kodoulian, at the scene of last night's murder attempt in Junktown. This is Franklin Young for Zarathustra News Service. Back to you, now, Hal."*

"Thank you, Frank. And now, here with the weather, is ZNS's own meteorologist, Doctor George."

Christiana appeared in the doorway, pushing up the sleeves of Grego's too-large spare robe she was wearing. "What was *that?*" she asked.

Grego smiled. "The weatherman," he replied. "I like the way he throws himself into his work."

She came over behind Grego's chair and put her arms around his neck from behind, kissing him on top of the head. "You're not so bad, yourself. Hungry?" she said, nuzzling around his ear.

"Ravenously," Grego said and took a sip of his coffee.

"Don't worry," Christiana said. "I'll get you to work on time, but I want you well-fed. You have to keep up your strength."

Grego leaned back in the chair and kissed her again.

She stood up straight, again. "Breakfast is almost served, my dear," she said, "but if you distract me very much more, I just may pounce upon you and let it burn."

"Is Diamond up and about?" he asked. "I haven't seen him at all this morning. He's usually jumping up and down on my stomach at dawn."

"Fuzzies are very discreet creatures," she said in a tone of mock-seriousness. "Actually, he's out playing on the terraces somewhere. Later on, I'm going to take him over to the Pendarvis's. He's gotten very keen about teaching Pierrot and Columbine the fine points of eating with silverware, and Claudette Pendarvis is quite charmed about the whole project."

Grego frowned. "Does he—?" he began.

"—know about us?'' She finished the question. ''Of course he does. You can't keep secrets from a Fuzzy, Victor. I talked with him while you were in the shower, although I didn't really need to explain. He understands that Hagga are much like Fuzzies—they prefer privacy when mating.''

Grego suddenly sat bolt–upright in his chair. *''Mating?* I hadn't quite thought of it as—*mating!''*

''Well, Fuzzies do, and Diamond does too, darling, so we might as well get used to it.''

He was about to reply when the private communications screen chimed. ''Now, what the Nifflheim,'' he said irritably and motioned Christiana to move out of the pickup range.

She made cooking motions with her hands and blew him a kiss as she returned to the kitchen, shoving up the sleeves of her robe.

Grego opened the access key. *Hmmmmm. Have to do something about getting her one of those that fits, I suppose.*

The image cleared and became that of Harry Steefer. ''Good morning, Victor,'' he said. ''Sorry to disturb you before you get to the office.''

''Quite all right, Harry,'' Grego said. ''What's up? Have you picked up Ingermann yet?''

''Not yet, sir,'' Steefer replied, ''but he can't get out of Mallorysport. Ian Ferguson has the city buttoned up tighter than a new airlock, and Al Earlie and I have a cop on every esplanade and escalator in town. I expect they're all equipped with the wanted photo by now, and we have detectives combing Junktown; we're putting the pressure on all his known associates and watching his haunts.''

''Mmmmmm,'' Grego said. ''How about a reward? The Company will put up forty thousand sols. I'm going to be talking with Gus Brannhard and Ben Rainsford later today. I'll see what I can do about getting a similar amount posted by the Colonial Government.''

''Rainsford'll rant and rave about the money,'' Steefer said. ''You know how expense conscious he is.''

Grego smiled. ''Yes, Harry,'' he said, ''I know that. I also

know that Gus has been trying to sink his fangs into Ingermann's throat for a long time. I'll just bring it up, and let Gus
do the convincing. That's my department. In the meantime,
get hold of Max Fane and see what the Marshal's Office can
work out with Judge Pendarvis about immunity from pros-
ecution to the rat who turns Ingermann in. That's your department.''

Steefer stroked his chin. "Yes, yes," he said. "I can see
that. Eighty thousand sols and amnesty ought to get one of
Ingermann's pals to blow the whistle on him.''

"Any other developments?" Grego asked.

"Well," Steefer said, "we've still got the two Marines in
the bucket. So far, no one has showed any interest in getting
them sprung.''

"I'll get around and have a chat with them; might not make
it today, though. Have Nifflheim's own itinerary today.''

Steefer grinned. "No rush, Mr. Grego," he said. "Bert
Eggers is staying on for a few hours after his duty shift. He's
not real fond of Marines to begin with, and he takes a fiendish
delight in interrogating suspects who are hung over.''

Grego chuckled. "Anything else?"

Steefer's grin disappeared. He inclined his head and
frowned. "You remember our man on Beta?" he asked.

Grego nodded. "Did he get anything yet?"

"He got nailed," Steefer said.

"What do you mean?" Grego asked.

"I mean," Steefer said, "that he got caught. George Lunt
has him in jail at Holloway Station.''

"Mmmmmm," Grego said. Then, "Ghu! Harry. We've
got to get him out of there before they can sweat him down.''

Steefer shrugged. "I'm doing what I can, Mr. Grego.
They've got to turn him loose tomorrow—I don't think
they've really got a charge they can hold him on. But, under
the—well—the circumstances, I can't bring any real pressure
to bear.''

Grego was silent for a moment. "Well, do what you can,
Harry, and see that he's de–briefed before he talks to anyone

here—especially the damned news media. We will, of course, lodge the stiffest possible written protest with the Native Affairs Commission.''

"Holloway won't like that,'' Steefer said, ''and neither will George Lunt.''

"Well, then, they'll just have to lump it, won't they?''

"Uh—yes, sir,'' Steefer said.

Grego caught a glimpse from the corner of his eye of Christiana standing in the kitchen door, with a worried look on her face. At first he thought that meant breakfast was starting to get a little black and crisp around the edges, then he realized why she was listening. "Harry,'' he said, ''how's Miss Ramsey doing? Anything new?''

"I talked with the doctor this morning,'' Steefer replied. "She's officially not out of danger yet, but he says she's young and strong, doing nicely, and should pull through with no complications.''

"Good, Harry,'' Grego said. "I'm very pleased to hear that. I'll get back to you sometime before lunch.'' He blanked the screen and got out of the chair.

XL

The charge nurse punched a series of numbers into her console and scrutinized the readout on the screen. "I'm sorry," she said. "Miss Ramsey is not having visitors at this time." She looked crisply at Christiana. "She's in protective police custody until such time as the Attorney General can take her statement."

Christiana frowned and squinted at this most efficient lady in immaculate white. "I have an authorization," she said; "in writing," and pushed the sheet of paper across the desk.

The nurse held up her hand, still looking crisp. She was a floor charge nurse and was not accustomed to anything contrary to her own orders—except from a physician. "I'm very sorry, Miss Stone," she said, "but the orders are quite specific."

Christiana pierced her with an irritated look. It felt good. Slowly, she tapped her finger on the piece of paper. "The authorization which I have," she said in measured tones, "is from the man who issued the original orders."

The nurse raised one eyebrow and dropped her gaze to the paper. "Oh," she said, "you're from Mr. Grego's personal staff. You should have said that to begin with."

"I've been trying my best to do just that," Christiana said. "Now will you please find out if the patient is awake, and inform the police guards?"

Christiana was not prepared, even though she intellectually knew what to expect. A tiny white form lay very still in a white bed. Her skin was almost the same color as the sheets. The elementary sensors of a robomedic were still attached to her body, the multicolored wires and tubes making a crazy pattern on the white sheets.

323

Christiana stepped forward hesitantly. "Gwennie?" she said softly. "Are you awake?"

Gwen said something unintelligible and tried to lift her head. Blonde hair cascaded across the pillow.

Quickly, Christiana stepped to the bedside. "Don't try to move, Gwennie," she said anxiously. "They've still got part of the machine plugged into you."

Gwen smiled thinly. "Chris? Chris—is that you?"

Christiana took one of Gwen's hands in both of hers. "Yes, Gwen, yes," she said. "I'm right here. How do you feel?"

Gwen opened her eyes, blinking for a moment. "Rotten," she said, "but I'm going to beat the house on this one." She smiled, again. "All I've got to do is whip two bulletholes in me. It'll be a snap."

Christiana began to cry.

Gwen smiled again, showing just the edges of her upper teeth. "Chris," she said, "it's not your fault. I was helping to find out what had to be found out because I wanted to. It's not your fault. I just made a mistake."

Christiana dried her eyes on a corner of the sheet.

Gwen coughed hoarsely. A monitor light on the robomedic flickered briefly, then went out as the nasal cannula made adjustments of air pressure in her lungs and their rate of respiration.

"They're going to get Ingermann," Christiana said. "They have an eyewitness to the shooting."

Gwen blinked again. "Of course," she whispered. "The old man on the bench. He was right there."

"Victor has put up a reward on Ingermann," Christiana said. "They've got it fixed so he can't get out of Mallorysport. They're going to get him—for sure."

Gwen moved her body and head into a more comfortable position, so she could look straight at Christiana. "Victor, is it, now?" she asked. "Something has happened, hasn't it?"

Christiana tried to say something, but couldn't. She nodded her head and sniffed. "He forgave me," she said. "He forgave me everything. No one has ever done that before . . ."

Gwen reached up and touched her shoulder.

Christiana nodded her head again. "I've never been so happy—except that you're here—all shot up—and it took *that* for me to get my guts together."

"I'm going to make it," Gwen said. "I'm so happy for you, Chris. I'm so happy for you." She coughed again, and the monitor light on the robomedic flickered briefly.

Christiana leaned down and touched her cheek to Gwen's cheek. "Get well, Gwen," she said. "Just get well; and don't worry about anything else. We'll find some way to get you where you'll be safe as soon as they let you out of here."

Gwen looked at her questioningly. "How?" she asked. "Where is safe, now?"

"Well, Great Ghu!" Christiana said. "You can't go back to Junktown. Ingermann surely has friends left down there. Just don't worry about it, Gwennie. We'll figure something out. I feel strong, now. Ghu, it's the first time in my life that I've felt strong, and I'm still getting used to it. Now, you get strong again, while Victor and I find someplace for you to be safe."

Gwen smiled, again. "Why, Chris? Why?"

Christiana pursed her lips. "Because you're my friend, that's why. You stuck your neck out for me." She paused. "I stuck my neck out last night when I went to Victor. It feels good, because now I know I can do anything I want."

"Were you scared?" Gwen asked.

"Scared?" Christiana said. "I was afraid my legs were going to go out from under me every step of the way. Part of the time I would try to say something and I couldn't get any noise to come out of my mouth."

"I know what you mean," Gwen said. "It does feel good, doesn't it?"

"I never felt better," Christiana said, "except that you're hurt. Why did you have to get hurt? It's not fair—it's just *not fair*."

"Don't worry about that," Gwen said. "I told you; I can do this standing on my head. This isn't the first time some guy's tried to take me out. What's important is that you've found a wonderful man—one who's good to you. That's all there is to life, really.''

Christiana started to cry, again.

With an effort, Gwen reached up and, with the other corner of the sheet, wiped Christiana's eyes. ''Don't cry, Chris. Please don't cry. You've found what everyone is looking for—sometimes for their whole life—someone who's good to you that you can make a life with. That's what you have to look at, now. I'll be fine; really I will.''

Christiana nodded. ''Yes,'' she said, ''yes. Oh, my God, Gwennie, I love him so much . . .''

''I know you do,'' Gwen said. Her head rolled slightly on the pillow and her eyelids fluttered.

Christiana quickly grasped Gwen's hand, again, in both of hers. ''Gwen?'' she asked. ''Are you okay?''

Gwen nodded, almost imperceptibly. ''I'm fine,'' she whispered. ''I'm just fine.''

''This must be tiring you,'' Christiana said. ''I'm going to go, now, so you can get some rest.''

Gwen nodded, again, very slightly. ''I wear out pretty fast,'' she whispered, ''but I'm going to be just fine.''

Christiana bent down over the bed and brushed her cheek against Gwen's. ''Get some rest, now. I'll be back as soon as I get them to let me back in.''

Hugo Ingermann had not shaved.

His clothes were rumpled from spending the night on a cot in the storeroom of his ''charity'' mission. He couldn't go home. He couldn't go to his office. The police were watching, it seemed, everywhere. Thank Ghu he had some money tucked away in blind–account deposit boxes at various banks.

He had risked much to come skulking in the back door of *The Bitter End*—like a common criminal—and have to beg entry to Raul Laporte's office.

Presently, Laporte entered. He was not pleased. ''What in Nifflheim are *you* doing here?'' he demanded. ''Don't you know they're turning over every damp rock in town trying to find you?''

Ingermann's eyes were wild. ''I've got to have some help,

Raul, until this blows over. You've got to find me a place to hide.''

Laporte sat down behind his desk. There was no trace of emotion or reaction on his swarthy face. ''Why don't you just get out of town?'' he asked.

Ingermann was astonished. ''They've got the place velled up tight, Raul. You must know that. I've got to get out of sight, and you've got to help me.''

Laporte leaned back in his desk chair, pulled out his pocket knife and started cleaning his fingernails. He did not look at Ingermann. ''I don't *have* to do a thing, Hugo,'' he said.

Ingermann was a little miffed at the familiarity of using his first name, but he knew he couldn't afford to show it. ''My back is killing me,'' he said. ''Damned cot.''

Finally, Laporte looked up at him. ''Hugo,'' he said evenly, ''for years now you've had the idea that you were in charge of something around here. The rest of us have gone along with it because it didn't hurt anything—and it was profitable for all concerned. Now, you've brought the law down on all of us. They're leaning on everyone in Junktown like I've never seen before, and it's your fault—because you did a stupid thing.''

''*Stupid!*'' Ingermann snapped. ''How dare you call me stupid!''

''I call you what I please, Hugo,'' Laporte said. ''If you had to have the girl shut up, why didn't you use your brains and have it done quietly, without any fuss, and especially not while she was making a screen call in public.''

''Why—I've made you all rich,'' Ingermann said huffily. ''I've—''

Laporte cut him off. ''*You've* been the best crooked lawyer I ever had,'' he said. ''That's what you've done for us—until you managed to get disbarred. Now, you're not even any good for that.''

Ingermann leaped out of his chair, his face white with rage.

Laporte snapped his fingers, and a very large man appeared from an adjoining room. Ingermann sat down.

''What it comes down to,'' Laporte said, ''is that we just

can't afford to be associated with you any more. They're out to get you, and they will. There's an eighty thousand sols price on your head, and I wouldn't give you six-to-five one way or the other who will be the first to turn you in for it. The safest thing for you to do is stay clear of everyone you know.''

"Why, this is preposterous!" Ingermann fumed. "I will *not* be treated this way!''

Laporte's patience was wearing thin. He sprang to his feet, put the flat of both hands on his desk—with the knife near his right hand. *"And that's not the worst of it!"* Laporte shouted.

Ingermann shrank back from the verbal attack.

''The *worst* of it,'' Laporte said, ''is that you had to go and shoot the only decent singer I've been able to hire for this joint in the last five years!''

There was a moment of silence.

Laporte made a gesture of dismissal. ''Now get out of here—before I have you thrown out.''

After a shaken Hugo Ingermann had left the office, Laporte turned to his assistant. ''I don't think Mr. Ingermann is quite in his right mind,'' he said. ''It might be better for everybody if some kind of accident happened to him.''

The large man nodded and left the room by a side door.

It was unusual for Alex Napier to attend to business outside his own office. He preferred—as a matter of protocol—to have people come to him. He had visited Colonel Tom McGraw in his own quarters as a matter of insuring privacy.

''What's your readiness status, Tom?'' he asked. Then, he held up his hand. ''Not on record, but in fact.''

''Coffee, Alex?'' McGraw asked. Napier technically out-ranked him, so he was practicing some protocol of his own.

''Certainly,'' Napier said and arranged himself in one of the large chairs in McGraw's cabin.

As soon as they were comfortably situated, McGraw said, ''We're fine, Alex. I've stepped up re-supply to the First Battalion. We have the company you ordered on board the *San Pablo,* and I can load the rest of the brigade on two hours notice—combat ready.''

Napier nodded reflectively. "Good," he said, then re-peated it. "Good."

"You expecting things to blow up, again?" McGraw asked.

Napier set down his cup and shifted his weight in the chair, so he could reach his pipe and tobacco. "I couldn't sleep last night," he said, carefully packing tobacco into the bowl, "so I went down to commo and monitored the traffic for a while. I can't put my finger on it, exactly, but I don't like it, Tom. I don't like it."

Hugo Ingermann did not customarily drink, and almost never before cocktail hour, but it was past the middle of the afternoon, now, and he didn't know what else to do. Besides that, the weather was hot and uncomfortable, he felt as though his brain had cooked inside his skull, and he could not recall the last time he had eaten.

It was dim and comfortable inside the bar. Ingermann rolled the cold highball glass across his forehead after he took his first swallow. He began to feel better, but he still didn't have any idea what to do next.

There was a news broadcast on the large communications screen at one end of the bar.

Ingermann decided he would listen to the news and have another drink.

When the barman brought him the audio outlet, he affixed the earpiece and plugged the other end into one of the pickup jacks across the front edge of the bar.

" . . . *with more reports of street fights in Junktown. Authorities maintain that these incidents are unrelated, and say they expect the situation to quiet down with the onset of cooler weather—and cooler tempers.*

"Efforts to verify rumors of a sunstone strike on Beta are still unsuccessful at this hour. Colonial Governor Bennett Rainsford's office issued a statement earlier today to the effect that the matter was still in the area of pure speculation. We'll have tape on that a little later."

Ingermann did not notice the person who slid silently onto the barstool next to him. An idea was about to form itself in his mind and he was trying to focus his attention on it.

"Meanwhile, the search for Hugo Ingermann continues, with police expecting an early arrest. Here with a live interview on that story is News Director Franklin Young. Frank. . ."

"Good afternoon, Mr. Ingermann," the man in the hat whispered. "May I join you?"

Ingermann jumped as though he had been stabbed. He turned to stare incredulously into the colorless eyes of the man next to him. There was terror on Ingermann's face.

Joseph Weisberg made a reassuring gesture toward Ingermann as he signalled the barman.

Ingermann took a gulp from his drink.

The barman set down Weisberg's drink in front of him, but Weisberg didn't pick it up right away.

"Who—who are you?" Ingermann finally managed to stammer.

Weisberg smiled humorlessly. "Ah," he said, "you don't remember me, do you?"

Ingermann nodded dumbly.

"Well, it is a matter of no importance," Weisberg said. "What I felt you should know this afternoon," he leaned closer and lowered his voice still more, "is that Raul Laporte has taken a great interest in the state of your health."

Ingermann turned pale. He knew what *that* meant. Ghu knew he had hired Laporte's services in such matters himself, many, many times in the past.

Weisberg leaned forward and took a sip from his drink.

"Why—why are you telling me this?" he asked. It made no sense. Everyone in town, it seemed, was out to get him, yet here was this stranger giving him information that might well save his life.

Weisberg shrugged. "It is not an incident of great concern to me—one way or the other—but I felt you would consider it useful."

Ingermann's eyes narrowed. "What do you want in return?" he asked.

Weisberg shrugged again. "Nothing," he said.

Ingermann still did not comprehend. There had to be a way

out of this. Money, of course, could buy anything, but he had no way to get at his own—except for a few small sums he had put away in the event of just such a blowup.

Suddenly, the rest of the puzzle dropped in to place in his tormented mind. His face brightened. "Blowup," he said softly.

"I beg your pardon?" Weisberg asked.

Ingermann didn't hear him. "Blowup. Heat wave. Riot. Sunstones. Of course," he said. Without another word, he slid off the barstool and scampered out the front door of the lounge.

The barman came hurrying over. "Hey," he said. "That guy didn't pay for his drinks."

Weisberg smiled across the bar at him. "That's all right," he said. "I'll take care of it and collect from him later."

XLI

The Rev keyed the next item of data onto the screen. "We've had one hundred ninety–four arson fires this year, sixty–six in the past six weeks, and six last weekend," he said to the group of men in his office. "Things are starting to strain."

Emmet Taylor held up his index finger. "My cheese shop has been broken into twice this month," he said, "and they didn't even try to find money. They just stole some merchandise."

"These crimes aren't being committed by common thieves and footpads," Floyd Kalisher said. "These people are getting hungry."

"And there's no work for them," added Sam Quo.

Irv Schneider spoke up. "They're borrowing money like crazy in my pawnshop," he said, "on just about anything that can be carried. I know some of it is stolen, but there's no way to prove it—so I have to look over each situation individually."

"The saloon business has never been better," Dan O'Hara remarked. "The place is packed most of the time—but it's not a crowd that laughs and jokes and enjoys themselves. They mostly just sit and stare and mutter to each other."

"What's the government doing about this—if anything?" Mike Morgan asked.

The Rev shrugged. "As much as they can, from what I can tell," the Rev said. "Governor Rainsford and Victor Grego both strike me as being decent, honest men—men who are caught in the middle. They're spread pretty thin. The police are spread pretty thin—"

"—And we're spread pretty thin," George Patterson interrupted. "Every centisol I have is plowed into my business. If that goes up, I'd have to go find a job to support my family."

"Except there are no jobs," Sam Quo repeated.

The aircar grounded quietly on the esplanade, then lifted off a few inches to adjust its position so the light from above would fall on the contragravity housing.

Hugo Ingermann still had a few henchmen he felt he could trust. He peered anxiously out the door. Good, good. Early in the evening. Hot, sticky, uncomfortable weather. There was a splendidly large crowd of people outdoors tonight. These were his friends; they wouldn't let the police get him.

He climbed out, carrying the audio pickup for the external hailing system, and hopped up on the contragravity housing. The esplanade lights shined down on him. "My . . . *friends,*" he began, and the crowd started to accumulate in front of him.

As Ingermann spoke, another aircar proceeded slowly north through Mallorysport, keeping low to the ground and moving under the trees in the open spaces whenever possible. In it were three rough–looking men and an accumulation of cataclysmite, incendiaries, and detonators. By the time it had wound its way to Mortgageville, Ingermann had the ever–increasing crowd in a very unhappy mood and was about to reveal how they could alleviate their sufferings.

Lolita Lurkin burst into the Rev's office. "Father, Father," she gasped.

Everyone in the room turned toward her. There was a bruise on her left cheekbone and tearstreaks on her dirty face.

The Rev got quickly to his feet and came around the desk to her. "What is it, Lolita?" he asked anxiously. "What is it?"

"It's Uncle Charley," she blurted out. "He's goin' crazy. I tried t' stop him, but he knocked me down the ramp."

The Rev frowned. "But why, child?"

"I don't know," she said. "He came runnin' in to get his gun. I asked him what was goin' on, and he said somethin' about we was all going to be rich—and then he knocked me down and ran out, again.'' She started to cry. ''I think he's goin' crazy.''

The Rev turned back to the group. He sighed. ''I guess we can knock off working on the list of aims and goals,'' he said. ''Let's see if we can keep the hatch down on this.''

The others were already moving toward the door.

''Lolita,'' The Rev said, ''you go down to the dispensary and have them take a look at you. And, stay here until I get back.''

Out on the esplanade, smoke was drifting low to the ground from several bonfires that had been lighted. The light from them flickered across Ingermann's face. There was a strange look in his eyes.

''Citizens of Zarathustra!'' he shouted. ''We are all—all—citizens of the Federation. Zarathustra is Federation territory; we *its* citizens. The Federation doesn't want you to be broke and without work, but the Colonial Government surely must; else they would do something about it. My friends, *they haven't lifted a finger!* All *this* while they are sitting on a deposit of sunstones out on Beta—them and *Old Man Holloway!*—that is huge beyond imagination!''

He paused, to assess the muttering of agreement. ''What right,'' he said in measured tones, ''has this damned jackleg government to tell us—*its* citizens—that we have no right to the comforts of life?'' The sound of the hailer speakers echoed between the buildings. ''My friends, there's enough for everyone. Why should *we* go without? Why should *we* break our backs to dig sunstones, when they're lying on Beta—waiting to be picked up?''

''Whatta we gonna do about it?'' shouted a voice from the crowd.

Ingermann smiled, inhaling deeply. *''Go out there and TAKE them!''* he shrieked. *''NOW!''*

There was a moment of silence. *''Take the sunstones!''* the crowd, which had just turned into a mob, chorused raggedly.

The people began to break up, milling about and running in every direction at once—rushing home to get weapons and pile into anything they could put on contragravity.

The Rev found Charley Walker on the outskirts of the crowd, where he was gleefully jumping up and down. The Rev grabbed him by the shoulders. "Charley!" he shouted above the din of voices. "This is crazy!"

Charley glared at him. "Gettin' rich ain't crazy!" he barked.

"Can't you see he's just using you?" The Rev shouted.

Charley's lip curled back from his upper teeth.

The Rev began to shake him by the shoulders, but he knew it was useless. "Charley! *Charley!* Use your head!"

Charley hit him in the jaw with a roundhouse punch.

The Rev fell to the pavement and the crowd surged over him.

Already, aircars, boats, jeeps, work buses, cargo scows, and anything else that would fly, were beginning to rise in clumps from the shack–rows, jumbled old log buildings, and the low buildings that made up the old part of Mallorysport. Their running lights and bottom floods bathed the esplanade and all of Junktown in an eerie light.

When Harry Steefer screened him, Victor Grego was tossing a ball back to Diamond, who sprang at it as though it was something to eat. He had brought some papers from the office to go over, but decided to play with Diamond for a while. He hadn't spent as much time with Diamond lately as he might have, and Grego didn't want him to feel neglected. Christiana had gone to the hospital to visit Gwen. When she returned, they would have cocktails while Diamond watched his favorite bloodthirsty 'screenplay in the Fuzzy room, and then the three of them would have dinner together in the apartment. It would be a nice, quiet evening with everyone together.

When the screen chimed, Grego tossed the ball out onto the terrace through the open doors. Diamond galloped after it as fast as his little legs would carry him.

"Yes, Harry," Grego said when the image cleared.

"Thought you ought to know, Victor," Steefer said. "Most of Junktown is in the air—in a bob–tailed fleet of civilian vehicles. They're heading for Beta to *take* all the sunstones they can lay their hands on."

Grego compressed his mouth. So, things had finally cracked open down there. Well, a hot, uncomfortable night would be the time for it. "Do we know how this got started, Harry?" he asked.

"No one seems too sure, but the word is that Ingermann whipped the crowd into a mob frenzy," Steefer said.

"Ingermann, Ingermann!" Grego exploded. "When we get that son of a khooghra, I'm going to hang him high." He recovered his composure. "They can't get out of Mallorysport, can they, Harry? The Colonial Constabulary is supposed to have the town sealed up tight."

The image of Harry Steefer shook his head. "I wouldn't bet on it, sir. Ferguson's men have been doing just that, but we're talking about hundreds of vehicles, here. Some of them are bound to get through. In fact, quite a few of them are bound to get through."

"Are we lending a hand?" Grego asked.

"Mallorysport P.D. and us are doing as much as we can," Steefer said. "But, there are some fires in Junktown, some street fights, and some reports of looting."

Grego shook his head in disbelief. "So this disorganized gang is heading for North Beta to raid for sunstones. It's like a—what did they call those little animals that committed suicide by the whole herd running over a cliff? Well, no matter; that's what it is. Harry, they haven't got a chance. They're going up against trained Marines."

"I know that," Steefer said. "You know that; but, no one has told *them* that."

"Has any of the rioting leaked up into Mallorysport, yet?" Grego asked.

Steefer shook his head. "Not yet," he said, "but I've increased security around Company House. They may make a try for you, so we're watching your residence very close. I don't want you to leave your apartment without telling me. I'll likely be here all night—or at least until this is over."

"In that case," Grego said, "you'd best put a couple more men on Miss Ramsey's hospital room. They may make a try for her, too."

"Good idea," Steefer said.

"And, Harry," Grego said.

"Yes, sir," Steefer said.

"Christiana's over there right now," Grego said. "Send a Company Police vehicle for her and bring her back here." He leaned back in the console chair. "Any other trials and tribulations?" he asked. "I mean, something minor, like a volcanic eruption in the center of town?"

Steefer smiled crookedly. "One other thing . . ." he said.

Grego didn't like the tone of gallows humor in Harry Steefer's voice. "Which is . . . ?"

"Mortgageville's burning," Steefer said. "Big fires. Has to be arson."

Grego clenched his teeth. "Ghu's guts!" he intoned.

As soon as the transmission cleared, Grego rushed out onto the north terrace. Silver–trimmed maroon Company air jeeps, with POLICE lettered on their sides, were already circling over Company House.

To the north of Mallorysport, great, leaping flames hundreds of feet high were dancing against the night sky, with clouds of dense, black smoke rising above them, already beginning to blot out the stars with a stygian curtain of darkness. Ingermann had unleashed the demons of hell and the misshapen ogres of brutality that still lived deep inside the Terran human spirit, and their primal forebears were now cavorting for joy a few miles north of Mallorysport. Grego had the uneasy feeling that they were, perhaps, the shadows of things yet to come.

In the distance, darting lights showed the location of firefighting vehicles as they sought to close on the fires. One could occasionally catch a glimpse of one of them, illuminated from below by a new billow of flame or explosion.

Grego rolled his eyes upward. "Bill Zeckendorf is going to *love* this," he said to himself.

Diamond had stopped playing with his now–forgotten ball and was watching, too. He thought it was a splendid show and spectacularly entertaining.

As soon as Alex Napier finished the communications abstract which a yeoman had just delivered to his cabin, he grabbed his tunic and began to put it back on. "Another quiet evening shot to Nifflheim," he muttered. With his arm in one sleeve, he punched up a screen–call combination with that hand while he fumbled behind him for the other sleeve.

"Connie," he said to the image of his Exec that came on screen, "have you seen this abstract?"

"Just finished reading it, Alex," Captain Greibenfeld said. "I was just starting to call you."

"Full staff call in my office," Napier said, "in thirty minutes—to include McGraw, his Exec, O'Bannon, and Helton."

"An enlisted man?" Greibenfeld interrupted.

"I want his opinion," Napier said coldly.

Greibenfeld said nothing.

"Signal Akerblad to put *San Pablo* ready to lift off on my order. Situation estimate from Steve Aelborg—he can refine it later; I want what he has in thirty minutes. When you find McGraw or his Exec, I want the rest of the Second and all of the Third Battalion to saddle up and stand by in their quarters for further orders. All supply and support elements to be on their stations as soon as possible."

"Isn't this a bit much, Alex?" Greibenfeld asked. He honestly felt Napier was over–reacting. "I mean this beat–to–quarters–and–man–guns? It sounds to me like just a rather elaborate series of civil unrest incidents."

"It's a mob, is what it is," said Napier, closing up the front of his tunic.

"But, still—" Greibenfeld began.

"Dammit, Connie," Napier said. "A mob is like mud; it has no mind, no form, no reason—only movement. If you don't stop all of it, you haven't stopped any of it. It'll roll over you, smother you, and kill you without ever knowing anything was in its way."

XLII

"We did the best we could do," Colonel Ian Ferguson said into the communications pickup. He was screening from his command car. His tunic collar was open. He looked haggard. "As it is, Governor, we'll be the rest of the night charging and booking the ones we have in custody—if the town doesn't burn down first."

Ben Rainsford wanted to take a handful of his own whiskers in each fist and pull them out. "Ingermann—*Ingermann—INGERMANN!*" he raged. "That fat little son of a khooghra has caused me more grief than the entire planetary government put together. I hope they can hang something with mandatory death sentence on him; I want to be the one that pulls the trigger. How many got through, Ian?"

"As nearly as we can tell," Ferguson said quietly, "almost two hundred vehicles. We have no idea how many people that involves, though."

Rainsford had been lighting his pipe. He waved his hand to clear the dense cloud of tobacco smoke between himself and the communications screen. "You better—no, you're busy enough—I'll screen Napier. Keep me posted, Ian. And don't worry; if you did as good as you could, you did good."

Jack Holloway was nearly two hours south of Fuzzy Valley, almost to Fuzzy Divide. The stars were bright, overhead, and Xerxes had climbed almost halfway from the horizon to the zenith. He had been busily making lists in his head of things to do and was happy to conclude that during the week or so that everyone was going to be on Xerxes, he could just about handle all the work that had piled up since the afternoon when Ahmed Khadra gave a whoop and shouted that he had found an enormous titanium object buried under the soil of

339

what was now called Mount Fuzzy. Now, who could be calling him on the screen? No one knew he was in the air, except . . .

"Major Stagwell, here, Commissioner."

"Yes, Dick," Holloway said. "What's up?"

As Stagwell spoke, Holloway laid Gerd's airboat over into a long, flat arc that would take it back to a reverse course.

"What do they have to shoot with?" he asked as soon as Stagwell had outlined the situation.

"We don't know yet," Stagwell answered. "My guess would be nothing heavier than individual weapons, but I expect they'll have some automatic stuff—maybe a few machine guns."

"I'm on my way, Dick," Holloway said. "Have you raised Xerxes yet?"

"We've signaled and are waiting for the authentication code," Stagwell said. "I've done a lot of riot work, but I want guidance from upstairs on this one."

"Makes sense," Holloway said. "Look, when you get them, tell them I'm returning. I'm the Commissioner; that's where I belong. And tell them I'm going to raise George Lunt—see how many men he can send up. It's his jurisdiction as the ZNPF head cop."

The Rev walked unsteadily into the dispensary at his own mission and sat down heavily in a chair at the nurse's station. There was blood on his face and he felt as though every bone in his body had been broken.

The evening nurse, a volunteer in street clothes, dropped the stack of files she was moving from one desk to another. They went skittering and sliding across the floor in a jumble of forms. *"Father Gordon!"* she said. "Are you all right? You look like you'd been trampled by a veldbeest stampede."

The Rev managed a smile. "I was," he said.

She keyed the automatic page that summoned the doctor. She brought a wet cloth to the chair. "Let's get that cleaned up and see what else we have, here," she said.

"Double vision," The Rev said, shaking his head vigorously. ''Funny. I usually don't get that till the next morning.''

''Jack, they haven't got a chance,'' George Lunt said over the screen. ''They're going up against three companies of trained troops.''

''I'm sure the thought never crossed their mind, George,'' Holloway said. ''This is a mob. A mob never thinks; it just charges like a damnthing. By being totally unaware that they don't have a chance, they just might make it. You see?''

George nodded. ''I'm afraid I do,'' he said. ''I've seen it work. Okay. I'll round up as many men as we can spare without leaving ourselves wide open down here. If there are as many variable unknowns as you say, we may have to fight at Holloway Station. People seem to identify you with sunstones, you know.''

Stephen Aelborg had just finished delivering his situation estimate to the meeting. As Intelligence Officer he was naturally cautious, but had to admit that for thirty minutes' notice, it wasn't too bad.

''Gentlemen,'' Napier said, ''we have a still–developing set of actions here. It remains in a fluid state, not yet fully formed. Therefore we want to keep our ability to respond flexible but quick. Another thing we have to consider is the lag–fac between decisions we make here and the travel time needed to put troops on the ground on Zarathustra.''

Helton had noticed Greibenfeld look at him in an odd way when Napier used the term ''gentlemen.'' He was amused, but made a mental note not to trust Greibenfeld any more than was absolutely necessary.

Napier turned to Helton. ''Gunnie,'' he said, ''what is your evaluation of the First Battalion in terms of weapons and readiness?''

Helton felt his ears flush slightly. He got to his feet. ''First rate, Commodore,'' he said, and proceeded to concisely outline his views.

When Helton sat down again, O'Bannon realized—and felt slightly foolish about it—that he had been holding his breath. Quietly, he exhaled.

"Good," Napier said. "I still want the balance of the Second Battalion loaded aboard the *San Pablo*. Even if the First won't be needing any hand–holding, I'd feel better about having additional men on the surface. Ops will alert another suitable vessel, and the Third will board it and remain there for further orders."

McGraw's Exec was making notes.

The Operations Officer paused, his pencil above his own notes. "Do you plan to intervene, again?" Carl Johnsen asked.

"Emphatically *not*," Napier said. "Only in the case of the most extreme emergency or at a request for assistance from the Colonial Government. It's something that has to be planned for, in any event, although the very thought of it gives me the willies. I don't want to infringe on First Battalion's operation, but I don't want to leave them out on a limb. The doctrine that applies here, gentlemen, is one of minimums—minimum show of troops—minimum show of force—and minimum *application* of force. If the colonial population gets the idea that we're going to step in every time there's a fist fight on Zarathustra, they never will get around to forming a completed government. They'll just look up at Xerxes when the going gets a little rough, sit down, and wait for us to tell them what to do. That's not the kind of attitude that colonized all these worlds in the first place, and I refuse to foster it."

XLIII

Jack Holloway stood, with his feet slightly apart and his hands on his hips, puffing his short pipe and looking eastward. He had given his rifle—he was carrying his 6–mm Stecker in the airboat—a part–way takedown and cleaning. Have to tear that thing down to the last screw and really go over it. Someday soon. Time. Time. Never enough of it these days. That's all he wanted when he came out to Cold Creek Canyon—time by himself. Funny how you never got what you wanted when you searched for it; only when you stopped and let it find you.

Nothing to do now but wait. Everything that could be done was already done. He liked the way Stagwell had laid out his forces; it showed a businesslike knowledge backed up by experience—same kind of attitude that let Helton calmly blow in that tunnel face without knowing what, or how much of it, was on the other side. Holloway chuckled in the back of his throat. He particularly liked the idea with the riflemen on the bench at the north end of the site; a separate group of sharpshooters made up of picked marksmen from each company, placed at an elevation from the rest of the area.

Stagwell came up beside him, his boots blowing up little puffs of dust ahead of the toe. "Anything?" he asked.

Holloway shook his head.

"How soon, do you think?" he asked.

"Can't say," Holloway replied, keeping his gaze on the horizon. "Depends on how fast they're going and whether they really know where we are. They may not have a definite course. If they just cast about till they find the valley it could be quite a while."

Stagwell nodded, sighed, and was silent for a moment. "By the way, Mr. Commissioner—" he began.

"Jack," Holloway said.

"Jack," Stagwell corrected himself. "I've been meaning to ask what your tobacco is."

"OLD TERRAN CUT," Holloway said. He jerked a thumb to his right. "But they grow it down on South Beta."

"Can I get it in Red Hill?" Stagwell asked.

Holloway nodded. "I get it from Walt Davis. Got a little gun store and tobacco shop there."

"Mmmmmm," Stagwell said. "I'd like to pick some up before we leave."

"Try some of mine, first," Holloway said, handing him the pouch without taking his gaze from the horizon. "If you like it I'll bring you a big tin on my next trip up."

"Thanks," Stagwell said, digging out his pipe.

Several minutes passed without conversation. Then, Holloway pointed to the east, where a little gob of light was coming over the horizon. "I think that's company, coming to call," he said.

Presently, the light separated into several, then separated again—and once again—until it was a cloud of lights, each one indicating a separate vehicle in the mob that had gotten out of Mallorysport.

Stagwell turned and looked over his shoulder. "Sergeant Major Miller!" he said.

The battalion sergeant major appeared out of the darkness. "Sir," he said.

"Pass the word to look sharp," Stagwell said. "They're almost here."

"Yes, sir," Miller said. He sat down on the housing cover of a nearby vehicle and began talking to net control, his voice relayed throughout the tactical position on pocket radios like the one he was using. "All right, jarheads; get both eyes open. They're coming in. Don't get enthusiastic. First man fires without orders, I'll have him up on battalion punishment and cut a stripe off him. Remember, these are civilians, but they're a little dockered out . . ."

Five minutes later, the air cars and scows began to land in a ragged, jumbled disorder about seventy meters from the line Stagwell had established.

Holloway shifted his weight, and crossed his left foot over his right knee. He knocked out his pipe on his boot heel, blew through the stem, and put the pipe in his pocket. He unslung his rifle.

Stagwell signaled his engineer sergeant. Floodlight portables illuminated the scene with a blue–white light from about sixty feet overhead, where their contragravity sleds bobbed at the end of umbilical tethers.

"Uh—Major," Miller said from his location behind the nearby vehicle, "hadn't you two better find cover? You're awfully easy to shoot at out there."

"What?" Stagwell said, grinning. "And let them think we take them seriously?"

ZNPF Captain Joe Holderman stood looking out the window of the headquarters and smoothed his flawlessly groomed mutton–chop whiskers. Outside, in the barracks quadrangle, the floodlights reflected garishly off the vitrilite paving of the drill yard. A few hours ago, the yard had been swarming with men as George Lunt assembled forty constables and led them off in patrol jeeps toward Fuzzy Valley. Behind him, he heard footsteps as someone entered the room. That would be Jordan Nuñez, coming in a half–hour ahead of the watch–change to get up–to–date on what was happening before he relieved Holderman and took the new watch.

Nuñez sat down and started scrolling incident–log items up the readout screen. He let out a whistle and muttered something when he ran onto the entry about Fuzzy Valley.

Holderman didn't turn around. "Too many rats in the box, Jordy," he said.

Nuñez stopped the scrolling. "Rats? Whattaya mean, rats, Joe? You know there's no rats around here."

Holderman turned and looked at him. "Too many rats in the box, Jordy," he said again. "In Mallorysport. You get too many rats in a box, they start to eat their way out."

The mob was milling around. Holloway could see Hugo Ingermann in the forefront. Poor, crazy Ingermann. Sunstones had finally done it for him—unhinged his mind.

"It's your territory, Mr. Commissioner," Stagwell said, and handed Holloway the audio pickup.

The mob swirled aimlessly for a few minutes, humming and buzzing with the conversation of anger and indecision, as Ingermann harangued them from the open cargo floor of a work scow. There were periodic shouts and curses from individuals, unintellible at this distance, and a good deal of fist–shaking. Presently the crowd turned and began to surge like a thick lava flow toward the Marines' positions on the line.

Holloway had earlier had reservations about the overhead lighting, but now he saw why Stagwell did it. Misdirection; it gave the mob a focal point to keep their attention in more or less one place—the place Stagwell wanted them positioned. Good thing they had sent all the Fuzzies down into the woods at the south end of the valley. This could turn pretty ugly before it was over.

The vanguard of the mob moved forward perhaps thirty meters, still being swelled by people from among the grounded vehicles, before Holloway stopped them. There appeared to be close to a thousand of them.

Holloway raised the audio pickup to his mouth.

The mob moved another ten meters, their pace punctuated with muted shouts and muttered curses.

"HOLD IT!" Holloway's voice boomed and reverberated as it was amplified over the loudspeakers of a dozen or so of the Marine vehicles strung across the valley. *"This is Jack Holloway,"* the amplified voice said, *"Commissioner of Native Affairs. This is a legally established Fuzzy Reservation."* His words made ghostly echoes as the sound of the amplified voice coming from different locations reached the listeners' ears at slightly different times. *"Your presence here is a violation of law,"* he said. *"I order you to disperse."*

"Nifflheim with you, Holloway!" Ingermann yelled. "We came for sunstones! Sunstones that belong to the people!"

"Yeah! We want what's ours!"

"You got no right . . ."

"Gonna keep 'em for yourself?"

"This for your reservation!"

Ingermann turned to the mob. *"You see?"* Ingermann hooted. "Why should we starve while they get rich from sunstones?"

The mob was rumbling viciously, like an angry volcano. Weapons were being brandished in the air.

"I warn you!" Holloway said into the pickup. *"We will use force. GO HOME!"*

Ingermann turned back toward Holloway and made a derisive gesture. "You can bully your Fuzzies and your flunkies, old man," Ingermann jeered, *"but you can't bully us!"*

More clamor from the mob. "What're we waitin' for?" "We can take 'em." "Come on!" *"Sunstones, SUNSTONES!"* In the front of the mob, a few knots of people took two or three steps forward.

"You'll be the first to get it, Ingermann," Holloway said. The rolling, amplified voice made it plain that he meant it. Just to punctuate his point, Holloway clipped the pickup onto his pocket, twisted his feet to dig his boots in, and levelled his rifle from the offhand position—taking a sight picture on Ingermann's chest.

"Okay, okay," Sergeant Major Miller said into his pocket radio. "Take your line of sight. Let's put the volley shot about two feet over their heads. If that doesn't stop 'em, pick your targets and go for it. On my mark, now—ready—ready."

Ingermann turned pale, but he was a desperate man, now, and he had already come this far. If Holloway broke up his mob, he would very likely be arrested on the spot before he could get away. Surely they, too, must know he was wanted for attempted murder in Mallorysport. He grabbed a rifle from someone, raised it to his shoulder, and fired.

Standing where he was, Holloway was a slightly higher elevation than the mob. The shot took him from below, in the upper left arm. The impact spun him. When he felt the *slap* of the bullet hitting him, he tried to get off his shot on Ingermann, but he was already in motion and only succeeded in dropping the man next to Ingermann.

Holloway spun halfway around and went down.

Ingermann raised the rifle triumphantly over his head and waved the mob forward.

There was a roaring, deafening noise, drowning out the screaming mob, as all the Marines fired a single shot at the same time, sending a sheet of bullets shrieking over the mob's head. They hesitated and ducked, then began running forward, firing as they came.

Rows of people in the front began falling. The charge slowed, faltered, and then broke, as the mob turned and ran back to take cover in the maze of grounded vehicles. From there, they began shooting again. Buried in the rabbit warren of vehicles, as they were now, it was going to be Nifflheim's own job to root them out.

Stagwell got down on one knee and lifted Holloway's head. "You get elected, Jack?" he asked.

Holloway coughed through colorless lips. "No, but I got nominated pretty good," he whispered.

"Are you okay?" Stagwell asked.

"I'm going to be fine," Jack said. "The thing damned near bounced off me. Get me out of this draft." Bullets were whining through the air around them.

"Hey, Roy," Stagwell shouted to his sergeant major. "Bear a hand, here."

Miller came over in a short, crouching run.

Stagwell stood up. There were flat, *splatting* sounds and little geysers of dirt shot up around his feet. They picked up Holloway and carried him over behind the vehicle where Miller had been. Stagwell still had his pipe in his mouth.

"Better get a medic over here," Stagwell said to Miller. Miller was already talking into his pocket net radio.

Blood was soaking Jack's left sleeve. Stagwell reached into his hip pocket and got out a wireman's clasp knife. He slit the sleeve from wrist to shoulder and pulled the fabric away. "Hold your arm over your head, Jack," he said. "It'll slow up the bleeding."

"I can't move it," Jack said.

Stagwell wiped the knife blade on his pants leg and folded it up. "Mmmmm," he said. "It's probably busted, then."

He sat back on his haunches and re-lighted his pipe. "Well—medic'll be here in a minute."

"Where's Ingermann?" Jack asked through gritted teeth.

Stagwell put the knife back in his hip pocket. "When they started to charge, he disappeared in the crowd," he said. "They just enveloped him."

Holloway made several unsavory remarks of along the lines of hoping Ingermann was among the people in the front who had been shot.

A medic came to a sliding stop on his knees. He was festooned with pouches and packs of supplies and equipment.

"Take a look at the Commissioner, Corey," Miller said. "He copped one."

Corey got out an osteo-sono-scan and jacked one end of a wire into it. He ran the sensor head up and down Jack's upper arm. "Bullet's not in him," he said in a businesslike way, "but I get an interruption in the pattern. I think it broke the bone and ricocheted back out. Let's see." He put the sono-scan away, then dug a wrap-scope out of his musette bag. He fixed the lensatic cuff around Jack's arm at the wound site and energized the field. In the direct view the flesh appeared to melt away from the bone, showing a ragged break much like a greenstick fracture, with little chips floating around it.

Corey made some adjustments that weakened the field of the device, and a network of blood vessels and nerves appeared in a web around the bone. He sat back at watched it for a few seconds, then turned off the field. "You got a busted humerus, Mr. Commissioner," he said as he began restowing the wrap-scope. "The fracture's kinda nasty, because of the shattering, but it's not completely separated— and none of your big vessels or nerves got clipped." He wiped down the wound with an antiseptic/anasthetic solution and sprayed the entry and exit wounds with a fibrous aerosol that would make the blood cells web together and stop the bleeding. He put a cuff around Jack's wrist and stapled it to the front of his shirt. "Come on," he said, standing up and helping Jack to his feet. "We'll get you over to the aid station and start to work on you."

Jack stood, weaving slightly on his feet. "Wait a minute," he said. "Where's m'rifle?"

Stagwell got to his feet and looked out to where Jack and himself had been standing. "I see it," he said. "Stand fast a minute." He walked out into the open, puffing his pipe, and picked up Jack's 6–mm Stecker. He blew the dust away from the bolt as he returned and handed the weapon to Jack. "I'll be around and see you in a while," he said. "Right now, I gotta mind the store."

The firing had died down to an occasional rattle of shots an hour later when it started to rain.

The Marines had the mob pinned down among their vehicles. They made no attempt to flush them out, sleep gas them, or mount any kind of attack.

Stagwell's orders were to render assistance—if requested by Commissioner Holloway—make no offensive moves, use the minimum force necessary to protect his own men and keep the mob from the hypership wreck and the cavern, and, should the mob fail to disperse peaceably, keep it bottled up so no one got away. He had a canopy of combat cars overhead to see to the latter point. Occasionally, one of the mob's vehicles nervously attempted to lift off; it was systematically disabled on the ground. Things were getting downright quiet.

Stagwell looked up at the sky, letting the first big drops strike his face. "Wouldn't you know it," he said. "The whole damned place is drying up and blowing away for want of rainfall—but let us get into a little action and right away somebody sends us some mud. I swear; mud follows Marines around like fleas follow a dog."

The rain started coming down harder, steadily. Then, with his face still upturned, Stagwell saw the spherical shape settling toward them. Well, it was about time. He had begun to think the Navy had lost the bus schedule. That's the way it was; the Marines get their work done while they're waiting for the Navy. Stagwell turned his pipe upside down so it wouldn't get put out with a wild raindrop.

In the claimjumpers' camp everyone was wet and nervous.

They couldn't make headway against the Marines and they couldn't escape from where they were. And now it was raining.

Thump. Thump. Thump. "Ingermann never told us about this part," Harris said as he occupied himself with sticking his pocket knife into the wooden deck of the work scow—over and over again.

"I wish to Nifflheim they'd just *do* something," Joey said. Joey was Harris' partner. "This waitin' is gettin' on my nerves something awful."

"Well, stick your head out and see if it's still raining," Harris said. "That'll give you somethin' to do."

Joey heaved a big, moist sigh and opened the side hatch of the scow. Miraculously, the rain seemed to have stopped. "Hey, Harris," he said. "it ain't rainin' no more, but I can't see any stars."

Harris came over to the hatch and stood beside him, looking upward. He held out his hand. "You're right, Joey," he said. "It's stopped."

Suddenly, they were both blinded by an intense light.

A two-thousand-foot diameter light cruiser hovering at one hundred feet will shed the rain from a rather large patch of ground, and that was exactly what the *San Pablo* was doing. She kicked on all her bottom lights at once, illuminating the scene as brightly as high noon on a sunny day. The loudhailer sounded like the crack of doom as the click of the pickup switch was transmitted over speakers powerful enough to carry sound for a mile.

"CEASE FIRING—OR WE'LL VAPORIZE ALL OF YOU WHERE YOU STAND!"

XLIV

"*Vee–dahl*, dammit! You're gettin' to be an old woman."
Helton stood with his feet apart and his arms folded across his
chest.

Sergeant Beltrán re–located his cigar in the exact
mathematical center of his mouth. "Now, you listen here,
Gunnie. My boys just swabbed down the deck of this mess
tent, an' now that we got this wet weather, there's only two
ways anybody comes in here—with clean boots or in their
sock feet; an' that goes for you, the Colonel, the Captain, an'
the corporal of the guard. So, you either go over to the
water–point, there, and clean 'em up with a stiff brush or you
peel 'em off and put 'em back on when you leave." He
pointed to the pile of muddy boots under the tent fly in front
of the inflatable dining tent.

The rain was still drizzling on Hugo Ingermann. Mud and
water had gotten inside his shoes and it gooshed rhythmically
through his socks as he trotted into the deep woods. He was
certain that he had contracted at least double pneumonia,
from the way his lungs wheezed each time he took a breath,
but he kept moving—because the only way to get away from
the fiasco at Fuzzy Valley was to take off on foot and hope for
the best, whatever it might be.

He was momentarily frozen with fear when he saw the
aircar hovering over him. But then he realized that it had no
police markings—and there was no way to escape from it in
any case. He stood there, dumbfounded, with his face turned
toward the sky and the rain falling on him as the vehicle
settled down toward him.

Rain beaded on all the surfaces of the aircar as it hovered a
few inches off the ground, so that Hugo Ingermann could not
see who was inside at the controls, but the side hatch opened

from the inside control and a friendly voice said, "Come in, sir, and out of the rain."

Hugo Ingermann would have climbed into that aircar with the devil himself, just to get in out of the rain—the rain that had been beating on his skull ever since he left Fuzzy Valley. In the dim light he could not make out the face of his benefactor, but the friendly voice said, "Climb over in back, there, and get out of those wet clothes. You'll find some blankets in the locker."

Hugo Ingermann did just that, wringing the water out of his sopping clothes and he took them off and arranged them over the warm air inlet to dry. He curled up in a warm cocoon of blankets and slept.

"Hey! You're not supposed to be up and around," Stagwell admonished.

Jack Holloway gave him a haughty stare. "I'm the Commissioner," he said. "It's my *job* to be 'up and around,' as you put it."

George Lunt had set up a command post at the approximate spot where Stagwell drew his battle line and his ZNPF cops were systematically disarming and making arrest reports on the members of the mob that were still on their feet. George was wondering where in the world he was going to find detention space for all of them until he could turn them over to Max Fane and the Central Colonial Courts for arraignment.

Holloway was squatting on his heels next to the field table where George Lunt was processing paperwork. "Did you find Ingermann yet?" he asked, for perhaps the hundredth time.

Stagwell caught up with him there. "Jack, dammit, you're under the care of my medical officer. Now, will you get back to the hospital tent and lie down?"

"I will not!" Holloway said. "I feel fine—and I have things to do." He waved his broken arm defiantly in the sling.

"Oh, hell," Stagwell said. "I wish Ingermann had shot you in the leg. At least we could take your crutches away."

Holloway turned back to Major Lunt. "Now, George," he said, "what about Ingermann?"

George Lunt spread his hands. "What can I say, Jack? He's not among the dead. He's not among the wounded; and he's not among the prisoners. He's copped out on foot and hit the woods. He'll get hungry, sooner or later, and we'll get him. Now, go lie down, like Dick says. You look all feverish to me."

"Dammit all to Nifflheim!" Holloway said. And he said some other things, more profane, as he tried to hold down the butt stock of his rifle with his forearm while trying to chamber a fresh round one-handed.

"What are you trying to do, now?" George said. He took the rifle away from Jack and slammed the heavy bolt of the Stecker back, then forward, chambering a fresh round. He handed the weapon back to Holloway. "Now, what do you think you're doing?" he asked again.

Jack stood up. "I'm going to find that fat little son of a khooghra," he said. "He's bound to have left tracks in this mud, and I'm going to find him. He got a whole bunch of poor, dumb slobs killed—whose only crime was being out of work and hungry—and I'm going to find him." He *sloshed* off over the muddy ground, in a still-slight drizzle of rain, toward the deep woods.

George Lunt got to his feet and started to say something, then let it be. He knew Jack Holloway well enough to know that there wasn't much point in reasoning with him when he was in this kind of mood.

The dawn in Mallorysport was a dingy gray, partly from the overcast and the light rain, and partly from the pall of smoke that still hung in the heavy air after the fires in Mortgageville had been put out.

There were puddles of water on the weed-infested esplanade where the aircar set down. Hugo Ingermann, wearing now-dry-but-wrinkled clothes hopped out of the side hatch, then leaned back into the aircar to profusely shake the hand of his rescuer. "I won't forget you for this," he said. "I promise you, I'll see that you're taken care of very well indeed—just as soon as this blows over. It'll blow over, you know. These things always do. And when it does, you'll be on my team—and on my payroll. I promise you that. Oh, yes. They've got Hugo Ingermann down right now, but he's not out. You'll see.''

The man in the hat, behind the controls of the aircar, smiled cryptically, but his colorless eyes showed no emotion. ''I wish you the very best, Mr. Ingermann,'' the man in the hat said. ''But please don't feel that you're obligated to me.''

''Oh, but I *am*,'' Ingermann said. ''I never forget a debt of gratitude. That's the way I am about gestures of friendship. You'll see. I won't forget this.''

''I sincerely hope not,'' the man in the hat said. ''Be seeing you.'' He pulled the side hatch shut and watched for a moment as Hugo Ingermann ran off through the puddles of rainwater on the esplanade.

XLV

Joe Holderman stood, again, looking out the window at the drill yard, sipping coffee from a white porcelain mug with no handle. He heard footsteps behind him. "Too many rats in the box, Jordy," he said. "Too many rats in the box."

Jordan Nuñez threw down a stack of printout on the watch commander's desk. "Dammit to Nifflheim, Joe," he said. "What are you doing back here? You're not on duty station again till 1200 today."

Holderman didn't move his gaze from the drill yard. "Can't sleep, Jordy," he said. "Too many rats in the box. I can see it coming. We're going to have to cut down a lot of poor bastards whose only crime is that they can't make a living. Too many rats in the box."

Nuñez hooked his thumbs into his hip pockets. "You're lettin' this get to you, Joe," he said. "Why don't you just have a couple of stiff drinks and go to bed?"

"Tried that," Holderman said. "It doesn't work any more. I'm never wrong. I don't like what I see. Too many rats in the box."

"Oh, hell," Nuñez said irritably. "I'm going to call the Doc and have him give you a shot that'll put you out for twenty–four hours. I'll pull your shift. You've got to get off this."

"I wish to Ghu you would," Holderman said. "I sure don't want it on my record."

Nuñez punched up a call combination on the screen.

When it cleared he said, "Get Doctor Bob." A pause. "I *know* you'll have to wake him up. I've got an officer here that needs a sedative—I.V.—and I want it stat. What? I'm the *watch commander*. Now, get Bob Morton up and get him over here. I don't want to file paperwork on this."

"Son," Napier said, "you've got the whole bag in that portfolio."

Lieutenant Moshe Gilbert nodded.

"Now," Napier said, "I want you to take seriously what I told you. You keep that packet on your lap. You take it with you when you go to the head. You sit on it when you eat, and you keep it tucked under your arm—with a pistol in your hand—when you sleep. You deliver it by hand to Admiral Peterson—nobody else—and you require him—on my authority—to verify thumbprint before you put it in his hands. And then you wait—a week, a month, however long he may take—for the instructions. And then you get those instructions back here—and you burn out the drives on *The Ranger* if you have to. Commander Hesser is at your disposal in that respect. *The Ranger* is powered up and ready to lift out. She'll strain every rivet to get you—and that packet—to Terra in four months' time—if that's humanly possible. Do I make myself clear, Mister?"

"You do, sir." Gilbert saluted.

"Understood, aye," Napier said and returned the salute. The two men shook hands.

"*Ghu!*—you smell good," Victor Grego said as he pitched the file folder of work onto the dappled marble hall table in his penthouse foyer and slung his other arm around Christiana, pulling her close to him as he kissed her on the neck.

"Victor!" she said in mock surprise. "Aren't we ardent this evening."

Grego regarded her at arm's length. "I know enough to grab onto a good thing when I find it. How do you think I became Manager–in–Chief, anyway?"

"I love it, and you know it, you old dog," she said.

"I know it, and I know you love it," he replied. "Cocktails before dinner? Where's Diamond?"

"Yes," she said. "At Government House with Flora and Fauna—in that order. We'll have a drink and then go over there to fetch him—and the Fuzzies will have their evening romp together, and we will dine with Governor Rainsford.

He wants to talk to you about this Navy reception that's coming off tomorrow.''

"Ah," Grego said, accepting the frosted glass she handed him. "Alex Napier is going to *tell us all*. Is that it?"

"More or less," Christiana said, "as I understand it. It's to be done with a certain amount of pomp—and from what I have been able to pick up on the coffee–pot–and–water–cooler telegraph, there's a good chance that you can get the Company's fingers back into the operation of the planet."

"Oh–*ho*," Grego said. He put his arm around her waist and walked her out onto the south terrace, from where they could view the Zarathustran sunset, blazing red and gold in the western sky. "So, this insurrection and gun battle thing over on North Beta is a little larger than the news media let on to the citizens, is it?"

"It certainly looks that way to me," she said.

Grego patted her, just below the ribs. "Maybe I should fire Harry Steefer and put *you* in charge of the Company Police—the way about you that you have of ferreting things out and—oh—managing people—including me."

She giggled quietly and smacked Grego on the shoulder with her fist. "Ingermann got away, you know," she said, turning suddenly serious.

Grego raised his eyebrows. "No. I hadn't heard that. It'll be Nifflheim's own job to dig him out and arrest him, now."

"That's why I think we should send Gwen over to Holloway Station as soon as she's ready to leave the hospital," Christiana said. "She's the star witness in the case, and where would she be safer than sitting in the middle of the entire ZNPF? Perhaps we can arrange for her to stay with Lynne Andrews—who is an M.D.—and who lives next door to the van Riebeeks—who are also both M.D.s. And I understand Gerd van Riebeek is experienced in the bush and a good hand with a gun."

Grego took a pull at his drink. "You've figured it all out, haven't you?"

She smiled a tight little smile and nodded.

Grego nodded. "I'll speak to Pappy Jack at the reception."

XLVI

When Fuzzies talk among themselves, they generally sit down on the ground—or the floor—in a circle and proceed with the conversation. When they are in attendance at a social function with the Hagga, though, they have learned to make their talk-circle in a place where they are not apt to get stepped on accidentally. In the case of parties held in places with outdoor terraces, such as Victor Grego's penthouse or the Colonial Governor's quarters at Government House, there always seemed to be heavy circular tables made of dilon in use as outdoor furniture. These became a favorite place for Fuzzy-talk while the Hagga made Big-One talk.

Starwatcher and Little Fuzzy were deep in serious conversation with Diamond, who would occasionally nod his head slowly. All of them frequently lapsed into *Lingua Fuzzy*, audible to Terran ears only as a series of *yeeks*. All three were soon to be disturbed by Commodore Napier—who referred to them as the Big Three Fuzzies—as he would require their presence in the Governor's conference room.

The reception that Alex Napier had laid on at Government House could, as Christiana had predicted, be accurately described as having a certain amount of pomp. The first inkling that this was a military affair came from the posted—and armed—Marine sentries in dress blues. They positively glittered. They were affable, incredibly polite to the civilians, and all business as they checked the identification of every person entering the building.

Through Governor Rainsford's cavernous private conference room and out on the terrace, Navy messcooks in spotless whites had laid out a buffet that would rival the most elaborate do that Jerry Panoyian could assemble. The bar was open, but the presence of more Marine sentries, posted like statues around the terrace fenceline, seemed to indicate re-

straint. Napier had carefully orchestrated the affair to indicate convivial co–operation while at the same time underscoring the point that civil unrest was still a cause for concern. He had only invited The People Who Counted, and the
quick realization that they were *all* there indicated that this
would come to more than some little Public Relations party
the Navy was tossing.

Ordinarily, Napier would have been resplendent in his
gold–braided Space Navy black uniform, but he looked like
an undertaker alongside Marines in dress blues. Phil Helton,
in particular, was blindingly easy to find, with Master Gunnery Sergeant of Fleet Marines chevrons—three gold ones
up, three more upside down under them, and two straight
gold bars through the middle, all on a crimson background
with a flaming bomb at the center of the two straight bars.
That took up most of each sleeve, but on the left one he had to
cram in a string of gold hashmarks and off–planet service
bars (which were called hershey bars for some reason no one
remembered any more). The high, tunic collar, piped in red,
was set off with the TFMC anchor–and–spiral–nebula
insignia—"clanker in the stars," as it was referred to by
insiders.

Jack Holloway sidled up to Helton. "That's a mighty
gaudy—I mean—ah—colorful uniform, Phil," he said.

Helton smiled a tight smile and took a sip of his drink.
"That's because you've never seen a senior Marine NCO in
full drag before," he said.

"Full drag?" Holloway was awash to the term.

"All dressed up," Helton said.

"No," Jack said, "as a matter of fact, I never have.
Great Ghu," he said, eyeing Helton's medals, "that's quite
a string of gongs you've got there, too."

"Well," Helton said, "no matter how careful you are, you
can't avoid collecting a few in twenty years."

"What's your next move?" Holloway asked. "I suppose
you'll be shipping out pretty soon."

"Yes, sir," Helton said, reiterating their private joke.
"My work's done here, now. Time to move on to the next
job."

"How long before they put you out to pasture?" Jack asked.

Helton puffed his cheeks and exhaled noisily. "I'm supposed to get my double–dec chip any time, now," he said. "I haven't made up my mind whether to pull the pin then or stick for thirty. It all just gets to be the same after a while."

Holloway looked off into the middle distance. "I know what you mean, Phil," he said. "I know what you mean."

The band—in Navy full–dress—had returned to the platform and struck up a slow waltz called *Baldur's Rum Rats*. Holloway recognized it, but had no notion at all of why it had come to be written or what it meant.

As Holloway stared across the terrace, he could see Grego and Christiana coming toward them, accompanied by Ben Rainsford—who was wearing his usual rumpled bush jacket and short pants. With his bushy red whiskers and knobby knees—at that distance—he looked rather like an obscure species of khaki emu. Odd—how he and Victor Grego had become something of friendly enemies, once each understood that they were both working toward the same goals. Grego seemed to be getting positively mellow—and everyone noticed how impossible it was for himself and Christiana to conceal their obviously deep devotion to each other. Even in public, at the most formal of affairs, they were like a pair of water spaniels that had mated for life—totally wrapped up in each other.

Holloway smiled as unobtrusively as he could. *Wonder what goes on when there's no one else around,* he thought. *Looks like there'll be another wedding reception pretty soon—and Grego won't be losing his Fuzzy–Sitter–In–Chief at this one.*

He turned to Helton. "I hope you'll consider coming back to Zarathustra when you leave the TFMC," he said.

"I heard that," Grego said jovially, "and I concur. Zarathustra needs men like you, Helton. We're getting ready to grow, again. This little pot of mud that Ingermann has stirred up will settle out pretty soon, and—"

"And Ian Ferguson is griping about retirement," Rainsford interrupted. "I've been talking to Alex Napier about you, young man, and he agrees with me that you'd be a perfect choice for the next Commandant of the Colonial Constabulary.''

Helton grinned broadly and took a hurried gulp of his drink. "You overwhelm me, gentlemen,'' he said. The only thing I can say at the moment is a verse that comes to mind.

> 'When foxes eat the last gold grape,
> And the last white antelope is killed,
> I shall stop fighting and escape
> Into a little house I'll build.' ''

Helton was relieved from dealing further with Ben Rainsford's expansive suggestions by the ringing of a ship's bell over the portable public address speakers—*ding– ding—ding–ding*—and the amplified voice of a Navy Chief Petty Officer. *"Four bells and all's shipshape. Those with individual invitations to the briefing should turn to in the ward room—''* pause*"—I mean—assemble in the Governor's conference chamber.''*

1800 hours. The band resumed playing, softly—light classics, mostly: *Like Loki is my Home, Buried in the Stars, Hyperspace Heaven, Senchant Star*—that sort of thing. People were filing into the conference room and taking seats which had small cards taped to the backs with each individual's name printed on them.

The room had been re–arranged, with the long conference table turned at a right angle across one end of the room. Alex Napier and his principal staff were seated behind it, like judges in a court.

As soon as everyone was comfortably situated and the Marine guards had closed the outer doors to the conference room, Napier rose. "Ladies and gentlemen,'' he said, nodding toward Little Fuzzy, Diamond, and Starwatcher, who were seated in the front row, to indicate that he included them in the appellation, "you may have noticed that there are quite a lot of Marines on Zarathustra.'' There was a ripple of laughter. "To be more precise,'' Napier said, "there is a full brigade of them, assigned to Xerxes Base and under the command of Colonel Thomas McGraw.'' He indicated

McGraw, who stood so that everyone might get a good look at him. "I wish to emphasize," Napier continued, "that this military presence in no way indicates that I have again assumed temporary control of the civil government. The Marines—and a contingent of Naval personnel from Xerxes—are here in answer to the specific request by Governor Rainsford for assistance in maintaining law and order during a period of civil unrest. When complete order has been restored, and on the request, again, of Governor Rainsford, we will withdraw."

Jack Holloway nodded. *Ah,* he thought to himself, *Ben has made a deal with Alex Napier—a deal that will not bring down a Board of Inquiry on either one of them, but will get us all out from under this insurrection business as gracefully as possible.*

"The situation is, I must say, quite serious," Napier was saying, "but nothing—in the view of Governor Rainsford, Mr. Victor Grego, or myself—that warrants a declaration of Martial Law."

Oh–ho, Holloway was thinking. *All three of them put it together over cocktails last night.*

"I will elaborate on this later during the briefing, but it is not the central reason for calling you together.

"As most of you know, there has been discovered—in conjunction with a wrecked hypership of alien design—a certain body of equally alien communications and information storage gear on North Beta. The Navy has impounded this gear under the provisions of Priority One, in order to examine it and decipher as much of the information as our cryptography and psycho–medical personnel could manage. The results of our investigations will be presented in the briefing by Lieutenant Commander Ybarra, Liaison Officer, and Lieutenant diCenzo, Chief Psychologist—whose portion of the briefing will follow immediately after me. Gentlemen . . ." Napier sat.

Ybarra stood, and Joe diCenzo moved to the projection console.

Pancho Ybarra made the protocol–appropriate preferatory remarks, and began his portion of the briefing. "Basically," he said, ''the problem is divided into three parts. First, we had to decipher the Fuzzy language as completely as possible. Working from the vocabulary we accumulated when doing our sapience tests, and from basic number identification, we were able, using computers, to compile a lexicographical profile of Actual Fuzzy from the keys found in Zarathustran Fuzzy. Secondly, we took phonetics and mated them with sounds to decipher the Fuzzy alphabet. Finally, we continually played side systems in and out of the data present in order to catch the subtleties of nuance and idiom. As a result of this program, we have assembled what we believe to be a fairly clear picture of the history of Fuzzies on Zarathustra.''

Slide projections and film strips played across the readout screen, underscoring the technical remarks to which Commander Ybarra referred.

''I won't bore you,'' Pancho Ybarra said, ''with technical details, although I will be available later to answer specific questions by qualified researchers.

''To place the matter in a simple narrative form, the events are as follows. Very nearly a thousand years ago, a hyperdrive spaceship was wrecked on the northern part of Beta Continent. The passengers and crew were all Fuzzies. Fuzzies were at that time—and if they have survived on what we will call Fuzzyhome planet, still are—a star–traveling race of intelligent beings. They are, we suspect, more intelligent than Terran Humans, but we are not yet certain of that point.

''In any case, the cracked–up ship came to rest about halfway up Mount Fuzzy in Fuzzy Valley. Some were killed, but most of the Fuzzies survived.

''We don't know where Fuzzyhome is, because no navigational equipment survived the crash, and, as nearly as we can tell the vessel was off course when it crashed—or made its forced landing. In any case, there was some trouble with the drives. The vessel sent out a distress call, and that is logged, but no other Fuzzy vessel ever found them, so the position given must have been wrong.

''At any rate, the surviving Fuzzies were stuck in Fuzzy Valley and on Mount Fuzzy. However, there was a nice cave in the mountain. Geothermal heat kept it warm and it is lighted all the time; the same geothermal heat excites sunstones to thermofluorescence, and the entire interior of the cave is liberally studded with sunstones. I can explain the geology of this phenomenon, but I shan't go into it deeply unless there are specific questions later. Basically, North Beta and South Beta were once separate continents. As the tectonic plates drifted together, they raised up the mountain range to which Mount Fuzzy belongs. The flint layer was on top of a limestone layer; ground water leached away the limestone, over some megacenturies, leaving the cavern roof and its layer of sunstones exposed.

"It was a very nice cave.

"The shipwrecked Fuzzies took as much gear as they could from the ship into the cave, to help them survive. They set up housekeeping for a few generations. They lived from the surrounding countryside, eating what they could catch, and augmenting that with stores salvaged from the ship. They built some huts and suchlike, but mainly they headquartered in this fine cave."

Jack Holloway hadn't heard any of this before. He wasn't upset about being left out, because while this wonderful little social gathering was being put together, he had been very busy in the hospital getting his arm put back together.

Ybarra continued. "The ship—as nearly as we can tell—was a cargo–passenger vessel with a crew *we* would call paramilitary. This is not an accurate term, because Fuzzies don't think in military terms the same way that Terran Humans do. The crew, though, was trained to teamwork, whereas the passengers were not.

"At first, the castaways didn't care too much for the lush plants that grew in Fuzzy Valley, but as time went by, they began to taste better and better. The titanium hull of the ship was slowly being eroded away by ground water, which oxidized it and leached titanium salts down into the soil of the valley, where the native plants picked the stuff up.

"Even after all the ship's stores were gone, there was still an abundant supply of a spice shipment the vessel was carrying on its cargo manifest. We might call it a kind of 'titanium pepper,' but, in any case, it made things taste good to Fuzzies, and they sprinkled it on everything they ate.

"So far, so good. The castaway Fuzzies weren't exactly living in the lap of luxury, but they were making do—and they were reproducing at a reasonable rate as they adapted to the alien environment of Zarathustra.

"Then, catastrophe number two arrived.

"An earthquake caused a landslide which buried the mouth of the cave and covered the wrecked ship. Those Fuzzies in the cave were wiped out. The only survivors were the ones who happened to be out gathering nuts or picking the lettuce in the valley. They were completely cut off from all the items of salvage, the remnants of their technology, and their parent culture.

"Now they know nothing of their own history except what is in their own minds. Hard times and a lot of survival pressure conspire to accelerate the erasing of that memory."

Holloway could tell, from looking around the room, who had already been exposed to this knowledge. The ones who were not looking astonishedly at Ybarra and the visual presentation that accompanied his remarks were obviously the ones who already knew. Little Fuzzy was serenely smoking his pipe. Starwatcher had his arms folded across his little chest, his legs crossed, and his khaki barracks cover hung on one knee. Diamond was fascinated—because he had only heard the news at the Fuzzy Conference earlier in the afternoon.

"Water from the mountain, though," Ybarra was saying, "continued to leak down through the rocks covering the wreck of the S.S. Fuzzy—and continued to leach titanium compounds down into the valley. There wasn't any more spice, but by this time the native vegetables weren't so bad, and the folks were making do.

"Several centuries passed. The main group of Fuzzies continued to stay in the valley. Colonies that tried to form satellite settlements always died out in a couple of generations. By this time, Fuzzies have forgotten that their metabolisms require titanium and that it is a vital component of their biochemistry. Titanium, as you may or may not know, is very scarce in Zarathustra's crust—*except in the soil of Fuzzy Valley."*

The tape–chip slowly lap–dissolved into an image of the recorded pickup of the Big Blackwater Project.

"And, now," Ybarra said, "here comes catastrophe number three. The Chartered Zarathustra Company started to drain a half–million square miles of swamp on the coast of Beta. That caused a drought in the Piedmont—where Jack Holloway had a camp in Cold Creek Canyon, near where Cold Creek joined the Snake River. New maps refer to Cold Creek as Holloway's Run, and a scientific study center has grown up there, along with the Zarathustran Native Protection Force headquarters. The place is now commonly referred to as Holloway Station. The drought also extended—" He outlined the geography on the projected map with his light–pointer. "—into the volcanic foothills and Piedmont of Northern Beta Continent, where we see Fuzzy Valley, north of the Fuzzy Divide.

"The valley dried up for lack of rain. The native vegetation began dying off. Dry weather for two winters in a row did, however, hatch out a bumper crop of land–prawns. The land–prawns migrated into Big Woods, and, eventually, down across Fuzzy Divide into Deep Woods, since a principal component of their food chain on Zarathustra is the forest moss that bears traces of titanium.

"Land–prawns are about the only thing left that tastes good to Fuzzies, so they followed that general *volkerwanderung* southward."

Ybarra switched off his light–pointer and held up the index finger of the hand which still held it. "But, you say, the Upland Fuzzies didn't follow the *volkerwanderung,* and they have different cultural habits—like large–scale co–operative hunting. Why is that?

"The Upland Fuzzies belong to a different social class. They are mostly descendants of the paramilitary crew of the Fuzzy ship. They long ago forgot why the crew should stick close to the site of the crashed ship—they just know that they *should.* The 'passenger descendants' are oriented toward individualism, *laissez–faire,* and those sorts of things. The 'crew descendants' are conditioned to ritualized activities, such as complex teamwork, close–order drill, and such–like.

"Parenthetically, land–prawns aren't native to Zarathustra, either. They also fall under Garrett's Theorem, by virtue of their preference for the Zarathustran moss, which only grades about ten atoms of titanium to the ton. Land–prawns are native to Fuzzyhome—where they are considered to be a culinary delicacy by Fuzzies. A dozen pairs of them were being shipped to a colony—the location of which we do not know—to be bred in captivity for expensive lobster dinners. On Fuzzyhome, it was well known that there is no hokfusine in land–prawns that can be converted into NFMp. Land–prawns utilized the titanium in their diet in a way that is non–nutritive to Fuzzies, but they taste good.

"With their simpler metabolism and a much less critical need for titanium in the diet, land–prawns managed to spread around quite a bit before the big drought. During the casta-way period of Zarathustran Fuzzy history, the Fuzzies be-came quite adept at killing them—for two reasons. First, they tasted good, and had nourishment in them other than hok-fusine. Second, they had to be kept out of the vegetable garden because of the crop damage they do. Thus, land–prawn hunting became a traditional chore of adolescent Fuz-zies, and, hence, its universal adeptness among contempor-ary Fuzzy adults at this point in time, which is not quite three years after the start of the Big Blackwater Project."

After Ybarra called for questions, he sat down. That seemed odd to Jack Holloway; then he caught on. Napier was answering the questions—unless they were highly technical in nature.

Jack held his pipe in his left hand, a little clumsily, since he wasn't used to it, and since his left arm was in a sling and a cast that prevented articulation of the elbow, and raised his right hand.

Napier rosed suavely and nodded his head in Jack's direc-tion. "Mr. Commissioner Holloway," he said deferentially.

Jack stood, "Commodore," he said, "it appears to me the Navy put this all together damned—I mean—in mighty quick order. Are your team and yourself certain that these deductions are correct?"

"Reasonably so," Napier replied. "Once we figured out how the Fuzzy instruments worked—that was the hardest part, by the way—we found their language to be not greatly different from the native speech of *Fuzzy f. holloway zarathustra*. The rest of the reconstruction was fairly simple. There were records, and passenger lists, and freight manifests, and mail, and official reports en route to what we might call the Fuzzy Colonial Office, and reference manuals, and—in short—just about everything you would expect to find on a hypership of the Terra–Baldur–Marduk Spacelines. Something, though, happened to the navigator's station. We don't know where Fuzzyhome is. After a thousand years, there may be no more Fuzzies alive there. Perhaps something happened to Fuzzyhome and its culture—since no rescue vessel ever appeared—so that the Zarathustran Fuzzy is the only surviving example of the race. But—Fuzzyhome is out there; somewhere."

Holloway was still standing. "How can we find it?" he asked.

"Patiently," Napier said. "Very patiently. We are now logging all the differentials we can isolate between recorded Actual Fuzzy morphology and Zarathustran Fuzzy morphology. By making detailed computer comparisons, we may be able to extrapolate how Fuzzies have evolved on Zarathustra to become slightly different from the parent group, and thus sketch a profile of Fuzzyhome and its star. If we can do that—and don't make any mistakes—then we only have to make physical inspections of—maybe—as few as a hundred thousand star systems before we find Fuzzyhome and make contact with the parent culture. However, none of us in this room should figure on being around to shake hands with Pappy Fuzzy when we finally find him."

Napier looked around the room. "No more questions on this portion of the briefing?" There was silence. "Very well," he said. "The next portion of the briefing will be conducted by Dr. Gerd van Riebeek, director and chief xeno–naturalist of Fuzzy Institute. Dr. van Riebeek . . ."

He sat.

Hmmmmmm, Holloway was thinking. *Napier is keeping all this on a close leash. But, why not? If anything goes haywire out here, he's the guy who's going to have to stand good for it. Federation Constitution; Federation Citizen Colonists; legally defined sapient natives. I wouldn't have his job for all the honey–rum on Baldur.*

There followed some rather complex comparisons by Gerd between the metabolisms of Zarathustran Fuzzies and the other eight extrasolar races of established sapience. He concluded on an explanation of how the difference between an antigen and an antibody had bearing on NFMp utilization in Fuzzy biochemistry and mentation. Jack didn't understand most of it. Then, Gerd asked for questions.

This time, George Lunt stood. He made no pretense at formality. "I don't get it, Gerd," he said. "How could the Fuzzies have dropped back so far? How could they have just forgotten everything?"

Gerd smiled. "What you're saying, I suppose," he said, "is that you're a little alarmed about the fragility of civilization, advanced though it may seem at a given moment?"

George nodded. "I suppose that might be it."

"Well," Gerd said, staring thoughtfully out over the room, "put yourself and a bunch of other Terran humans on a desert island for a couple of hundred years, during which time everything begins to wear out and what you can use is nothing more than what you can make with your hands. Then, bring along a typhoon, or something, and wipe out everything you have—all your tools. If you stay alive long enough to make a few simple weapons so you can get enough to eat, and if your natural enemies—most of whom are three times your size—don't snap you up for breakfast, where do you think the thrust of your daily activity is going to be? What will be more important to you—showing the flag or getting a decent lunch; one which will provide you with the energy to get a decent dinner?

"You'll keep alive some stories about the old days, but nothing more than can be passed by word of mouth. You don't have anything to write on, and you don't have anything to write with, and you can't spare the time to do it if you had the equipment—you're too busy staying alive.

"So, your stories become legends, and your legends become myths, and your myths gradually become fiction, and your fiction gradually becomes fairy tales.

"Finally, you become Little Fuzzy, and you're damned glad to find a *Hagga* who is a strange and powerful creature, who lives in the *Hoksu–mitto*, and who is willing to help you for nothing.

"So you will love the *Hagga* and do everything you can to help *him*—because there is a dim memory buried in you of a time when you didn't have to kick, bite, and scratch, and run from your enemies—just to keep breathing.

"Does that answer your question, George?" Gerd said.

George nodded, but did not say anything.

There were no more questions. A few people in the room had handkerchief tissues concealed in their hands and were dabbing unobtrusively at their faces. Jack Holloway was one of them.

Suddenly a little hand—holding a little, smoldering pipe—shot up from the front row.

When he was acknowledged, Little Fuzzy stood, realized that almost no one in the room could see him, and vaulted into a sitting position on the edge of the conference table, facing the assembled People Who Counted.

There was a murmur from the fifty or so persons in the conference room. Little Fuzzy held up his hand for silence. Jack Holloway suppressed a grin. *Ghu! He's the original Herr Doktor Professor Fuzzy, all right*.

"Fuzzies," Little Fuzzy said, indicating Diamond and Starwatcher, "*heeva gashta so–washa*. We so–say things we have found at Place where jump–so–high. I so–say for all Fuzzies: we do best can do to help; any way can. We must know who Fuzzies are, where come from . . ." His voice broke a little bit. " . . . what Fuzzy mean. Fuzzies make do learn anything—*eve' thing*. So much for Fuzzies to learn. We so–say want to begin—now."

Holloway got slowly to his feet, favoring his left arm. "As

a duly appointed official of the Colonial Government,'' he said, ''I here and now specify for the record of these proceedings that this verbal petition is to be duly noted as a legitimate request from the other human race, *id est Fuzzy f. holloway zarathustra,* and I solemnly pledge the assets of my office to the fulfillment of the said request. Much for Big Ones to learn, as well. Big Ones must learn to be like Fuzzies—more and more. If we do not, the galaxy itself can drive us crazy.'' He paused. ''So log it.''

There was a moment of silence. Then, Little Fuzzy came dashing down the aisle and flung his arms around Holloway's knee. *''Pa–pee Jaaak! Pa–pee Jaaak!''* he said, in the same tone he had used at the sapience trial—the first time Jack had ever heard him speak Lingua Terra within the range of human hearing.

He picked Little Fuzzy up and hoisted him onto his own shoulder.

Ben Rainsford jammed his pipe in his jacket pocket and thumped the arm of his chair. *''Concur!''* he said. ''So log it.''

There was a few seconds' pause.

''Concur!'' Victor Grego said. Christiana squeezed his arm warmly. (Grego had refused to attend the briefing if Christiana wasn't included.) Diamond abandoned his chair in the front row, rushed back to Grego's seat, leaped on his lap and began to pummel his stomach playfully. When he got his breath back, Grego said, ''So log it.''

From then on, the concurrences had to be taken in order by show of hands by the recording yeoman. The military all abstained, according to regulation. Frederic Pendarvis abstained, according to the oath of his office.

XLVII

"Well, I certainly have no objection to Napier's suggestions."

"The meeting after the briefing seemed to go all right as far as I was concerned."

"Actually, he's got a pretty good idea, there—an interim government, by the common consent of all involved—with a three-way authority involving the Navy, the CZC, and the Colonial Government."

"Sure will put a stop to all this jockeying for power that's been going on in the Constitutional Convention."

"What'd he mean with 'troika,' anyway?"

"Oh, that's some kind of three-headed animal from Old Terran mythology."

"It certainly cuts down on *my* paperwork. We won't know what's *really* happening until the whole thing has run through the courts, anyway. . ."

"That's going to take years, you bet."

"Besides, there's commonality of assets—and the Terran Federation Navy has sols to *burn.*"

"For a case with no precedents in Colonial Law, they do, you bet."

Gus Brannhard was standing with Jack Holloway as they listened to the conversations swirling around them on the terrace. Gus rumbled quietly as he quaffed a rather large belt of brandy. "Damned fools," he muttered in Jack's ear. "There's *nothing* that has no precedent in Colonial Law. Well, Nifflheim with it—it's certainly going to be the most interesting case I was ever a noble pleader for."

Holloway took a small sip of his highball. He was still so full of chemicals from surgery that he didn't want to try anything too chancy. "So, Gus," he said, "you want to stick to the limit?"

"Are you kidding?" Brannhard asked incredulously. "Jack, this suit that's coming up is a lawyer's *dream*. I don't even know for sure which side I'm going to be on—and won't until I spend about four months poring over the body of case law. Does the Charterless Zarathustra Company get back its charter? Can it be demonstrated that sapient beings, *to wit*, Fuzzies who are not native to Zarathustra, but who have been living here for a thousand years—with *de facto* proof thereof—can be said to be natives *de jure*. Oh, Jack; young lawyers lay awake at night dreaming of a case like this one is going to be—and praying that they never get into it until they are old, experienced, cynical, and sodden appropriately." He laughed a great, phlegmy laugh that seemed to shake the windows.

"I take it," Holloway said, "that you plan to be on the winning side."

"You bet your sweet—" Gus chopped the sentence short as Liana Bell came hurrying up to them.

She had a 'writer in her hand. Her cheeks were slightly flushed and she appeared to be short of breath. "I just heard, Mr. Commissioner—"

Holloway cut her off. "Jack," he corrected.

"I'm sorry," she said. "Jack. I just heard how you got your arm hurt, and I want to know if you would mind if I signed my name on your cast." She suddenly put her hands behind her and twisted nervously, swiveling at the ankles.

Holloway smiled. The points of his mustache turned up and creases appeared at the corners of his eyes. "Why, no, Miss Bell—"

She cut him off. "Liana," she said. She looked him dead in the eye when she said it.

"Yes," he replied, "Liana. I think that would be very nice, and I appreciate the thought."

She slowly inscribed something in Latin on the upper part of his spray–web cast, and then very elaborately signed her name in a flourishing hand.

He couldn't quite read it, because he was looking at it

upside down. And the Latin would have made no sense to him, anyway. But, no matter; he could get Ben Rainsford or Gus Brannhard to translate it for him later. They both made their living from Latin.

She began to speak while she was still doing her signature. "You know that project with Fuzzy sociology we were talking about?" she asked.

"I recall we mentioned something like that at the van Riebeek's that night," Jack said.

"Well," she said, "I've got approval from Dr. Mallin and Juan. Science Center is going to loan me out to Fuzzy Institute for a year to do a complete rundown on the system differences between Upland Fuzzies and Woods Fuzzies." She finished and looked at him directly, again. "That means I'll be moving in with Lynne Andrews next week."

Holloway smiled, again, holding her direct gaze with his. "I'm very pleased to hear that, Liana," he said.

She tapped his cast with the 'writer. "And I'm going to keep an eye on you and take care of you till this comes off—you poor old bear. You got yourself hurt doing something very fine, and I'm going to see that you get well."

Gus had been reading the inscription. He turned suddenly, rumbling into his beard as quietly as he could, and wandered off toward the bar.

Nearby, Little Fuzzy, Diamond, and Starwatcher were seated in a circle on a table.

Little Fuzzy leaned toward Diamond. "What Pappy Jack make do?" he said. "Have fun?"

Diamond leaned closer. He said *"Dishta,"* then whispered something in *Lingua Fuzzy*. By this time, Starwatcher had leaned into the conversation to hear what was being said.

A certain amount of giggling and shoulder–slapping followed the whispered conversation.

Then Starwatcher leaned back upright and tilted his khaki barracks cover onto the back of his head. Then he shook his head slowly. "So many things for Fuzzies to learn," he said.